VIRAG
MODERN CL
718

© Evening Standard/Getty Images

Nancy Spain was a novelist, broadcaster and journalist. Born in Newcastle-upon-Tyne in 1917, she was the great-niece of the legendary Mrs Beeton. As a columnist for the *Daily Express* and *She* magazine, frequent guest on radio's *Woman's Hour* and panellist on the television programmes *What's My Line?* and *Juke Box Jury*, she was one of the most recognisable (and controversial) media personalities of her era. During the Second World War she worked as a driver, and her comic memoir of her time in the WRNS became an immediate bestseller. After the war she began publishing her acclaimed series of detective novels, and would go on to write over twenty books. Spain and her longtime partner, Joan Werner Laurie, were killed when the light aircraft carrying them to the Grand National in 1964 crashed close to the racecourse. Her friend Noël Coward wrote, 'It is cruel that all that gaiety, intelligence and vitality should be snuffed out when so many bores and horrors are left living.'

DEATH GOES ON SKIS

Nancy Spain

Introduced by Sandi Toksvig

TO

HERMIONE GINGOLD

VIRAGO

This paperback edition published in 2020 by Virago Press
First published in Great Britain in 1949 by Hutchinson

1 3 5 7 9 10 8 6 4 2

Copyright © Nancy Spain 1949
Copyright © Beneficiaries of Nancy Spain 1964
Introduction copyright © Sandi Toksvig 2020

A CIP catalogue record for this book
is available from the British Library.

ISBN 978-0-349-01396-1

Typeset in Goudy by M Rules
Printed and bound in Great Britain by
Clays Ltd, Elcograf S.p.A.

Papers used by Virago are from well-managed forests
and other responsible sources.

Virago Press
An imprint of
Little, Brown Book Group
Carmelite House
50 Victoria Embankment
London EC4Y 0DZ

An Hachette UK Company
www.hachette.co.uk

www.virago.co.uk

'Always to be a Governess and always to be in love is a severe handicap in a world where so many people are neither one thing nor the other.'

VIRGINIA WOOLF

Introduction

'The world of books: romantic, idle, shiftless world so
beautiful, so cheap compared with living.'

NANCY SPAIN

I never met Nancy Spain, and I've been worrying that we might
not have got on. It bothers me because I'm a fan. That's probably
an odd start for someone writing an introduction to her work, but
I think it's a sign of how much I like her writing that I ponder
whether we would have clicked in person. The thing is, Spain
loved celebrity. In 1955 she wrote, 'I love a big name ... I like to
go where they go ... I always hope (don't you?) that some of their
lustre will rub off against me ... '

I don't hope that. I loathe celebrity and run from gatherings of
the famous, so I can't say I would have wanted to hang out with
her, but I should have liked to have met. I would have told her what
a brilliant writer she was, how hilarious, and I'd have said thank
you, because I also know that I might not have had my career
without her. I've been lucky enough to earn a crust by both writing
and broadcasting, and I do so because Nancy Spain was there first.

During the height of her fame in the 1950s and early 60s she did something remarkable – she became a multimedia celebrity at a time when no one even knew that was a desirable thing. She was a TV and radio personality, a novelist, a journalist and columnist for British tabloids. She did all this while wearing what was known as 'mannish clothing'. Although her lesbianism was not openly discussed, she became a role model for many, with the closeted dyke feeling better just knowing Spain was in the public eye being clever and funny.

I am too young to have seen her on TV, but the strange thing about the internet is that people never really disappear. Check Nancy Spain out on the web and you can still see and hear her performing in a 1960s BBC broadcast on the panel of *Juke Box Jury*. She has the clipped tones of a well-bred Englishwoman of the time, who sounds as though she is fitting in a broadcast before dashing to the Ritz for tea. It is a carefully contrived public persona that suited Spain as a way to present herself to the world but, like so much of her life, it skirted around the truth. She was selling the world a product, a concept which she would have understood only too well.

In 1948 Spain wrote a biography of her great-aunt, Isabella Beeton, author of the famous *Mrs Beeton's Book of Household Management*. Although it was an encyclopedic presentation of all you needed to know about running the home, Isabella Beeton was hardly the bossy matron in the kitchen that the book suggested; in fact she wrote it aged just twenty-one, when she can hardly have had the necessary experience. Isabella probably knew more about horses, having been a racing correspondent for *Sporting Life*. The truth is that she and her husband Sam saw a gap in the book market. So, rather than being the distillation of years of experience, Mrs Beeton's book was a shrewd marketing ploy. I wonder how many people know that Isabella never did become that wise old woman of the household because she died aged just twenty-eight of puerperal fever following the birth of her fourth child? There are parallels here too, for Spain's background was also not what it seemed and she, like Isabella, lost her life too early.

Far from being a posh Londoner, Nancy Spain hailed from Newcastle. Her father was a writer and occasional broadcaster, and she followed in his footsteps quite aware that she was the son he never had. Her determination to come to the fore appeared early on. As a child she liked to play St George and the Dragon in which her father took the part of the dragon, Nancy marched about as St George while, as she described it, her sister Liz 'was lashed to the bottom of the stairs with skipping ropes and scarves'. No dragon was going to stop Spain from being the hero of the piece.

From 1931 to 1935 Spain was sent, like her mother before her, to finish her education at the famous girls' public school, Roedean, high on the chalky cliffs near Brighton. It was here that her Geordie accent was subdued and polished into something else. She didn't like it there and would spend time getting her own back in her later writing. Her fellow classmates seem to have varied in their attitude toward her. Some saw her as exotic and clever, while others found her over the top. It says something about the attitude to women's careers at the time when you learn that in his 1933 Prize-Giving Day speech to the school the then Lord Chancellor, Lord Sankey, congratulated Roedean on playing 'a remarkable part in the great movement for the higher education of women', but added, 'In spite of the many attractive avenues which were now open to girls', he hoped 'the majority of them would not desert the path of simple duties and home life'.

Deserting that path was Spain's destiny from the beginning. It was while at school that Spain began writing a diary of her private thoughts. In this early writing the conflict between her inner lesbian feelings and society's demand that she keep them quiet first stirred. She began to express herself in poetry. Some of her verse-making was public and she won a Guinea prize for one of her works in her final year. This, she said, led her to the foolish notion that poems could make money.

Her mother harboured ambitions for Spain to become a games or domestic science teacher, but it was clear neither was going to happen. Her father, who sounds a jolly sort, said she could stay home and have fifty pounds a year to spend as she pleased. She joined a women's lacrosse and hockey club in Sunderland because it looked like fun, but instead she found a fledgling career and her first love. She became utterly smitten with a fellow team member, twenty-three-year old Winifred Emily Sargeant ('Bin' to her friends) a blonde, blue-eyed woman who could run fast on the field and rather glamorously seemed fast off it by drinking gin and tonic.

The Newcastle Journal decided to publish some reports about women's sport and almost by chance Nancy got her first job in journalism. Touring with the team meant she could both write and spend time with Bin. When she discovered her feelings for Winifred were reciprocated, she was over the moon.

> *Dearest – your laughter stirred my heart*
> *for everything I loved was there –*
> *Oh set its gaiety apart*
> *that I may feel it everywhere!*

She bought herself a second-hand car for twenty pounds and began making some local radio broadcasts, getting her first taste of fame when she played the part of Northumberland heroine Grace Darling in a local radio play. Meanwhile she and Winifred found time to escape. It was the 1930s and they were both supposed to be growing into 'respectable' women. The pressure must have been unbearable as there was no one with whom they could share the excitement of their feelings for each other. They went off for several weeks to France on a touring holiday, which Spain described as idyllic. It was to be a one-off, for they returned to find Britain declaring war with Germany. They both joined up, with Spain enlisting in the Women's Royal Naval Service, the Wrens.

She would later describe her time in the service as the place where she found emancipation. She became a driver, scooting across the base and fixing the vehicles when they faltered. Based in North Shields, where many large naval vessels came in for repairs, it was often cold and there was no money for uniforms. Some trawlermen gave her a fisherman's jersey, and she got a white balaclava helmet that she was told was made by Princess Mary. She also got permission to wear jodhpurs on duty. It was the beginning of her feeling comfortable in men's clothes.

At the end of 1939 news reached Spain that Winifred, aged twenty-seven, had died of a viral infection. Unable to bear the grief, she didn't go to the funeral, but instead wrote poetry about the efficacy of drink to drown sorrows. The Wrens decided she was officer material and moved her to Arbroath in Scotland to do administrative duties. It was here that she began to shape the rest of her life. She became central to the base's many entertainments. She took part in broadcasts. She wrote. She was always busy. She did not talk about her life with Winifred. Years later, when she wrote about their dreamy French holiday, she wrote as if she had gone alone. Her only travelling companions apparently were 'a huge hunk of French bread and a slopping bottle of warm wine'. The descriptions of the trip are splendid, but they mask the painful truth.

After the war, Spain was set to be a writer. An outstanding review by A. A. Milne of her first book, *Thank you – Nelson*, about her experiences in the Wrens, gave her a first push to success. She sought out the famous, she lived as 'out' as she could in an unaccepting world. I don't like how the tabloids sold her to the public.

The *Daily Express* declared about its journalist, as if it were a selling point: 'They call her vulgar ... they call her unscrupulous ... they call her the worst dressed woman in Britain ...'

She called herself a 'trouser-wearing character', with her very clothing choices setting her apart as odd or bohemian. I suspect she was just trying to find a way to be both acceptable to the general public, and to be herself. It is a tricky combination, and was much harder then. She may not have known or intended the impact she had in helping to secretly signal to other lesbians and gay men that they were not alone. She lived with the founder and editor of *She* magazine, Joan 'Jonny' Werner Laurie, and is said to have slept with many other women, including Marlene Dietrich. Fame indeed.

I am so thrilled to see her work come back into print. Her detective novels are hilarious. They are high camp and less about detecting than delighting, with absurd farce and a wonderful turn of phrase. Who doesn't want to read about a sleuth who when heading out to do some detective work hangs a notice on her front door reading 'OUT – GONE TO CRIME'? Her detective, Miriam Birdseye, was based on Spain's friend the actress Hermione Gingold whose own eccentricities made her seem like a character from a novel. Miriam's glorious theatricality is complemented by her indolent sidekick, the (allegedly) Russian ballerina Natasha Nevkorina, who has to overcome a natural disinclination to do anything in order to do most of the actual detecting. They work incredibly well together as in this exchange:

'And she is telling you that you are going mad, I suppose?' said Natasha.

'Yes,' said Miss Lipscoomb, and sank into a chair. She put her head in her hands. 'I think it is true,' she said. 'But how did you know?'

'That's an old one,' said Miriam briskly. 'I always used to tell my first husband he was going mad,' she said. 'In the end he did,' she added triumphantly.

There is something quintessentially British about these detective novels, as if every girl graduating from Roedean might end up solving a murder. The books contain jokes that work on two levels – some for everyone; some just for those in the know. Giving a fictitious school the name Radcliff Hall is a good queer gag, while anyone might enjoy the names of the 'intimate revues' in which Miriam Birdseye had appeared in the past, including 'Absolutely the End', 'Positively the Last' and 'Take Me Off'.

Seen through the prism of modern thinking, there are aspects of Spain's writing that are uncomfortable, but I am sad if they overshadow her work so thoroughly as to condemn it to obscurity. P. G. Wodehouse has, after all, survived far worse accusations. Thomas Hardy is still recalled for his writing about 'man's inhumanity to man', even though by all accounts he wasn't nice to his wife. Should we stop reading Virginia Woolf because she was a self-confessed snob? I am not a big fan of the modern 'cancel culture', and hope we can be all grown-up enough to read things in the context of their time. Of one thing I am certain – Spain was not trying to hurt anyone. She had had too tough a time of her own trying to be allowed just to survive the endless difficulties of being other. My political consciousness is as raised as anyone's, and I see the flaws, but maybe it's okay just to relax in her company and succumb to being entertained.

Nancy Spain died aged forty-seven. She was in a light aircraft on her way to cover the 1964 Grand National when the plane crashed near the racecourse. Her partner Jonny was with her and they were cremated together. Her friend Noel Coward wrote, 'It is cruel that all that gaiety, intelligence and vitality should be snuffed out, when so many bores and horrors are left living.' She was bold, she was brave, she was funny, she was feisty. I owe her a great deal in leading the way and I like her books a lot. They make me laugh, but also here I get to meet her alone, away from the public gaze, and just soak up the chat. Enjoy.

Sandi Toksvig

To find out more about Nancy Spain, you might like to read her memoirs, *Thank you – Nelson*, *Why I'm Not a Millionaire* and *A Funny Thing Happened on the Way*. Also the authorised biography, *A Trouser-Wearing Character: The Life and Times of Nancy Spain* by Rose Collis.

Characters in the Story

Barny Flaherté — *Manufacturer of the famous scents 'Nine Times Too Far', 'Whew!' and 'Pong'*

Regan — *his wife*

Toddy — *his cousin*

Kathleen — *her sister*

Joyce ⎱
Margie ⎰ — *his children*

Miss Rosalie Leamington — *governess to the children*

Fanny Mayes — *Film Star, mistress to Barny Flaherté*

Sir Edward Sloper, K.B.E. — *an architect, her husband*

Johnny DuVivien — *a night club proprietor and ex-all-in wrestler and a detective of sorts*

Natasha — *an ex-ballet dancer, his wife*

Pamela — *his daughter*

Miriam Birdseye	*a genius*
Roger Partick-Thistle	
Morris	*her friends*
Watson-Birchwood	
M Lapatronne	*proprietor of the Water Station Hotel, Katsclöchen, Schizo-Frenia*
Mme Lapatronne	*his wife*
Hans Grübner	*a policeman of Kesicken, Schizo-Frenia*
Kurt Vital	*a doctor, also of Kesicken*
Trudi	*chambermaids*
Nelli	
Mr Field	*deputy to His Britannic Majesty's Ambassador to the country of Schizo-Frenia*
Kiki	*a thug*

Chorus of skiers, enthusiasts, waiters, railwaymen, brakemen, newspapermen, etc.

BOOK ONE

THE JOURNEY

I

The Winter Sports Express

In Calais half a dozen trains waited for the tourists who were leaving for the Winter Sports. The trains were labelled A, AB, B, BC and so on.

Among the tourists Kathleen Flaherté failed to manage her Passport and a lot of little travel agency brochures. She stared about her wildly and felt desperately in her pockets and all her various shoulder bags and wallets. Her black, brilliant eyes showed all the whites round them, like an anxious animal. Her black page-boy bob flew behind her in elf locks, in the cold wind that came off the sea. The effect was hysterical.

'DE,' she said to her sister, Toddy Flaherté, who stood glumly beside her. 'That's what it *said* . . . '

'*I* expect that's what it meant,' said Toddy reasonably enough. She was a tough, gentlemanly young woman in Glastonbury boots with a polished Eton crop. She was about thirty-four and she was ten years older than her sister Kathleen. They were both unmarried.

Toddy was lazy and she usually allowed Kathleen to do all the work. Nevertheless she had good ideas. It had been her idea, for example, to leave England for Schizo-Frenia, a small mountainous Central European Country, much given to winter sports. England was clenched in the expensive grip of the electricity and gas crisis of February, 1947, and Schizo-Frenia would probably be better organized and sunnier. It would certainly be more expensive.

'I expect that's what it means,' said Toddy again, elbowing aside a young gentleman dressed in fleeces, carrying two aluminium ski sticks. 'Here. Give *me* the damned thing . . . '

She snatched the green cardboard wallet with the tickets and the itinerary from Kathleen and quite suddenly assumed command. Kathleen followed her towards the Schizo-Frenia express (labelled DE) which lay ahead of them, steaming slightly.

A small fierce man in coffee colour admitted the existence of a sleeper with two berths called Flaherté and said something confused about Thomas Cook and Son. While this was going on Kathleen had time to think about something else. She tossed her head. A more unconcentrated human being has seldom existed.

'Look . . . ' she said happily, pointing up the platform through the half light. 'Surely that girl was at St Anne's with us. In Viola's House. Or at least, I think so . . . '

'For God's sake,' said Toddy, shortly, pushing ahead of the little man in coffee colour. 'Twenty-two and twenty-three. Sorry, Kathleen, later.'

'Pamela,' said Kathleen, dreamily. 'Pamela Something. In Viola's. She was good at games.'

'So what?' said Toddy rudely, over her shoulder.

'Don't be beastly,' said Kathleen, vaguely. 'She was rather nice. If it's the girl I thought it was.'

Toddy's square, sullen face went a dull red as she slowly lost her temper. 'I want to get settled,' she said. 'Eh? *Then* we'll have time for Pamela what's her name.'

'DuVivien,' said Kathleen with a brilliant smile. '*That* was it. I knew I'd remember.' She followed Toddy's stocky shoulders along the dark corridor of the *wagon-lit*.

'If she's on this platform she's probably on this train,' said Toddy, without turning her head. 'There we are. Twenty-two and twenty-three. Now we're all set.'

She pulled her sister into the little sleeper. The beds were already made up. Kathleen complained. The attendant shrugged his shoulders. He said it was the war and that the young misses could perfectly well have dinner like everyone else and go to bed. Or play cards. He disappeared into his own little compartment with a leer.

'Or tell fortunes,' said Kathleen, happily. Toddy turned her back and climbed into the top bunk like an angry dog. She started to pull off her long, heavy boots.

'Our porter's number is 169,' she said, tartly. 'Go and find him and see he hasn't dropped my big pigskin bag. Then you can find your precious Pamela what's her name. And bring her back here if you like.'

Kathleen, at the window, looked wistfully out at the platforms, at the light clouds of steam in the clammy air and the tourists who ran unclaimed among the piles of luggage.

She heard a voice calling: '169. 169.'

'OK,' said Kathleen. 'I'll bring him back.' She went to climb down the steep steps from their sleeping-car.

II

Pamela DuVivien noticed the sinister figures of the two Flahertés under the dim platform lights. Toddy looked extremely grim and Kathleen, wearing an eccentric overcoat with a hood, appeared far from elegant.

'Well I'm damned,' said Pamela.

'What?' said Natasha, her stepmother, vaguely. 'I am hoping *so much*, dear Pamela, that you will not be forced to share a sleeper with a not very nice class of person?'

'Oh, it'll be all right,' said Pamela, casually. She was a leggy young woman, with a promise of good looks. 'It's those Flahertés, those awfully rich Flahertés the scent makers ...'

'Where?' said Natasha. 'But it *may* not be all right. If only that wicked Johnny had decided to come next *week*. Do you mean the Flaherté part of Flaherté, Havard and Yale, Scent Importers, London, Marseilles, and Grasse?' she went on inconsequently. 'Whew! and "9 × 9" on all the bottles?'

She stood still and stared up at the long, dusty Schizo-Frenia express which towered over them. Natasha's wide hazel eyes were like a cat's and her light brown hair was always beautifully groomed.

'Yes, the people who make "Nine Times Too Far" and "Whew!" and "Pong",' said Pamela, putting down a heavy suitcase. 'They were at St Anne's with me. At least the young one was. The old one came down at half-term. They were up that end of the platform near the *Douanes* ...' Pamela pointed. 'They've gone now. I'm sure it'll be all right, Natasha. Do stop *fussing*.'

'Fuss? Who? Me?' said Natasha, shocked. And she did not speak again for some time.

Natasha was the second Mrs DuVivien and a Russian ballet dancer into the bargain. Her husband, Johnny, owned a great many night clubs and one roadhouse in Yorkshire. He was very proud of Natasha and he had always wanted to spend three weeks winter-sporting in Schizo-Frenia. Natasha considered this English of him. She had given in, saying they would meet 'unpleasant soldiers and sailors from Colchester and Frinton-on-Sea and Budleigh Salterton'. It had been decided that it would be good for Pamela's health.

'I am knowing,' said Natasha, climbing up the steep brass-bound ladder to their sleeper; 'that there will be no drama in Kesicken, in our hotel.'

If there was one thing that Natasha loved it was a little drama.

Johnny, her husband, appeared with a number of suitcases and a small porter in a blue smock, saying 'Wee' and 'Mercy' at intervals. He looked up at Natasha and grinned.

'Dunno, puss,' he said, slowly in his pleasant Australian twang. His big red Indian's nose had turned a little blue with the cold. 'There may be any amount of broken legs an' arms an' that ... '

'Broken legs is not drama,' said Natasha, haughtily. A large pullman car man hauled her in. He brightened considerably as he looked at her. Mr and Mrs DuVivien. Ah yes. And *Miss* DuVivien will be next door to them, sharing with a Miss Leamington, who was attached to the Flaherté party.

'*There* you are, Natasha,' said Pamela, 'it's going to be all right.'

'You are sure these Flahertés are nice?' said Natasha.

'They're very *rich*,' said Pamela.

And there the matter rested for the time being.

III

Pamela stared round her sleeper.

She was in temporary, undisputed possession of a narrow bunk, neatly made up with very clean sheets and pillow cases, with two blankets called '*wagon-lit*'; an interesting wash-basin that emptied back into itself; a jug of French, dubious, drinking water; and a small cupboard with a looking-glass let into the front of it. There was also a small, plush covered ladder for climbing up into the top bunk and there were various complicated slots and shelves upon which Pamela balanced her suitcases.

As she worked away she heard voices and pattering feet that approached her door. She winced. She didn't like children.

To her horror, outside the door, the footsteps halted abruptly.

'There you are, Miss Leamington,' said the first voice, which obviously belonged to an adenoidal girl of fourteen. 'It says so on the list that man had. Eleven an' twelve.'

Another voice broke in, younger and more shrill.

'With a Miss P. DuVivien. I expect she's quite *old* an' eighty years of age an' very, very feeble an' you'll be up *all* night . . . '

There was a giggle and some snuffling and the scraping of feet.

'Hush, Margie . . . ' This was a deep, slightly husky, definitely adult voice. It was quite pleasant. 'Come away. We'll go back to your cabin and you shall brush your hair . . . '

Pamela began to think that Natasha had been quite right to fuss.

'*I wonder where Auntie Kathy is?*' came a nasal whine from outside.

'And I wonder where Auntie Toddy is?' was the reply. The two voices sounded like Strophe and Ante Strophe.

'Somewhere up the train I expect, dear,' said the soothing governess's voice. 'Come Joyce. Come Margie.'

They evidently went into the cabin on Pamela's right and presently a muffled series of small taps, clicks and crashes (and an inaccurate rendering of 'Lili Marlene') indicated that Joyce and Margie were having their hair brushed.

Pamela cautiously opened her door and peered up and down the corridor. To her amazement she saw Natasha's head, on her left, doing the same thing.

'My poor Pamela,' said Natasha. 'To share with the governess and these dwarfs. We will have you changed.' And she laughed gently.

'Oh, I dunno,' said Pamela. 'The governess may be quite nice.'

'But these dwarfs will be in all the time to have hair and teeth brushed and shoes buttoned and *worse* done for them.'

'Aw, hush up,' said Johnny behind her. He looked very big and purposeful. He wore a green shirt and a very extraordinary pair of braces. 'They were older'n that. Don't tease, honey chil' . . . '

'All right,' said Natasha. 'But if *you* had not been selfish and had been going by beastly unsafe aeroplane, none of this would ever have been happening to Pamela.'

Johnny pulled her inside the sleeper and shut the door. Pamela laughed. At that moment Kathleen Flaherté, looking something like Paganini, came stalking down the corridor towards her.

'Pam?' she called. 'It *is* Pam, isn't it? From St Anne's? I'm Kathleen Flaherté of Portia House . . . '

9

Kathleen was about a half inch over six feet and her face seemed very sharp and pointed and white in the gloom. Pam stood her ground bravely.

'I remember you well,' she said. 'And I'm sharing a sleeper with your governess.'

'What?' said Kathleen, disconcerted. 'Who?'

'A Miss Leamington,' said Pam a little self-consciously.

'Oh. Rosalie Leamington. Hm,' said Kathleen. 'Is she there now?'

'No,' said Pamela, vulgarly jerking her chin. 'She's in *there*. With two children.'

'Joyce and Margie,' said Kathleen. 'I rather like them.'

'Do you?' said Pamela, politely. 'I think they're brushing their teeth.'

Kathleen frowned.

'Come and see Toddy, my sister,' she said. 'She wants to meet you again.'

'Toddy,' said Pamela, thinking back into the past and various Old Girls' Committee Meetings. 'She was good at sketching, wasn't she?' she added.

'Good Heavens, no. She's a surrealist now,' said Kathleen proudly.

'Natasha will like that,' said Pamela.

Kathleen began to lead the way back to their cabin.

'She was Natasha Nevkorina, wasn't she?' she said, over her shoulder. 'We know lots of ballet dancers. Two great friends of ours and my cousin Barny's are on this train. Those are his two children.'

'Who are?' said Pamela, reasonably enough. 'Your cousin or his chums?'

'They *all* are,' said Kathleen. 'And their wives.'

'How many does that make?' said Pamela, bewildered.

'Of the Flahertés?' said Kathleen. 'Well, there's Barny. He's my cousin. And his wife Regan. And their two children.'

'Joyce and Margie,' said Pamela, 'and their governess.'

'Yes. And the two friends, Sir Edward and Lady Sloper.'

'Not *the* Sloper?' said Pamela. 'The architect?'

Sir Edward Sloper was the newest and most spectacular architectural knight and his wife (Fanny Mayes) was a film star in her own right.

Kathleen nodded.

'Why wasn't there a brass band and red carpet at Victoria, then?' said Pamela.

'For Fanny, you mean?' said Kathleen. Pamela nodded.

''S matter 'f fact,' Kathleen lowered her voice and became confidential, 'my cousin Barny, whose kids' governess you're sleeping with . . . '

'I beg your . . . Oh, I see what you . . . ' said Pamela.

'Fanny's frightfully keen on Barny. I happen to know.'

'Good Lord,' said Pamela. She felt very sophisticated.

'Yes,' Kathleen wagged her head. 'Of course Barny's *awful*. Thinks of nothing but sex. Here we are.'

They had arrived at *Numéros* 22 and 23. Kathleen kicked open the door. Pamela was instantly aware that the Flahertés had somehow made their sleeper look exciting and cosmopolitan. Her sleeper and Miss Leamington's was merely dull.

Toddy's grim, handsome face peered over the bunk at her. Both Flahertés wore little gold rings in their ears, which had been pierced when they were children. The gold rings looked quite feminine in Kathleen's ears. They made Toddy look like a buccaneer. Pamela was non-plussed. Toddy shook hands with her in a frank, manly way and Pamela sat down on a very much labelled suitcase.

'My dear,' said Kathleen, falling gracefully into the bottom bunk. 'She's in a sleeper with Rosie.'

'Rosalie Leamington,' said Toddy with a slow, subtle smile. 'Well, she's not too bad. She doesn't smell or anything and she's intelligent. She has a madly complicated Cambridge Degree in Modern Languages, too . . . '

'Oh?' said Pamela.

'How do you know she doesn't smell?' said Kathleen.

'I just *know*.' Toddy swung her legs over the side of the bunk. She wore buckled shoes like a sailor. Pamela was a little worried.

'Well then, where are Barny and Regan?' said Toddy. 'Regan surely hasn't let the brats out of her sight for a *second*? I hate children, don't you?' she added with a sudden tigerish gleam of very regular, very white teeth. Pamela felt she might be able to talk to Toddy.

As she sat looking with interest and admiration at the Flahertés, the great train gave a little jolt and a small shake and pulled effortlessly away from Calais. Toddy lounged across to the window and peered out into the winter evening.

'Nothing like it,' she said. 'A train starting.'

'Most exciting thing in the world . . . ' said Pamela.

IV

Fanny Mayes, the film star (Lady Sloper), had already worked up a considerable claustrophobia. She was a beautiful, precise and elegant blonde with small features, a narrow chin and the second most beautiful figure in the world.

She lay fretfully on the top bunk, whining, while Sir Edward Sloper went methodically through the luggage. He was trying to find the little bottle of pills that Fanny took when she felt this way.

Fanny bit holes in a small lace handkerchief and looked miserably at the ceiling. From time to time she switched the lights on and off. There were a great many of these. Otherwise she just attacked her husband verbally:

'Oh Ted, if you'd allowed me to bring Françoise, *this* would never have happened,' she said in her small, querulous voice. '*She* always knows where everything is . . . '

'Naturally. She packs it,' said Edward. 'But that's very unfair of you, you know. You decided to leave her behind yourself.'

Edward Sloper was a big, middle-aged man with a broad, average face and flat mouse coloured hair. At present his face was anxiously puckered and he was slightly out of breath. He stooped over a large canvas zipper bag. He was wearing a heavy tweed overcoat. Although they had been married three years he had not yet learned that it was best not to reply to his wife when she was nervy. She promptly had hysterics.

'Oh, *Hell* . . . ' said Edward. He suddenly thought a good bat on the head would be a cure for claustrophobia. He was (he thought) very much in love with his wife.

V

Two compartments away, where Barny Flaherté and his wife, Regan, were getting tidy and organized, the positions were characteristically reversed.

Barny, head of the firm of Flaherté, Havard and Yale, lay flat on his long elegant back with his beautiful hands locked behind his head. His horn-rimmed glasses were pushed up on his forehead, his long-lashed eyes (vague with various dreams) were half shut. One lock of straight, ash-brown hair had already fallen into his eyes. Even in his shirt sleeves, and a little lemon coloured slip over, Barny Flaherté looked romantic. He considered it a great burden.

Regan Flaherté, a passionate red-haired woman, knelt on the floor, wondering all the time, out loud, how the children were and whether Miss Leamington was as good a teacher as her references.

Regan's restless hands plucked and twitched all the time at the straps of the luggage, at Barny's and her sponge-bags, at the odd cake of soap as she dropped it, at her hair and her neck. She wasn't really a clumsy woman, but she always gave an appearance of busy-ness. Things nearly always fell on the floor round her.

'After all, that Cambridge Languages Degree must mean *something*,' said Regan, ' . . . but it doesn't necessarily mean she's kind and good with the children, really . . . '

'They seem to like her,' murmured Barny.

'Well, they've only been in London with her at the flat, and an intelligent woman is always OK in London . . . '

'Why are we going to Schizo-Frenia then?' said Barny, lazily. He opened one eye. 'My pipe would be nice,' he said.

'Here it is, *darling*,' said Regan, fondly.

'And tobacco pouch,' said Barny.

The two objects lay beside him on the bed. He began to fill the pipe absently, without saying 'thank you'. He wondered how

Fanny Mayes was. He decided she was thinking about him. As it so happened he was perfectly right.

VI

His two girl cousins, spreading a pack of cards on Toddy's bunk, were discussing Barny Flaherté. Indeed, they usually did.

'Yes, he *is* selfish,' said Kathleen. 'Cut, Pamela. But he was nice enough, you know, when he was a young man. Before the firm made all that money . . . '

'But he was *wild*,' said Toddy. 'Remember that wonderful story about his trip to Dublin to see The Cousin?'

'Another cousin?' said Pamela. She was sitting on the top bunk and her legs dangled helplessly. Toddy held the pack of cards firmly on her knee and stared at Kathleen. She was wearing small agate cuff-links.

'I should think we could tell her, couldn't we?' she said.

'Oh heavens, yes,' said Kathleen. 'The Cousin is a bit of a swell. An Irish Lord, you know. Last Prince of all this and all that. Lord Cranford. Has a very beautiful wife, younger than him . . . '

'And no children,' went on Toddy taking up the story. 'Couldn't have any, you know. So they thought they'd like to see Barny. They thought they'd make him their heir. They had masses of money and a great big house and miles of bog. *You* know the sort of thing . . . '

Pamela didn't, but she thought it was all very grand and she nodded enthusiastically.

'So Barny went over to Dublin to see them,' said Kathleen. 'He wasn't married then. That was when he was so awfully in love with Elizabeth, remember?'

'Elizabeth?' said Pamela, helplessly.

'His cousin,' said Toddy, shortly. 'Go on, Kathleen.'

'Help,' said Pamela, under her breath.

'Well, on the boat, my dear, he met a marvellous and most beautiful woman who *adored* him. They didn't tell each other names. Only Christian names. Apparently Barny called himself Bertram. It was most romantic,' said Kathleen. 'Anyway . . .'

' . . . They had an affaire,' said Toddy rapidly.

'What? On the boat? But . . . ' said Pamela.

'Uncomfortable?' said Toddy. 'I don't suppose *that* would stop Barny, would it, Kathleen?'

'Should say not,' said Kathleen, staring round her for a cigarette.

Pamela's eyes nearly popped out of her head.

'So they were *mad* about each other, my dear. And everything was so perfect they agreed they'd never see each other again and never write or anything . . . '

'A beautiful interlude in the middle of the ocean . . . ' said Kathleen. 'And,' she went on triumphantly, 'Barny arrived a bit late at Cranford because he was so upset by the beauty of it. He sent telegrams. And he drove all the way out to the house in one of those awful jaunting cars. And he got there at tea-time . . . '

'It was a beautiful evening,' went on Toddy. She was enjoying herself thoroughly, working up atmosphere with a heavy hand. 'And the setting sun made the drawing-room all golden. He was shown into the drawing-room, d'you see?'

Pamela saw.

'And a parlourmaid came in, carrying silver teapots and trays

16

and everything; and then Lady Cranford came in, who he was going to be heir to ... '

'And what do you think?' said Kathleen intensely.

Pamela didn't think at all. She was enchanted.

'Why ... ' said Toddy. 'She was the woman on the Dublin boat.'

'Goodness,' said Pamela.

'Well, that was all right,' said Toddy briskly, 'because of course they liked him *awfully* and of course they made him their heir, but ... '

'Nine months later she had a little son and so of course he was disinherited,' said Kathleen, her strange, black eyes glowing.

'What?' said Pamela, aghast. 'Heavens. It's like a story by De Maupassant.'

'Oh, it's nothing,' said Kathleen, carelessly. 'That sort of thing happens to Barny all the time ... '

'Goodness,' said Pamela again. Her eyes stood out on stalks.

A bell, clanging dismally, like a muffin man, began to approach along the corridor.

'Dinner,' said Toddy. She jumped down from the bunk and held out a square, brown hand with a signet ring on the little finger. It matched her cuff-links. Pamela took her hand and jumped down.

'And let that be a lesson to you, young DuVivien,' went on Toddy, grinning. 'Don't do anything with strangers on ship-board.'

'Oh, I won't,' said Pamela, fervently. And they began, banging slightly from side to side, to go along towards the dining-car.

II

Dinner on the Train

The waiters in the dining-car on the Unteralp express were far from dapper and wore piqué coats. The head waiter was the only one with individuality. He had a round, wise, fawn face that occasionally twisted with curious passions and always glistened with sweat.

The dining-car was noisy because the tables were not fenced off from one another with high padded walls. Every diner, if he tried, could hear some part of the shouted conversations at the tables on either side of him. Also, there were no tablecloths to muffle the clattering and clinking of knives and forks.

Edward Sloper and Fanny were the first to arrive for dinner. Fanny led the way down the big, echoing metal car. She sometimes screamed a little as the movement of the train flung her against a table; and she sometimes (from purest habit) flung a brilliant smile at the head waiter. Fanny was extremely chic. She wore a little black suit that fairly glittered with diamond clips. The head waiter was unimpressed. He liked his beauties to come naturally.

Edward and Fanny settled themselves in two seats, rather too near the kitchen. Edward had taken off his overcoat. He still looked extremely large in a dark blue double-breasted suit. He wore large, very clean wash-leather gloves, which he now removed and laid beside his plate. His hands were good. He was innocently proud of them.

He linked his fingers together, leaned his chin on them and smiled ingratiatingly at his wife.

'And *there* we are,' he said, cosily.

Fanny looked sour. She said nothing. Her round blue eyes watched the doorway, endlessly, for Barny Flaherté. They seemed to Edward to be very hard and quite unswerving.

II

Rosalie Leamington and Joyce and Margie arrived next. Both children were unattractive, but Joyce was the elder.

She had straight brown hair like her father's. Her teeth were lashed tightly into place with a strong plate of metal-fencing. When Joyce felt that no one was looking she picked at it methodically with her forefinger. The rest of the time she sucked at it furiously, to dislodge the cement that held it in place. This gave her the unhealthy look of a young rabbit. Joyce was a fast worker on a plate and it usually only took her six hours to loosen one. It would spring, twanging furiously, from her mouth and then her sister Margie would run, sneaking, to the nearest authority.

Margie was a red-haired and faintly insanitary prig. Her name, incidentally, was short for Margaret and was therefore pronounced with a hard G, as in Handel's Largo. How she had lived for twelve years no one shall ever know. Joyce was fairly well liked, but Margie was an object of terror to one and all. Even Regan, her mother, unnaturally devoted, was bewildered by her. Barny positively detested her.

Rosalie Leamington propelled the two children by a light hand, one on each shoulder. She was nicely dressed in a tweed coat and skirt and a fawn jumper and small pearl necklace. Five years' work in the Admiralty had bred in her a tendency towards tuberculosis and an unnatural detachment. She did not think of the children at all, except as physical phenomena, like earthquakes or rainstorms. This was just as well. They were a naturally unkempt pair.

Margie asked shrilly if Auntie Toddy would come to dinner and Rosalie said she expected so.

'P'raps she'll forget,' said Margie, nipping Joyce, who hit her arm. 'Auntie Kathie often forgets. Joyce *loves* Auntie Kathie.'

Joyce sucked her plate.

Fanny Mayes watched the head waiter approach, skirt the two children defensively, and put the whole party at a much better table than Fanny's. She scowled and looked down.

'That governess,' she said viciously to Edward, 'gives herself *airs.*'

'Oh?' said Edward, amiably, crumbling bread. 'I'm hungry. Barny thinks the world of her—'

'That's what I mean,' said Fanny. Her eyes, which looked exactly like two round, bright decorative buttons, had swerved back to the doorway.

Rosalie Leamington, with her well-scrubbed hands folded on the table in front of her, sat with her head bent. The light caught her large, pink-rimmed glasses and her hair. This was fair and nondescript, but not unattractive. Each sixth hair was already prematurely grey. Rosalie did not look delicate, but the work in the Admiralty Mappin Terraces and the long hours had sapped her vitality. The family doctor had ordered her abroad. She could only afford to do this as a governess, or a paid companion.

She considered herself rather too good to be a governess. Nevertheless she was impressed by the Flahertés, by their glamour and their money.

Behind them the restaurant-car filled up. Kathleen and Toddy came in, saw Rosalie and their two nieces and cheerfully insisted that the head waiter add a fifth chair to their table. Margie lost her head and screamed a lot of directions that no one obeyed. Joyce sucked her plate. Rosalie began to feel a headache coming on, so she smiled in a very civilized way and suggested that Toddy might like some bread. Toddy stared at her.

Johnny and Natasha came in. Natasha cowered slightly to allow a bouncy young man in tight black ski-ing trousers and a yellow sweat shirt to push past her. He was with a brusque young woman and they shouted such things as 'Telemark' and 'Stem-Christie', at one another.

Over dinner Pamela began to tell Natasha the story of Barny Flaherté's early disinheritance. Natasha listened, enthralled.

'That,' she said, with her mouth full of black-market *poulet*, 'is just what I mean by drama. It is my cup of tea altogether.'

'And mine,' said Pamela.

'But this,' said Natasha, suddenly crestfallen and sad, 'is already happened. There is no chance of further drama from him, I am afraid.'

'Dunno, honey,' said Johnny. 'Is this chicken or is this cat?

When *one* thing like that'll happen for a feller, things like that'll go on happening all of his life. You see.'

'Just what Kathleen and Toddy said,' said Pamela gravely.

'And which are they, now, these Toddies and Kathleens?' said Natasha.

'Well, those over there,' said Pamela, a little dubiously. 'With those two nasty little girls and that gentlewoman in spectacles . . .'

Kathleen was laughing, rather too widely and foolishly. She was feeding Margie with a fork. Toddy had twisted a cigarette into a very long holder and was biting it savagely. Joyce was sucking her plate. Rosalie Leamington was looking at the door, where Barny Flaherté had just come in and was waving to Fanny Mayes. Fanny was now all smiles.

'Dunno, I'm sure,' said Johnny, solidly. 'They look pretty screwy to me, your friends.'

'They can tell fortunes,' said Pamela, defensively. 'With cards,' she added as an afterthought.

'That is always good,' said Natasha.

There was a pause, while plates were taken away and the smell of death filtered through the dining-car. This was easily traced to camembert cheese, now handed round with small warped pears. Natasha suddenly brightened. 'After supper the kiddies shall be sent to bed,' she said, 'and their Aunts will tell my fortune. And everybody else's too . . .' she added with a bright, unselfish smile. And oddly enough, Natasha got her own way.

III

Natasha had said, somewhat confusedly (for she referred collectively to Joyce and Margie, Miss Leamington, the Slopers and

22

Mr and Mrs Flaherté): 'when the grown-ups are gone to bed we can *all* play with the two aunties and the cards.'

The restaurant-car slowly emptied and the fumes of cigarette smoke as slowly dispersed. The head waiter seemed to like Kathleen and Toddy and he allowed them to stay on at their table. This may have had something to do with the enormous quantities of brandy that Toddy Flaherté was absorbing.

Johnny and Natasha and Pamela moved over and joined Toddy and Kathleen. Johnny even began to drink brandy. Among the wine stains, the old pieces of bread and the scratches left by the knives and forks during the last five years, Kathleen Flaherté dealt out Natasha's fortune.

Natasha was *so delighted* to get the King of Hearts (who was *not*, she insisted, Johnny), the thoughts of the King of Clubs and also the Knave of Diamonds.

'He does no one any good at all, that one,' said Natasha, with her lovely head on one side, pointing to the vicious-looking Knave of Diamonds.

'No indeed,' said Toddy, filling her glass from the bottle and bending forward. 'But everything will be OK Look. There is admiration and flattery and a great personal success. And drops of drink and excitement.'

'Quite a party,' said Johnny, sourly. He looked at Toddy under lowered lids, decided she was merely a *poseuse* and looked away again.

After this they told Pamela's fortune. It was more than obscure and meaningless. Johnny was bored by his. Both Flahertés had already told their own that day and said it was unlucky to re-tell them.

'All right, then,' said Pamela. 'What's wrong with someone else's? The governess? Or your cousin Barny? Or his wife?'

The sisters looked at each other.

'I don't know,' said Kathleen. 'We haven't told Regan's for ages. But it's always so unhappy it depresses me.'

'Perhaps it will be quite *gay* this time?' said Natasha, hopefully.

'I doubt it,' said Toddy, handing the Queen of Diamonds to Natasha to hold. 'Well, then, here she is.'

'Here is Regan,' said Natasha. She placed her solemnly in the very middle of the table. 'She is this woman with red hair who has sat here . . . ' she pointed, 'and who is so nervy?'

'I thought you knew her. Yes, that's her,' said Toddy, gulping brandy. She lit another cigarette and screwed it into her uncomfortable holder.

I do not understand the intricacies of fortune telling, nor can I ever remember what the smaller cards mean. In Regan's first round there was, apparently, misery, torment, jealousy and soul weariness.

'As usual . . . ' said Kathleen as Toddy dealt briskly. 'But look, here are the parties and the excitement and flattery just as in Mrs DuVivien's. There must be going to be a good time at Katsclöchen.'

The hearts and diamonds fell in a small shower round the Queen of Diamonds, but she faced away from them.

'Oh,' said Johnny flatly. '*You're* going ter be at Katsclöchen too?'

'Yes,' said Pamela, quickly.

'And the dear little kiddies too,' said Natasha in her slow soft voice.

Johnny poured himself a stiff drink. He began to wonder if there might not be alternative accommodation in Kesicken or Mönchegg.

'How odd ...' said Toddy, in a thick, strangled voice. 'The party is all *behind* Regan ...'

'That's what the Catholics call *turning the back on the world*,' said Kathleen, tossing her long black locks behind her shoulder.

'Do you *know*?' said Toddy with just the tiniest hint of drunkenness, 'If I didn't know Regan as well as I do I'd say she was going into a nunnery. A what's name? Convent?'

Kathleen dealt more cards. She tried out more combinations. The cards fell over and over again in the same pattern. Finally she sighed and complained that her eyes ached. She pushed the cards into the middle of the table and stood up.

'No good,' said Toddy.

'No,' said Kathleen. 'I'm going to walk the whole length of the train to stretch my legs. Then I'm going to bed.'

She looked down at the cards and shivered.

'Poor Regan,' said Natasha.

Toddy looked at her sharply.

'What do you mean?' said Toddy.

She slapped the cards into a pack and put them in her tweed pocket. She corked the brandy bottle and tucked it under one arm.

'Oh, it is such a little thing,' said Natasha. 'A bad fortune. But I am always hating it so *much*. Aren't you?'

IV

Pamela in the top bunk opened her eyes and stared round her. The great train had stopped. Someone a long way away called

25

out 'Schröster and Unteralp' and slammed a door. Unhurried, shuffling feet went up and down the platform. Pamela turned over and prepared to go to sleep again.

Instantly the light in the bunk below was turned on. Miss Leamington groaned and sat up and lay down and groaned again.

Pamela wanted to giggle.

Miss Leamington reached a long, thin arm down to the floor and picked up a notebook, a writing-pad and a fountain-pen. Pamela, watching her covertly in the looking-glass over the wash-basin, was fascinated. The notebook she knew. She had already looked at it, furtively, from a distance. It was bound in stiff, red cardboard and was called, 'Elocution – up to the age of 17'. It contained such fragments as 'The Thief of Spring' by Humbert Wolfe, 'Riouperoux' and 'The Dying Patriot' by J. Elroy Flecker and 'For the Fallen' by Binyon. Most lyric poetry gave Pamela 'the sick'. Moreover, Pamela suspected, Miss Leamington was one of those women who wrote verse herself.

Pamela now decided that she was in for a disturbed, but probably amusing, night. She was absolutely positive that Miss Leamington was in the middle of a Sonnet Sequence and might ask her any minute for six rhymes for 'lust'.

V

Miss Leamington was not writing verse. She was writing a letter (or, as she would have called it, 'a note') to a girlfriend in Cambridge, a Miss Sewingshields. Miss Sewingshields was a lady don.

Dear Barbara,

Well, it is all just as you warned me. 'Mr Rochester'
(Barny Flaherté, my employer) is devastation itself. Vague,
charming and utterly bored with his wife and children.
Regan, the wife, is one of those women who would drive a
governess to drink!!! Mr Rochester is, so far, immune, but
his cousins all drink a great deal.

I suppose the children are all right. They are much
like any children. Rather unintelligent and dirty and
unattractive compared with what we were at our age,
when at St Sepulchres, and I hate red hair, anyway.

On the train, as I have said, are Mr Rochester's cousins
and the children's aunts and that rather famous architect
who built St S's. You remember? Edward 'Ally' Sloper who
was 'up' with Tom: Your Tom, I mean. I haven't spoken to
him yet, but no doubt I will.

I am sharing this carriage with a nondescript young
woman, who (I must say) is a very quiet sleeper . . . '

The train went forward here with a sharp lurch. After one
or two abortive blots and scratches Miss Leamington laid down
her pen with a sigh. It was always so difficult, she found, to go
to sleep when she had waked up. Soon she was snoring faintly.

That 'quiet sleeping, nondescript' young woman, Pamela
DuVivien, lay awake for an hour or so. She would have liked
to hear the train cross the Schizo-Frenian Frontier. She would
have liked to be able to say to herself, 'Now I am in Schizo-
Frenia.' By the time, however, that the French Customs were
tramping up and down the train, Pamela, too, was fast asleep.

III

Schizo-Frenia

With the dawn came the Schizo-Frenian Customs, who could hardly have been more anxious to find large quantities of francs in Natasha's stockings. For some reason they thought poor darling Natasha looked like an International Currency Runner. They stayed in her sleeper for about half-an-hour, and more or less ignored the rest of the train.

By the time that they had gone away and Natasha and Johnny had restored a little order neither of them wanted to sleep any more. They looked out of the train window at a strange, pale landscape, something like Northumberland. There was not a teaspoonful of snow anywhere in sight.

Johnny dressed himself in his coupon-free Gamage's pilot's fleece. It made him seem even bigger than usual. He filled half the carriage as he stooped and looked out into the unsympathetic dawn.

'Say ... ' he said, gloomily, to his wife, who was curled up and watchful, in the top bunk. 'Berkeley Square was better'n this for snow ...'

'You could so *easily*, I am thinking, have stayed in Hampstead, my poor Johnny,' said Natasha, 'and done the ski-running by the Spaniards.'

'I'll go away,' said Johnny, miserably, 'if you're goin' to get up.'

Natasha blew him a kiss and he jerked open the door and stepped out, shivering, into the draughty corridor.

II

As Johnny walked down the corridor, heads bobbed out at him and back into their sleepers again. Here and there a half-open door showed scenes of indescribable confusion. Johnny passed Toddy and Kathleen Flaherté's sleeper. He glanced in by mistake and saw Toddy, partially disrobed, skipping about in an attempt to dry herself. She was examining her waist. Johnny hastily recoiled.

He reached the dining-car considerably shaken and found that it had been changed in the night and was now under Schizo-Frenic control and quite different. There were apparently unlimited quantities of butter, bread, cherry jam and omelette. Johnny sat down and began to eat an enormous breakfast. Everyone was extremely civil. And then the bill was presented.

'I have only English money,' said Johnny, searching his trouser pocket.

'OK' said the waiter, with a sweet smile, taking a ten shilling note from Johnny. He made no effort to produce any change.

'Well. Damn. The most expensive I ever ...' began Johnny.

Miss Leamington and her little charges banged against him as they stumbled by. Johnny winced and stood up. He felt defeated. He brushed some bread crumbs from his lap and lit a small black smelly cigarette. He was about to warn Miss Leamington about the expensive breakfast when she drew in her breath with a sharp hiss. Johnny sighed and lounged out.

He met Natasha and Pamela in the corridor. Pamela clutched a twenty franc note in one hand and Johnny marvelled at her.

'It costs ten bob English,' he began, 'how did you know to get some Frenic money?'

'They told me at the agency,' said Pamela.

Johnny flattened himself against the window as Barny Flaherté and Fanny Mayes tried to pass them.

'It's too *bad* of you, Barny,' Fanny was saying in a high, metallic voice.

'Shut *up*, Fanny,' hissed Barny. His voice was still attractive and caressing, but there was a subtle menace behind his words. 'With Ted about I can't ...'

'I only *came* to Schizo-Frenia because ...' went on Fanny. Her voice was very near breaking-point. Barny shrugged his high, thin shoulders. They went away to the restaurant-car.

Then Edward Sloper, looking amiable and not *really* following on his wife's heels, appeared at the other end of the corridor. He was carrying a copy of the *New Yorker*. His wash-leather gloves remained miraculously clean and fresh, like daisies. Behind him, her face now etched and outlined by railway dirt, came Regan Flaherté. She ran past him like a high-stepping mare, saying, 'Excuse me, Ted.' One of Regan's Things was a super sensitive skin. She was therefore unable to wash in French water, and she had forgotten to pack her cold cream. Consequently she looked wildly unattractive.

Natasha shook her head as she passed.

'I am hating *so much* scent in the early morning,' said Natasha. 'Even when it is the famous Flaherté "*Whew!*" Ten shillings? My poor Johnny. It is not true.'

'It was true,' said Johnny, crossly. 'Smelt more like "*Pong!*" to me . . .'

'If you made as much money out of "*Whew!*" and "*Pong!*" as the Flahertés do,' said Pamela solidly, 'I bet you'd stink in the early morning too . . .'

'Your stepmother would do no such thing,' said Johnny.

'It is not money that I mind people stinking of,' said Natasha and moved gently away.

'Thirty-five pounds,' said Johnny morosely, his hands deep in his pockets, 'won't go very far at this rate.'

III

In the diner everything was tumultuous and frightening. Toddy Flaherté told her sister that her shingles had returned. Barny had escaped Fanny Mayes and had seated himself at a table with his children and governess. Rosalie Leamington was instantly aware of the dirt in her finger-nails.

Regan and Fanny and Ted Sloper were a difficult and silent party. Of them only Ted pretended to be happy. He read his *New Yorker* and laughed, rather irritatingly, at the jokes. Sometimes he showed his wife what he had found and she scowled at him.

'This is good,' he said, with a deep cheerful laugh. 'This sheriff. With "Gone to Lynch", written on his door.'

'I *don't* like coffee,' said Fanny, chewing her underlip. 'I want tea. My liver is like hell without tea.'

Across the car came Toddy's voice, sharpened to several fine points by her sleepless night.

'I call you *madly* unsympathetic, Kath,' she said. 'Shingles itch like hell as it so happens. I might have known this journey'd bring 'em on.'

'All you've got to do is put very strong surgical spirit on them,' said Kathleen. 'Or gin. Or whisky.'

'Or "*Whew!*" or "*Pong!*",' said Toddy.

IV

Joyce and Margie were utterly overcome by their father. They had become almost imbecile with shyness. Joyce now had a splendid purchase on her plate. She worked steadily at it and made distressing noises like a dredger at low tide. Margie's hair already needed brushing. Joyce suddenly, foolishly, tried to ingratiate herself with her father.

'You know my mouse?' she said, suddenly.

'No, thank God,' said Barny.

Rosalie Leamington laughed. Barny looked gratified, but a little ashamed of himself.

'I hate mice,' he said. 'What about it?'

'Nothing,' said Joyce. She looked glumly at the floor.

'I believe you've got it here *with* you,' said Rosalie Leamington sharply. 'Have you?'

Joyce didn't reply.

'Have you?'

'Of course she has,' said Margie. 'It's up her sleeve.'

The mouse was very small, but when it was suddenly released by shaking it caused a lot of trouble. It ran, shrieking furiously, along the table through the plates and plunged to the floor in a swift, scrabbling flash. Fanny Mayes screamed and sprang on a chair. She had good, neat legs.

Rosalie Leamington seized Margie's wrist.

'No,' she said, sharply. 'You shan't go after it. You know perfectly well you shouldn't ever have brought it with you. Now you must take the consequences . . .'

'Admirable,' said Barny, nodding. Then he added under his breath, very quietly: 'When you're angry, you know, you're jolly good lookin' . . .'

And Rosalie Leamington blushed fierily and let go of Margie's wrist.

'Someone will hear you,' she said, softly.

V

Toddy Flaherté' was fighting a dreadful impulse to scratch her shingles. She suddenly felt an extra tickle on her ankle. She was wearing slippers.

'What the hell?' she said, bending down to it.

Kathleen also bent down.

'A white mouse,' she said. 'How extraordinary.'

The mouse chase, which had lasted just seven and a half minutes, had, it seemed, raged round the Flaherté' sisters unobserved. Even the head waiter, flicking viciously with a tea towel, had escaped Kathleen's notice.

'It is *not*,' said Natasha, leaning forward. 'Not extraordinary at all. It is your niece's mouse. Yes.'

'Niece's mouse?' said Toddy. She lifted it up gently on the palm of her hand. 'It's a nice mouse,' she said. 'Thanks for telling me. I must give it back.'

She looked round the compartment.

'I shouldn't do that,' said Pamela, anxiously. 'Not if you like mice, that is . . . '

'Oh?' said Toddy.

'They'll only kill it . . . '

'They?' said Toddy.

'Your cousin Barny and the governess . . . '

'Barny?' said Kathleen, suddenly interested and concentrating. 'And the governess?'

'Are they . . . ?' said Toddy. They both turned round and stared at Barny.

Margie was now weeping noisily and horribly. Joyce was looking haughtily out of the window. Barny was paying the bill and Rosalie Leamington was looking up at him as though she had never seen him before.

'Oh God!' said Toddy. 'How squalid.'

And slipped the mouse into her pocket.

IV

Miriam Birdseye

The train thudded along toward Gulich and Unteralp comfortably enough. Most of the passengers, however, were by now extremely hungry. Johnny DuVivien, for one, refused to go anywhere near the dining-car again. He would not spend his daughter's money on his own stomach. Or so he said.

'And so *much* of it,' Natasha said, vaguely, looking out of the window. 'So splendid. So little snow.'

In the hay-coloured meadows there was still only very occasional snow, usually lying under the lee of small black pine woods. Johnny, smoking endless black Russian cigarettes to 'fix' his hunger, became more and more depressed. Eventually, with bells clanging for crossings and for the station itself they drew slowly into Gulich.

Pamela promptly sprang unselfishly from the train and chased after a gentleman with a small glass wagon. On the wagon she had seen rolls, ham and a form of sausage. Even at this distance she could smell the garlic.

A block of small pale blue food tickets had been issued to all travellers at breakfast. Pamela was determined to buy as much food with her remaining money as she was able. She bought eight hard-boiled eggs, eight rolls, some very good praliné chocolate and two fawn, garlic smelling sausages. There was no butter.

Johnny's face lighted up as Pamela climbed back on the train clasping her purchases. It was agreed that this was not the same thing as spending money on Johnny's stomach.

The next part of their journey was punctuated by rhythmic chewing and by the dropping of small pieces of silver chocolate paper on the floor at their feet. Outside, as they climbed towards Unteralp, snow began to appear in larger quantities. It was not yet, however, lying deep and crisp and even. And Johnny was too taken up with peeling the hard-boiled eggs to notice the lack of it. This was just as well.

II

Fanny Mayes was one of the few people who took luncheon in the dining-car. She determinedly thrust herself in between Barny and Regan. Regan moved uneasily as she approached and clenched her long, thin hands.

Ted Sloper caught Barny's eye with a grimace. He ordered two bottles of claret. The meal therefore went off a little better than might have been expected.

Regan, abstractedly tearing bread, thought out loud that it was so nice that Joyce had taken such a fancy to Toddy. Regan had, she said, been along to borrow cold cream from Kathleen and had found Joyce playing Beggar-my-neighbour with Toddy.

It had been decided that Toddy would keep the mouse for the rest of the journey, but Regan did not know this.

'That god-damned mouse,' said Barny suddenly. 'At breakfast. Hah. That was funny.'

Regan winced, considering herself snubbed. Barny turned to Fanny and filled up her glass again.

'Fanny, here, looked idiotic,' he said. 'Jumpin' on chairs. Didn't she?'

He looked at Edward, who said he hadn't noticed. Fanny shook her smooth golden head and spoke. She spoke unkindly, taking it out on Ted.

'Ted never notices *anything*,' she said meaningly. 'Do you, Ted?'

'Oh, I dunno,' said Ted. ''S'much's the average chap, I suppose.'

They had reached the coffee stage. Barny was looking about him and flicking his fingers for brandy.

'Extraordinary, how *dumb* Ted is, considering he's quite fairly famous,' said Fanny bitterly. ' . . . Oh damn.'

'And *now* what?' asked Barny, perhaps a little viciously. He did not (he said) enjoy seeing Fanny bait Ted Sloper. In this respect Barny was unfair to Fanny. It was exactly her vixen-ish quality that had first attracted him. Now it repelled him.

'I've forgotten the sugar. *Darling* Ted, could you? It's in a little screw-top glass jar in our sleeper somewhere.'

Fanny still had a pretty smile and now she used it. Ted sighed. He was perfectly able to use saccharine himself. 'But there,' he said miserably, 'I can't tell the difference between Napoleon brandy and brandy.'

'You *know* it's not the same thing at all,' said Fanny,

37

beginning to whine. 'Saccharine tastes *beastly*. How *extra-ordinary* you are, Ted.'

'Oh very well,' said Ted.

He got up and carefully pushed his chair against the table. He put on his gloves. They were no longer immaculate and showed grey marks on the fingers. He left the dining-car slowly, a stiff, obedient, resentful figure.

III

Margie suddenly knocked over a coffee-pot with her elbow and the coffee, leaping in a great jet from the spout, severely scalded Joyce on the knee. Joyce screamed. Margie screamed. And Regan sprang across the carriage like a leopard, also screaming.

'Oh!' shouted Regan. 'These Frenians. Leaving the coffee unattended and leaving it boiling hot, too.'

'So unlike England,' murmured Barny, 'where it is always stone cold and never unguarded for a single instant.'

Regan swept out of the diner, pushing Margie and Joyce and Miss Leamington in front of her. She called rather wildly for picric dressings, carron oil and butter. The confused shouting became fainter and fainter and finally disappeared altogether. Fanny and Barny were left together.

Fanny slid one soft, white hand into his and regarded him through long, mascara-ed eyelashes.

'Now then,' she said, fairly gently. 'An explanation of this behaviour, please?'

Barny shrugged his shoulders and looked away. He also tried to withdraw his hand. Fanny's knuckles gripped it.

'Why you ... you *animal*,' she said, furiously, and then in a quieter, more penetrating tone, 'Don't you love me any more?'

'Love you, Fanny?' said Barny, lightly. 'But I never did. And I *hate* the way you bully poor Ted. Ted's nice. I like him.'

'Oh *you*,' snapped Fanny. She threw away his hand pettishly. 'And this is my *congé*, I suppose.'

'Your what, dear?' said Barny.

'My brush-off, my goodbye, you're giving me the air,' said Fanny rapidly. And then, with a little bitter laugh, 'Throwing me aside like a worn-out glove?'

'I never throw gloves away,' said Barny. 'This is very disagreeable and Ted will soon be back. Do shut up, Fanny.'

'You *bitch*,' said Fanny.

'I'm *not* a bitch,' said Barny, amiably. 'I'm a gorgeous domesticated chap with kiddies to whom I'm *devoted*. Hullo, Ted. Got the sugar?'

'Yes,' said Ted, edging back into the table, holding the little glass bottle gingerly. 'Took me ages to find it. Shut up in Fanny's sponge bag.'

'Say thank you,' said Barny, maddeningly, turning towards her. Fanny promptly burst into tears, climbed over Regan's empty chair and stumbled, weeping copiously, out of the diner.

'God,' said Ted. 'Aren't women hell? I needn't've got the sugar at all. *And* me coffee's cold.'

'Poor old chap,' said Barny. 'Let's get you some more. What's up with Fanny?' he added in a kind voice.

Ted looked down at the table.

'Nerves, I guess,' he said.

IV

'Women hell?' said Barny, banging from side to side as he worked his way all alone, back to his sleeper and his ever-loving wife. 'Hell indeed,' he said. 'And this is hell nor am I out of it.' He stopped for a second and rested his head on the cool glass of the window. The landscape outside was becoming whiter, but there was a brittle and lowering dampness in the air. In England he would have said there was a thaw on the way.

'I shall live quite alone,' he said, suddenly, to the pine trees and the grey, hanging sky. 'I shall live alone on a desert island and see no one. Except at tea-time.'

Some pine trees wearing white snow-hats now appeared and cheered him slightly.

'At tea-time,' he said to himself, 'I shall see people. A native girl?'

He thought a little about native girls and decided against them.

'No. No native girls. A nice quiet intellectual woman,' he said to himself, 'who knows all the arts of living. She can pour tea out of a silver teapot.'

V

At Unteralp they changed, angrily, running down the platform with phlegmatic porters ... These pushed large, flat wagons covered with valuable luggage (which they handed to all the wrong ladies and gentlemen) and talked indistinctly in German.

Joyce Flaherté limped, leaning heavily on Rosalie Leamington.

Rosalie carried several suitcases herself, being of the opinion that death from natural causes (like heart failure) would be less of a strain than the porters. Margie was run over by a luggage wagon, was shouted at by a porter and again burst into tears.

Natasha waited serenely in the near-funicular. It would presently carry them away from Unteralp to Kesicken and Katsclöchen itself. Natasha announced that she could stand no more German. Fanny Mayes heard her and leant forward eagerly. Her narrow, nymphomaniac chin went up and down like a nutcracker as she agreed with Natasha.

'The first sympathetic word that anyone has said for *hours*,' said Fanny. 'Now, I, too, hate German. It gives me claustrophobia.'

Natasha said that she could see what Fanny meant. Johnny and Pamela clambered into the carriage, bullied by a cross, unshaved blue blouse, who said, in German, that he had no use for half-a-crown.

'OK,' said Johnny. 'Give it back, then.'

The carriage was simply furnished with hard, wooden slatted seats, each covered lightly with patterned carpet. Natasha caught some of the heavy beaver wraps that she had spread around her. Johnny and Pamela, flushed and dishevelled, sank beside her and weakly clasped heavy zipper bags on their knees.

'Oh, do look,' said Fanny Mayes, clearly. 'There's Miriam surely. Miriam Birdseye. *She's* a long way from "The Ivy".'

'Huh?' said Ted Sloper, laying down a copy of the *Tatler*. 'Who? Where?'

'Coming up the platform. With all those very young men. In that *hat*,' said Fanny, jealously.

A bizarre procession now wound in view. It was odd that

no one had noticed it earlier. Fanny said she expected Miriam Birdseye had been in bed during the whole journey. This was most probable, for Miriam looked as fresh as paint.

This brilliant revue artiste was famed as much for the youth and number of her lovers as she was for her hats and her heart of gold.

Her *galère* today consisted of four or five young gentlemen, each one more beautiful than the last, slightly worn and *cerné* about the eyes. The average age of the party was about twenty-three.

Miriam saw Natasha from the platform, said: 'Look, there's Nevkorina, the dancer,' and waved furiously. Miriam was tall and not strictly beautiful. Her long black gloves looked as inconsequent in that setting as the paws of a Siamese cat. She was a genius.

'See, Johnny,' said Natasha, waving back. 'Miriam Birdseye. She is always so *careful* of her health.'

'Comin' to Katsclöchen?' said Johnny, brightening. 'That so? You never told me ...'

Johnny for the rest of the journey was quite gay. He could see the *point* of Miriam.

VI

All the way to Unteralp Regan Flaherté made a scene to her husband. She was obviously as overwrought as Fanny Mayes: and probably for the same reason.

The scene started rather quietly: about the children, whom Barny did not love (or so she said). It went on in a half voice about his selfishness and cruelty and ended with a wild, hysterical outburst to the effect that he was no gentleman. Nor, it seemed, had *any* Flaherté ever been a gentleman, however often they had all gone to Eton.

'I was at Winchester,' said Barny.

And this did not help matters.

VII

At Unteralp Miriam Birdseye cantered from the near funicular to the funicular. She ran, an easy first of her little school of chums. They were none of them athletes.

She looked very spectacular and cheerful, with her lovely long legs moving like a race-horse. Her ridiculous hat (something like a coal-black church steeple) threw a fantastic shadow across the platform.

The sun had now come out and everything seemed altogether gayer. Miriam often had this effect on the weather.

Fanny Mayes was not pleased.

'I hear she drinks like a fish,' said Fanny. Her lip curled as she watched the squeaking, scampering young men in their American army duffle coats, tumbling into the funicular.

'*That* is only showing you do not *know* Miss Birdseye *at all*,' said Natasha. 'She is not touching spirits since 1925. There is no need for her to drink' – she added, scowling – 'as she was born drunk.'

As it was well known that Fanny Mayes had been hopelessly intoxicated in her only stage show *(Mascara 1936)* she no longer thought Natasha sympathetic.

VIII

Regan had now reached the point in her accusations where *all* Flahertés (male *and* female) were ill-bred. Kathleen and Toddy heard her in the distance and climbed hastily into the third class. Toddy was still carrying the mouse in her pocket. Regan said she had already begun to detect signs of the hairy cloven hoof in Joyce and Margie.

Barny said he *quite* agreed and thought Margie would grow a tail any minute now. This silenced poor Regan. She walked ahead of Barny, chewing at her lips, while Miss Leamington ducked out of sight with Margie and Joyce. Joyce had stopped whimpering about her scalded legs and was back sucking her plate.

They were a miserable and dispirited lot who climbed into the Kesicken-Katsclöchen-Mönchegg funicular, but they were in Schizo-Frenia.

Natasha and Johnny sat on the fringe of Miriam's entourage, next to two young gentlemen called Roger and Morris. They seemed very fond of each other. Morris was tall and thin with a sallow face. Roger was small and handsome. Miriam suddenly leant across their laps and spoke to Johnny.

'The eagles,' she said, 'are flying very low this winter.'

IX

In Kesicken it was thawing. On a small, melting slope of slush a lady was drawn up on a sledge with a broken leg. Miriam pointed her out and Roger and Morris capered over to the window to see. Their eyes seemed wide with fear. Or possibly it was some other primitive emotion.

'The others will be playing,' said Johnny, inarticulately, turning to Miriam, 'but you will be working, I'm positive. I never forgot that show *Hips and Haws*: Terrific, that's what.'

'Roger and Morris and I,' said Miriam, primly, 'are writing a musical version of *Dracula*.'

X

The Kesicken thaw depressed everyone but Natasha and Miriam. They remained in tearing spirits for the rest of the climb. The mean sound of water dripping from eaves, of picturesque cow bells and sleigh horses running, squelching, through the slush was left behind them as they jerked upward to Katsclöchen.

At Katsclöchen there are two hotels, advertised as 'mountain hotels of the simple kind'. It was at the newest of these (just below the Water Station) that most of the party got down. Here, facing the three mountains of Brauzwetter, Schwab and Glöchner, the snow lay a little better. After all, it *was* a few feet higher up than Kesicken.

The snow here seemed thin, carefully polished and icy: extremely dangerous.

On the right of the railway line was a steep, snow slope, covered with hillocks and nastinesses (known collectively as 'The Bumps') that confounded skiers. On the right of these was a straight, sharp drop, from a sinister crevasse, to an equally sinister wood. It was marked out with red and green flags and showed the International Championships Ski Course. For the championships were to be in Schizo-Frenia this year. Very few skiers were expert or intrepid enough to shoot down this course like bullets. Mostly, they twisted miserably in and out of the Bumps, falling down each time they tried to turn.

Miriam Birdseye wrapped herself in the only fur coat that the burglars had left her. She kept it in the oven when at home. She breathed in the mountain air and stared up at Brauzwetter, across the valley.

'I can never see,' said Natasha, pointing at the Brauzwetter, known locally as 'The Frau', 'why people are not *admitting* she is exactly like a woman.'

Miriam said that mountains were always sexy.

Everyone's luggage was now piled on a sledge by a Schizo-Frenian giant. He pushed it ahead of him up the little icy slope to the hotel.

'Well . . . ' said Ted Sloper, suddenly. 'Let's hope there's some snow tonight, what?'

Natasha stared at him.

'Why?' she said.

'For ski-ing, madam,' said Ted, briskly. 'I'm no expert, God knows, and *I* can't cope with ice, for one. Haven't been on 'em for five years, either. Hopin' to get some practice on the Mönchegg nurseries before I go over Glöchner Glacier.'

'Don't understand, don't understand, don't understand,' said Miriam Birdseye rapidly under her breath.

Slipping, and holding each other up, she and Roger and Morris went hand in hand up the slope to the hotel.

The Water Station Hotel

The 'simple little mountain hotel', known as the Water Station Hotel, was a nice, square, well-built house, standing well back from the railway. It was decorated round the eaves with a lot of 'filthy fretwork'.

There were thirty-six bedrooms, with well-planed pitch-pine floors each furnished with a bed, a wash-hand basin with hot and cold taps and a sofa or a small table. Sometimes the room was double and then instead of the sofa or table there was another bed. Sometimes the room was called 'and bath', and then it was a larger, better thing altogether, with two beds and no wash-hand basin, a mat and a door leading into a small green bathroom.

Natasha and Johnny had one of these 'and baths', on the first floor, at a corner of the house. The windows looked out to the right on the railway line (and therefore towards the Glöchner, Schwab and Brauzwetter) and to the left on the snowy slopes of the Southern shoulder of the Bleaderhorn.

Natasha said she wanted tea more than anything in the

world and lay down quite flat on one of the beds. Johnny wagged his head and said it would be sure to be Extra. He went to find M and Mme Lapatronne to order it.

The Lapatronnes (who owned this hotel) were lovely, quiet people with a great many children. M Lapatronne was small, dark and agile and had been a great ski champion in his time. Mme was tall and thin and exactly like the German tennis player Frau Sperling. The Lapatronnes lived mostly in the glass-fronted office in the hall and also in a dim, unnoticeable room beyond it. Often the children had measles and whooping cough and bronchitis in bed in this room and were therefore neither seen nor heard. More rarely they were quite well and slightly out of control, rampaging round the hotel outside on *luges*. During Natasha's and Johnny's stay they were (on the whole) ill, invisible and inaudible.

The ground floor consisted of a large, well-shaved wooden room with a small bar in one corner and seats running round most of it. Dances were suddenly held here with a piccolo, a cornet and an accordion. There was also a hall, paved with scratchy coconut matting, a dining-room, a servants' dining-room and the office. The kitchen was alongside the office and opposite the dining-room.

All round the hotel, outside, ran a sort of duckboard with long chairs (for sunbathers and tuberculosis patients) and small hard iron chairs and small hard iron tables for the casual and healthy Schizo-Frenians. There was a vast pile of firewood, neatly stacked, sawn off into two-foot lengths. With the wood went a two-handed forester's saw and a small axe. The whole thing was looked after by a gnome in a wool hat. He had very bandy legs.

Johnny found Madame Lapatronne very easily and explained about Natasha and the tea. He didn't even have to speak French. Morris and Roger were before him, doing the same thing. For Miriam.

He gathered that they were on the third floor and also (from their complaints) that Joyce and Margie were next door to them. Elaborate arrangements were made for Miriam and Morris and Roger to use the servants' dining-room instead of the true (and therefore overcrowded) dining-room. As Johnny left he saw Roger tuck a bottle of champagne under each arm.

Johnny's and Natasha's room was next door to the parlour, writing-room, drawing-room, or lounge. It was labelled 'Saloon'. Johnny looked in, half expecting spittoons, Dangerous Dan McGrew and the Lady Who's known as Lou. Instead, there were sofas, heavily upholstered in brown brocade, and arm-chairs and a fumed oak writing-table. On the mantelpiece was a clock (oddly enough, made in Birmingham, England) which didn't work. It was a brass figure of Justice, carrying a pendulum, ill disguised as a pair of scales.

Johnny crossed the room and touched it nervously. It gave a clear, bell-like note and Johnny retreated.

By the time he arrived in their room Natasha was already sitting up and tucking into a vast tea of rolls, butter and cherry jam. She looked up and waved gaily. Her mouth was quite full.

Hoarse cries floated in through the window. Johnny looked out. A flight of skiers in bright, impossible garments were shuffling past the hotel, propelling themselves awkwardly on skis with ski sticks. They looked like ludicrous, painted clockwork birds.

II

By Barny's arrangement Regan and Barny Flaherté had two single rooms on the top floor. Regan was very hurt about it.

Barny graciously allowed her to unpack him and she fidgeted in and out while he lay on his bed with his hands clasped behind his head.

'Well, dear,' he said. 'You know I *have* been sleeping very badly. But I shall get all my health back here.'

'Of course,' said Regan. She put his shirts in neat heaps in the chest of drawers. She wanted so much to trust him.

'I think that's all,' she said, finally. She straightened her back and rubbed one reddish hand across her forehead, 'Shall you get a little sleep before dinner?'

'Expect so,' said Barny, closing his eyes. 'Could do with it after last night.'

He held out one hand to her.

'Of course,' said Regan. She took his hand and slowly unwrinkled her forehead. Last night he had woken at least twice in the sleeper and had once asked Regan for a glass of water. Women always wanted to make fools of themselves looking after him.

She went out of the room and across the passage to do her own unpacking.

Years ago, when she had been the much-run-after rich Miss Regan Menzies of Montreal, she had tried to sort out the young men who truly cared for her and those who cared for the Menzies millions. In the end she decided she could only marry someone who had as much money as she had. Or even more.

So, she had thought (innocently enough), they might start

equally and she could really have someone to look after. And eventually this turned out to be Barny Flaherté. Regan thought that all she wanted was someone 'to look after'.

She quite forgot she also liked them to be grateful to her and dependent on her and admiring of the admirable way she *did* look after them. So unobtrusively, she thought.

Barny was utterly ungrateful, completely independent and often unfaithful. The children were no help. It was no wonder that Regan was often depressed. Each night she took several red pills (compound of Barbituric) to make her sleep. Unaccountably, since she arrived in the Water Station Hotel she had been unable to find them.

She wandered round her little clean cell, putting away her clothes. She had few possessions. As Regan Menzies she had had more than her fill of beauty boxes and enamelled brushes and combs. As Regan Flaherté she had a plain wooden hair brush and a black, utilitarian comb. She put them on the dressing-table with a sigh. If thinking of others was happiness, Regan wondered, what the hell would misery be?

'Perhaps,' she said to herself in the looking-glass, cleaning her face with suspect Schizo-Frenian cold cream, 'I think about them in terms of *myself*. I don't know. I wish I was clever. I wish I hadn't married Barny when I knew quite well it was Elizabeth he was in love with . . . I wish I could have a decent rest tonight . . .'

She wiped the railway dirt from her slightly bulging forehead and cleaned it a second time with astringent lotion. Her hair tingled all along the roots and she began to feel a little better. Perhaps the pills had been put in a drawer. They had not. She made up her face methodically, shading her eyes above and below with green before she realized she hadn't had a bath.

She had beautiful eyes, large and green, like malachite. Barny had stopped considering them at the time when Joyce was born. Tonight Regan looked for a long time at her snow-white neck and arms.

'Surely I am still beautiful?' she said. 'Can no one help me? I suppose I had better have a bath.'

She rang for the chambermaid and ordered a bath, speaking in careful German. She asked her if she had seen the pills. The chambermaid said no and hurried away. She had a lot to do before dinner. Her name was Trudi.

Afterwards Trudi said that she had heard Mrs Flaherté say in German before she switched out her light:

'It is all quite hopeless. Not even Kathleen can help me this time . . . '

III

Kathleen Flaherté was putting photographs and coloured miniatures of their father and brothers along the dressing-table. Kathleen's father was still alive, sitting morosely in some yacht club along the South Coast of England. Her adored mother was dead. Toddy wandered in.

'I wish you'd knock,' said Kathleen.

'Why?' said Toddy. 'Don't be silly.'

'Because . . . because,' said Kathleen, dusting the miniature of her mother, 'because I might not want to see you.'

'Don't be silly,' said Toddy again, crossing to the window. 'I'm your sister. The air is good here.'

She walked over to the window, opened it and stared out across the valley. Brauzwetter and the other two stood out, enormous and white in the blue evening light. The sky was already the colour of blue-black ink.

'They say Schizo-Frenia clears the mind,' she said gruffly.

'Yes,' said Kathleen. She flung a nice dark red corduroy dressing-gown on the bed.

'Poor Regan,' she said.

'Why poor Regan?' said Toddy. She leant against the dressing-table. One of the miniatures fell to the floor with a tiny crash.

'Oh, *do* be careful,' said Kathleen. 'I *said* I might not want to see you. You are *clumsy*.'

'All right. I'm clumsy,' said Toddy. She replaced the miniature. 'Why poor Regan? She's jolly lucky, actually. She's going to lend me 10,000 ...'

'Francs, pounds or dollars?' said Kathleen. 'Are you really so much in debt, poor Toddy?'

'Hellish ...' said Toddy with a grin. 'Dollars.'

'Lor',' said Kathleen. 'That Casino at Monte Carlo, I suppose. And the drink?'

'And the drink,' agreed Toddy.

'Does Regan know yet?'

'No. I'm goin' up to tell her now.'

'Have a bath first,' said Kathleen. 'And for goodness' sake take off those boots. They get on *my* nerves, so goodness knows what they will do to poor Regan's. She's an absolute gibbering wreck.'

'Who isn't?' said Toddy, with a quick, bright, cruel grin. 'What about you?'

'Me?' said Kathleen, starting.

'Uh huh. Barny said today that he really ought to have

married *you* and kept the temperament in the family ... You know, the family ardour ...'

'But I'm not arduous; I mean, ardent,' said Kathleen, mumbling; 'I don't know what you mean ...'

'Poor Regan,' said Toddy, and slouched off to her bath.

IV

'Poor Regan,' ran into Miriam Birdseye on the stairs. Miriam carried a bottle of champagne in one hand (for Roger's heart she said) and a champagne glass in the other.

'Oh!' said Regan, passionately. She stopped on the top step and looked down at Miriam's extraordinary hat. *'You're Miriam Birdseye, don't attempt to deny it ...'*

To Miriam, looking upward, Regan seemed equally extraordinary. Her red hair was piled high on her head, to avoid bath water. Her angular figure was wrapped in a pale green flannel dressing-gown. Bath towels, loofahs, sponge bags, dangled from her sharp elbows like Christmas tree ornaments.

'Yes?' said Miriam. She was startled, and who can blame her.

'You're Miriam Birdseye,' said Regan again. 'I would know that hat anywhere ...' Miriam touched it with the champagne glass and simpered. Her manner was a strange compound of nervousness and arrogance.

'Oh you needn't look like that,' said Regan, walking slowly and menacingly toward her. 'Don't you remember Roddy Menzies?'

'Rather a boring Canadian in the Navy?' said Miriam considering. 'I *think*. Or was that Charlie Mackenzie?'

'Roddy Menzies is my brother,' said Regan, colouring up, for he was indeed a Canadian sailor and he was (indeed) rather boring. 'My baby brother. You know quite well who I mean. Roddy was hardly old enough to be *your son* . . . '

Regan's voice rose to a high shrill scream, above the noise of bath water thundering into baths, which had been a background to this conversation. This now abruptly stopped. The chambermaid, Trudi, stood a little way along the passage, able to hear everything that went on between these two ladies. Trudi understood English perfectly well.

Miriam stared steadily at Regan for about five minutes. Then she poured out a glass of champagne. It was a divine, detached gesture.

'He's my little brother and you've *ruined him* . . . ' continued Regan, incoherently and vehemently. She clenched a fist and struck it into the palm of the other hand.

'If he's the boring Canadian *I'm* thinking of,' said Miriam, swinging the champagne glass round and round, 'there was certainly no talk of *ruin*. He was richer than Rockefeller.'

'Cruel, unpleasant woman,' said Regan, savagely, advancing.

'Such language,' said Miriam, primly. And she slowly and elegantly poured the champagne on Regan's head. Laughing lightly, she went upstairs.

Regan was left, licking the champagne as it trickled down her chin. She spluttered and shouted various words that no one who was educated at Cheltenham Ladies' College should know.

'Your bath, madam,' said Trudi, suddenly, in English.

V

After her bath Regan felt no better. Indeed, if anything, she felt slightly worse. The contemplation of her long, white body, in the bath, had distressed her. It always distressed her.

She covered it up imperfectly with flannels and loofahs. As she washed herself she tried not to look at it or think about it.

When she was back in her bedroom she had to reset her hair. It had gone quite straight from the effect of the bath steam. She was almost sure she could taste champagne on her nose and she thought her hair was sticky with it, too. She sat a long time in front of her looking-glass in an unhappy daze.

Toddy broke into her dream with a firm, cautious knock. It was not a feminine knock. For half a second Regan thought it might be Barny.

'Come in,' she called, 'darling.'

Toddy paused on the threshold indecisively. Regan scowled.

'Regan?' said Toddy. 'Are you busy?'

Regan began to answer 'yes', but Toddy was already in the room and closing the door behind her. Regan changed her 'yes' to 'well?'

'I've come to ask you a favour ... ' began Toddy.

She could hardly have asked her favour at a worse moment. In a few days' time Regan might have been lulled into fairly healthy optimism. Ski-ing agreed with her and made her quite attractive to look at. Barny might even have noticed her again. And she might have said 'Yes' to Toddy's request.

Tonight the benefits of her holiday were not yet apparent. Regan was only aware of the tiresomeness of travelling,

56

unpacking and packing and of her own personal unhappiness. So she was *bound* to say 'No' to Toddy.

'I've come to ask you a favour . . .' said Toddy again.

'Oh?' said Regan, coldly.

'Yes,' said Toddy. 'I'm overdrawn about twice the overdraft I'm allowed,' she said, slowly and heavily, 'and there's no hope of paying it back . . .'

'Oh *Toddy!*' said Regan sharply, in the tone of an angry school mistress. 'Honestly you *are* a bore. How much do you want?'

'Ten thousand,' said Toddy.

'Francs or dollars?' said Regan.

'Dollars,' said Toddy.

'Impossible!' snapped Regan. 'I wouldn't mind if it were any *good* giving it to you. If it weren't to get swallowed up the same way everything else has . . . if you *weren't* going to gamble it . . . or drink it . . .'

'Or pay it straight in to the Bank Manager,' said Toddy, grinning.

'That *isn't* funny,' said Regan coldly. 'You know quite well it's a waste of my money. *I'm* not going to fork out ten thousand dollars to soothe your bank manager . . .'

'But Regan . . .'

'Yes, I *know,*' went on Regan, tartly. 'I've left you about forty times that amount in my will. Well, then, why the hell can't you wait until I'm dead? Eh? Or borrow on the amount of your expectations? Eh? Or leave me alone?'

'Anything you say, Regan,' said Toddy, dangerously calm.

'Why can't you be like everybody *else?*' said Regan passionately. 'And get married? And have children?'

'*Kiddies* . . .' said Toddy in a tone of withering disgust.

'Yes, *kiddies*,' said Regan. 'And spend your money on something more worthwhile than drink or gambling?'

The fact that Toddy considered drink and gambling the only worthwhile things in the world would never have occurred to the utterly unsympathetic Regan. She had never put money on a horse in her life.

'I don't think that's my sort of thing, actually, marriage,' said Toddy. 'I have no sense of possession.'

Regan stared at her.

'And if you want to know . . .' said Toddy, suddenly losing her temper at Regan's smugness, 'I think that you and Barny are a particularly poor advertisement for marriage.'

'Toddy!' said Regan.

'Well,' said Toddy, scarlet with rage and still furious. 'You are a damn silly fool, Regan . . . I come here and ask for a loan . . . a small loan that won't embarrass you a bit . . .'

'Yes?' said Regan.

'And you more or less advise me to murder you,' said Toddy. She moved to the door. 'That's all. Goodnight, Regan.'

The door closed.

VI

Regan Goes For a Ski Run

By the time that everyone had got used to the Schizo-Frenic routine they found the Water Station Hotel extremely comfortable.

The funicular, clanking up and down from Kesicken to Mönchegg, started at eight in the morning and stopped at six in the evening. The nights were utterly undisturbed. They were almost ecstatic periods of calm. The mountains made everything even quieter. When it snowed (and it sometimes snowed in the night) Natasha felt that she lay in a deep, dreamless sleep at the bottom of a pleasant pit, full of grey wool, muffled by central heating. Only outside the wool was the cold stillness of a wrapped, white world. Natasha liked this.

Johnny, also, began to feel about half his age.

On the first morning at Katsclöchen he and Pamela went up to Mönchegg in the funicular to hire some skis. Pamela was, as Natasha frequently pointed out, 'a gamesy girl'. Natasha thought it only right that she should do 'the ski-ings'.

It was a very beautiful morning. No wind, footprint, or ski track disturbed the snow. About two inches of it had fallen in the night.

Johnny and Pamela waited outside the little wooden hut that served as a station shelter. They stood in the full blaze of the early morning sun. It made Pamela blink. Presently she put on her dark glasses. Seen through these the world was still fantastically coloured. It was painted a sharp white and blue, very like the robes of a madonna or a Roman Catholic Saint in plaster.

In the distance the funicular appeared. It was about half a mile away, worming its way through the distant shadows of the trees in the valley below them. The dark pine trees seemed cut out of untidy black paper against the white, curved banks and drifts of snow. The brakeman (another warped dwarf in a wool hat) had already shot away down the track on a small sledge to deal with the points. He rode with his feet sticking sharply out in front of him, like shafts.

The train was fairly full when it arrived. The first truck was flat and open. It had an iron centre piece. Skis and ski sticks leaned here, negligently unattended.

Two early, hard-faced skiers sprang out of the train. They snatched their skis from this truck, put them on, all in a flash, and set off over the bumps like dark, humped birds. Pamela sighed as she stood in the doorway of the carriage and watched their flight. It looked easy and graceful.

They had climbed together into a third class carriage already filled by Schizo-Frenic guides of all ages, shapes and sizes. Mostly, these wore grey-green waterproof trousers and jackets, and sinister hats. They all smoked a most villainous sort of crackling sulphuretted tobacco. Such part of the carriage as did not appear stuffed with their large, brass tipped boots was thick with the very unpleasant smoke from this tobacco. Pamela and Johnny climbed out and got hastily into an empty second class carriage. The seats here were covered with elegant carpet.

The funicular ascended roughly in a spiral, winding round and round the lowest snowfields of the Bleaderhorn. Pamela tried hard to open the windows, but these were shut, crossly, by the conductor who came to punch their tickets. 'To keep fuel and not waste réchauffage,' he said obscurely. Pamela and Johnny were too awed to argue.

After this little episode the windows quickly fogged up with tobacco and carbon dioxide. Pamela sank back exhausted on her seat. And the beauty of the white landscape, the blue sky and the fantastic curves of ski tracks etched on the snow, went unobserved behind the windows, which were now completely opaque.

II

At Mönchegg the funicular ran into a large, grey station, much spread about. It seemed to be nearly all *buffet*. In the distance a vast hotel, flying a small house flag, and some ski and knick-knack shops surrounded a curling-rink. On their left and ascending to the top of the Bleaderhorn was a trembling, sinister ski lift, already working. There was hardly anyone about.

A porter from the hotel, in shirt sleeves, waistcoat, and trousers, was brushing up and down the curling-rink. The rink looked grey and foolish and isolated in the snow. Some blue sky reflected in the south edge of it.

Pamela and Johnny clumped across the snowy, lumpy paths to the ski shop. They felt stiff and awkward in their new boots. There was a very old unshaved man inside the ski shop, polishing something; and there was a very young man rubbing a ski with wax. They were both only *just* pleasant-looking enough. The young man had a rush of white teeth to the head when he smiled.

Johnny and Pamela hired skis and ski sticks. Pamela's seemed to be split (they were made of thick bamboo), but she was too humble to make a scene about them. Someone suggested they might join the Mönchegg Ski School. Johnny said he had played that game before, thanks very much, and he wanted a guide.

'To rub up what I learned ten years ago ...' said Johnny. 'Telemarks an' such.'

The young man sneered.

'No one,' he said, rubbing a hand across his black hair, across the seat of his pants and down his sweater. 'No one does telemarks now. They are quite out of date.'

Pamela wondered what a telemark might be and reflected that she would probably never find out. She was perfectly right.

Johnny paid no attention. He explained very slowly and loudly where he was staying. If he couldn't have the guide until tomorrow that was OK by him he said. He thought of tumbling about on the nursery slopes by himself. Expense was no object, see? The old man promptly became quite obsequious.

'Hans Walter ... that is *little* Hans ... will be free tomorrow. I shall without fail send him down to the hotel,' said the old man. 'Hans has held for many years the championship for running, *slalom* and jumping.'

Johnny said again that that would be OK by him.

'He sounds as though he would be very expensive,' said Pamela, 'and what is *slalom?*'

'I knew once, but I've forgot,' said Johnny. 'I think it's when you go in an' out of poles like on ponies in a gymkhana . . . '

Pamela was silent.

III

She walked with Johnny to the nursery slopes. They lay just below the railway line and almost on top of the station. They were approached, as Johnny now pointed out to Pamela, by one of the nastiest little slopes for a beginner that he, Johnny, had ever seen. Pamela nodded and thanked God that her skis were safely in the shop.

Johnny looked at the slope and went rather white.

Then he stuck his ski sticks savagely into the snow and bent down to loosen the wire springs on his skis.

These, in theory, coil *round* the heels of the eager skier and hold them in place with a *splendid* locking device. In practice this device swiftly undoes itself and the coils of spring then slip unobtrusively (or spectacularly) *under* the heels of the eager skier, who quietly breaks his neck. Or so it always seems.

Johnny spent some time unravelling them and, later, the theory upon which they worked. When he had finished learning about them he was very red in the face and quite hot.

'Thank God your stepmother ain't here,' he said to Pamela.

'Yes indeed,' said Pamela, who had not spoken before.

'Well, *why?*' said Johnny.

'Well, she'd only say my poor Johnny there was, you say, no

skis like this ten years ago and how difficult everything is. Or something like that. And either way you'd feel foolish.'

Johnny nodded gravely. He wasn't in a good temper when he stamped his heels into the springs and clamped the lock back to hold them fast. He picked up his ski sticks and stamped quite crossly on the snow. He promptly fell elaborately, flat on his back, with one ski behind his right ear. Pamela said nothing.

'*Take my skis off!*' cried Johnny.

'You look like a cat washing itself,' said Pamela. Johnny, oddly enough, did not think this funny.

IV

By and by, from the next funicular, and the one after that, tourists and others descended at Mönchegg, put on their skis, stamped on the snow and flew like birds down the track to Lavadün. Johnny had reached the nursery slopes. He had achieved them by taking off his skis and walking methodically sideways, placing his feet like a rock climber. Pamela had watched him go, standing safely and squarely on her two feet by the railway. Then she had turned away to the hotel.

The flocks of skiers, swooping and turning in neat half circles, went past Johnny with grace and maddening precision. He watched them sourly.

'No call,' he muttered to himself, 'f'r people to behave like French aristocracy jest on account of they're able to do a Christie. Pride comes before broken necks, as Heath says. Yes sir.'

And he plodded to the top of a small hillock and went slowly down the other side of it with great and ponderous dignity.

V

Suddenly, with little cries of distress a female figure, sharply dressed in navy blue, came flying down the slope towards him at about 45 miles an hour.

'Help! Help!' it cried.

'Damn you, madam,' replied Johnny, who had lost his head. 'Keep away. Keep away.'

And then, possessed by a strange will of their own, his skis galloped furiously in all directions. His ski sticks crossed themselves behind his neck. He fell forward on his face. And the lady rushed by, still screaming. Her skis flew off. She turned two violent somersaults. She lay moaning in a dishevelled heap about fifteen feet to his right.

'If,' said Johnny to himself, 'if'n she can moan she's still alive.'

He took off his skis. He sat up safely. He felt he had finished for the morning.

The lady slowly sat up too. 'Bit my tongue,' she said miserably. Blood ran slowly down her chin. She was a forlorn sight. Tears started in her eyes. 'Bit my tongue,' she said again.

It was Rosalie Leamington.

'Foolhardy,' said Johnny glumly. He watched her pick herself up, 'Might-a killed us both. We ain't broke nothin'. *But* she deserved to . . . '

VI

Pamela sat happily in the sun beside the rink and drank coffee. She was perfectly happy. Presently a young man in a pair of tight green ski-ing trousers and a short white jacket strolled out of the hotel with an accordion in his hands. He began to play 'Tales from the Vienna Woods'. He played very well. His music made the sunlit morning a special thing for Pamela to remember always: a very small vacuum of perfect pleasure.

She stretched her legs. She lay back in her chair and watched the people as they came and went. Mönchegg, as each successive funicular belched forth its skiers, became busier and busier. Soon there was no snow to be seen, except as occasional background to these brightly dressed people. They had much time to waste. Pamela noticed there were definite fashions among them. All children, for example, under the age of ten, wore red. And most of them seemed to come from Weybridge.

The Flahertés arrived without Barny. They were therefore miserable. Kathleen and Toddy wandered into the Old Schizo-Frenic Knick Knack and Woodwork shop and bought postcards. They wandered out again. Regan, who could ski very well, stood and wasted time. She stared unhappily at the waiters, gay as grigs, who darted in and out among the crowd carrying trays with glasses.

'Come *on*, Regan,' said Kathleen, kindly. 'Come and sit down here and listen to the music and drink some coffee.'

Toddy, her heavy shoulders humped round her ears, presently slouched up into the hotel. She went towards the entrance called 'American Bar'. She didn't even say goodbye.

'I suppose,' said Regan, bitterly, 'she will now get into a poker game.'

She kicked at a loose piece of snow. Kathleen admired her long slim legs in their tightly fitting black ski-ing trousers.

'At *this* hour?' said Kathleen. 'Don't be silly, Regan. No

one plays poker in the *morning*. No. She'll just get drunk and *arrange* a game for tonight ... '

'How disgusting,' said Regan.

'Don't be so silly and bitter, darling,' said Kathleen, still kindly and (perhaps) a little maddeningly. 'It doesn't suit you. Makes your face all hard and nasty. Drink your coffee.'

'Kathleen,' said Regan, helplessly and miserably, 'I *know* I'm becoming a bitch. I *know* I am. I can't help it. I used to be so nice, didn't I? Didn't I, darling Kathleen?'

'Of *course* you did, Regan,' said Kathleen, cosily. She laid a hand on Regan's shoulder. Regan jumped like a frightened horse.

'And now I'm so miserable I'm quite beastly, I *know* I am. I quite feel it and I can't help it ... '

They were by now sitting at a table quite near Pamela.

'Drink your coffee,' said Kathleen.

'Oh Kath, I *can't*. I'm so miserable I can't even swallow. Or eat anything. I wish I were *dead*. And where can Barny be?'

'Listen, Regan,' said Kathleen, very slowly and distinctly. 'No one person is worth all that misery. *No one*, I tell you, is worth it, do you hear?'

'Oh Kathleen,' said Regan. 'It's all very well for *you*.'

'What do you mean?' said Kathleen.

'Well ... ' said Regan, 'you've never really been in love with anyone, have you?'

Which, as Pamela said to Johnny and Natasha afterwards, was a big laugh, for Pamela had never seen anyone in love if Kathleen Flaherté was not in love with her cousin Barny.

VII

Natasha sat outside the hotel on a long wickerwork chair. Her hands (in catskin mittens) were folded in her lap. She contemplated the Brauzwetter, Schwab, and Glöchner. She thought quite a lot about the other people staying in the hotel and she discussed them with Miriam Birdseye, who spent ten minutes of the afternoon with her.

Miriam looked astonishing. She had on a pink silk man's shirt with short sleeves and a navy blue slipover with 'Miriam' and the Flags of all Nations embroidered on it. She said she was pleased to see Natasha and sat down beside her.

'And what do you think of the Flahertés?' she said.

Natasha removed her dark glasses and looked at the top of Miriam's celebrated head. Her thick, pale hair was blown helplessly by the wind.

'These Flahertés?' said Natasha. 'But you must know there are so many of them even in the one hotel. *Which* Flaherté particularly?'

'The man,' said Miriam, shaking her hair out of her eyes. 'Barny. Rather a dish I'd say?'

'A dish,' said Natasha, slowly. 'Now *would* you, dear Miriam? It seems in this hot sun that the snow already on the roof will so *soon* be melting on to us . . . '

'I expect so,' said Miriam, looking at the snow without interest. 'Not that he notices anything *I* do. At the moment, anyway. He's all taken up with that dreary governess.'

'Dreary?' said Natasha. 'My Pamela shares a sleeper with her and says she is quite pleasant enough . . . '

'I daresay she is,' said Miriam, scowling. She waved a hand

and an opal ring flashed and caught the sunlight. 'I always like people for all the wrong reasons. To me she seemed dreary. Yes.'

Roger and Morris now approached them round the corner of the hotel. They looked self-conscious in racoon-skin coats. Miriam looked them over. They smiled politely at Natasha. They thought they were going to be too hot in their fur coats and they said so.

Natasha said the *only* thing was sitting still and then one was so *sure* one was dressed right. She turned to Miriam again.

'I am knowing very little,' she said, 'about this Barny. What I have been told by my Pamela is *bizarre*. He definitely only looks at the governess today?'

'Yes, rather, dear,' said Roger, with enthusiasm. He looked up at Morris. 'And Fanny Mayes is *biting* her nails inside there with vexation, isn't she? Hardly said good morning to her *or* Mrs Flaherté. I *am* too hot ...'

He took off his little fur coat and appeared in a lumberjack's shirt made of dark, queer tartan.

'*What* a nasty woman that Fanny is, dear,' said Morris. 'They tell me she causes more trouble than anyone else in B.I.M.'

'B.I.M.?' said Natasha, vaguely.

'The films,' said Miriam, rapidly. 'Fanny Mayes is a neurotic little Welsh witch, that's what she is. Ugh. How I hate her.'

'And Miriam hates Mrs Flaherté too, don't you Miriam?' said Roger.

'And Miriam poured a glass of champagne over her last night, wasn't that wonderful?' said Morris.

'Goodness,' said Natasha.

'Oh, it's nothing,' said Miriam carelessly.

VIII

By the time that everyone was eating their dinner in the Water Station Hotel a lot of ground had been covered. Natasha was the only person who did not move all day.

Miriam and Roger and Morris had gone down to Kesicken by train, changed all their Travellers' Cheques and had bought a cuckoo clock.

The two children, Joyce and Margie, had spent a happy afternoon throwing boulders and branches into the Luge Track that runs from Wasser Station down to Kesicken. They hoped very much that someone might break their leg. Their father and Miss Leamington had disappeared with two packed lunches into the woods above 'Siding' and had left the children quite uncontrolled. The arrangement suited everyone perfectly.

Toddy and Kathleen had sat about in the sun at Mönchegg for most of the afternoon. They had met a small, bouncy black West Indian prince whom they had not seen since Monte Carlo, 1938. He was exactly like a squash rackets ball and he lent Toddy 5,000 Schizo-Frenic francs.

Regan appeared very late for dinner, unchanged, with snow crystals in her hair. She had, she said, skied from Glöchner Glacier to Verboden to Lavadün. She never remembered a run she enjoyed more. She had had the time of her life.

'The *peace* of the snow above Verboden,' she said enthusiastically to Barny who was changed and civilized in a dinner jacket, eating chicken casserole. He had also had quite a lot to drink. He frowned as Regan continued her narrative like an excited schoolgirl. 'I can't tell you what heaven it was . . .' she said. 'Barny, I *wish* you'd been there. Do you know I *can* see some point in the world if one's allowed to enjoy it like that?'

Regan's enthusiasm had made her quite pretty, but Barny looked at his plate.

'Extraordinary,' he said, drily. 'Meanwhile' – he added, meaningly, looking at his wife's soup-plate – 'we have reached the chicken, while *you* . . . '

'Oh dear,' said Regan, gulping soup, stopping, looking worried and miserable and gulping again. 'I *am* sorry. Oh dear. How *selfish* of me . . . '

And thereafter Regan seemed unable to enjoy a single mouthful. In fact she ate nothing more. Barny told the waitress that she had lost her appetite.

IX

'Where have you *been* all day, Miss Leamington?' asked Margie, in her faint nasal whine.

'Yes, Miss Leamington,' said Joyce, chipping in. 'And have you had a nice time?'

Joyce had worked her plate off early that afternoon and had dropped it, after the branches, into the Luge Track. No one noticed its absence. For the rest of her time in Schizo-Frenia Joyce was untormented.

'And how is Joyce's mouse?' countered Rosalie Leamington, swiftly. There was no conversation after this, and Miss Leamington did not have to describe her afternoon to the children.

X

Johnny helped Natasha to a pleasant little piece of veal with white wine sauce.

'Johnny did magnificently coming down from Mönchegg to the hotel,' said Pamela, 'at least as far as I could see. Until he got to that little dip under the railway bridge.'

'My poor Johnny,' said Natasha, absently, 'so brave . . . '

'Oh, that little dip,' said Johnny. 'I thought I'd broke me neck . . . '

He laid his knife on the side of his plate and ate briskly with his fork in the American fashion.

'Look for me, now, at the Flahertés . . . ' said Natasha suddenly, in a penetrating whisper.

Johnny glanced across the dining-room. Regan pushed her plate of food from her. Barny squeaked his chair back along the floor.

'Finished, dear?' he said, in a charming, modulated baritone. He lifted his horn-rimmed spectacles up into his forehead. 'D'you feel like changing, hm?' he went on, speaking rather louder, to the room in general, as it seemed. 'There's a dance tonight, they say, and I think it would be polite.'

His voice died away as they went into the hall. Natasha looked at Johnny.

'That young man, that one, he is odd,' she said.

'So detached, it's almost inhuman,' said Pamela.

'So selfish,' said Johnny.

'So attractive,' said Natasha. And Johnny, as usual, was mildly astonished, by women in general and his wife in particular.

XI

In the distance the sudden, happy noise of a saxophone, a piano, a clarinet and an accordion went bouncing into a rare old Schizo-Frenic Square Dance. Roger and Miriam Birdseye, clucking with pleasure, hurried, with their heads down, along the corridor to the bar. This had been converted into an admirable dance floor and all the little tables had been thrust back against the walls. The band sat round the piano, near one of the windows.

The music even penetrated to Regan Flaherté's room, where she was changing in a hurry. She looked furiously for her sleeping pills. They seemed to have disappeared.

Trudi and the barmaid, Nelli, very spruce in clean white aprons, jigged up and down behind the bar and sometimes put an extra polish on the tumblers that were all laid out, ready for hideous excesses. The floor was tantalizingly empty.

Roger and Miriam burst on to it and spun suddenly round the room, leaning well away from each other. They beat their feet neatly at the corners. Barny Flaherté came in and leaned against the bar beside Morris and ordered a *very* large brandy. He watched Roger's and Miriam's progress. Obviously he was thinking of something quite different.

Miriam danced with unnecessary precision and panache and was (perhaps) a little aware of Barny's Byronic presence. He seemed in a perpetual dream.

'Perhaps,' thought Morris, looking up at him covertly through long, silky lashes, 'this is charm. Always to make people wonder what you are thinking about . . .'

More people came in. The floor began to fill.

Johnny danced with Pamela, complaining about the stiffness in his calves and thighs ... Kathleen came in and said she would dance with Barny. She pulled him away from the bar. She talked to him all the way round the floor with great animation and Barny obviously did not hear one word. Then he suddenly seemed to make his mind up about something. His face changed and he bent and listened to Kathleen and laughed at her jokes and praised the little band.

Toddy came in, in a very clean, simple navy-blue dress with a severe white pique collar. She sat down beside Natasha with her knees slightly apart.

'Good evening,' she said, politely.

'Is it not?' said Natasha, literally.

'I'm missing a very good game of *chemmy* with Roff Bandra, the West Indian, you know.' Natasha inclined her head, although she could hardly have known him less. 'Because of this dance. Silly, really, when I'm not a dancing girl. However, care to have a small bet, eh? One must do something.'

'Must one?' said Natasha, absently.

Toddy laughed.

'Not if I looked like *you*, I needn't ... ' she said, gruffly. 'Thought you might care to take me at two to one that when that governess comes in, Rosalie Leamington, you know, that Barny'll drop my sister Kathleen cold an' dance with the governess for the rest of the evening?'

'That,' said Natasha, blandly, 'sounds like betting on a certainty. In Russia we do not care to bet *against* such things. It is a principle. Forgive me if I am rude ... '

'Rude nothing,' said Toddy, crossing her legs, leaning back

and whistling tunelessly. 'Well, it's one way of making money, you show y'r sense, that's all.'

'Not at all,' said Natasha, politely.

XII

Rosalie Leamington, as it so happened, was a non-starter. She sat upstairs in the Saloon and finished her letter to her friend Miss Barbara Sewingshields.

Wed. night.

Well, I suppose I can say I am settling down, although I am hardly standing on my head or my heels. I should need all your philosophy, my old one, to deal with the situation that is arising . . .

I am unused, as you know, to emotional entanglements and stimuli. But it is early yet to pour out anything I feel and it would be presumptuous. You might not be interested. So I admit nothing, not even to you. Pray forgive me, Barbara, for my incoherence, it is due to *les nüits blanches.*

This is a lovely place and Mr Rochester, alternately glooming and dreaming and taking flattering interest in Poor Little Me, is certainly *a very pleasant companion.* I shall say no more.

I escaped from my little charges a whole afternoon today and the peace of the high snows was unbelievable. So many things have happened I shall have with me always. Just as you said it would be. You are a wonderful

person, Barbara, and I hope you will understand this
letter, my dear, for I don't. I wish I slept better.

With my love,
Rosie.

Rosalie Leamington blotted her letter and moved over to the
window. It had begun to snow. The light from the bar streamed
out and made square warm patches of golden light where the
snowflakes dazzled and spun, whirling down. The noise became
louder and more exciting. The piano beat, the clarinet called,
Rosalie felt a sudden *pull* towards gaiety and the company of her
fellow human beings. This also, was something she had never
experienced before.

XIII

Barny Flaherté swung Kathleen nearly off her feet and they
both roared with laughter. The music stopped and they
clapped, feverishly, to make the band start again. The band
cleared its (collective) throat and beamed nervously. It broke
into a very quick quick-step.

'I wonder where Regan is?' said Barny, holding Kathleen a
little closer. He danced a couple of steps.

'And where's my sister?' said Kathleen, tripping over his feet.
'They were both here a minute ago. Sorry.'

'Hold up,' said Barny. 'No. My wife hasn't come down yet.
She went up to change . . . ' He stopped and let go of Kathleen.
'I think I'll go and find her,' he said. He moved towards the door.

'Oh,' said Kathleen. She looked after him. 'Shall I stay here?'
she said, under her breath.

The door swung to and fro behind him. The light winked and flashed on the glass panels. Kathleen stood for a second. Then she followed him.

XIV

'No,' said Natasha to Miriam Birdseye and Roger and Morris, who were standing about trying to persuade her to dance. 'I cannot say *why*, but I am not in a dancing mood. I am not happy.'

'But surely,' said Roger, with a swift smile, 'the Great Nevkorina should always be in a dancing mood?'

'I was *never* the Great Nevkorina,' said Natasha, severely. Nevertheless, she looked pleased. 'I was not bad, but I was not *great*.'

The bright little band played a jig while Natasha, in her slow, pedantic English, started to explain quite everything that she felt about dancing, and ballroom dancing in particular. Johnny and Pamela danced quite close to them and waved as they went past. Miriam suddenly said inconsequently:

'I wonder why everything is so pleasant?'

'Because Fanny Mayes isn't in the room, I expect,' said Roger.

'Neither she is,' said Morris and looked round him. Everyone laughed. Miriam suddenly went very still, like an Irish setter making a point. 'Barny Flaherté,' she said. 'Look. In the doorway.'

XV

His eyes seemed blank behind his glasses. His face was expressionless. He looked astonished. Pamela and Johnny stopped opposite him and Pamela realized that something was wrong.

'What is it?' she said. 'Something's happened, Johnny. Mr Flaherté, what *is* it? Tell us please . . . '

'I went out,' began Barny, in a slow, dead voice.

'You went out . . . ' said Johnny, encouragingly.

The music halted. The dancers stopped. The room was silent. Everyone leaned forward and listened. Natasha and Miriam had got up and came forward. There were snowflakes in Barny's hair that melted and fell in small, shining drops on the shoulders of his dinner jacket.

'Go *on* . . . ' said Pamela, urgently.

'Give me a drink,' said Barny. He gulped and then swayed.

Johnny went to the bar and came back with a bottle and a glass. He poured out a stiff brandy and Barny drank it off.

'Before I went up . . . ' he gasped. The words seemed to have no meaning for him. It sounded as though he were thinking of something else. 'Before I went up I went to the front door. It's under my wife's room. She sleeps . . . slept . . . on the third floor . . . '

'Slept . . . ' breathed Miriam.

'On the snow,' said Barny. His mouth seemed stiff and frozen. 'In the snow, nearly covered, you see, it's still snowing . . . '

'Yes, yes, go *on*,' said Morris, passionately.

'On the snow was Regan,' said Barny. 'My wife. She must have fallen. Dead. From the window.'

And his head seemed to slip sideways as he half turned and fainted away.

BOOK TWO

———————

THE FIRST WEEK

I

Barny Flaherté

It was indeed snowing. The wind, whirling up the valley from Kesicken, or down from Mönchegg, was unable to make up its mind which way it was prevailing. Clouds of snow blew off the pile of firewood, like spray. Little drifts formed behind chairs on the wooden duckboard and shifted backwards gradually. The outlines of everything outside the hotel slowly became muffled.

Johnny could see Regan Flaherté's body ahead of him, outside the front door. It lay curiously twisted, already half covered with snow. The wind blew in his face and soaked him.

Golden light from the open door blazed out round him and showed him all he wanted to see. He turned Regan over very carefully. Her neck was certainly broken.

She had been wearing a green evening dress cut very low and her red hair was piled on her head. She wore green earrings and her fingernails were newly scarlet and varnished. Her right arm seemed to be broken. She had not been dead long. In spite of the cold night her body seemed faintly warm.

Johnny shivered.

'She certainly was dressed up to meet death, po'r lady,' he said to himself. 'Sunday go to meeting. Yes *sir*.'

He straightened his back and stared around him. Edward Sloper had come to the front door. He stood, silhouetted against the light. He was square, worried and anxious to help.

'Is she really . . . dead?' he said and swallowed. 'Funny thing,' he added, and coughed nervously, 'two wars an' all that an' I *still* think it's awful.'

'What's awful?' said Johnny, sitting back on his feet. 'Something more *odd* about young married women fallin' outer windows. Woman with two kiddies, too . . . '

This feller, he reflected, was a friend of the family, too. Johnny looked up at him.

'Corpse . . . ' said Ted Sloper. 'Death an' all that.'

He came cautiously towards Johnny, moving his feet carefully as though he were afraid of falling. He looked around him and up at the hotel roof. He glanced down the valley into the twirling snow. He looked anywhere but at Regan Flaherté, lying broken at his feet.

He blinked continuously, trying to keep the snow out of his eyes.

'Wind stings rather, doesn't it?' he said at last, in a careful conversational tone.

'Uh huh,' said Johnny. 'Let's see? How does the police work here?'

'Police?' said Ted Sloper. '*I* don't know. *Well* I expect. But is that necessary? You surely don't mean . . . ?'

'It's an accident, isn't it?' said Johnny, heavily. 'It happened to a friend of yours, didn't it? Means b'rights, in England, we'd have the police. I mean ...' Johnny stopped wondering what Ted Sloper could be thinking. 'She might've ...' he went on slowly.

'Committed suicide?' said Ted, his eyes wide and dark.

'Yeah,' said Johnny. 'Or been murdered,' he said briskly, looking at Ted's face for a reaction. There was none.

'Suicide'd be worse,' said Ted, glumly.

'For heaven's sake ...' said Johnny appalled, '*Why?*'

'Flahertés are all Catholics,' said Ted, and put his hands in his pockets.

II

Five minutes later Johnny finished a thorough examination of Mrs Flaherté. She wore nothing under her evening dress but a pair of openwork knickers and a brassière. Her earrings were emeralds.

'Worth a bit,' said Johnny, peering at them. 'What I should really like,' he said, 'would be a camera. I mean, we c'd floodlight her easy enough an' then we c'd move her in. Up to her own room, maybe. No police force in the world'd mind *that*. They'd have how the body lay when first discovered 'n' everything.'

'What *I* should like,' said Ted Sloper, 'would be a double brandy.'

Johnny looked up at him and grinned. Ted looked white and sick.

'As a matter of fact,' went on Ted, nervously. 'I *have* got a camera. A good one. A German one. It can take pictures in flood or flash, whichever you like. That'd do, wouldn't it? I'll take the picture if you like. I expect we could flood-light ...'

He stopped and swallowed uncomfortably and looked at Regan and looked away again. Johnny nodded.

'Too right that's the best way,' he said. 'Too right. And I guess the hotel will agree, too. Does Monsieur Lapatronne know anything yet, for example? Anyone told him what's happened?'

'I really couldn't say,' said Ted. 'I don't feel very well. Excuse me. I'll come back with the camera.'

And he bolted, slipping through the snow in his thin evening shoes. Johnny looked at his watch. It was exactly 11.15. He suddenly became unpleasantly aware of his wet feet and his wet knees. He was now shivering as badly as Ted Sloper. He wanted a double brandy himself.

III

Pamela came slowly out of the door and approached her father. She seemed detached, intelligent and amiable. She was wearing a fur coat, ski-ing trousers and boots and several sweaters. Johnny was very glad to see her.

'Natasha says to go in,' said Pamela. 'And change into proper clothes. She thinks this will be an all-night party.'

'She is so *certain*,' said Johnny at this point, and they both laughed. Pamela checked instantly and looked down at her feet.

'Sir Sloper said he was goin' in fer his camera,' said Johnny.

'Yes, I know,' said Pamela, 'an' Monsieur Lapatronne says he will floodlight the hotel and poor Mrs Flaherté. Then the picture can be taken. But Natasha says for God's sake to get properly dressed and don't catch cold. I'm to stay here an' watch.'

'OK,' said Johnny, standing up and dusting his knees. 'But Natasha thinks I'm right to make all this fuss, huh?'

84

'Gracious, yes,' said Pamela. 'She's up there right now.'

'Up where?' said Johnny.

'In Regan's bedroom,' said Pamela.

IV

Regan's bedroom was turbulent with the effects of someone who had dressed in a hurry for dancing without the help of a lady's maid. Her ski-ing trousers were in a heap on the floor where she had stepped out of them. Her wet socks lay on either side of her ski-ing boots. The boots were already white round the toes. They had dried too fast.

Natasha paused on the threshold. She locked the door behind her. It was an old-fashioned lock with a hole in the latch for a pin. It did not rattle, yet she felt guilty.

She gazed round the room. Her mild hazel eyes seemed bigger than usual as she tried to fix each detail of the small cold room on her sensitive mind. The curtains were alternately sucked outside into the storm or sharply billowed back into the room. Natasha did not want to shut the window. So she shivered. She wished fretfully that she had thought of taking the advice that she had given to Pamela and Johnny.

She started very seriously to recreate the movements of someone who has just come in from a long, tiring ski run. She put herself in Regan's place: tired and told off by her husband to change and get downstairs as quickly as possible. To please him. Natasha, in her imagination, went over to the wardrobe for her evening dress.

The wardrobe was tidy enough. There was a space on the shelf where a pair of evening shoes might once have been.

And there was an empty coat-hanger, swinging by its hook, amongst Regan's other clothes. There was a lot of loose, rustling tissue paper on the floor that fluttered and tinkled in the wind. Natasha shut the cupboard door and mentally pulled her dress over her head, crossing in a hurry to the dressing-table and looking-glass.

'It is, you see,' said Natasha, to herself in her quiet, soft voice. 'It is just possible that Mrs Flaherté has been like me. This one could be loving the gesture of dressing up to jump out of the window. If *I* were to do this I should be dressed right to the teeth. I should . . .'

Natasha stared at herself in the looking-glass. For a second it almost became a white, ravaged, unhappy mask. She started back. The idea had been too vivid.

'It will be an accident?' she asked herself. 'Or murder, even?'

The white death mask of Regan Flaherté which she fancied she had seen had melted for ever. Natasha looked at her own reflection with relief. She did not care to test her intuitive power any further. She examined Regan's anonymous brush and comb.

Three or four moist hairs in the brush showed that Regan had brushed her hair that evening. The damp on the hairs was quite unmistakable. Regan's hair must have been very wet when she came in from her ski run.

'After all,' murmured Natasha, wrinkling her nose with displeasure. '*All* women are not being like me. Why, *I* should commit suicide if anyone made me *wear* skis. Leave alone to go on the ski-ing runs. So it may be she has not dressed herself up to die at all.'

She went on looking at the dressing-table. There was a box

of creamy white foundation cream and a piece of rather dirty cotton-wool that had applied it. The cotton-wool was stained and damp.

'It is,' said Natasha, 'inconceivable therefore that this woman, *such* a woman, would kill herself after the perfect ski run she has been mentioning at the dinner-table. Or is it? Perhaps she is this rare perfectionist philosophical thing?'

Natasha reflected that the little she had seen of Mrs Flaherté had not pointed to a rare perfectionist philosophy. She pushed with her forefinger at the face powder. It was still in its expensive cardboard container. It was perfectly tidy. No one had spilt it, or even used it. And a lipstick lay beside it with the cap still on.

'Now I ought . . . ' said Natasha, staring down at these somewhat repellent little objects, 'to be able to learn something from all of this. I am *so sure* I should . . . '

Someone knocked at the door.

Natasha's heart gave a convulsive leap into her throat and went on beating there for some time.

'Who *is* it?' she called as though it were truly her room and she had no clothes on.

'It's Toddy. Toddy Flaherté,' said a deep boyish voice. Toddy's voice, however, always sounded as though she were being strangled by something. Perhaps it was emotion, or indigestion. Or both, thought Natasha, and she opened the door.

V

'I say. This is pretty awful, isn't it?' said Toddy. 'So sinister.'

'Yes,' said Natasha, who wondered if Toddy meant that her

presence in Regan's bedroom was sinister. 'Why?' she added, after a moment's consideration.

'Because of that future? Remember?' said Toddy abruptly. She sat down on the bed and screwed a cigarette into her long, embarrassing holder. She glanced round the room. Her sharp black eyes looked like pin-heads. 'She turned her back on the world, didn't she?' said Toddy bitterly. 'Us being Catholics makes it worse.'

She pulled fiercely through her holder like a small child at a lemonade straw. She seemed to become calmer as she did so. She drew back from the edge of her hysteria with a defiant little puff of smoke.

'You are meaning,' said Natasha, maddeningly, 'that she is committing suicide?'

'Oh yes . . . ' said Toddy. 'Of course. The cards showed it.'

'Well, I am telling you,' said Natasha viciously, 'that this woman is probably *murdered* . . . '

For a moment blank surprise showed in Toddy's face. Then she looked angry.

'What makes you think so?' she said. 'Why shouldn't it be an accident? It had better be.'

'I am saying *nothing*. But first I am feeling it very strong in this room and then I am knowing I shall find the clue to back it up with.'

'Oh,' said Toddy angrily. 'Is that all? Scaring the life out of me. I thought you really *had* something.' Her voice took on a hard, cynical, unpleasant quality. 'I heard all about you and your precious husband's behaviour at poor Old St Anne's.* *The*

_____

* *Death Before Wicket*

Original Crime Intuition Committee, aren't you? Floggin' round the countryside with a corpse behind every tree. Looks fishy to me, *I* can tell you. Mind *you* don't get arrested, that's all ...'

'This is rude,' said Natasha.

'It's meant to be,' snapped Toddy. She got up, scowling, and lurched towards the door. Then, without warning, she burst into tears and almost ran out, gulping and sniffing, like a schoolgirl. 'Jolly fond 'f old Regan,' she said, as she went.

Natasha sat down on the bed, mildly astonished.

VI

Downstairs, M Lapatronne, dressed simply and oddly in a calico night-shirt, telephoned to the Schizo-Frenic *Gendarmerie* in Kesicken. Morris and Roger held the door of the telephone box and were very inclined to giggle.

'I thay, Morrith,' said Roger. 'The Thkidtho-Frenic polith dithmitheth uth.'

'I wish you wouldn't,' said Morris, 'I know it's only nervousness makes you behave like that, but I do so want to laugh. Miriam is being so serious about the whole thing, too.'

'Miriam,' said Roger, sobering, 'is a very nice person. So, not unnaturally, she takes death very seriously *indeed*.'

M Lapatronne emerged from the telephone box. His hairy little legs ran in and out under his night-shirt like a spider's. He had been roused by Ted Sloper from his bed, where he had been asleep. He always went to bed when gaiety descended on his hotel. He did not care for it. He was very keen on the death of Mrs Flaherté.

'My friend Hans,' he said, '(this is Big Hans of the Gendarmerie). He says all is OK now that this photograph is

89

taken in flood lighting. He has seen, he says, the hotel floodlit from his house and we are looking very pretty. This event will much custom attract.'

And M Lapatronne beamed with simple pleasure all over his little face. Roger and Morris were astonished.

'Big Hans he say: move by all means the corpse lady into the hotel and he will be up tomorrow. There are no funiculars tonight now. He is suggesting a room where she may lie in state and where people may see her most easily. I am thinking the servants' dining-room ... perhaps ... ?' M Lapatronne put his little bald head on one side.

'But that's *our* dining-room,' said Roger, horrified.

'Miss Birdseye *must* have her meals in there,' said Morris.

'She is so sensitive,' said Roger.

'And a Very Great Artist,' said Morris.

'So,' said M Lapatronne, pulling at his lip.

'Not that I mean to be tiresome,' said Roger again, 'but what about that rather dreary old saloon upstairs, dear? No one uses *that*.'

'My saloon,' said Mr Lapatronne, drawing himself up. 'No,' he added, deflating. 'It is quite true. No one uses that. She shall lie in the saloon.'

And it was so.

VII

The photography went off very well indeed.

From one angle, Regan's pale-lipped face looked extremely beautiful against the snow. Ted Sloper quite forgot his nerves as he wandered around, trying to make a good picture. He also forgot his subject and behaved in a most callous way, fussing with filters and gauges to get the length of exposure exactly right. Johnny and Pamela were rather shocked.

Then they carried Regan indoors.

Her thin body lying along their shoulders, the long folds of her green evening dress, her white face, made a picture like a *macabre* and dreadful ballet. Carrying her, Roger and Morris and Ted Sloper seemed unaware of her weight. They stood straight and moved very slowly.

As they went across the dance floor silence followed them. Guests, who had collected in nervous little groups, broke away from each other and more than one person looked fearfully toward Barny Flaherté. He was slumped on the top of one of the bar stools, leaning forward across the bar. He was very drunk indeed.

The four figures went across the hall, the staircase and the saloon. Johnny came last of all, carrying the precious camera in both hands. His naturally jaunty walk was much subdued.

Barny glanced up. His eyes were glazed and half open. His elbow sent a wineglass spinning to the floor, where it shivered into fifty pieces. He lurched off his stool and stepped forward, clenching his twitching hands, and screamed something incoherent. He spun back to the counter and buried his face in his hands. Johnny came up to him. He gathered him into an enormous hug, like a bear.

'Now, now you-all,' he said, very gently. 'Bed's the place f'r you, boy. Bed an' nice long rest ...'

'Nice long rest,' said Barny, obediently.

Johnny's arm slid across his shoulder. He ran him across the floor to the hall. The inner door swung behind them. And the horrid tension instantly eased. A little sigh ran round the room through the silent dancers. Someone turned to the band and suggested it should play again. The band leader shrugged his shoulders and said: 'Why not?' A heartless little jig began beating through the hotel once more. And it was as though Regan Flaherté and her unhappiness had never been.

II

The Unused Lipstick

The sweetish smell of the quantities of white Alpine flowers and the narcissi that M Lapatronne had scattered for Regan Flaherté merely accentuated the general airlessness of the saloon.

Regan lay with her hands by her sides. The flowers had been heaped around her on the sofa, breast high. All the English people in the hotel were embarrassed by the idea of this lying in state. But really it was the extraordinary behaviour of M and Mme Lapatronne that upset them. In England, when death troubles an hotel, the hushing up is extreme, the loss of custom legendary. The ghoulish and practical reactions of M and Mme Lapatronne had to be seen to be believed.

Monsieur procured the flowers (from goodness knows where, in the middle of the night). Madame renamed half the dishes on the next day's menu: Potage Funèbre was her most alarming choice. And they both sat up until two in the morning, mapping out an itinerary for tourists, that included this new attraction. In fact, they showed all the basic instincts of

Devonshire peasants extracting the last brass farthing of profit from Uncle Tom Cobleigh.

That night, in turn, members of the party stood in the saloon doorway and looked at Regan.

Only Joyce and Margie and Barny failed to appear. Joyce and Margie were safely asleep in bed and so was their father. He slept, of course, a little differently, white-faced, twitching and muttering all night. None of these people woke until ten the following morning.

II

Toddy and Kathleen stood in the doorway and stared about them.

'Regan *was* beautiful, you know,' said Toddy. She had set her feet rather wide apart. Her hands were thrust deep into the pockets of the jacket, which she now wore over her little black dress. She looked incredibly sinister.

'Poor darling Regan,' said Kathleen, vaguely. 'She *was* so unhappy. And she committed suicide, poor darling, I expect she *still* is . . . '

'Mrs *DuVivien* doesn't think she committed suicide,' said Toddy glumly. '*Do* you, Mrs DuVivien?'

Natasha smiled her sweetest smile. She walked towards them along the corridor. She knew quite well that Toddy was overwrought and like many sensitive people she now looked around her for someone to hurt. Natasha nodded.

'I'm glad you don't think that,' said Kathleen. 'It's charitable of you. I shall watch with Regan tonight.'

Kathleen walked towards the flowers and the bier and

the candles which M Lapatronne had lighted. They burned quite straightly and cleanly behind Regan's head. Kathleen's pointed face and her dark eyes seemed pitying and soft. Natasha thought she looked kind and nice. She said so. Toddy scowled.

'She wouldn't look so kind and nice,' she snapped, 'if she thought you thought her "poor darling Regan", was murdered ...'

Natasha shrugged her shoulders.

'As you say,' she said, amiably. 'She was, however, certainly murdered. It is not only thinking. I am knowing, now.'

'Indeed ...' sneered Toddy. 'Why?'

'Because she couldn't have fallen out of the window by accident at that stage in her toilet. Now it isn't likely, is it, that she would open a window and fall out of it in the middle of making up her face?'

'No ...' growled Toddy, 'that's what I ...'

'And if it is suicide she is committing, then she would have *used* the lipstick. For vanity? Do you see? So it is *neither*. And as her face is *half* made up she was pushed, therefore. And by someone she knew *well*.'

'Good Lord,' said Toddy, 'I see what you ... Good Lord. But she might still fall by mistake, mightn't she? Make-up, or *no* make-up?'

'On a night like this? To open a window at all? Even for a fresh air *devil*, this is *madness*. Why, the snow blows right in and wets *everything*.'

'I suppose so,' said Toddy, thoughtfully. 'These windows like little doors with latches are hard to control, though. Certainly she had no lipstick on when she was brought in. I particularly remember I noticed.'

They went over to the sofa-bier where Kathleen already sat, her head lowered. Both of them looked, before anything else, at Regan's mouth. Both of them gasped. Natasha with astonishment. Toddy with horror, and loudly.

For Regan's mouth was heavily painted, a deep crimson. It glowed in the candlelight like a monstrous red flower.

III

Toddy turned to Natasha and spoke in an undertone.

'My ... ' she said. 'You are right, aren't you? I mean, this *makes* you right ... '

'This is not any such place to discuss a matter and disturb your sister,' said Natasha. 'Come away downstairs and we will be going to my husband. He is so *practical*. He will be wonderful about it.'

Kathleen sat quite still beside Regan with her hands folded. She said nothing. She seemed not to hear them. But she smiled at Toddy as they went.

'Kathleen is a *religieuse*,' said Toddy, bitterly, as they went down the corridor together. 'I expect she will be a nun one day.'

Toddy seemed to have changed her mind again about Natasha and was looking at her with a mixture of respect and defiance that was ludicrous in a woman of her age. Natasha was again reminded of a very young schoolgirl as Toddy creaked along the landing. She nodded. Toddy stopped at the top of the stairs to light another cigarette and swore as the wind blew out her match. Natasha, smiling, watched her, partly understanding the fascination of the Flahertés.

In the bar Johnny and Ted Sloper drank hot rum punch called *gluvine*, much sprinkled with nutmeg. They discussed mutual acquaintances on the Stock Exchange. Their conversation consisted chiefly of the phrase: 'I know who you *mean*.' They were in fact, playing the old social game 'Do you know the Poodles of Pom?' which Natasha disliked so much.

Fanny Mayes, in a simple black evening dress that must have cost Ted about fifty guineas, leant back against the bar beside them and kicked fretfully at a leg of one of the stools. Even this nasty trick did not achieve her the limelight. Both men had drunk enough to be quite indifferent to a further assault on their nerves. Fanny was therefore extremely angry.

'You are *extraordinary*, Ted,' she said, carefully watching him. 'I do think you're extraordinary. *How* you can sit there talking about Jimmy James like that when poor Regan ...'

'That bloody Fanny Mayes,' said Miriam Birdseye, further along the bar in a savage undertone. 'What hell she is. Nasty little Welsh witch.'

'Miriam, do be careful ... she'll hear you,' said Roger.

'Doesn't matter if she does, dear,' said Morris. 'She'd never admit to being *Welsh*.'

'Mum *isn't* well,' said Miriam, suddenly, 'Mum's tum's not right. Hullo, Natasha Nevkorina,' (with a complete change of tone) 'what's the *news*?'

'The news is not good at *oll*,' said Natasha, who had come into the room with Toddy. And suddenly, in this company of actresses who could appreciate *nuances*, she was unable to resist a little drama. 'This *poor* Mrs Flaherté is murdered. Yes.

And by someone in this hotel now. Someone who knew her well.'

'Lor' . . . ' said Ted Sloper. And his mouth fell open.

'Oh, poor sweet,' said Miriam Birdseye.

'I don't believe you. The woman's mad. She's showing off,' said Fanny Mayes, rapidly. 'She's hysterical,' she added coldly.

'Natasha,' said Johnny sternly. 'Are you *seein'* things again?'

'Oh yes,' said Natasha, seriously. 'I see this one all right.'

'Perfectly true,' said Toddy, suddenly, gruffly. 'Mrs DuVivien has the whole thing taped, most reasonably. An' I agree with her.'

'Isn't that *splendid?*' whispered Miriam to Roger. Roger choked over his *Gluwine* and had to be patted on the back.

'*Come over here,*' said Johnny, grimly, to Natasha. 'You too, please, Miss Flaherté,' he added to Toddy. And sternly he marched them to a little table by the band.

The band was playing, very quietly, an American foxtrot. Noone paid any attention and noone was dancing. By and by the band put its instruments down and folded its music and softly stole away.

Johnny sat down and dragged Natasha down beside him.

'Now then, honey chil',' he said. '*Give!*'

V

And so, encouraged by Johnny, her narrative punctuated by gruff expressions of approval and admiration from Toddy, Natasha told her story, in her curious, halting, pedantic English.

Johnny, once he had grasped the principle involved in making up the human face, nodded and said he saw her point.

'Kind of like laying out a hard lawn tennis court . . . ' he said, wagging his head. 'First the foundation, an' then the ash, an' then the top dressing. Sure, I see . . . '

'And so, you see, Johnny,' said Natasha, 'when I have realized this I go *up*stairs to look. And here are Kathleen and Toddy (if I may call her so) . . . '

'Please do,' growled Toddy.

'And Mrs Flaherté's mouth has been painted *since* she is dead.'

'By the murderer,' said Toddy.

'It ain't necessarily so,' said Johnny firmly. 'One er these young fellers, Roger, or Morris (why are these sort of young men always called after motor cars?) *he* might er done it to make her look nice. Sir Sloper. He an' Morris an' Roger they carried her up. Or Monsieur Lapatronne with the flowers. One of 'em oughter know, any old how. I'll ask 'em.'

'Bring them over here,' said Toddy. '*Ted!*' she called sharply, 'Come over. We need you.'

Ted came over. He came thankfully, to escape his wife. She could be heard right across the room, saying to his retreating back how *extraordinary* she thought he was.

Johnny told him what had been discovered and what had been decided from it, and he sat very still.

'Can't say, I'm sure,' he said. 'Never notice things like that.'

'Oh rot, Ted. You must've noticed her face when you photographed her.'

'I didn't,' said Ted, and looked down.

'Hey!' shouted Johnny. 'You – all. Morris! Roger! Miriam, bring your boy-friends here. I want to ask 'em a question.'

Miriam, Roger and Morris turned together and approached the table, entwined.

'Did either of you two see Regan's mouth when you carried her up to the saloon? Hey? Was it made up, d'ye remember? With lipstick?'

'Oh, no, it definitely wasn't,' said Roger.

'I particularly noticed how *awful* she looked,' said Morris. 'I mean, kind of white.'

'Well then ...' said Toddy, firmly. 'Monsieur Lapatronne?'

'Oh, damn it ...' said Ted Sloper, exploding suddenly. 'You don't suppose he did it, like a bloody undertaker? My God. To attract tourists, I suppose. It really goes *too far*.'

'What's the matter with you, Ted?' said Fanny, laying a hand on his shoulder. She had approached with a subtle undulation of the hips. 'Are you playing "Murder"? Or what? Who's detective?'

Which, as Miriam said at the time, was in the worst possible taste. But she need not, perhaps, have said it quite so loud.

VI

''s matter 'f fact, madam,' said Johnny, tartly, in the horrified silence that followed Fanny's remark, 'we *are* having a little Game of Murder, as you call it. An' *I* am detective. An' Mrs Flaherté is the victim. An' you shall be the first player to say where you were when they screamed.'

'I must point out that only the *murderer* is allowed to tell lies,' said Toddy, rudely.

'Yes,' said Miriam, firmly. And she looked hard at Fanny Mayes, whose thin red line of a mouth dropped open in astonishment.

'Where were you when Mrs Flaherté fell out of the window?' said Johnny grimly.

'Haven't the remotest idea . . . who says she was pushed? And what time, anyway, and how dare you?' said Fanny Mayes, very angry and slightly out of breath.

'We can't go into how we know *why* she was pushed all over again,' said Johnny coldly, and perhaps a little unfairly. 'We estimate she must've fallen some time from 10.30 to 11 p.m. Well, where were you during that time?'

'I absolutely refuse to say,' said Fanny Mayes. Her mouth quivered and she closed it like a rat trap. 'And I'm not staying here to be insulted. By that . . . *mountebank tart.*'

'Mountebank Tart is good,' said Miriam, nodding.

Fanny Mayes said 'Pchah' and spun round and turned her back. She ran out of the room, her small neat feet in their elegant black evening shoes pattered across the dance floor as she went. She closed the door haughtily. They could hear her going away in the distance along the hall.

'In itself this seems to me *so* suspicious,' said Natasha. 'If you will excuse me, Sir Sloper,' she said to Edward, 'why should *she* want Regan Flaherté dead, I am thinking?'

'Forgive me, Ted,' said Toddy, 'but this is so interesting.'

'Not at all,' said Ted, and drank all his glass of brandy and poured himself another. They had the bottle on the table and Ted was drinking far too fast. 'Help 'self, Toddy . . . '

'Well you might say,' said Toddy, 'that Fanny, being keenish on Barny and all that, she might've thought she could *get* him for ever with Regan out of the way, mightn't she? Not' – she added hastily, turning to Ted again and speaking as comfortably as she could – 'that there ever *was* anything in that affaire you know . . . '

'Oh yes there was,' said Ted Sloper miserably. 'Was plenty

in it. I'd give Fanny any mortal thing she wanted. Always would . . .'

'But I don't think she could ever quite have *got* Barny,' said Toddy, earnestly. 'That's what made her so cross, wasn't it?'

'Changed, hasn't she?' said Ted miserably. 'She's *nastier* now. I don't like her so much.'

The little circle round the table was silent, appalled, listening to Ted.

'Shut up, you fool, you're drunk,' said Toddy savagely.

'I'm drunk . . .' said Ted. 'But, you know, Toddy, that *is* true. Fanny's such heaven when she's gettin' her own way. Sh' can be heaven, *really*.'

He turned confidingly to Natasha.

'*I'd* have given her Barny, if it would've made her happy. I would *honestly*. I did, in 'manner 'f speaking. Barny's m' best friend, you know . . .'

'He *is* drunk,' said Miriam, wonderingly.

'And even murdered his wife to do it, I suppose? Don't be such a fool, Ted,' snapped Toddy.

VII

'Thank you, Miss Flaherté,' said Johnny with a sigh of relief. He turned away from Ted towards her. Ted's head slumped forward on his chest and he seemed to fall asleep. 'Suppose you tell us where *you* were?'

'In between 10.30 and 11.00?' said Toddy. 'As it so happens I was in the Ladies' Cloaks all the time. Reading a book.'

'Thanks,' said Johnny laconically, writing it down. 'Well, Pamela and me were dancin' till Mister Flaherté burst in, so *we're* all right. An' Natasha here, she was sittin' watchin', so *she's* all right. An' Miriam an' Roger an' Morris were here, too, for we *saw* them ...'

'So *we're* all right,' said Roger. 'And anyway, if I'm not being offensive, dear, none of us have any motive for ... er ... *it*. I mean, have we?'

And he looked confidingly round the circle, his big blue eyes large and innocent.

'No,' said Miriam rapidly. '*I* had. She had an awfully *beastly* attitude to a Dear Friendship she thought I had with her Brother. Baby Brother. And I poured some champagne on her.'

'Jolly good,' said Ted Sloper in his sleep, and began to chuckle.

'No, Miriam, that won't *do*,' said Morris. 'That's not a motive.'

Miriam pouted. This is incredible, but it is a fact.

'All the rest of us, though,' said Toddy's deep rough voice, 'have perfectly good reasons for getting rid of Regan. About 40,000 francs' worth. Some of us *more*. Anyone got any brandy?'

'You are meaning?' said Natasha, 'that all Flahertés will benefit from Regan's death? It cannot be true?'

'However,' said Toddy, nodding, 'the Menzies money was invested in the business, you know. We make scent and sell it. She owns a lot of shares in it now, you see. Like a dowry, really. And on *her* death, instead of Barny gettin' it all, it's divided among all the Directors. And re-invested, it's a family rule.'

'It seems silly,' said Johnny.

'It isn't really,' said Toddy, drinking her brandy, 'it's a better return on your money than ½ per cent.'

Rosalie Leamington crossed the floor to the hotel post-box and posted her letter to Miss Barbara Sewingshields, Oxford

University, Angleterre. She nodded to them. She looked white and rather drawn round the mouth.

'Well, Miss Leamington,' said Johnny comfortably. 'Have a drink. Expect you need it ... '

'Thanks,' said Miss Leamington. 'Ai don't maind if ai do.' She laughed. 'That's what that character in Itma says, isn't it?'

Johnny silently held out the brandy.

'We are all making a plot of our movements,' said Natasha.

'Silly, isn't it?' said Miriam.

'Where were you, Miss Leamington, when Mrs Flaherté' fell out of the window?' said Johnny.

Rosalie Leamington drank her brandy and sighed deeply.

'I was writing that letter,' she said, 'that I just posted. To a Friend. And I happened to look out of the window and I saw ... something dark fall past. It was ... Mrs Flaherté. It was *awful*.'

She stopped and shuddered and Johnny said 'Poor kid, poor kid' and poured her another drink.

'I leant out and shouted,' went on Miss Leamington very fast, 'an' she didn't move. So I ran downstairs. And I bumped into Mr Flaherté and I told him and he went out to her ... '

'How very disagreeable for you,' said Natasha softly. 'So what are you doing then?'

'I was sick,' said Rosalie Leamington promptly. 'In the Ladies' Cloaks.'

'?' Johnny looked his question at Toddy.

'Someone certainly came in and was sick,' said Toddy stoutly. The two girls looked at each other and both of them blushed.

'Didn't see the time by any chance?' said Johnny.

'Yes,' said Miss Leamington. 'It was twenty-five to eleven.'

III

Kathleen and Fanny

Margie went to see Joyce the following morning. Her sister was sitting up in bed, playing with her mouse. She adopted toward it the slightly revolting attitude of a witch with her familiar and Margie was always shocked by it. The mouse ran unhampered about the bed clothes or sat on Joyce's shoulder behind her ear. It could hardly have been nastier.

'You are *revolting*, Joyce,' said Margie. She jumped up and down in the middle of the room. She had no bedroom slippers on.

'And so are you,' said Joyce automatically. 'Your feet are filthy and you'll sneeze again or catch a real cold again and Miss Leamington will *be furious*.'

It was another fine morning. The early sun struck on the window and it became hot. It fell in a square, warm patch on the floor where Margie stood. She wriggled her toes in it luxuriously.

'Shut *up*,' she said, moving towards the window. 'I'm Ever so Healthy.'

'Miss Leamington says Ever so is Common,' said Joyce.

'So it is. But I put it in inverted commas,' said Margie.

'*Fowler* says inverted commas are the commonest thing of all,' said Joyce.

'Oh, shut up,' said Margie again. 'No one cares what you or Fowler think. Do you suppose we'll give 'em the slip again today? An' go back to the Luge Track?'

Joyce brightened.

'P'raps someone *will* break their leg today,' she said with relish, and eagerly.

'Or their *neck*,' said Margie. 'Still, we can't go to the Luge Track now and I'm *bored*. After all, you've got your blasted mouse. *I* never have *anything*.'

'All right,' said Joyce, 'let's go an' tell Miss Leamington we both feel ill. We can hit ourselves all over with the hair brush like the cousins did an' say we've got scarlet fever ...'

'Goody, goody,' said her astonishing sister. And so Joyce bared her chest and her sister beat a neat tattoo on it with the set of hairbrushes that she was given on her eighth birthday and they were no longer bored.

II

About this time Rosalie Leamington also wakened. The bright light dazzled her. She felt exhilarated and wondered why. Then she remembered she was in Schizo-Frenia. And then she remembered, also, with a sinking heart, that she had to tell her charges about the violent death of their mother. She winced and put her head under the bedclothes. After a second or two in hiding she sat up.

'No,' she said to herself. 'Barbara would never behave like this.' And she reached a hand down to her writing-pad and found a fountain-pen.

She began to make a list of her responsibilities. Inevitably they took the form of a letter to 'Dear Barbara'.

I cannot think (*she wrote*) how I can tell them. Or what will be the best form to use. Joyce had hysterics over her mouse and its death, so you can imagine, Barbara, with what trepidation I approach the whole subject (of Death). It isn't (even) as if you or I believed in God or Heaven. The Child Mind ... '

inscribed Rosalie Leamington in her careful scholar's hand, with her head on one side.

And instantly the door opened about half an inch and the Child Mind, represented by Margie's repellant face and unbrushed hair, peered round it.

'*Can we come in?*' said Margie.

'Yes, dear,' said Rosalie. 'As a matter of fact I have something to tell you both.'

She screwed the cap on her fountain-pen and laid it and the writing-pad on the floor again.

'Oh?' said Joyce, following Margie into the room. 'What about?'

'Your mother,' said Rosalie. She hesitated and made an attempt to pick her words. 'She's ... '

'Oh, we know all about *Mother*,' said Margie, contemptuously.

'You mean she's *dead? We* knew that last night,' said Joyce. 'We went into the saloon and I must say she looked awfully pretty.'

'Auntie Kathleen,' said Margie, 'says she's with God's Holy Angels. Which is much nicer for *her*.'

Joyce noticed that Miss Leamington was looking distressed.

'We came to tell you we had scarlet fever, actually.'

In the whole of her thirty-two years Rosalie Leamington had seldom been more completely shattered.

III

Meanwhile, Kathleen, sleepy from her vigil, had been relieved by Madame Lapatronne in the saloon.

Together they opened the window and let in the glorious morning air and light. The saloon began to shine like gold and a shaft of sunlight glowed on top of Regan's head. It was a beautiful and solemn moment.

Kathleen and Madame Lapatronne said nothing, but each felt respect and understanding of the other.

Kathleen went out and closed the door behind her. She hesitated in the passage. Then after a minute's reflection she climbed the stairs to Barny's room.

He was awake when she went in. He lay face downward with one arm crooked to keep out the light. He looked up at her. His eyes were vague and luminous and not at all bloodshot.

''Lo, little Kathleen,' he said. 'Why are you still in your evening things?'

Kathleen looked down at her dark crimson dress and then, astonished, at Barny.

'You don't *remember*?' she said.

'I got drunk,' said Barny. 'I suppose. I often do. Was I very bad?'

'But Barny ...' said Kathleen. 'You weren't drunk. At least, not when it happened, that is. You *must* remember ...'

Barny half sat up and twitched the pillow from behind his head.

'So something happened,' he said slowly. His eyes were uneasy, watching Kathleen and waiting for her to say something else.

'Regan's dead,' said Kathleen.

Barny drew in his breath very slowly and sighed.

'I thought that was a dream,' he said. 'Oh, my God. She fell out of the window.' He nodded. 'Who's with her now?' he added, as though something were expected of him.

'Madame Lapatronne,' said Kathleen. 'I came to tell you so that you could do *your* share.'

'I won't,' said Barny instantly. 'I just won't. Oh, no. Sooner I get her home an' buried better pleased *I* shall be ...'

'Barny!' said Kathleen, horrified. 'You mustn't say things like that.'

'Oh, rot,' said Barny, 'she might've committed suicide or had an accident. Let's face it.'

Kathleen began to sniff.

'Pull yourself together, dear,' said Barny sharply. 'What's the matter with you? You needn't worry on *my* account.'

'The matter is,' said Kathleen, gasping like a fish, 'that *I've* been up all night while you (as usual) have been shirking. *You* just got drunk, like you always do. Your children ...'

'I hate my children,' said Barny. He turned his back on her. 'It's all too difficult,' he said. Kathleen stood shaking in the doorway.

'Barny,' only two inches of his tufted head could be seen above the sheet, 'it's not a bit of good. You *must* face up to it.'

'Oh, go to Hell,' said Barny. He put the pillow on his head. 'None of my business. Too difficult. Go away.'

'But, *Barny,*' said Kathleen. And from tiredness and exasperation a faint suspicion of a whine crept into her voice. 'When the gendarmes come you'll have to say *something.* If you'll only tell me what to say ... Oh, *Barny* ...'

'Kathleen,' said Barny, sitting straight up in bed, 'you are talking the most awful b—— rot. Very kind of you, I'm sure. And now, clear out, there's a dear ...'

Kathleen, tears starting in her eyes, moved to the door, hating Barny and his facile charm, furious that he neither wanted nor needed her help.

'Since you're *up,*' he added with a winning smile, 'there's a black tie in the wardrobe. Will you ...'

Kathleen had actually moved a foot or two towards the wardrobe when she lost her temper. Her gasp of rage could have been heard in Mönchegg.

'You selfish, loathsome swine,' she said. 'I loved Regan, I tell you ... I loved her. I was her best friend.'

And the door slammed behind her.

Barny sighed and burrowed into the pillows and sheets.

'Why is everyone,' he said to himself, 'always so angry when one tells the truth?'

IV

Five minutes later there was another light knock on Barny's door. He was still in bed, lying this time on his back. Fanny Mayes stood in the doorway, dressed in a white silk kimono.

'Barny ... darlingest ...' she said, with an edged smile.

She looked like a golden fox. 'We're free, my darling. We're free ...'

And she sat down on the bed and bent over him. Barny sat up and snatched furiously for his dressing-gown and his glasses. He put on the glasses first and glared through them.

'Go *away*, Fanny,' he said. 'Go away at once. What about Ted?'

'Oh, Barny darling,' said Fanny, leaning over him. 'We needn't go on pretending now. We're free, Barny. Free. Kiss me, kiss me, darling, darling Barny.'

He sprang out of bed and fled towards the door. There was a moment's terrifying struggle when he forgot that it opened towards him, and Fanny's arms came round his neck from behind.

'Go away!' he shouted. 'Leave me alone! Help!'

The door flew open and he shot down the passage, his bare feet smacking flatly on the floor as he went. His ankles and wrists looked brittle and extremely thin.

'Dear, unselfish boy,' said Fanny. 'Doesn't want us talked about. Bless him.'

And Barny, panting, flung himself into Rosalie Leamington's bedroom and slammed the door behind him. He leaned back against the door, gasping, and stared round the room. It was empty.

V

Toddy Flaherté stood at her looking-glass and smacked at her head with a couple of men's hairbrushes. She was looking sinister, even for Toddy. She had on a pair of dark, tight trousers and a white shirt, and the trousers were held up by decorated Tyrolean braces. Her olivine skin had already acquired a smooth and gentlemanly tan. She leered at herself in the glass and then took up a pair of nail scissors. She began to cut away large chunks from her Eton crop. The door opened and Kathleen came in.

'Hullo, old dear,' said Toddy, past her reflection to her sister. '*You* look pretty down in the mouth ...'

Kathleen sat down on the bed.

'What's up?' said Toddy, roughly.

'No one,' said Kathleen, sniffing. 'No one in our family seems to think one pays respect to the dead except *me* ...' Her chin began to tremble with tiredness. Tears began to trickle slowly down her chin. Toddy laid down the nail scissors, aghast.

'But *Kathleen*,' she said. 'You *never* cry.'

Kathleen gulped and tried to stop, but she went on crying.

'Barny's been *awful*,' she said. 'And now *you* are being awful too.'

'Oh, do stop,' said Toddy. '*Please* stop, Kath ...'

She strode over to Kathleen and put her arm round her.

'C'm on,' she said. 'Blow your nose an' tell me ...' She extracted a large white silk handkerchief from her cuff and gently blew Kathleen's nose. Kathleen gulped back her remaining tears.

'Well then. Jus' because Regan's fortune came out like that, doesn't *prove* she committed suicide, does it?'

'Goo' Lor' no,' said Toddy. 'Rather the reverse I expect, just like Freud. But it *was* sinister, wasn't it?'

'Yes,' said Kathleen. 'It was. And there seems a chance, you see, it wasn't an *accident*. I believe it looks like murder to some. Or so they say.'

Toddy, with her arm still round her sister, seemed surprised.

'Fancy that,' she said. 'And we all trying to keep it from you. And you being so fond of Regan and that . . . '

'Well, if it's murder,' said Kathleen, 'Barny ought to be told he's the first under suspicion. I mean, he's bound to be, isn't he? Isn't he? Isn't he?'

Toddy was silent, looking at the ground. Kathleen began to sniff again.

'He *would*,' wailed Kathleen. 'And he won't defend himself. Not even to me. And he'll never see how suspicious it all looks, he's so dreamy. And oh, Toddy, I love him so *much* . . . '

And Kathleen's tears broke out again and soaked Toddy's braces and the bosom of her white shirt, and even fell as far (in great wet drops) as the knees of Toddy's smart black trousers.

'*There*, there, there,' said Toddy, in the most motherly manner possible. She could hardly have sounded sillier.

VI

Rosalie Leamington stiffened in alarm when she came into her bedroom.

'Oh . . . ' she said gruffly, '*you're* here.'

'Yes,' said Barny. 'I was being *hunted*.'

He shuddered and looked out of the window.

'Perhaps I could borrow your bedroom slippers or your dressing-gown or a book or something, if someone comes in,' he said.

'No one will come in, but I think you need a dressing-gown,' said Rosalie, sternly. She took her own dressing-gown down from the door. It was a heavy woollen number, in lumberjack's tartan. It might have been more unbecoming.

Barny huddled it round him.

'I'll buy you a new one,' he said. 'A pretty one.'

'You'll do no such thing,' snapped Rosalie Leamington.

'Good Lord,' said Barney. He pushed his glasses up on his forehead and surveyed her, dreamily. 'Intellectual womanhood,' he said vaguely. 'Why ever not? Hurt, or something, because I don't think this *horror* is pretty? Eh?'

And he ran a hand slowly down the woollen dressing-gown, and as slowly took Rosalie Leamington by the hand. She shook her head and bit her lip. Her hand seemed very dry to him.

'Well, *why*, then,' said Barny, caressingly. 'Why? Mmm?'

'Because . . . ' said Rosalie, looking away from him, past him, over his head to the snow outside, 'because people are *equal*. Even men and women.'

Barny's arm tightened round her.

'And some,' he said, 'are more equal than others.'

VII

'Who was it?' said Rosalie, 'who was hunting you, Darling?'

'Eh?' said Barny. 'Oh, yes. Sorry. Didn't hear. *Hunting* me. Of course. Fanny Mayes.'

'Has she some claim on you?' Rosalie sounded suspicious.

'What? I don't think so. No more than anyone else. She *has* started to say that this is my child she's going to have . . . '

'Going to have a child?' said Rosalie, horrified.

'Why yes,' said Barny, surprised. 'Everyone knows *that*. That's why she's come to Schizo-Frenia. Don't suppose it's old *Ted's*, but it certainly isn't *mine* . . . '

'I should hope *not*,' said Rosalie, tartly.

'Oh, certainly not, definitely not,' said Barny, hastily. 'But she seems to *think* she has a claim. So I don't *feel* free . . . '

There was a pause.

'Ah,' he said, slowly. 'If only I were free, what *fun* we could have. Just you and me. You and your intellect . . . '

Rosalie sighed.

'And me and my vitality,' said Barny, happily.

'I suppose,' said Rosalie, tentatively, 'that you *are* free, in a manner of speaking.'

IV

Ted Sloper

By the time that she had returned to the bedroom *and* bath that she shared with her husband, Fanny Mayes was furious. She now realized that she had been humiliated by Barny Flaherté. She only realized this dimly. Her fine, handsome conceit of herself was her greatest theatrical asset.

'Why ...' she said, shutting her door behind her. 'Barny liked me better, I do believe, when Regan was alive.'

II

Downstairs in the servants' dining-room, incredibly announcing that she didn't want a second cup of Schizo-Frenic tea by saying, 'Chib, chib,' Miss Miriam Birdseye observed the arrival of the *gendarme* from Kesicken. He was a stout, roundabout little man with a stout, fawn face. He was obviously madly healthy and had a pair of skis with him. He leant these against the wall by the front door and briskly came in by the servants' entrance, banging slightly with his feet.

'Good morning,' he said to Miriam. 'You have put the body upstairs?'

Miriam's mouth fell slowly open and she nodded. The *gendarme* disappeared towards the office, whistling between his teeth and asking for his *good* friend, Adolph Lapatronne. He evidently found him, because the murmur of their voices became subdued and finally died away altogether when they went into the room behind the office.

After this Miriam could only hear an occasional burst of admiration and excitement as the *gendarme* looked at and exclaimed over his good friend Adolph's beautiful kiddies.

III

Ted Sloper hung about the ordinary dining-room, reading a four-day-old *Daily Mail*. He had done this quite long enough and he became sick and angry, waiting for his wife. He threw the paper down and slowly went upstairs, apprehensive of the scene which he knew would burst around him if he disturbed his wife when she was dressing.

'Can't help it,' he muttered. 'Sh' mus' see this is a thing 'f importance. We should *all* map out about where we all were yesterday evening.'

The night before Ted had been unable to approach Fanny about any subject at all, and when he went upstairs she was in bed already. He had asked her if she wanted anything and she had snarled at him 'To be left alone.' So he had shuffled miserably about the room, taking off his clothes in the dark.

Now he entered his own bedroom delicately and closed the door behind him with the gentlest of clicks. He could not have been more irritating to Fanny had he tried.

Fanny was in bed. Her shoulders were humped up crossly, her feet could be seen, muffled by the eiderdown, drawn up as though she were in pain.

'I say . . .' said Ted Sloper nervously. 'Are you all right?'

'Oh go *away*,' said Fanny's weary voice. 'Do you suppose I should be in *bed* if I were all right?'

'Yes,' said Ted Sloper, losing his head, 'I do . . . I mean, no. Well, I'm not sure. *Are* you?'

Fanny turned round and sat up. She was very angry indeed. Tears glittered in her eyes unshed. She was wearing a black lace night-dress that Ted was almost sure she had not worn the night before.

'Yes I am,' she said. 'But I want to spend a morning in bed. Can't I spend a morning in bed without the whole world disturbing me? What do you want?'

'Well, it is quite important, actually,' said Ted miserably. He sat on the edge of the little bedroom chair.

'Oh . . .' said Fanny wearily. Her voice was, as usual, metallic and unpleasant. 'You *are* such torture. What can be important at a time like this?'

'Where *you* were last night at twenty-five to eleven,' said Ted, grimly. He clenched his hands and anticipated the stream of fury and abuse that was so sure to come.

It came all right. Fanny would like to know, she said, who the sweet hell Ted thought he was to ask a question like that, and just because she was pregnant he supposed she was going to become the Victorian wife and *he*, Ted, the Victorian male ?

Well, he was very much mistaken, and all Fanny could say was she damn well wouldn't tell *him* her movements. Nasty jealous beast. And if he wanted to know where she was he could damn well find out. And so could that Miriam Birdseye.

'A policeman has just arrived, dear,' said Ted Sloper, gently. 'From Kesicken.'

He had, had he? Well then Ted could take his blasted policeman *and* his blasted title and he could shove them ... Not that a Knighthood or ship or what had you *was* a title, and she was sick of being Lady Sloper, anyway. She had had enough. She was going back to England ...

'Never mind, dear,' said Ted, gently. 'The doctor *said* you'd be a bit nervy for the next few weeks ... '

And it wasn't really surprising at all that Fanny hit him over the head with the bedside light.

IV

Natasha and Johnny met Hans Grübner in the bar. He was the *gendarme*. He smelt vaguely of old nuts and fish, and at first Natasha liked him. He wasn't wearing uniform, and they all sat together in the bar and drank *gluvine*. To begin with they were quite cosy and M Lapatronne spoke of Johnny and Natasha as 'famous criminologists'.

'Yes,' said Hans Grübner, shaking his head. He had not shaved, but he still looked cleanish. 'I have been told of Monsieur DuVivien. And I hear he has taken photographs of the corpse? And that *Madame* DuVivien suspects the heavens know what?'

A faintly sarcastic note crept into his voice and Natasha inclined her lovely head and did not like him so much.

'Now me, I do not. And with what my good friend Adolph here is telling me I think it is so obviously an accident. Isn't it?' Hans Grübner lit a cigarette, which he took out of a rather battered tin box. Almost immediately he knocked the ash off on the polished floor.

'I am quite sure,' said M Lapatronne, sycophantically smirking at Hans Grübner, 'that the relations of this lady would *wish* it accident. They are the Flahertés, the scent makers. And very rich.'

'Ah,' said Grübner. He half shut his eyes and looked sleepy. 'I must see everyone and question everyone,' he said. 'There is no doubt of this at all.'

'Jest a second, pardner,' said Johnny.

His chin had gone tense and white and his mouth was quite thin with rage. Natasha, observing these signs of 'Johnny's crossness', thanked heaven that All-in wrestling had taught him, at least, patience.

'Jest a second,' said Johnny again. He turned to Adolph Lapatronne. 'Did *you* make up Mrs Flaherté's mouth with lipstick?' he said.

'Lipstick?' said M Lapatronne, obviously bewildered by a new idea. He moved his eyes sideways to catch the glance of his friend, Hans Grübner. 'I know nothing of lipstick,' he said.

'Make-up?' said Hans Grübner. 'This is significant?'

'*Yeah*, chum, significant right enough,' said Johnny. 'Significant enough for m'wife to spot, any old haow ...'

Adolph Lapatronne simpered and looked out of the window.

'The ladies,' said Grübner, with a gentlemanly bow, 'are always so *clever* ...'

If it were possible for Natasha to contort her exquisite features into a scowl, that is what she did.

'Skip that,' said Johnny. 'Point is this. Corpse fell out of window in middle of night, in middle of makin' up her face. Point Number One. She hadn't put any powder on. Point Number Two. She hadn't put any lipstick on. Point Number Three ...'

'And later, oh so much later,' said Natasha in her plaintive Russian sing-song, 'poor Mrs Flaherté is taken to the saloon and she is laid out all in flowers and I go to see her.'

'An' someone's jest made up her mouth. Point Number Four,' said Johnny. He, too, lit a cigarette.

'And so previous to all this I have announced my discovery quite generally to so many people who would be so much better off if Mrs Flaherté were dead ...' wailed Natasha. 'It is not nice.'

'An' so me wife thinks, an' vurry natural too, that if it ain't Monsieur Lapatronne or his good lady has put the lipstick on her, it's the murderer definite. An' probably the definite murderer whodunit.'

'Used the lipstick, he means,' said Natasha with a sweet smile. Hans Grübner smiled back warily. Someone kicked someone under the table. Adolph Lapatronne suddenly came to life.

'Oh,' he said suddenly. 'Lipstick. Oh yes. I am using lipstick. On poor Mrs Flaherté. To make her look pretty. You know. For the bier.'

Which, as Johnny afterwards said, no one could refute, particularly when old man Grübner made gorgeous notes in his book about it.

V

Johnny and Natasha went out on to the snow terrace that surrounded the hotel. They were both in an overpowering rage.

'I am so *angry*,' said Natasha, 'I could almost learn to ski.'

'Don't go too far,' said Miriam Birdseye. 'Don't lose your head.'

'No dancer should ski,' said Roger, and nodded wisely.

So Natasha told Miriam why she was upset and Miriam looked up at Brauzwetter with large, lustrous eyes. Adolph Lapatronne and Hans Grübner could be heard going upstairs to the saloon.

'It is like a feather bed, foreign justice,' said Natasha. 'Once you are oil in it there is no *hope*, no hope till the morning.'

'And Natasha,' said Johnny, 'is just like Dunlop tyres, of course, British as the flag.'

They sat in the long wickerwork chairs and discussed the situation endlessly and hopelessly. Miriam agreed with Natasha it was most certainly murder, and pointed out, in passing, she had no axe to grind. Morris thought the lipstick incident *olly* fishy and said he was sure it was murder, too, and *Roger* had seen Barny Flaherté go roaring upstairs with a very queer look in his eye. He was positive it was murder and sure it was Barny who had done it, to get rid of an unwanted wife.

'No one wants a woman with red hair,' he said. 'Look at Queen Elizabeth.'

'But I should have been *crazy* about Queen Elizabeth,' said Roger. 'I *know* I should.'

And the conversation became general, and historical, and no one referred again to the death of Regan Flaherté' until they saw Barny Flaherté come out of the hotel and hurry down to the funicular. His head was lowered and his eyes were fixed on the ground two feet ahead of him.

'My *dear*! the dish!' said Miriam instantly, pointing after him. 'Going down to Kesicken. How simply splendid.'

'Who's coming, too?' said Roger. And oddly enough *everybody* was.

VI

The funicular, groaning and banging, came roughly to a halt opposite Miriam and her little party. They stood in the snow at the Water Station Halt. Miriam, bless her, looked extremely odd. She was, as usual, wearing the only fur coat the burglars had left her, short and boxy, made of baby seal. She carried her hands clenched tightly in her pockets. Under the coat her slacks looked incongruous and charming.

Barny Flaherté climbed into a third-class compartment and sat in a morose heap with his thin shoulders hunched round his ears. He was sulking. Miriam instantly climbed in beside him. He raised his eyebrows. After all, the rest of the train was empty.

'Well really,' he muttered. 'I shouldn't've thought the whole of *Schizo-Frenia* wanted to get into this *one* carriage, damn it all . . .'

Miriam could hardly hear him. She stared at him intently under her outsize false eyelashes. The gaze in her enormous pale blue eyes was wide and innocent and utterly devoid of any sort of coquetry.

When the train stopped with a jerk at 'Siding' Barny rose to his feet and tried to get out. Miriam instantly laid her hand on his knee. The big opal ring that she wore on her fourth finger flashed. She was promptly lost in admiration of it, her head on one side.

'Oh *please*,' she said, watching the ring and flashing it idly about. 'Don't *go*. I've been dying to meet you ever since I saw you at the hotel. I'm so *glad* to have this opportunity of speaking to you.'

Barny hesitated and was lost. The train started with its usual jerk and flung him into the seat beside her. Morris and Roger, who were penned off like cattle behind her, put their heads forward and grinned. Johnny and Natasha, huddled together on the other side of the carriage, pretended to admire the scenery.

'Couldn't be keener to meet you,' went on Miriam steadily.

Barny looked up and saw flattering interest flaming in her eye. He had never failed to respond to such a flame.

'Oh . . . ' he said. 'Why?'

'Well, I just liked the way you *looked*, you know,' said Miriam earnestly, and her explanation went meandering off into a series of phrases like 'That little waistcoat' and 'So young and yet so old,' 'So wise and yet so *silly*.'

She made very little sense, yet Barny seemed quite satisfied. Possibly this may have been because he was the subject under discussion. Sometimes he nodded his head and his straight, light lock of brown hair fell into his eye. Sometimes he said 'Penetrating, penetrating'. But he seemed pleased.

Bit by bit Miriam and Barny shuffled along the wooden seat until they were next to the window. They were now isolated from the rest of the party. Roger quickly shuffled along in *his* pen until he was looking out of the window behind them. Natasha murmured to Johnny that Roger was going too far.

'Nobody except us should be allowed to be detective and listen to other conversations,' she whispered, and Johnny quite agreed.

'Mrs DuVivien *says*,' said Miriam, about to approach the subject of Barny's wife's death.

'Mrs DuVivien?' said Barny, puzzled.

'Why *yes*,' said Miriam. 'Mrs DuVivien. You must have noticed *her*. She's the most beautiful woman in the hotel.'

'Oh?' said Barny, bored. 'Well ...'

He stared wildly around him and suddenly gave a sigh of relief.

'Look ...' he said, leaping up, 'there's old Hans Grübner skiing down to Kesicken ...'

He opened the window and leaned out. He spent the next twenty minutes giving a running commentary on Hans Grübner and his speed, which was faster than that of the train. Roger confided in an undertone to Morris that Barny was indeed 'a dish' and Miriam 'a goner'.

'Who's Hans Grübner?' said Miriam, frowning at Roger and Morris. Barny paid no attention. She turned to Natasha and repeated her question.

'It is this ver-ry bor-ring policeman who is coming this morning to be making the enquiries,' said Natasha. 'About Mrs Flaherté.' And she, too, frowned.

'Goodness,' said Roger. 'He's been quick. Why, he didn't even bother to interrogate *me*.'

And he cocked a chest and laughed sideways at Miriam, who promptly put her feet up on the seat beside her. Her eyes were all the time on Barny's slim, elegant, backview. He was staring out of the window.

'No necessity,' said Barny suddenly, spinning round to face them all. 'For mass interrogation. Death was an accident. We were all agreed about *that* . . . '

'But . . . ' said Natasha and Roger absolutely simultaneously.

'Yes, *indeed*,' said Miriam. 'But . . . '

'She was my wife, wasn't she?' shouted Barny. 'And I shall have all the trouble of the funeral and the travelling and taking her home to England and everything . . . '

And he scowled like a child that knows it has been naughty. He stumbled over Miriam's feet to the carriage door as the train drew slowly into Kesicken. At the door he turned.

'Miss Birdseye?' he said, 'could I buy you a drink?'

And Miriam, who had been teetotal for the last two years, went over to the station buffet to drink double brandies with Barny.

Natasha and Johnny disembarked and, standing arm-in-arm beside the train, were lost in admiration.

VII

As usual in Kesicken, it was thawing, but no one noticed for some time. Miriam and Barny went to the door of the station buffet. As they went in Miriam waved and made a face at Roger and Morris.

'Calloo Callay,' said Roger to Natasha.

Natasha was not listening. 'She is a clever one, that Miriam,' she said to Johnny.

'Sure is,' said Johnny, stoutly.

The DuViviens began to walk along the main street of

Kesicken. The sun came out and for a minute or two everything seemed gay and like a film-set. A horse, pulling a sleigh, trotted by, its bells ringing. A band somewhere played 'The Skaters Waltz'. Two young men on skis slapped along the street beside them. People, strolling, talking and smoking, in bright ski-ing clothes achieved the excitement and unreality of extras. And then the sun went in again.

Instantly, in the chill, Natasha noticed that there was no snow for the skiers to slap on, but only a little mud. She pointed this out to Johnny, who agreed that they looked very foolish. They reached the ice-skating rink and there was quite a deep pond on top of it. And the people who passed them in the street were, most of them, English.

'Noice, i'n't it?' said a young man to a girl.

They both carried cameras. He wore a white sweater called 'Scarborough O.F.C.'

'Christmassy,' said the girl, nodding.

And the gramophone (for it was *not* a band, but only a simple mechanical device with an amplifier) broke noisily into a horrid tune called 'Bobbity Bob, Rebob'. The enchantment was gone.

Natasha put her hand in its catskin mitten into the crook of Johnny's arm. He grinned down at her.

'It is more real this way . . . ' she said.

Johnny quite often had no idea what Natasha meant. He just grinned again.

'Wonder how Miriam's progressin' with that there Flaherté?' he said.

'If *anyone*,' said Natasha, 'can be making sense of that one, it will be Miriam. I am surprised, however, certainly. In England she would be thinking him *quite* dreary.'

'Ah well,' said Johnny. He stared around him at the sparsely scattered snow, which was dotted here and there with tiny holes where moisture had fallen from the eaves of houses. 'Different standards in Kesicken.'

VIII

Miriam and Barny sat together in the station buffet and drank pink gins instead of brandy. Miriam had pointed out that angostura bitter was good for the liver and also that it was luncheon time and she was hungry.

Barny ordered an enormous omelette, golden with butter, stuffed with green peas and sprinkled all over with dear little cubes of ham. Miriam quite forgot that 'Mum's tum wasn't right.' Her mouth watered furiously. Barny divided the omelette scrupulously and for a moment there was no conversation between them. There was merely the extremely pleasant noise of two people enjoying their food.

'You *are* a strange young man,' said Miriam, finally, when the waiter had come with coffee and doughnuts and Barny had ordered brandy and poured it into the coffee. 'Your po-ah wife is dead and your appetite is so go-od ...'

Miriam nearly always pronounced words like 'good' to rhyme with 'food'.

'I never liked her very much,' said Barny, candidly. 'She was awfully difficult, you know. So *moody* and cross always lately.'

'She was all right, was she, when you married her first?' said Miriam.

'I don't know ...' said Barny. His forehead wrinkled. 'I can't

128

remember. So long ago. And then we had those *dreadful* children. I do hate them so . . . '

He smiled at her wickedly and Miriam smiled back.

'Shocked, I'm sure,' she said. 'But I suppose she'd been meaning to jump out of a window for some time?'

'Eh?' said Barny. He was disconcerted. 'Oh *no*. I don't think so. She got a bit fed-up over Fanny, but so did I in the end, you know. I say, isn't Fanny *awful*? You know her too, don't you?'

'She's a horrible little Welsh witch,' said Miriam, scowling until she looked like a gargoyle.

Barny drank his brandy in a gulp and Miriam poured hers into his coffee as he turned his back to call for more.

V

The Cheque

When her father and stepmother impulsively left in the funicular, Pamela was only slightly startled. Johnny had certainly been bespoken to go ski-ing with her and the expensive new guide; but Natasha's whim had always been law, and Pamela was one of those people who are quite happy by themselves.

She stood a little insecurely outside the hotel, poised on her hired skis, and wished that her trousers were as smart as those of the other ladies and gentlemen. Then Hans Walter, the new expensive guide, came briskly round the corner of the hotel. He did a neat and exciting Christie, sent the snow up into the sunlight like spray, and said:

'You know Mr DuVivien, no?'

He was a thinnish young man with rounded shoulders and an angry face like a bird, all beak and eyes. His jawline was blurred by a three days' growth of golden beard. He wore a greenish-grey hat with a flat aggressive peak that accentuated his bird-like appearance.

'He is my father,' said Pamela politely. She pointed down the hill with one of her ski-sticks and spoke slowly and distinctly as she might to a child or an idiot. 'He has had to go to Kesicken in a hurry. So will you please take me alone instead?'

'Sure,' said Hans, and smiled a bright, hard, unkind smile.

Pamela suddenly thought, with some apprehension, that he was a cruel young man.

'OK,' he said, and 'We too will go to Kesicken now, on skis.'

Pamela was appalled.

'Oh!' she said. 'Do you think? I mean, I never was *on* skis before ... I mean, don't you think that a little practice might be ... '

'Running is best practice,' said Hans, viciously. 'Running and stemming. Also I have people in Kesicken to see. Now then. Lean AWI from the hill ... '

And Pamela, whether she liked it or not, found herself promptly proceeding down the hill, away from the safety of the hotel, into the unknown, with this strange, beastly young man.

As she went she was mortified to see Rosalie Leamington with Joyce and Margie come out on the terrace, presumably to watch her progress. (In fact none of them saw her at all.) Instantly her feet began to gallop and she fell heavily on the back of her head and bruised herself severely.

Hans twirled past her, did a superb Christie and *glared*.

'You lean towards the hill as I have *not* said,' he cried furiously, beating with his stick in the snow. 'I say AWI. I mean AWI.'

And for the rest of the day, from sheerest terror of Hans, Pamela leaned AWI from the hill.

Rosalie Leamington was getting rid of her two charges, who seemed unusually unattractive to her. They were both slightly purple and shivering. The shock of their mother's death had at last penetrated their nerves. Moreover, Rosalie had spent the last hour giving them hell through a quill about their abortive pretence of scarlet fever.

'It shows,' she had said in her dry, caustic Cambridge manner, 'a definite arrested development. My friend, Barbara Sewingshields, and I did that trick when we were *eight*. How extraordinarily young for your age you must be to do it when you are *fourteen*.'

Joyce was quite abashed and awed by Miss Leamington after this. Even Margie wondered if she had not at last met her Waterloo.

'I suppose you will both be going luge-ing?' said Rosalie with some distaste.

'Oooh, *yes*, Miss Leamington,' said Margie sycophantically. There was a pause.

'And you aren't going to ask me if I am coming too?' said Rosalie, bitterly.

'Oooh, yes, Miss Leamington,' said Margie, without enthusiasm. 'I didn't think you'd care to . . .'

'Well, thank you very much,' said Rosalie, coldly, 'but I find I am unable after all to accept your kind invitation. And *that*, Joyce, is what *we* call good manners.'

Joyce began to wish she still had a plate to suck. It gave a girl something to do. Rosalie walked back to the hotel. The children were badly shaken.

'Not a bad sort, the Lem Bug,' said Margie, her teeth beginning to chatter. 'Have you got that luge?'

'Oh, do you think so? I think she's *hell*,' said Joyce. 'It's in the ski-hut.'

They took it out of the hut and tobogganned furiously down the ski-run to the luge track. On the way they ran into, and became hopelessly entangled with, Pamela and Hans Walter.

Hans evidently cared for kiddies. Or at least he wasted a good ten minutes of Pamela's time calling after them 'Bubchen' and 'Schoene Kinder'.

III

Back in the hotel Rosalie went upstairs very slowly. Her vitality seemed quite sapped. So much had happened to her in the last few days. Barny . . .

For once she felt she could not use Barbara as her safety valve. She wanted, she felt, a *new* sort of friend. Someone who was sophisticated and perhaps rather wicked. Someone who was married, possibly, and who certainly knew all the answers to the questions that she (Rosalie) had never asked herself before. And at the bend of the stairs she met Fanny Mayes.

Fanny was now fully dressed and looking more like an angry golden fox than ever.

'Seen the corpse yet?' she said chattily.

IV

'It was accidental death, that *gendarme* says,' said Fanny. 'We ought to be celebrating. He's gone away to get the death certificate. Or so they say ... The only doctor's heaven knows *where*, delivering kiddies or something. *Splendid*, isn't it?'

'Oh,' said Rosalie. 'I'm rather sorry. She was quite a good employer. Do you think it's too early for a drink?' she added, shyly.

'My God,' said Fanny. 'The girl's human. Of course it's not too early. Have it on me.'

Rosalie reflected that some people (and, she supposed, especially actresses) often spoke very coarsely indeed. However, if she played her cards right, here was advice and information ready to hand. She followed Fanny into the bar.

'What'll it be?' said Rosalie. She vaguely recollected the half pints of mild and bitter she had swallowed at Girton. 'You don't drink beer, I suppose?'

'No,' said Fanny. 'I just busted my old man over the head, so it'd better be brandy.'

Rosalie thought this must be some very sophisticated catch-phrase she had never heard before.

'Certainly,' she said, and approached the bar very quietly. Trudi was behind the bar, knitting. 'Two brandies, please. Men can be very tiresome, can't they?'

She returned with the two drinks to Fanny, who seemed quite to have forgotten her momentary jealousy of Rosalie on the train. During the next hour and four brandies she poured out her opinion of her husband, her fury at having a child and her determination to avoid all possibility of this in the future. Rosalie Leamington, quietly disapproving, paid for most of the brandies and learnt from Fanny Mayes everything she wanted to know.

V

Ted Sloper sat outside the hotel in the sun with a piece of cotton wool and witch hazel held tightly against his eye.

Around and above him the aching loveliness of the dark blue sky and the blinding snow seemed to mock him. Other people, he reflected bitterly, had been able to lift up their eyes to the hills and receive strength. But *they*, he told himself, probably had not had a black eye.

He told himself that he was through with Fanny. He was sick of her. He was sick of everything. What on earth was the use of making sacrifices and taking risks if everyone else behaved so badly? Why did *anyone* try to be good? *He* didn't know.

It was no good saying man was only mortal and the world eternal and that such things had been going on for years. His quarrel with his beautiful bitchy wife (and therefore with his own inadequacy) utterly absorbed him. That and the pain in his bruised eye . . .

VI

Toddy Flaherté put a hot water bottle beside Kathleen's feet in bed and gave her a nice hot cup of coffee and a couple of aspirins. She went over to the window to draw the curtains, against the bright sun. She looked down on Ted Sloper's despondent shoulders.

'Ted's down in the mouth,' she said.

'Poor Ted,' said Kathleen sleepily. 'That awful woman. Fanny an' Barny were at least a match for each other in bitchiness . . . '

'Hey, steady on, old girl,' said Toddy, moving about the room remarkably quietly in her heavy ski-ing boots. 'No Flaherté could ever be as bad as that common little vixen.'

'Maybe,' said Kathleen. She was almost asleep. 'Maybe she's the murderer. Murderess, I mean. Maybe she pushed poor darling Regan out of the window ...'

'Well, maybe *you* did. Or *I* did,' said Toddy, turning round at the door, holding it half open in her right hand. 'Now, do shut up, Kath, an' go to sleep.'

'Maybe,' mumbled Kathleen, and fell asleep.

VII

Meanwhile, downstairs in their office, surrounded by enough of their 'schoene Kinder' to make the heart of Hans Walter as glad as *anything*, sat Monsieur and Madame Lapatronne. They were waiting for the doctor who would come and sign the death certificate.

In front of them, on the desk, and representing a lakeful of cod liver oil and orange juice and butter and other essential kiddies' food, was a cheque for 750 dollars, payable on a New York Bank. It was signed, demurely enough: *Barny Flaherté*.

VI

Fanny Gets Drunk

When Toddy Flaherté wandered downstairs at about four o'clock that afternoon she was wearing a smart Tyrolean youth's jacket of black leather, fiercely trimmed with silver buttons. Kathleen had given her fifty French francs for a drink, and until she could see Barny that evening she was quite broke. However, she was quite defiant, too. At each bend on the staircase she did a little dance with her feet, like a clog dance, scraping on the coco-nut matting that is common to every hotel in Schizo-Frenia. It protects the polished floors from the ski-ing boots of the English visitors.

Downstairs in the bar Fanny Mayes was argumentative drunk. She was lecturing Rosalie Leamington about George Black and the Littlers. Rosalie was already tired of her new, sophisticated friend, and there was a look of faint distaste behind her pink-rimmed glasses. It changed to a look of gratitude as Toddy came in. Toddy might rescue her from this unpleasant, tipsy woman.

'Hullo,' said Toddy. She stood with her hands in her pockets and her head flung back. 'How's about a drink?'

Rosalie went to the bar to get it. She was longing to escape.

'Where're the kids?' said Toddy heartily. 'I'm downright *fond* of those two . . . '

Rosalie didn't reply.

Fanny said: 'Little bastards'.

'Oh, surely *not*,' said Toddy, looking at her meaningly. 'We all know that Barny's perfectly capable of fathering his children. Don't we, dear?'

Fanny winced and went white and said something about 'Bought that one'.

'Thanks, Miss Brodington,' said Toddy to Rosalie, taking her drink.

'Leamington,' said Rosalie. 'The children are luge-ing. They seem to like it.'

A fit of shivering seized her and her teeth began to chatter. Toddy stared at her.

'You're not well, Miss Leamhurst,' she said. 'Thanks for paying for my drink. Jolly D of you. I think you ought to be in bed.'

'I think so, too,' said Rosalie, still shivering.

'Extraordinary how poor Regan popping off like that has affected us all,' said Toddy. She turned to Fanny. 'And what's up with Ted?' she asked. 'He's sitting out there with his head in his hands looking exactly like hell? As if the world had come to an end.'

''Spect he's tryin' to leave me, dear,' said Fanny, and giggled. She was just drunk enough to put no guard on her tongue. 'Decides to leave me about once a week. Writes me little poems 'bout it.'

'Good Heavens,' said Toddy, plainly meaning 'That's no occupation for a man'. 'And *then*,' she added, 'I suppose you get Barny, huh?'

'That's right,' said Fanny, and giggled again.

'Excuse me,' said Rosalie. 'Will you forgive me?' And she went quietly out of the door.

''S Right,' said Fanny. 'Poems. Wha' 'bout this?'

And she recited a little piece of verse in theatrical and maudlin tones, beginning, 'My soul says I must leave you.'

'Wha' you think of that, eh?' she said as she came to the end of it. 'Isn't that a lot of nonsense, eh?'

And she sent a tumblerful of brandy spinning across the table. Toddy sprang on it like a leopard.

'Thank you, Fanny,' said Ted's quiet voice behind them. Toddy looked up and gasped. She had seen his black eye. It was very nasty and contained several interesting combinations of blue and black and green.

'Whaffor?' said Fanny.

'For broadcasting our dirty linen,' said Ted. His voice was still quiet, but there was menace behind it. He had gone very white and his hands were shaking. Nevertheless, he left the bar with some dignity. Fanny giggled uncertainly. Toddy ordered another drink and watched her.

'Well, you bought *that* one, old girl,' she said.

'Whatcher mean?' said Fanny. 'Hey, Trudi, bring that brandy.'

'Well . . . ' said Toddy, carefully. 'I mean he'll leave you.'

For a moment a little fear showed in Fanny's eyes. Then it was replaced by her usual bravado.

'Think so?' she said thickly. 'Well, I don't. Fool's in *love* with me.'

'What?' said Toddy, exasperated. 'I thought you were going off with Barny?'

'Oh, for*get it*,' said Fanny, all in one word.

II

Six brandies later Fanny's head slipped forward on the table and she began to fall asleep. Toddy was not non-plussed. She picked her up and frogmarched her (just as Johnny had frogmarched Barny) towards the staircase. At the staircase Fanny woke up and said passionately:

'On-y wanter lie *down* . . . Le' go' me,' and staggered away from Toddy to lean against the wall.

'Don't be such a fool, you fool,' said Toddy, and picked her up.

By a miracle they encountered no one on the stairs. There was also no one in the passage, and Ted had left their bedroom deserted and miserable. The two twin beds were neatly made and the curtains were drawn. Outside it was getting dark very quickly.

Toddy half lifted, half pushed Fanny on to her bed. Fanny dropped her hand-bag. It burst open as it hit the floor. A lipstick, a compact, a small bottle of scent, a lace handkerchief and about three thousand Schizo-Frenic francs fell or fluttered out. A bunch of keys came last.

'———,' said Fanny. She twisted her head round. 'Ugh,' she said. She fell asleep again.

Toddy put the eiderdown over her.

'Disgusting bitch,' she said to herself. And then: 'What an extraordinary lot of money disgusting bitches always seem to have.'

She looked wistfully at the francs at her feet. She looked down at Fanny, snoring like a pig.

Then she stooped quickly and peeled off a thousand-franc note. She stuffed it into her trousers pocket and left, noisily.

III

About an hour later Fanny Mayes woke up and dimly saw a dark figure bending over her.

'Ugh,' said Fanny Mayes.

'How do you feel?'

'Sick,' said Fanny Mayes. 'Headache,' she said, and hiccuped.

'Here,' said the voice, 'drink this . . . '

'Beas'ly taste,' said Fanny Mayes, gulping it down. 'Wha's time?'

'About six,' said the voice. 'It may be beastly. It'll settle your stomach.'

It settled Fanny Mayes' stomach all right. She fell asleep immediately and never woke again. There were thirty sleeping tablets dissolved in the water and Fanny Mayes died in her sleep at about six-twenty.

BOOK THREE

————————

ON THE SKIDS

I

Miriam Turns Detective

The doctor arrived at five-forty-five, inconsequently stepping off the funicular and announcing that he must stay the night. M Lapatronne ran down from the hotel to Water Station Halt to greet him, with happy cries of 'Vital, my friend, Kurt Vital!'

Kurt Vital was a tall, strong, slab-like man with a blue chin. During the summer months he was occupied in bringing Kesicken babies into the world. In the winter he was quite taken up with setting and (in some cases) rivetting all the Kesicken legs, ankles, arms and necks broken by enthusiastic skiers. Any departure beyond these two occupations vexed him very much.

He was therefore cross about Mrs Flaherté. He thought it was inconvenient of her. He did not (he explained) *mind* coming all the way from Kesicken to oblige his old friends Hans Grübner and Adolph Lapatronne, but (and here he laughed heartily, slapping his old friend Adolph on the back) he hoped they were not going to make a habit of it.

Dr Vital grumbled quietly all the way from the Water Station

Halt to the hotel, holding firmly on to M Lapatronne's shoulder with one hand, swinging a small old-fashioned satchel in the other. He spent the rest of his stay discussing the chances of his second son, Humbert, in the Schizo-Frenic Ski Championships.

II

A lot of people got off this train at five-forty-five. Barny and Miriam Birdseye were there (perhaps a little tired from an afternoon spent dancing at one of the Kesicken thé dansants). Pamela DuVivien was there, bruised but proud, and squired by Roger and Morris, who were madly impressed, my dear, by such a Gamesy Girl. And then there were a lot of unclassified persons in sweaters and ski suits of an old-fashioned pattern, who turned out to be army officers spending their gratuities.

Pamela descended stiffly from the train and was seized and embraced by Natasha. She showed as much emotion at her step-daughter's return as M Lapatronne had shown when he saw his friend, Kurt Vital.

'You *can't* have been worrying ...' said Pamela, taking her skis from the ski-truck. 'For goodness' sake. How long have you been home?'

'Johnny and I,' said Natasha, a little ashamed, 'we are getting *sick* of waiting in Kesicken for Miriam and her newest *chum*. So we come home at four o'clock, and we are sitting here ever since. We worry at *least* ten minutes ...'

Pamela laughed.

There were more people than usual in the bar. Most of them were strangers, just leaving to catch the last funicular up to Mönchegg, or the last funicular down to Kesicken. They milled around, talking and smoking and sitting on stools by the bar. Their eyes shone with health and the first stages of alcoholic poisoning. One of the young soldiers began to tell a long, loud story about how he had lost both skis at once on the Lavadün run. Ted Sloper came in and explained that he had got his black eye by falling on his ski-stick. No one was interested and he walked out again, presumably to go upstairs. Barny, after swallowing a quick gin and patting Miriam between her shoulders, followed him.

Pamela and Johnny and Natasha were quite relaxed. They sat and quarrelled among themselves about the relative claims of Pamela and Johnny on the first bath and what Doctor Vital would put on the death certificate.

'Forgery!' said Natasha, loudly and distinctly. 'Pamela must certainly have this. Against her stiffness and possible lumbago.'

'I don't see it,' said Johnny. 'Ah, anyway, I want a bath myself.'

'Ski-ing you have not been,' said Natasha. 'I suppose he will say heart failure like all doctors do.'

'I *prefer* a bath that isn't somebody else's, *honestly* I do,' said Pamela. 'I should have thought just "Broken neck" would have been enough ...'

'Dancin's just as bad as ski-in' for an old man like me,' said Johnny, nauseatingly. 'Fat lot a feller like that Vital cares if the lady fell or was she pushed. There's no justice like British justice. Flaherté's on a good wicket here, I guess ...'

And he began to sing to a tune out of *Annie Get Your Gun*, 'There's *no* justice like Schizo Justice,' and a hush fell on the noisy room. It was the sort of silence that sometimes happens in England, where it is known as 'An Angel flying over the house'. As usual, everyone looked at his watch and, also as usual, it was twenty minutes past the hour.

And into this unembarrassed silence there came a terrible scream of fear. A door slammed. Feet ran. There was another incoherent scream.

It was, of course, the chambermaid, Nelli, who had been turning down the beds. She had found the body of Fanny Mayes.

III

'The same eight people aren't here,' said Pamela, staring round her.

'Why d'y' mean?' said Johnny, angrily. The scream had penetrated his nerves more than he would like to admit.

'Well ...' said Pamela. 'Suppose this was a murder story. Someone'd have made a list of suspects by now and then we'd all look wildly round the room and see who wasn't here. And none of them are ...'

'None of who?' said Natasha.

'Oh, *rot*,' said Johnny. 'Prob'ly just that sinister lookin' medico scared the daylights outer someone upstairs ...'

Trudi came back into the bar. When she heard Nelli scream she had rushed from the room, trailing a ball of knitting wool behind her along the floor and round the door handle. Now she unwound it slowly and got it under control again.

'What is wrong, Trudi?' said Natasha.

'It is my sister Nelli,' said Trudi. 'It is Lady Sloper ...'

'Fanny Mayes?' said Natasha. 'Hit her or something, perhaps?'

'... dead,' said Trudi. She sat down and began to cry quietly into her knitting.

'Lor',' said Johnny. He looked at Pamela, who went rather white.

'That makes seven, but still none of them are here,' she said.

'*Who* in God's name?' said Johnny.

'Seven Flahertés and party,' said Pamela. 'Joyce an' Margie an' the governess, three . . . Barny, four . . . Toddy and Kathleen six an' Ted Sloper seven.'

'*Sir* Sloper,' said Natasha vaguely. 'But you are so *right*, Pamela. It is all wrong that Fanny Mayes is dead. She is the one I am thinking pushed Regan out of the window and made the mess with the lipstick . . . '

'What?' said Miriam. 'Fanny Mayes dead? Fanny Mayes the murderess? Roger, look after Mum, Mum's frightened.'

'Now she is dead she cannot have done it,' said Natasha petulantly.

'It ain't necessarily so,' said Johnny. 'We were goin' ter motivate the whole thing. Care to help, Miriam?'

'Motivate?' said Miriam coldly, 'I'm much too frightened to *motivate* . . . '

IV

Johnny took an enormous gold-mounted, purple fountain-pen out of his pocket and spread a bill on the bar. 'Volksbank Unteralp' was written on it and 'A.G. £5 and Fr 56'. He had no idea what this meant.

'Well then . . . ' said Johnny, writing laboriously, squinting down his nose at the paper, which he held a long way away from him. 'Crime Number One (or so Natasha says). Death of Mrs Flaherté. We assume it's murder. OK?'

'OK,' said Miriam, and suddenly put her feet in Johnny's lap. 'Look after Mum, Johnny, Mum may be murdered next.'

'Toddy,' said Johnny, writing and paying no attention to Miriam's feet. 'Kathleen, Barny, Fanny Mayes . . .'

'Oh, I see what you're doing,' said Miriam suddenly. She turned to Natasha. 'We can't rule Fanny out of the first one just because she's dead, you know.'

'No,' said Natasha. 'But I am wondering . . .'

'Ted Sloper,' wrote Johnny. 'The two kids an' the governess.'

'Where are those revolting children?' asked Natasha. 'I ask only so that I may avoid them.'

'They were in the luge track when *I* last saw them,' said Pamela. 'But I don't think children commit murders . . .'

'Oh, rubbish,' said Miriam, tartly. 'Little beasts. What about that little swine in Cleveland, Ohio, who did in his mum and dad with a meat chopper and then said to the judge "Have pity on a poor orphan"?'

'And "No Room at the Inn"?' said Natasha.

'Don't be silly,' said Pamela. 'That's a play.'

'Hush up, do,' said Johnny. 'Motives.'

'*Toddy*,' said Natasha, pointing at the list.

'She's very hard up,' said Pamela. 'And she expected a lot of money from Regan. I know that.'

Johnny wrote hard with his head on one side. When he had finished, his list looked something like this:

Toddy.
Ever so Squalid. Wants cash. Seems Queer, but kindly and unlikely to kill anyone for cash, let's face it.

Kathleen.
Equally Squalid. Because in love with Barny (Pam says) and
quite mad enough to do in Regan to get him. If she done it
she would be sorry probably and furious with Barny. Natasha
says Never happy again. Mem. Have a look and see if she
looks happy.

'The Governess,' said Natasha at this point. 'She has the
same motive as Kathleen. Put her in. I hate this one. She is *sly*.'
'You can't accuse people of murders on account of they are
sly, Natasha. Her name's Rosalie Leamington,' said Pamela.
Johnny wrote it in.
'Who else?' he asked, bored.
'*Sir Sloper*,' said Natasha. 'You remember he has said "I
would even give her Barny if she liked"? Well, this is one way
of doing it.'
'*Jolly* far fetched,' said Pamela, 'unless there's something
about him we don't know. That he's queer or something and
Regan knew.'
'Well he certainly isn't queer, dear,' said Miriam, 'and I ought
to know.'
'Pity,' said Pamela. '*Barny's* my choice . . .'
'What!' said Miriam. 'My darling dish a murderer. I *adore*
it, don't you?' And she shivered again and her teeth chattered
most realistically.
'I really *am* frightened now,' she said, surprised.
'Motive for Barny Flaherté,' said Johnny, scowling round at
Natasha.
'*Barny Flaherté*: to get rid of unwanted wife and more money,'
said Pamela.

'Oh think again, girls,' said Johnny, 'that boy uses his wife as a *protection*. Yes sir.'

'But he might not know that and not have worked it out,' said Pamela. 'After all, people make mistakes. And we don't know anything about the way Fanny Mayes died or *anything* . . .'

'Neither we do, and that may make a *lot* of difference,' said Johnny, briskly getting down from his stool. 'Well, which of us to ascend and find out?'

'Isn't he wonderful?' said Miriam, rolling her eyes. 'Me. Let me go . . .'

She swung herself down on to the floor and said, 'The game little trooper,' and went racing out of the door before anyone could stop her. In the hall she turned and made a hideous face like a gargoyle. Natasha crossed herself.

'Certainly she is the cleverest of us,' she said. 'But I am wishing so *much* she would not make faces like that. It has always worried me.'

V

The first of Pamela's suspects into the room was Toddy. She strolled up to the bar, put down her 1,000 franc note and smiled at Trudi, who looked startled.

'I have not change for a thousand,' she said. 'In the office, however?'

'Well, give me the drink, first, there's a dear girl,' said Toddy, easily. 'Brandy. Big one.'

Trudi poured it and Johnny picked up the note, very delicately indeed.

'These're rare . . .' he said slowly. 'How d'you come by it?'

Toddy, most disconcertedly, blushed and looked at her feet. It was as bad as a hippopotamus blushing. Her square-cut jaw positively *glowed*.

'Good*ness*,' said Natasha, softly. 'What about Fanny Mayes, Toddy?'

'Eh ...' said Toddy, gripping the bar and looking even hotter. 'Fanny? What about her?'

'Dead,' said Natasha, nodding owlishly.

'Oh!' Toddy gasped. 'You're mad. Don't be silly. She's dead *drunk* if you like. I saw her snoring like a pig upstairs about an hour ago. More, maybe. About five o'clock, anyway.'

'Madame is wrong,' said Trudi, standing with the change for the 1,000 franc note on a little plate, the marks of tears still on her cheeks. 'My sister find her dead. Doctor Vital with her now.'

'Good riddance, then,' said Toddy firmly. 'Drinks all round, on me.'

'What d'you know about that?' said Johnny, staring at her. And Toddy's right hand shivered as she lifted her brandy to her lips and her teeth chattered on the rim of the glass. She was frightened.

VI

The next two suspects in were the horrid children, Joyce and Margie. They were going blue at the edges like a piece of litmus paper under the effect of a strong alkali. Joyce's eyes were red and watering and Margie was sneezing violently. They were both obviously in the grip of a form of influenza.

'Ah—— tchoo! Where's Miss Leamington?' said Joyce, sneezing all over Natasha.

Natasha dusted herself down and said coldly that she did not know. 'Remove it, Johnny,' she said distantly, waving one hand at Joyce and speaking over the top of her head, 'before it has given each of us its loathsome disease.'

'Come along, you,' said Johnny, as though he were a policeman dealing with a drunk. 'Stop annoying this lady.'

Toddy, who was in the middle of a small bet with one of the soldiers about the number of matches in a Swiss match-box, collected her winnings and lounged back to the bar.

'Joyce, Margie, I'll help you find your keeper.' She spoke with an uneasy bravado. Natasha raised her eyes to heaven and said to Johnny how extraordinary Toddy was.

'I'm going to have my bath before I get this 'flu myself,' said Pamela. She followed Toddy and Joyce and Margie upstairs. She kept a respectful distance between herself and the unhealthy children.

Consequently she saw Rosalie Leamington encounter them and (very angry) sweep them away to their rooms.

'You would,' she cried as she went, 'choose exactly this one minute to get ill with the whole hotel in an uproar, and not enough hot-water bottles to go round ... '

The twilight outside the hotel was lovely. The dark evening mists, rising from the snow, penetrated the corridor and made everything beautiful.

'One of us can have yours, Miss Leamington,' said Margie, sneezing.

'That's what you think,' said Rosalie, hustling them into their rooms. 'Mustard baths and quickly, for both of you, believe me.'

Pamela faded away into the dimly lit middle distance. As she went she swore on her stepmother's head that she would never, never become a governess. Or (she added briefly in her own room, in her underclothes) a mother.

VII

Kathleen slowly waked from an aspirin-filled dream. She opened her large black eyes and saw her beloved cousin, Barny Flaherté, standing by the window. Her eyes instantly filled with tears and she turned her head away. She thought it was still a dream.

'*Kathleen*,' said Barny at once. 'I didn't want to wake you ...'

Kathleen shook her head as though she were wiping away the vision.

'About time I did wake,' she said slowly. And then she smiled. All the Flahertés had charming smiles. 'What do you want?' she said.

Barny crossed to the bed and sat down.

'Sorry,' he said. 'Was that your feet? There now, that's cosy.'

Kathleen tucked her feet up and switched on the little light over her head.

'What do you *want*, Barny?' she said again.

'Well, honestly to say I was sorry, about this morning. When I upset you. But when you came in to see me *everything* was a bit tricky. I hadn't been idle, I swear. I had to make' – he paused and looked towards the window and his little pointed chin suddenly went quite hard and strong – 'arrangements,' he ended, finally. He pleated the eiderdown between his finger and thumb.

Kathleen tossed her head.

'About Regan?' she said. She sat up rather straighter and went white.

Barny nodded.

'You see,' he said, 'we couldn't have a Flaherté suicide, now could we?' He smiled engagingly. 'It would have been so bad for *trade* . . .' he hurried on before Kathleen could complain.

'Oh,' she said, shocked. 'Oh. How awful.'

'Well, there were other reasons too, of course, more important ones,' hurried on Barny, quickly and plausibly.

'Oh . . . Yes,' said Kathleen. 'Well, suppose . . . What have *I* got to do with it?'

'You're a Flaherté, my dear,' said Barny. 'I thought you'd say that. As a matter of fact I'm in a bit of a mess with *Fanny* just at the moment . . . '

'Oh?' said Kathleen, coldly.

'Do *stop* saying "Oh", dear. It sounds so silly.'

'Oh?' said Kathleen. 'I mean, does it?'

'Yes,' said Barny. 'Fanny says I must act as correspondent in her divorce case, between her and Ted.'

'Well, why not?' said Kathleen bitterly. 'Don't let being a Catholic stop you . . . '

'Crikey!' said Barny. He raised his beautiful hand, to high heaven. 'Me marry Fanny? You must be mad. No. What I suggested was that *we* should get married. You and me.'

'?', Kathleen's question was not silent, nor was it articulate. She was obviously extremely moved. Barny hurried on.

'Well, we've always got on well, haven't we, Kath? And it would keep all that money in the firm, wouldn't it, dear?'

Barny had contrived to look sincere. As usual, his hair had fallen forward into his eye. As usual, he had pushed his glasses up on to his forehead.

'Well?' he said. 'What do you say? I mean . . . we needn't

announce it yet, or anything ... I think it's a solution myself. And you quite like those horrible children of mine, don't you? You wouldn't mind about my mistresses, would you? I mean, you never *have* ... '

Kathleen turned her back on him and buried her head in the pillow.

'For God's sake,' said Barny. 'What *is* it? Why are you crying, you silly little thing?'

He pulled her by the shoulder. She shook his hand free and sobbed helplessly.

'Oh do stop, darling. Darling Kathie, do stop ... ' said Barny, slapping at her hand. Muffled sobs shook all Kathleen's thin body.

The door opened and Toddy stood there, very forthright and grim, all her nervousness had vanished.

'Barny!' she said viciously. 'What are you doing here? That doctor man wants you.'

'Why?' said Barny, dropping Kathleen's hand as though he had been stung. He set his glasses straight on his nose. 'Why?' he said again.

'Because,' said Toddy, evenly, 'Fanny Mayes seems to have taken an overdose of some sleeping tablets ... '

'My God!' said Barny. 'That's torn it.'

'Why?' said Kathleen, turning her red-rimmed eyes round to peer at her sister over her angular shoulder. 'What's torn it?'

'Because,' said Toddy, 'Barny knows, and so do I, that Fanny never took a sleeping tablet in her life ... '

II

Ted Sloper Breaks Down

Miriam Birdseye went upstairs and followed the noise towards the Slopers' room. Ted Sloper, looking extremely sick, was standing outside the door. He had rested his head and his aching eye against the cool wall. When Miriam came up to him he said,

'They say she's *dead*. Fanny's dead. I can't believe it . . . '

'Is she?' said Miriam, playing for time. 'Here. Do sit down. You look kind of groggy.'

Ted collapsed into the tall-backed, old-fashioned chair that Miriam pulled forward for him. He sat in a heap. He looked grey and dreadfully drawn and ill. He started to shiver. Miriam patted his hand.

'Poor old boy,' she said. 'What happened?'

Ted looked up gratefully. Human sympathy and comfort were things to which he was unused.

'Seems she poisoned herself,' he said. 'Or someone poisoned her. She took tablets for claustrophobia and I expect she took an overdose . . . Oh, God, it's *awful* . . . '

'How do you know?' said Miriam, reasonably. 'I mean, you wouldn't until it was analysed, now, would you?'

'Suppose not,' said Ted. He put his head in his hands. 'The funny thing *is*,' he went on, 'that there was a bottle of empty barbituric tablets beside her. Labelled "*Mrs Flaherté as prescribed.*" They may have been *Regan's* sleeping tablets.'

II

'So that means,' said Miriam, later, excitedly to Johnny and Natasha, they were all in the bar, 'the same person who killed Regan killed Fanny Mayes.'

'An' that it was probably Barny Flaherté, who did,' said Johnny.

'My God,' said Miriam. 'You don't honestly think that, do you? I thought you were just *joking*.'

'I wonder how he'll get out of this one,' said Johnny.

Trudi was drawing the curtains all round the room, shutting out the snow and the dark. They were nice little curtains, made of royal blue folk-weave, embroidered all over with alpine flowers.

'Like he got out of the last one, I expect,' said Miriam, glancing round her. 'By paying up. Ted Sloper *said* Lapatronne *said* five thousand francs would see him out of it, Ted said to hell with him, Barny must pay, if anyone does. I thought someone passed just behind me. I feel cold,' concluded Miriam, with a shiver.

'It was Miss Leamington. Awful dangerous country this is to get murdered in,' said Johnny. 'Excuse me, miss . . . '

He leaned across Rosalie Leamington and took a couple of matches out of the match-holder on the bar. Rosalie said not at all and wasn't it frightful about Lady Sloper, Miss Mayes, she meant. There seemed to be a curse on the hotel.

'Dunno that it's the hotel,' said Johnny, 'but it seems more like the Flaherté party. Might involve you, ma'am. Best watch out.'

Rosalie said yes indeed and smiled warily. She carried her gin and vermouth, her fountain-pen and her writing-pad to a table at the other side of the room. Natasha watched her go. Natasha's eyes suddenly looked baleful, like an angry cat's.

'It is so *un*-natural,' she said. 'All that control in a servant. Now in *Russia*, in the Old Régime ...'

'I don't know, Natasha,' said Miriam, trying to be brisk and making a horrible face. 'She didn't *know* Fanny Mayes after all. I don't see why she need be upset. She was quite upset over Mrs Flaherté, I remember, and a governess isn't quite a servant.'

'Wonder what she'll do when she realizes her precious employer Barny Flaherté is prob'ly a murderer twice over ...' said Johnny grimly. 'Maybe she'll get upset *then* all right.'

'Oh, do shut up, you,' said Miriam. 'I'm sure it isn't Barny.'

'I do not suppose she will mind one little bit,' said Natasha. 'After all, she is in love with Flaherté herself. She will write the *whole* thing *home* to *mother*, or whatever that class of person *has* ... And a governess *is* a servant.'

III

As we know, however, Rosalie was already addressing herself to 'Dear Barbara'.

So far from pouring out the whole story in the uninhibited manner that might have been Natasha's (in writing to her non-existent old ancestral Russian mother), she was finding enormous difficulty in writing anything at all. Finally she drank her gin and vermouth in two hasty gulps and said bitterly to herself:

'Oh well, I can always tear the thing up and never post it.'

Dear Barbara (*she wrote*),

It is always an enormous difficulty, is it not, to write to each other when something *really* has happened? Do you remember that time when Freddy Sample went off his head playing the organ for Matins in John's and played 'Little Old Lady' and 'I'm just wild about Harry' instead of the Te Deum? You found it very difficult to tell me about that because of Freddy being in love with you at the time. It complicated things. Now I expect that is what has happened to *me*. You see, Barbara, I am in love with my employer ...

Rosalie stopped writing and glared round the room at Trudi and the bright little curtains, at Johnny, Miriam and Natasha, who were huddled closely together as though for protection. She wrote savagely:

What a curious *Jane Eyre* situation to be sure! My little charges are in bed with a pernicious form of Mid-European influenza and I am sitting beside one of their beds at this moment ...

Rosalie attracted Trudi's attention and bought herself another drink. Then, with furrowed brow she addressed herself once again to Dear Barbara.

Sometimes she stopped and picked nervously at the side of her thumb. Sometimes she ran her hands through her dim, lankish hair. No one noticed her again and she slightly resented this.

IV

At about seven o'clock, Kathleen Flaherté got up and forced herself to have a hot bath. She thought about Barny.

Why, after his proposal of marriage, had he not stayed and gone on talking to her? Because of Toddy? But surely the proposal was important to him and he could have asked Toddy to go away?

The bathroom had no window. It was filled, cosily enough, with steam. Kathleen felt safe in it.

Obviously he didn't love *her*, Kathleen. Well, she had never thought *that*.

She looked at her long, thin feet in the bath below the taps. But he would find such a marriage convenient.

Kathleen got out of the bath and began to dry herself. She was depressed. She pulled out the plug and the water ran away, making a revolting noise like a child chewing sweets.

Yes, Kathleen would be *convenient* to look after Joyce and Margie. Perhaps she would have a child of her own. Oddly enough, Kathleen would *like* this.

She put on her dressing-gown. It was long, made of velvet, and dark red.

Yes. If Barny were serious when he asked her again, she might say 'Yes'. It was quite true she would not mind him having mistresses. She was sorry about his immortal soul. She, Kathleen, could only pray for that. There was nothing else that Kathleen could do for immortal souls.

Kathleen swilled the bath round and wiped off her little tidemark. Then she opened the door and stepped out of the steam and went back to her own bedroom. The corridor seemed cold and she hurried.

'I wish,' she said unhappily to herself as she went, watching her feet because she was too frightened to look up, 'I had someone *else* to discuss this with who wasn't Toddy. How funny Barny is. I suppose he will be able to "arrange" about Fanny Mayes, too.'

And with this divine belief in the power of the Flaherté millions in Middle Europe, Kathleen reached her bedroom. She was too wrapped up in her dream to glance in the direction of the Slopers' bedroom. She only sensed the general uneasiness about the whole hotel and locked herself quickly into her room to escape it.

V

Pamela, on the other hand, went along the dark passage unable to take her eyes off the doorway of the sinister room. The door was half-open and showed a bar of bright yellow light. She could also hear voices. She paused and knocked on Kathleen's door and asked if she could come in. Kathleen's relieved and delighted voice was heard at once, inside:

'*Pa-amela!*' cried Kathleen. 'Oh, *do*. I am *longing* to see you ...'

She opened the door and dragged her in.

'I want to ask you something,' she said. 'And we must tell our fortunes, quickly, quickly ...'

And she locked the door behind them.

VI

In the middle of dinner, Ted Sloper flung down his table napkin and glared at Barny Flaherté and shouted:

'It's all very well for *you*, damn you. *You've* got a single room. I can't go up there to sleep, and I won't, I tell you, I *won't* . . . '

There was a shocked silence through the dining-room. The other guests stared at the floor, and tried desperately to disassociate their minds from further shock. Barny's voice cut through the silence like a sword.

'You *needn't*, Ted, I expect,' he said, calmly eating his soup. 'You've only got to ask Lapatronne if you can sleep in the bar or somewhere. There's no *need* for you to spoil *all* our dinners. It's not *my* fault, after all . . . '

'How do I know it isn't, damn you,' shouted Ted. 'Damn you for a mad, detached, unnatural *bitch*. If it hadn't been for you we shouldn't be here at all . . . '

'So rude . . . ' said Barny plaintively, watching him. Ted stood up, swayed uncertainly, kicked the napkin and almost ran out of the room. The napkin remained behind him on the floor, a little stained, crumpled ball.

'Oh dear,' said Kathleen. 'Oh dear, oh dear . . . '

She got up also and pushed away a half-eaten plate of beef. Her chair scraped back and she stumbled dismally from the room, sobbing and sniffing. Toddy followed her. She glared indignantly at Barny and then strode boyishly out.

Barny shrugged his shoulders.

'Have some more beef, Miss Leamington,' he said, politely.

'Thank you very much, Mister Flaherté,' said Rosalie. 'I don't mind if I do. That's what the Character in Itma says, isn't it?' and she laughed.

III

Natasha has a Hunch

Johnny sought out Barny Flaherté after dinner. He was still talking to Rosalie Leamington over their cups of coffee in the dining-room. The room was otherwise empty. Someone had picked up Ted Sloper's table napkin.

Rosalie looked animated and pretty, but seemed to be starting a cold in the head. She looked feverish.

'Is he all right, your friend?' asked Johnny. 'I mean, is there anything we can do, m'wife an' I?'

Barny stared at him. He took at least a second to recollect who Johnny might be. Then he smiled agreeably.

'Oh yes,' he said. 'Of course, I remember. You helped me upstairs when I got plastered ... Um. Kathleen was with your daughter at that awfully common school in Yorkshire ...'

'That's right,' said Johnny. He began to feel, resentfully, 'put in his place'. 'D'you think anythin' could be done for poor Sir Edward? A stranger sometimes ... better'n a friend ...'

In the face of Barny's detachment Johnny's voice trailed way.

'Impertinent 'f me, perhaps,' he ended, lamely.

'Not at all,' said Barny, coldly. 'Very kind of you. Ted seems to *mind* about his wife being dead.'

He looked at Johnny as though he expected him to go away.

'I thought he minded his wife being *murdered* . . .' said Johnny.

'Same thing,' said Barny, coolly.

'He feels the Schizo-Frenic police aren't doing a darned thing,' said Johnny.

'Yes,' said Barny, and laughed pleasantly. 'Funny, isn't it?' he said, turning to Rosalie Leamington. 'The Schizo Police dismisses it.'

Rosalie jumped and laughed brightly and looked adoring.

'I'm on his side,' said Johnny, heavily. 'I don't suppose you ever heard 'f me, but . . .'

'Toddy told me,' said Barny with some disapproval. 'You were mixed up in that Extraordinary Case at the Frightful School you mentioned just now. When Kathleen had to be taken away and the Games Mistress was murdered.* Such an extraordinary thing . . .' he added, turning to Rosalie Leamington with the beginning of what he obviously considered to be a good story.

'*I* was the feller,' said Johnny, controlling his fury with difficulty, 'who found the killer an' brought her to justice . . .'

'Indeed?' said Barny. 'I thought it was the police.'

He turned away from Johnny and back to Rosalie Leamington.

'I'm to take it that you're perfectly satisfied with the way the death of your wife has been investigated?' said Johnny. He picked up a table knife that lay on the table. He gripped

---

* *Death Before Wicket*

it hard and scratched it along the surface of the table. 'That so?'

'That so?' repeated Barny, elaborately puzzled. 'That so? Oh. I see what you mean. Well, do you know? I think I *am*.'

And he stared hard at Johnny under his long, dusty eye-lashes. He pulled his horn-rimmed glasses down from his forehead and turned back to Rosalie, who sat, silent and frozen.

'Oh ... ' said Johnny. 'Thanks very much ... '

A red mist of fury raced across his eyes like blood. He turned and walked out in a daze. He heard his feet bang distantly on the floor. When he got there he realized he was still carrying the table-knife.

'Extraordinary class of person,' said Barny's dry, maddening voice behind him. 'Steals knives, too.'

II

'It was No Good,' said Natasha, in the bar, greeting him. She observed the white marks of compression and fury round Johnny's nostrils and the thin line of his mouth. 'My *poor* Johnny.'

'It's damnable,' said Johnny, exploding. 'Cold-blooded selfish *swine*. Don't wonder poor Sloper lost control at dinner. My word.'

Johnny sat down beside his wife.

'He wants no help, that one,' said Natasha. 'Barny the Dish. It is curious how little help he needs. He reminds me *so much* of the Honourable Harrigon ... ' *

---

* *Death Before Wicket*

'Yeah . . .' said Johnny, 'but even so . . .'

'Pam *says* that he has been asking the long-haired Flaherté . . .'

'Kathleen,' said Johnny, nodding.

'Kathleen,' said Natasha, 'to marry him. To protect him from *Fanny*, Pamela thought.'

'Hey,' said Johnny, startled. 'That cat don't jump *now*, do it? He don't need protection from Fanny Mayes. She's dead.'

Natasha nodded slowly.

'Do you know,' she said, with infinite care, opening her lovely hazel eyes very wide, 'I think you will be getting so *much* more help and *interest* from Sir Sloper . . .'

'Natasha,' said Johnny, violently, as one who has suffered too much. 'Have you got a *hunch?*'

Natasha looked into the middle distance over the top of his head.

'Enough,' she said, 'to be asking Pamela for the next twelve hours not to be leaving Kathleen Flaherté alone ever . . .'

III

Johnny caught up with Ted Sloper in Madame Lapatronne's office. His eyes looked livid. His hands were trembling slightly. There was a bottle of aspirin open at his elbow.

'I am telling Good Lord Edward,' said Madame, like the start of a Traditional Old Song, 'not to be *fussing*. I tell him it is only ill he feels.'

Ted smiled wanly.

'I feel a cold coming on,' he said.

'And who would *not?*' said Madame shrilly. 'But Lord

Edward is to sleep in the servants' dining-room for tonight, isn't he?'

Ted Sloper nodded dumbly.

'Miriam won't be very pleased about *that*,' said Johnny.

'By tomorrow morning everything will be clear and the analyst's report on the tablets will all be come ... '

Madame Lapatronne checked the items on her fingers as though she were making out a list of groceries.

'The body will be descended to the Morgue in Kesicken,' she said.

Ted winced. His chin began to tremble.

'Ah, now then, Lord Sloper,' said Madame, putting an arm round him. 'Mister DuVivien is come here to look after you. Isn't that so?'

Her pale intelligent face was suddenly thrust up into Johnny's.

'C'm on, ol' man,' said Johnny. He put a hand under Ted Sloper's elbow and lifted him. 'C'm on. If you like I'll put you to bed ... '

'Would you?' said Ted Sloper, gasping. 'My God, that'd be kind 'f you. I honestly don't want to go *up* there even, an' get my night things.'

'Don't wonder,' said Johnny. 'Just forget it. Just relax ... '

'Mother's here,' said Madame Lapatronne, inaccurately.

IV

'My wife,' said Johnny, coming down the backstairs with his hands full of Ted Sloper's spongebags, pyjamas and hairbrushes, '*says* she has a hunch ... '

Brauzwetter glimmered menacingly across the valley

at them. They were in the cold, glass fronted servants' dining-room. It was possible to see the mountains beyond the window. A small, white, camp-bed had been put up in the corner. Trudi was dancing about with a stone hot-water bottle and Nelli was standing about with her arms full of blankets.

'Not warm, sirs, soon it will be warm,' said Trudi.

'*Service*,' said Nelli.

And the two little chambermaids bobbed and went skipping out of the door just as though Nelli had not found Lady Sloper's dead body two hours ago. Ted was slightly reassured.

'Sure,' said Johnny to their retreating backs. 'You be gettin' yer hot bath an' I'll bring you a nightcap. Hot milk an' brandy, or some'hing.'

'Your wife has a hunch?' said Ted Sloper. He turned his back on Johnny and stared out at the frightening moonlit snow. Something seemed to move in the shadows by the woodpile and Ted jumped. A shadow crossed the moon.

'Would you believe in an absolutely evil person?' said Ted suddenly.

'Dunno,' said Johnny. 'Never thought of it. Expect so. Believe most things. Me, I wanter investigate these nasty goin's on *properly*. Miriam ...'

Ted looked round.

'That leggy lady with the pansy escort, *she* says a bottle 'f sleeping pills actually belongin' to Mrs Flaherté was found beside Lady Sloper. That so?'

Ted put a hand up to his black eye and felt it tenderly.

'Yes,' he said. He looked hopeful. 'That *is* so. You know, Fanny never took anything but *nerve* pills in her life. Luminal they were called, I think. These sleeping-pills had nothing to do with *Fanny*.'

'Dirty work at the crossroads,' said Johnny.

Ted looked much happier.

'You know,' he said, 'I don't think it's right to bribe the police to turn a case up. I mean, it's *awful*. Let *alone* my loving Fanny.'

Two enormous tears, induced entirely by self pity, rose in his eyes and spilled down his taut, smooth cheeks.

'Damn,' he said, dabbing at them. 'Damn. Besides, they *hurt*.'

'Now, now, now,' said Johnny briskly. 'You have yer bath like I said. Then we'll make a plan. If we know *your* movements, it'll help with filling in the others ...'

'Do you believe,' said Ted suddenly in the doorway, his dressing-gown was over his arm, his flat fawn hair was already slightly on end, 'Do you believe *Regan Flaherté* was murdered too?'

'Uh huh,' said Johnny cosily.

'Then, my *God*, we must do our stuff,' said Ted savagely. He came back into the room. 'By the same person?' he said tentatively.

'I think. My wife thinks so,' said Johnny. 'I believe that's her *hunch*.'

'I'm *on*, then,' said Ted. 'I don't care *who* it is. We'll see justice done. We will. I'm your man.'

And he went upstairs to his bath, whistling *Forty Years On* through his teeth. He went as briskly as though he had not, for the last twenty minutes, given an excellent imitation of a gentleman in the first stages of a nervous breakdown.

V

Ted Sloper sat up in his little white bed. He had a rare old Schizo-Frenia dressing on his eye, held in place with a patch and a bandage. He looked less unhappy than he had before his bath. His cold feet moved restlessly, avoiding the perilously hot-water bottle that Trudi and Nelli had placed for them. He wore his dressing-gown. He held his hot milk in both hands. Sometimes he bent his head and sipped it.

Johnny sat on the bed by his feet and made notes with his vulgar purple fountain-pen in a small red penny notebook. He was surprised at the way that Sloper expanded under kindness.

'Well . . . ' he said, 'Natasha an' I still think there's one er two specially extraordinary things . . . '

'One or two!' said Ted with a sharp laugh. 'Huh! That's putting it rather low, isn't it?'

'Dunno,' said Johnny. 'Anyway, if'n you don' mind le's get some background. How'd you ever meet your wife, your late wife, that is. How'd you ever come to marry her?'

'Well . . . ' said Ted Sloper. There was a pause while he drank some more milk. 'I'm not her sort at all, really.'

'No,' said Johnny. 'I realized that.'

'Well. I was hired by B.I.M. Pictures, you know, as Consultant Architect. I did over all those places they bought up and I converted them for film studios. You remember? Whickham House? Caversham Lodge? All those places?'

'Uh huh,' said Johnny, 'I remember.'

'Well, when I was doing over Caversham Lodge, Fanny was there doing a film. *Pursuit of the Devil*. It was *very* bad. She was bored, I guess. Anyway, we went on one or two parties. To the dogs and so on. Then *I* got that job converting the Duke of What's it's house to the Ministry of Essentials. And after that I got knighted.'

'Uh huh,' said Johnny, who had now written the one word '*Sucker*'.

'And after that Fanny married me,' said Ted lamely.

'What kind of person was she?' said Johnny. 'Would being Lady Sloper mean anything to her?'

'Most actresses like titles,' said Ted heavily. 'She liked my having been to Harrow certainly. Can't see it myself.'

'Uh huh,' said Johnny. 'Women are funny. Well. You got married. Where'd you meet Barny Flaherté?'

Ted Sloper turned his head away.

'Last spring,' he mumbled finally. 'Riviera. Monte Carlo. But I think Fanny's known him before. Actually, I think she married me to try to make him *interested*. Less detached, you know. Of course, it *didn't* . . . '

'No, sir,' said Johnny. 'Nothin'd detach young Barny Flaherté short 'f a depth charge. But I thought you said he was your best friend. Why, you'd only known him a year.'

Ted Sloper nodded. He looked as though that had been particularly cold comfort to him.

'He gave me an awful lot of work to do,' he said defensively. 'Well paid, too. I designed the new Flaherté Scent Factory and a chapel for their house at Grasse, well *château*, it is really. I thought he *liked* me.'

'He probably did,' said Johnny. 'Uh huh . . . '

'Well, I *liked* doing the chapel,' said Ted. 'It was *pretty*.'

'Good God,' said Johnny to himself. He added something under his breath about 'how the other half lives'. 'Well, I suppose you were all pretty busy at Grasse, when you were *designing the Chapel*? Fanny was the only one with time on her hands, huh? An' it was a very hot summer?'

'Sounds so crude put like that,' said Ted despondently. 'Suppose I'm just *dull*, that's all, an' she got sick of me, let's face it ...'

Depression fell upon him like a cloud.

'Anyway,' said Johnny, 'you didn't murder her, did you?'

'No,' said Ted Sloper, gravely. 'As it so happens, I didn't.'

VI

Twenty minutes later Johnny's note-book showed the two words '*Honest*' and '*Sucker*'. They were both heavily drawn over and ornamented on both sides with small dahlias and fuchsia bushes.

'There's lots of things I don't understand,' he said. 'First. Where were you when Regan Flaherté fell out of the window?'

'Telephoning, I think,' said Ted. 'Yes, I was telephoning. About a guide.'

'And Mrs ... I mean Lady Sloper. Miss Mayes. Where was she?'

'She wouldn't say,' said Ted, looking unhappy. 'I thought ... Oh, well. I suppose she must've been with *Barny*, don't you? And didn't want to say so?'

'Uh huh,' said Johnny. 'Probably why she got so cross. Flaherté wasn't where he said *he* was, anyway.'

Ted Sloper moved his head a little. It was a tired little movement, like a sick child's.

'Barny wants to marry poor Kathie?' he said. 'Oh, dear. Isn't he hell?'

'The other thing,' said Johnny, paying no attention, 'about *that* case was the lipstick. Now *who* painted Regan Flaherté's mouth with lipstick after she was carried upstairs? Certainly wasn't the innkeeper ...'

There was a cold silence between them that lasted for about thirty seconds. And then:

'I did,' said Ted Sloper, quietly.

VII

'But what on earth *for?*' said Johnny.

The silence was as intense as the cold. Outside the piles of firewood threw their black shadow across the snow. Every now and then a cloud went over the moon. Johnny had sometimes made a part of settings that were more *bizarre*. He had never heard a more incredible statement.

'You see ...' said Ted Sloper, 'I know it sounds mad, but I thought *Fanny* had done it. Pushed poor Regan out of the window, I mean. And when I heard what construction you and your wife put on the lack of lipstick, then I thought ... Well, I nipped into the saloon and made her up. There wasn't anyone there. No one saw me. I'm quite good at that sort of thing, actually.'

Ted glanced down at his broad sensitive hands and rubbed them slowly through each other. He looked up at Johnny with a bright, childish smile. Johnny, not for the first time that evening, felt like 'Nanny'.

'*Very* good,' said Ted Sloper proudly.

'I'll be hanged for venison,' said Johnny.

'Thought it was sheep and lambs and goats,' said Ted Sloper, gaily.

'In England *awful* things c'n happen to you if you do *that*,' said Johnny. 'Falsifyin' evidence, it is. Didn't you know?'

'Yes,' said Ted Sloper, happily falling asleep. 'But this is Schizo-Frenia.'

VIII

Johnny turned away from the camp bed, where Ted Sloper was already asleep, snoring slightly. The moonlight stole across the floor and struck on the chair where Ted had hung his clothes. It showed an envelope, sticking out of the pocket of his jacket. It was a big, stiff, vulgar envelope, lined with brightly coloured paper. Johnny wrapped his handkerchief round his hand and extracted it. The flap wasn't gummed down. There was a letter inside. It said:

My dear Ted,

I couldn't be more sick of all this 'My Soul says I must leave you' stuff. Frankly, Ted, I don't care if you do. I've had it. I'm going back to England. Yrs. Fan.

PS – Sorry I hit you. I'll pay for the light before I go.

IV

Kathleen in Danger

'An' that, honey,' said Johnny to Natasha the following morning, 'just about proves that the lady didn't commit suey the pud.'

Natasha was still in bed, looking unnaturally beautiful. Johnny crashed about the room, dressing.

Natasha winced. She had always thought Johnny *most* vulgar, in the past, but she had not minded him. Nowadays she often felt he went *too* far. Suey the pud, for example, for suicide. It really went too far altogether. And they had sat *up* far too long (until two or three in the morning) to discuss the new evidence about Ted Sloper's behaviour with the lipstick.

'But this Fanny Mayes might still have done Mrs Flaherté,' said Natasha, drawling ever so slightly so that Johnny might not guess how irritated she was. 'And might then have been murdered. By someone else. But I think *not*.'

'Barny might still do both,' said Johnny, stoutly. 'An' I think he did. He was damn rude to me last night, any old haow.'

He flung his toothbrush with a little clatter into the tooth mug.

'Miriam,' said Natasha, 'is *positive* that Barny would never be caring about anything long enough so as to commit murders against it. And because Barny is rude to you does not make him *murderer.*'

'Aw, hell, Natasha,' said Johnny crossly. He wriggled his toes about in his ski-socks and tried to get his ski-boots on over them. 'Lay off of that psychic psychosis stuff, will yer? Gives me the sick.'

He sat on the side of his bed and dressed laboriously for his first long ski-run. He looked bigger than ever, and (thought Nastasha) more stupid.

'You are frightened,' she said suddenly. 'Afraid of the ski-ings. I know you are. It is funny that you, Johnny, can be afraid sometimes of something *physical.*'

Johnny grinned. Then he looked worried again.

'Sure can,' he said. 'I'm *bad* at ski-ing, see? If it were wrestlin' now,' he went on wistfully, 'or unarmed *combat,* or boxin' even ... Ah well, and I haven't got that guide today, Hans Walter. He's somewhere else. But how the hell c'n I keep an eye on Barny Flaherté, I'd like to know, if'n I *don't* go? Eh? Answer me *that* one if you can ...'

'Oh, I can *not,*' said Natasha. 'I have only found out one thing we have spoken of that I remember. *Who* stood to gain by Fanny *Mayes*' death? Someone you would not be expecting, I think ...'

'Well, the husband stood to gain some peace an' quiet, I guess,' said Johnny.

He creaked slowly towards the door.

'Too right,' he said, 'I am scared stiff of this ski-run. Well, who else for example? Honey?'

'Toddy Flaherté,' said Natasha simply.

'For crying out loud,' said Johnny, astonished. 'I'd never a thought of it. Why's 'at?'

'Well, she's been telling me how much she will be gettin'' from Regan in Regan's will, you remember ... ?'

'Yeah, yeah, I remember,' said Johnny rapidly. 'Vurry free an' open of her I thought at the time. Well, what of it?'

'I have found that she is owing Fanny Mayes £4,000 and Fanny Mayes has been starting to *rent* her for it.'

'Hey! Hey!' said Johnny frivolously. 'But if'n she has Regan's cash she could pay back Paul, I mean Fanny.'

'Oh no,' said Natasha, shaking her lovely head. 'These big estates such as poor Mrs Flaherté has been having, they do not pay off: Crash bang! Just like that.'

'Well then, who's to pay Toddy's hotel bill?' said Johnny, exasperated. 'Not me, I hope.'

'You are quite vulgar sometimes, Johnny,' said Natasha. 'Barny, I expect.' And she lay down again. 'Or so Kathleen tells Pamela. This Toddy, she is a gambler, you see, and she knows that Barny will not care for the Flaherté scent to have a bad smell in Schizo-Frenia. Gamblers,' said Natasha, reflectively, 'are brave enough to make quite good murderers.'

II

Johnny went downstairs, making a rude gesture that dismissed all murderers and all gamblers. He squeaked into the dining-room much preoccupied. To begin with, he was furiously shocked by the inconsequence of Barny Flaherté.

Barny was due to leave for Paris by the afternoon train, to escort the earthly remains of poor Regan to her funeral at the Madeleine. He would then return to Katschöchen for his children. (Luckily these were in bed with 'flu and the governess would look after them.) But meanwhile Barny Flaherté had elected to go for a *ski-run*, over Glöchner Gleicher and Verboden, in the morning if it were fine. He said there was plenty of time before the afternoon train left: at three-fifty-four.

Johnny was furious. Barny's disregard of everyone else's feelings. ('Just because *he* don't feel nothing, no call for anyone else to,' muttered Johnny sourly.) Barny's irresistible charm. Barny's unquestionable *chic*. All these things had exasperated Johnny into a near apoplexy.

Silly popinjay (thought Johnny). A man who can go on a ski-run with his wife lyin' dead, *there's* top marks for insensitivity. He surely must have special armour plating for the soul.

But Johnny was wrong. Barny's detachment arose from an extreme sensitivity. It had weakened him to a point where disassociation from the unpleasant things of life was the only bearable course. Much of his apparent callousness was product of a pathological escapism.

Consequently Barny came prancing down to breakfast, as gay as anything, thinking firmly of nothing but skis. Skis and snow and Miriam Birdseye. He saw Roger standing in the hall, and greeted him happily.

'Where's Miriam?' he said, going towards the breakfast-room.

'Good morning,' said Roger, nervously. 'Miriam's having breakfast in bed. Sloper's asleep in our dining-room, you see . . . '

Roger thought Barny looked like a pretty snake in his yellow sweater and his skin-tight black trousers. He wished his own figure were good enough for clothes like that.

'Beastly for you,' said Barny, casually. 'Oh well. Give Miriam my love. Hope I see her before I go this afternoon. If not, I'll write her a little letter . . . '

He went gracefully towards breakfast. Roger remained speechless in the hall with his mouth open. Johnny came up to him.

'Yeah, I know,' he said. 'I heard the whole t'ing. The feller's mad, let's face it. Must be.'

'Oh, he's not mad *yet*,' said Roger, firmly. Roger fancied himself as an investigator of the human mind. He started to explain, eagerly. 'I expect he will be mad one day.'

'Huh?' said Johnny.

'People as sensitive as *that*,' said Roger, holding Johnny by the elbow and talking unpleasantly near his face, 'go *on* until something happens that's unbearable. Falling in love, for example. And *then* they go mad.'

Johnny stared back at Roger as though he, too, were borderline.

'You better talk about that to m'wife,' he said. 'That's what *she* thinks. Don't see it misself.'

III

In the snows above Verboden everyone remembers the air clear and still and blue. When it snows there, it is soon forgotten. When it rains, no one can ever remember it.

And sometimes an early morning skier can gaze up into the blue and the dazzling sun and hear larks singing (any number of larks) by the Lavahorn; that little mountain that sticks out to the left of the Glöchner. But of *course* larks cannot sing above the snowfields in winter time. It must be a trick of altitude.

Barny Flaherté adored Verboden and the Glöchner Gleicher run. He looked forward to it with an endearing intensity. Going up, above the bump and thunder of the funicular, he fancied he could hear the larks. He just didn't like to mention it.

Johnny went up with the guide and Barny as far as Verboden and here he clambered out. They went on to Glöchen Gleicher, four hundred feet higher.

He watched them go sourly, perfectly aware that he was only just good enough to join in with the elementary run down from Verboden. So he sat gloomily in the sun by Verboden railway halt and stretched his legs in front of him. Far below him the snow-fields stretched across the valley in drifts and sweeps of unbelievable whiteness and softness. They went in curves, accentuated by the sharp black lines of ski-tracks, until they came to the other railway line, three hundred feet below him. Standing there on the other railway line there was a little pink hut. Every now and then, skiers, like ants, twirled down from the Glöchner, swarmed over the middle distance or fell, sending up tiny puffs of snow like smoke.

Soon Barny Flaherté and his guide would join them, christie-ing in and out of the hollows and hillocks that lie in the hardest snow. Johnny, wearing his dark glasses, kept his eyes fixed on the snow above him. Barny was wearing a scarlet cap. In his black trousers and his yellow jersey he ought to be easy enough to spot . . .

'Anyway, he's *safe* enough,' said Johnny, grimly. 'He can't get into any more murderous mischief between Glöchner Gleicher an' here, without me seein' him . . . '

By and by, however, Johnny fell asleep.

IV

'Natasha says I'm not to let you out of my sight,' said Pamela to Kathleen Flaherté. They were in Kathleen's bedroom and Pamela alternately looked at herself in Kathleen's looking-glass or fingered the miniatures that Kathleen kept all over her dressing-table. The fortune-telling cards, as usual, lay in a mess beside them.

'That's my father in his yachting cap, and that's my brother getting married,' said Kathleen. She pointed to an unpleasant picture of two people simpering in a high wind outside St Margaret's, Westminster, half obscured by an arch of swords.

'Have you *got* a brother?' said Pamela, startled.

'Oh, yes,' said Kathleen, combing her long dark hair, looking absently out of the window. She put down the comb and began to make up her mouth, pressing hard on the lipstick.

'Why aren't they out here with you then?' said Pamela, startled out of her usual good manners.

'Why should they be?' said Kathleen, reasonably enough. Then she added, as though for Pamela's interest, 'One's in the Army and the other has T.B. They don't work in the firm at all. They come and stay sometimes at Grasse, but it's very damp and they both hate it.'

'Oh . . . ' said Pamela involuntarily. 'Would either of them get any money, because . . . '

She stopped, horrified at herself and covered with confusion.

'Because poor Regan died?' said Kathleen gently. She looked gravely at Pamela as though she were a very long way away and only using her large black eyes as telescopes. 'Yes, of course they will. The same as Toddy and me. And it will all be re-invested and none of us will ever see any of it, unless, of course,' she added suddenly, 'if Toddy or I get married. Then there will be an awful row.'

Kathleen laughed and began to tie a red bow in her hair.

'I think I shall marry the Boss,' she said happily. 'That's the Boss.' And she pointed at a photograph of a man, wearing a bathing-dress, sitting in a deck-chair. He had what is known as a 'strong face'. His photograph was next door to that of her brother's wedding.

'I don't love him at all,' went on Kathleen gaily. 'So it would be *bound* to be all right. He's awfully nice, too.'

Pamela was too astonished to speak.

'Don't look so surprised, Pam,' said Kathleen. She started to brush her eyelashes upwards with Mascara. 'I know what I'm talking about. I do, honestly. Youth is an unhappy time. Love is an unhappy time. Marriage has nothing, thank God, to do with love, only with happiness. You know, children and security.'

Pamela still looked astonished, and who shall blame her?

'Oh, *yes*, Pam-amela,' drawled Kathleen, as though she were trying to convince a roomful of hostile people. 'Marriage for love is awful. Marriage with Barny would be awful. Beautiful and unhappy and insecure. Because he's mad, you see. Like all the Flahertés. Yes. I shall marry the Boss.'

It is impossible to convey the conviction with which Kathleen said these five words that denied her heart and her heart's true passion. Pamela sat on the bed and raised her hands to her face.

'I shall never believe it,' she said.

'What, Pam?' said Kathleen.

'That you mean what you say . . . ' said Pamela.

Kathleen thought they had better be going for their walk.

V

They disturbed Toddy outside the hotel. Curiously enough she was waxing a pair of skis. She jerked her head at them civilly

184

enough and then went on with her occupation. She seemed to be smoking a pipe.

'I didn't know,' said Pamela when they were out of earshot and walking down the railway line, 'that your sister could ski?'

Kathleen dug her hands deep into the pockets of her warm black overcoat and smiled pointedly.

'My sister,' she said, 'can do any dam' thing that she likes. She seldom wants to do anything at all.'

She promptly stopped thinking about Toddy and began to think about something else. By the anguish and the look of pain in her eyes, Pamela judged that she was thinking about Barny.

They walked down the track, breathing deeply. It was open here on both sides to the snow and plunged in a most frightening way along the side of the mountain, clinging to it with its eyebrows, as it were. By and by it plunged into a dark and sinister cutting. Pamela and Kathleen could see it some way ahead of them, yawning at their feet.

Pamela was bruised and stiff from her day's ski-ing, and Kathleen always walked as slowly as possible, from principle. They had not reached the bridge below Water Station Halt (where the dark cutting begins) before Toddy shot by them, side-slipping furiously on the icy snow by the side of the track. There was a pack on her back. She carried something small in one clenched fist beside her ski-stick. From time to time she glanced down at it, whatever it was.

'What's she doing?' said Pamela. 'Your sister? What's she carrying?'

'A stop watch, I think,' said Kathleen, startled out of her dream. 'She wants to make a lot of money at the Ski Championships this week. I expect she's working out the average times of the average skier. P'raps she'll like make an *awful* lot of money.'

Kathleen opened her eyes very wide indeed. Toddy disappeared abruptly into the woods above the luge track.

Pamela began to laugh.

'She's splendid, your sister,' she said.

'Is she?' said Kathleen, bored.

They were now reaching the part of the railway cutting that is overhung by dark, dripping woods. Eventually it passes below the luge track, which runs overhead in a sort of bridge, exactly like the West Bourne in Sloane Square Tube Station.

Every now and then, in the stillness, they could hear a piece of snow slip from a branch with a wet plop. Or a bough would crack suddenly from the weight of snow upon it. Both these things made them jump.

'Goodness,' said Pamela conversationally. 'Aren't we both nervy?'

Kathleen nodded and dug her hands deep into her pockets.

It was cold out of the sun. The little slit of sky that they could see above them when they looked up, seemed grey and unhopeful. They walked under the luge track.

An enormous boulder hurtled down. It seemed to be coming straight at Kathleen's head.

Pamela screamed and thrust her to one side.

They both fell in the snow.

The rock crashed into the middle of the railway line and broke into half a hundred pieces somewhere near where Kathleen had been a second before.

'Those god-damned kids,' said Pamela, flat on her face in the wet snow.

'It can't be,' said Kathleen beside her. 'They're safe in bed with 'flu.'

Yet both of them seemed to hear laughter in the luge track above them. Laughter, and a hurried, bumping noise that sounded exactly as though someone had ridden away on a sledge.

The little red bow that Kathleen had tied into her hair with such heart was draggled and damp. Kathleen shivered.

'We'd best go back,' she said.

VI

'Not on your life,' said Pamela in that rather boisterous tone that made Natasha and Roger and Morris speak of her as a Gamesy Girl. '*I* certainly haven't finished my walk yet. *And* I promised Natasha I wouldn't let you out of my sight. You've jolly well got to come with me ...'

Kathleen looked up at the shadow of the luge track, fifteen feet above their heads. She looked back at Pamela, fearfully.

'D'you think there's anyone up there now?' she said.

Pamela shook her head.

'Whoever it was was on a luge,' she said, 'or skis, an' if we run we should see them going across Jumping Hill Meadow ...'

Without waiting for Kathleen, Pamela began to run down the track, jumping from sleeper to sleeper, stumbling and swearing and often hurting herself.

Kathleen watched her go. She was afraid. Yet the fear of death was less horrid than the fear of spraining her ankle. She stood uncertainly for a second and then recollected a little sledge, used by the brakeman, which she had seen upended by the points fifty yards behind her.

Pamela had tripped and stumbled several times and was already quite out of breath when she became aware of Kathleen's voice, approaching from behind and shouting. She jumped clear of the track, only just in time. Kathleen shot past at about thirty miles an hour, sitting on the toboggan and piled up, with a little scream of terror, in a snowdrift. They were only a hundred yards above Jumping Hill Meadow and the station belonging to it.

Extricated from the snow, beaten down and the snow taken out of her ears, Kathleen was amenable to discipline. Yes, she would sit on the toboggan again while Pamela braked it and steered it. Yes, she was perfectly sure Pamela was quite, quite safe and used to such things. Yes, of course she wanted to see who had tried to murder her. And then she would like to go home, thank you very much.

'Well, never mind,' said Pamela heartlessly, 'a moving target is more difficult to hit.' She looked at her watch. It was half-past twelve.

Bumping and boring and every now and then bounding into the air with cries of alarm and shouts of rapture, Pamela and Kathleen, on the brakeman's sledge, descended towards Jumping Hill Meadow.

The meadow was covered with snow of a very inferior quality. There was a knot of students from the Kesicken Ski School learning the stem christie in one corner. There was no one on a toboggan at all. But there, careering down the very centre of the field, going at a tremendous pace, was Toddy.

And behind her, as though she had been born with silver skis in her mouth, was Natasha.

V

Natasha on Skis

Natasha descended Jumping Hill Meadow with extraordinary grace and poise and went very fast indeed across the little flat bit at the bottom. Here, gathered in a knot, as I have said, was the Kesicken Ski School, in the charge of an unshaven guide. To Natasha's surprise and embarrassment he now stepped forward and pressed a small, silver cup into her hand.

Natasha (who had just executed some of the most difficult gyrations that it is possible to perform on skis) quietly fell down.

'Time 27.3½,' said the guide, picking her up. He turned and spoke cruelly to his class behind him. 'Madame is faster than *any* of you,' he said, and his voice was savage and humiliating, 'and it is only her first day.'

Natasha clutched the little cup and moved anxiously aside. Toddy stood and waited for her, leaning on her ski-sticks.

'What was all that?' said Toddy, gruffly. 'I couldn't believe my eyes when I saw it was *you*. I didn't even know you could ski.'

'I can*not*,' said Natasha, quietly falling down again. 'I am putting on Pamela's skis and following *you*, and when I am reaching the bottom of this hill they give me this little cup.'

She held it up and Toddy took it from her. It was carefully engraved 'Kesicken Amateurs, 1947.'

'It is an insult, I think,' said Natasha, reading this, over Toddy's shoulder. 'And I who have danced for the great Sergei Pavlovitch himself.'

'You *must* have been going pretty damn fast to catch *me* up,' said Toddy, wonderingly. She looked at her suspiciously and turned the cup over and over in her hands.

'Oh, but I *was*,' said Natasha, wide-eyed. 'I was *terrified*.'

'What *was* yer time, d'y know?' said Toddy. 'Did that man say anything when he picked you up, eh? I'm working out the times for the course, you know, so that we can all make money at the Championships . . . '

'The man said 27.3½, but what he is meaning, I cannot say. Whether feet, inches, seconds, or my age, he does not mention,' said Natasha, with a sweet smile. 'But everyone cannot make money in betting.'

'All right,' said Toddy, grudgingly, 'so as one can make some money. Wouldn't care to have something on how much this cup is worth, would you?'

'No, I should not, it is *sordid*,' said Natasha.

They were clambering up the little hill to the railway track and Natasha was already bored.

'If ski-ing were only going down hills I should perhaps be enjoying it,' she said. 'So long as strange men are not trying to insult me with gifts. For Ama-teurrs—'

She spat out the word with all the furious contempt of the true, but retired, professional.

'Most people take weeks to do anything at all, and you aren't being *paid* for it,' said Toddy, gasping slightly. 'Must say you're lucky to be so fit. Mus' give up brandy. Don't think I can, though.'

'Fit?' said Natasha, lightly, and fell down. 'Nevertheless,' she said, flat on her back, 'I *do* find so long as I do not think about the skis but only about *you* who I am chasing, I am staying upright.'

Natasha picked herself up. Side by side they achieved the snow by the railway track.

'*Why* were you chasing me?' said Toddy. 'Jolly kind of you I must say. But *why*?'

'I am unable to say why,' said Natasha, foolishly. 'Because I do not know. But *this*, I know,' and she beat herself dramatically on the bosom with her fist, '*here*, that you and your sister Kathleen should *not* be left alone today.'

Toddy stared at her and crossed herself. Kathleen and Pamela, mounted on their ridiculous toboggan, now came slowly to rest a few feet away from them.

'How right you *were*,' said Pamela, who had overheard Natasha's little speech. 'Someone tried to murder Kathleen from the luge track. I thought it was Toddy at first, and then I thought, no, that is a very odd thing for one sister to do to another, and though I haven't a sister, I know *she* wouldn't if you know what I mean ... ' She stopped short and stared at Natasha and said, 'What on earth are you doing on skis?'

'I am,' said Natasha, with cold sarcasm, 'dancing the variations of the Sugar Plum Fairy in the *Casse Noisette Suite*.'

And she fell gently on her face alongside the track.

'Jolly lucky thing for me Mrs DuVivien *did* come ski-ing

then,' said Toddy, gruffly. She seemed to be the only person who had listened to, or made any sense of Pamela's extraordinary collection of *non sequiturs*. She helped to pick Natasha up. 'Jolly D of her,' she said. 'Establishin' my alibi like that. And besides,' she added, 'Mrs DuVivien is jolly good at ski-ing. Look at this little cup,' she said to Pamela. 'Bet you a shilling you can't guess how much this is worth.'

Pamela took the cup from her and turned it over and over.

'We'll pawn it,' said Toddy.

'But certainly *not*,' said Natasha, snatching it away from her. '*Blessed* little cup,' she crooned foolishly. 'The only little cup I ever had.'

'Someone *really* tried to murder Kathleen, Natasha,' said Pamela, keeping her head. 'Do pay attention. We were under the luge track where it goes over the railway line at half past twelve and someone in the luge track heaved a boulder over. Might have broken Kathleen's neck. They went off laughing. At least, we *think* we heard laughter.'

'Man or woman?' said Natasha, continuing to fondle her little cup.

'Don't be silly,' said Toddy, gruffly. 'How can anyone tell that? Besides, they didn't really hear. And men and women laugh awfully alike, especially in February when they all have colds.'

She looked at her sister, who shuddered.

'No,' said Kathleen, and tears began to rise slowly in her eyes. 'Oh Toddy, Toddy, isn't it awful? I thought it was you. Oh, Toddy, do forgive me. I'm so *sorry*.'

And the two sisters fell into each other's arms. For the next five minutes all funiculars to and from Kesicken and Mönchegg were held up by a disgusting and maudlin exhibition of family love and trust.

'Well,' said Natasha, considering, 'I *am* seeing Toddy in full view all the way down and she never goes near the luge track.'

She looked at the entwined sisters with affection. So, she imagined, did her *own* sisters behave and love each other back in the Russian home? The Old, White Russia . . .

'So I know she cannot be taking time off to throw boulders,' said Natasha. 'That idiot, Johnny, also, he is doing the same thing for your cousin Barny. So that will be two of you . . .'

II

Up at Verboden, That Idiot Johnny stretched his long legs and moved them in the sun. He woke up. He was very stiff. It was the clanking of the funicular that had intruded itself in his dream. He stared wildly round him.

A lot of people had climbed off the funicular. They were now getting ready to make the exciting, but elementary journey over Verboden, down to the Pink Hut.

Among them, with a little start of horror, Johnny recognized a tall, slim young man, accompanied by a faintly insanitary guide. The young man wore a red hat, a yellow jersey and tight black trousers. He turned, saw Johnny and grinned, pulling on his gloves. Barny Flaherté and his guide.

'D'you have a good sleep?' said Barny. 'We can all go down together this time.'

He smiled.

'This time?' said Johnny, 'how long ago did you get to Pink Hut the first time?'

Barny started.

'Why, *ages* ago,' he said. 'I've been right down to Jumping Hill Meadow below Water Station since then. This'll be our second run, guide an' me. We came up in the funicular. Only just time for one more run before luncheon,' he added.

'What's the time?' said Johnny, and then, answering himself, 'Oh, lor' 1.15.'

'Mister Flaherté,' said the guide, suddenly, 'is very fast for an Englishman. He is fast enough for Championship. He should be in them this week.'

'Oh, get on with you,' said Barny, pleasantly, pushing him with his ski stick. 'I'm all out of condition. They're worse than the Irish for flattery,' he added, turning to Johnny again.

'He *is* too fast for me, I can tell you,' said the guide. '*I* did not go down with him to Jumping Meadow. It was too much. I wait for him to come back to Mönchegg. I am getting to be an *old man*.'

Johnny stood up, feeling extremely sour. Together they made the glorious descent over Verboden to the Pink Hut.

III

'Sure, I get the point,' said Johnny to Natasha. '*Sure* I'm sorry I fell asleep. Sure I'm sorry I haven't gotten Barny his alibi. But Kathleen *wasn't* murdered. An' there's no harm done ... '

They were standing in the hall at the hotel, trying to sort the members of their party from the general Schizo-Frenic public, which had poured into the hotel with its luncheon in ruck sacks, or boxes. Later, it sat round the hotel very much unbuttoned, at the little chairs and tables and ate hard-boiled eggs in the sunshine.

'*Bête!*' shouted Natasha, instantly very angry. 'I do not want alibis. I want to attrap the lunatic who does all these *awful* things ...'

'Yes, Johnny,' said Miriam, apparently rising from the ground at their feet. Her tow-coloured hair was in wild disorder. 'You should have looked after my Darling Dish for me.'

Johnny went on being angry.

'Hell,' he said: '*You* ain't one to talk, Miriam. Ted Sloper was the one *you* was supposed to look after for the day. Where'd he get to?'

Miriam pouted and gave her imitation of a Notre Dame gargoyle.

'He went out on skis,' said Miriam. 'No one could expect me to do that sort of bestiality.'

'Natasha did,' said Johnny, proudly. 'Natasha got on skis and was given a little cup for it. Wonderful little skier, she is,' said Johnny, putting an arm along her shoulder. 'Toddy Flaherté made twenty francs bettin' me Natasha'd bin on skis. And I was *glad* to lose my money.'

Johnny looked proud and fond and rather revolting.

Miriam stared.

'Don't understand, don't understand, don't understand,' she said rapidly.

'It is *quite* true,' said Natasha. 'But I am ashamed of it and do not wish it referred to. At least, though, I do not allow Toddy Flaherté out of my sight, like I have said. You two, both of you, you have been doing very badly.'

She went sulkily into the dining-room. She moved a little self-consciously as the Great Catherine might have moved her first time in trousers.

The dining-room was fairly full.

Kathleen and Rosalie Leamington were eating their luncheon one each side of Barny.

'Hullo, Natasha,' said Kathleen, in a friendly way. 'Barny's coming back at the end of the week, isn't it lovely? An old British General, or someone, who's running the British Ski Team, saw him ski-ing and has entered him. Isn't it splendid?'

'Goin' to be pretty steep enterin' without proper trainin', said Barny, with his mouth full. 'Shall have to do something pretty drastic on the train to get myself into trim. And of course, no *drink.*'

Barny smiled in a manner that can only be described as impish. In spite of herself Natasha was shocked.

'But these ski-ings,' she said, loudly, looking at him in horror. 'They are only a *game.* But burying poor Mrs Flaherté. This is life. This *matters.*'

Barny looked worried. The light of enjoyment in his face went out like a candle. His eyes were haunted and distressed. He sat quite still. Natasha instantly wished she had not spoken at all. The intense distress and pain in his face was something that Natasha had only seen once or twice in her life before.

'I am sorry,' she said. She stepped forward and put one thin, white, beautiful hand on his shoulder. '*Please* do not be looking like that. Of course I understand. You mind too *much.*'

Barny looked up at her. His face slowly relaxed and his pained eyes became normal. They seemed to change from green to blue as they did so.

'You *are* very beautiful,' he said, just as though he had never seen Natasha in his life before and that someone had told him about her. 'I shall fly back from Paris,' he added inconsequently.

'Ah, good,' said Natasha, softly, 'and you shall *win* these ski-ings. I shall see to it myself.'

IV

'Natasha DuVivien has just got off with the Dish.'

Roger, outside the dining-room, in the passage had watched everything through a crack in the door and now handed on the information to his friend Morris. They were standing in the hall, giggling together about the crowd of wonderful Schizo-Frenics that were surging through and round the hotel.

'Look, dear,' said Roger, 'there's an awfully good character there. That old lady with all those kiddies.'

'I do think teeny weeny ski-sticks and teeny weeny skis are the absolute bottom,' said Morris, finicking slightly. 'Funny how all these girls are so crazy about Barny Flaherté ... '

'Who's crazy about Barny *now*?' said Toddy Flaherté's harsh voice behind them. 'Don't tell me. Wait a minute. Twenty francs I can guess who. Evens. Am I on?'

'You're on,' said Roger, spinning round. He alone admired Toddy's gambling proclivities. He held up a 20 franc note between his finger and thumb and looked at Toddy. She had her hands in her trousers pockets and a short clay pipe was clenched between her teeth.

'Natasha DuVivien,' said Toddy, slowly, removing the pipe from her mouth. 'I should think. Am I right?'

Roger shrugged his shoulders helplessly and handed over the money.

'I never win,' he said.

'Oh *rot*,' said Toddy. She put the note into her empty notecase. 'You won fifteen centimes from me yesterday.'

'Fifteen centimes,' began Roger, angrily. Toddy laughed and put the notecase away in a gentlemanly inside breast pocket somewhere under her armpit. 'And who,' she said to Morris, 'do you suppose is the next candidate for Murder, eh? Now, that'll be worth something. Specially to the victim, I guess, eh?'

And Toddy gave Roger a sidelong glance and a dig in the ribs and a corner boy wink that sent shivers racing up to the top of his head.

'Lor'!' he said. 'But you don't want to bet about a thing like *that*, surely, now, do you?'

'My dear boy,' said Toddy, boisterously, 'I'd bet on *anything*. Any damn thing.'

'I do believe you would,' said Morris, horrified.

'Toddy's the original old *crone*, knitting above the guillotine baskets in the Terror, dear,' said Roger, recovering himself. 'Betting on likely-looking aristocrats.'

Roger and Morris shuddered pleasantly.

'Isn't she *awful*?' they asked each other.

'Well, Mesdames, Messieurs,' said Toddy, striking an attitude with her pipe in one hand. '*Faites vos jeux*. The next *victime*? Anyone care to bet against Mr DuViven? Five hundred francs? Even Money?'

VI

Barny Starts For Paris

Natasha's moral courage was of the finest calibre. For example, she was the only inconsiderable female dancer known to outface the Great Diaghilev. This she had done in 1922 at Cannes. Ordered to wear a black wig in *Les Sylphides*, she had cheerfully disobeyed him and had danced in her own hair. It had caused a splendid scene.

A murder or two in a Schizo-Frenic hotel, therefore, would not be likely to shake her nerve or spoil her time. Yet, in the three hours before Barny Flaherté (wearing a black tie) set out on his *macabre* journey to Paris, Natasha was conscious of a feeling of disquiet.

There was nothing (or so she would have told you) upon which she could put her fingers. There was no *reason* for her to feel as she did. And yet, angry, jealous eyes followed her around, glaring at her from all the parts of the landscape. They even glared from Brauzwetter.

'It has something to do with Barny,' she said to Johnny. 'That I am *so certain* of. So you must go to Paris with him.'

'Was gonner do that, anyway,' said Johnny, firmly. 'Was gonner change some pounds sterling black and make a bit of money. If I use m'head.'

He looked at his wife. She seemed unusually quiet and pale. Even for her she appeared vague. She was obviously thinking about something else.

'What's the matter with you-all, honey,' he said, clumsily. 'Any'hing I c'n do?'

'No-o,' said Natasha, as usual irritated by his solicitude. 'No . . . I feel like I have felt when I dance the Doll in *Petrouchka* because Kasarvina is sick. Everyone is so cross about it . . . '

'Jealous, huh?' said Johnny.

II

Johnny left the hotel before 3.54 and slowly skied down to Kesicken. He thought he would get into Barny Flaherté's train without his knowledge. He whipped across Jumping Hill Meadow and (for the first time in his life) managed to do a stem christie round the post and rails. It was a mistake, but it was a definite stem christie. Johnny was delighted. He was only slightly worried about Natasha.

She certainly had seemed all steamed up about something. Johnny would give a bit to know *what*. Probably Natasha didn't know that herself. But with Monsieur Flaherté out of the way (thought Johnny) there'd be a chance of everyone settling down to their holidays.

After some unpleasant sloshing through mud and purest manure, Johnny arrived at Kesicken station. It was half past three. He took off his skis, lashed them together and wrote a little note to go with them. It was an odd little note, but the railway porters had no difficulty in understanding it.

'*C'est les skis de Monsieur DuVivien, S'il vous plait va monter les skis nacht Water Station Hotel.*'

He bought himself a return ticket to Unteralp. The booking clerk was perturbed at the thought of booking him to Paris and the whole thing got too difficult, so he gave it up and waited for the funicular. It was slightly late and came clanking into the station with little jolts and jars. Barny Flaherté leapt from the train and rushed into the Telegraph Office, waving telegram forms.

Johnny sat furtively in a third class carriage, peering along the platform. Had he worn a hat he would have slouched it across his eyes, like a writer of thrillers. He saw Barny dive out of the Telegraph Office and rush back to the train, carrying a copy of *Paris-Soir*. The train moved off. Johnny glanced round his carriage, under his eyebrows. He could hardly have looked more sinister.

He was surrounded by an entirely female party of tourists (English) who were booked (Thomas Cook and Sons) all the way through to Victoria, London. They had had the time of their *lives*, they said. And Ethel (who was in another carriage), *she* had bought enough milk chocolate and nylons to sink a Schizo-Frenic battleship.

'Look, Joan,' said the party leader, pointing out of the window at Kesicken. As usual it was engaged in a heavy thaw. 'The last of Kesicken. Roll on, Stafford Cripps.'

'Wish I'd managed to get some cups and saucers,' said Joan.

III

At the next station Johnny was in time to see Barny Flaherté rush out of the Telegraph Office, carrying another copy of *Paris-Soir*.

'P'raps it's the same one,' he said, savagely.

He ducked behind a milk chocolate machine and Barny went hurrying by to the train. He was whistling a little song that Johnny (in his rough uneducated way) identified with *The Scarlet Pimpernel*. It was '*Auprès de ma blonde, qu'il' fait bon dormir, dormir*', and Johnny was annoyed. Who was Barny Flaherté to have a blonde, as well as everything else?

Then he noticed that the chocolate machine was full of wrapped packages called Nestlé's. He hadn't seen such a thing for six years. He lost his head and five minutes later, as bells rang and the engine snored and the tram began to show signs of movement, he was still putting 20 centime pieces into the machine and taking out dear little slabs of chocolate. Out of the tail of his eye he noticed Barny clamber into a carriage and he dived into one behind him, dropping small blue and white and red packages in all directions. He was quite ashamed of himself. He settled down in his corner, ate a slab of chocolate and fell asleep.

Half-an-hour later a voice woke him. It was uncompromisingly British. It penetrated his dream and hurt him. He opened one eye, cautiously.

'Ah, Doreen,' said the voice. It belonged to a plump, middle-aged lady in a bottle green ski-suit. 'There you are. And now for Stafford Cripps.'

'I only wish,' said Doreen, 'that I had managed to get another cuckoo clock for mum.'

IV

The train ran into Unteralp with a small squeal and much ringing of bells. Johnny had eaten all his milk chocolate and was thinking wistfully of hard-boiled eggs. He moved into the corridor and thought tersely of sausage, flavoured with garlic. He stopped short with astonishment.

On the platform, in top hats and deep black frock coats and high, white stiff up and down collars, were two obvious mourners. The train heaved quietly to a halt. Barny Flaherté got down from the train and went up to them. They took off their hats.

'Quite,' one of them seemed to be saying, in French, wagging his head. '*Absolument.*'

They took off their hats again and both entered the train. Barny Flaherté waved to them gaily from the platform.

Johnny was furious. He had only just time to leap from the train before it pulled away from Unteralp. Barny approached a porter. He asked, 'When was the next train back to Kesicken and the High Mountains?' The porter said 'Tomorrow morning.' And Barny seemed quite pleased.

V

Barny Flaherté hurried out of the station. For a second he stood and stared round the station yard. It was a broad stretch of asphalt in rather bad repair. It was overgrown here and there with weed. There was an empty patch of grass by the permanent way where rusty tins and abandoned motor tyres lay about in a desolate tangle. The sun had been down for half-an-hour. The cold, blue twilight was unwelcoming. On the other side of the asphalt was a small pub. The windows were not yet lit up. The door seemed fast closed.

Barny approached it with a jaunty swing. The door opened as he came up to it. A man came out. Barny stepped aside for him. The pub was evidently open. For a second the light in the bar and the noise of the people drinking and talking streamed out. The evening was less lonely. The door closed behind Barny.

Johnny hesitated. He looked awkward and powerful in his ski-ing clothes. When he judged that Barny would certainly have had time to book a room, he crossed the asphalt himself and pushed the door slowly open.

The bar was dimly lit. It was a small room, scattered with tables and ill-made chairs. In the darkest corner the postman was playing draughts with a railway porter. There was a heavy mahogany counter and a barmaid with untidy hair. Johnny got the impression the room was lit with oil-lamps. He moved gently up to the counter and smiled uneasily at the barmaid. She turned away and began to pat her hair.

On the counter was a bowl full of hard-boiled eggs. Johnny became aware once again of his unnatural hunger. He ordered a drink and began to eat eggs. He had eaten six before a man, obviously the manager, came into the bar from the back. There was still no sign of Barny.

Johnny caught the manager's eye and offered him a drink, speaking in halting French. The manager looked surprised.

'*Avez vous une chambre pour ce soir?*' said Johnny firmly, when they had wished each other luck and drunk each other's healths twice.

'Well ...' said the manager, looking uncomfortable. He spoke slowly and distinctly in English. His English was better than Johnny's French. 'There is only the Guest Room. And there is one other gentleman in that already. There are, of course, six beds. But this gentleman. He is English also.'

'*Ça c'est OK*,' said Johnny. 'I'll share with him *avec plaisir. Absolument.*'

And such is the low level of integrity amongst Schizo-Frenic hoteliers that the manager didn't even bat an eyelid, but told Johnny that he understood him perfectly and that he spoke excellent French.

VI

'Here,' said the manager, 'is the other gentleman now. I am afraid I must ask you to share the room. But *Englishmen* will not mind?' At this appeal to his patriotism Johnny twisted his face into the sort of grimace he considered suitable for greeting Barny.

'Sure. No,' said Johnny, turning round. '*Absolument.*'

But the Englishman was a little short Jewish gentleman with a bald head. He did not resemble Barny Flaherté in the very least.

VII

'*Vous avez beaucoup de people ici? Anglais?*' said Johnny, rather desperately to the barmaid, who went on looking cross. 'I bet?'

'English? No. Seldom,' said the barmaid, glumly. She was certainly allergic to Johnny.

'Between *les* trains, I guess?' went on Johnny, grimly. '*Beaucoup des Anglais pour* drinks?'

'Well ...' said the Jewish gentleman, helping him out, 'you

know, Cici, there *was* another Englishman in today. For a drink. Trying to hire a car. Think he got one, too.'

'Good heavens,' said Johnny, with interest. 'A car? On a night like this? What an extraordinary thing. Where'd he want to go?'

'Kesicken I think,' and 'That'll be him now,' said the Jewish gentleman.

He wagged his head towards the window where the head-lights of a motor-car were suddenly apparent, shining brilliantly round the shutters. A young man in a small dark blue yachting cap and wearing a dirty grey polo jersey under a great coat appeared in the doorway.

'Flaherté?' he said, raising his eyebrows at Johnny. The barmaid said rapidly in French that the gentleman was eating his dinner and would be right out and the driver was to wait for him. The driver said a rude Schizo-Frenic equivalent of 'O Nerts', and that he wanted a drink. The barmaid shrugged her shoulder and gave him a pint of pale, innocuous beer.

Johnny edged over to the door and slid quietly outside. He wanted to have a look at this motor. It was a big old-fashioned open Oldsmobile with the canvas hood up. Pretty draughty, Johnny reckoned. He stood for a second, looking it over. He tried to work out how soon it would run out of petrol if he punctured the tank. And then if he hiked after it would he encounter the breakdown in a half-hour or an hour … He decided it would be more like six hours. He dodged round to the back of the motor as the pub door opened again, behind him. He heard Barny's voice saying that he'd like to get cracking as soon as convenient, thank you very much.

Johnny, now on all fours on the other side of the Oldsmobile, gently opened the back door and crawled in. He lay flat on his face in the back. The door shut gently, with a tiny, metallic click. There was a rug under him that smelt ferociously of car oil. He wriggled under it.

'*Alors. Partons nous?*' said someone.

'*Immediatement,*' said someone else.

The springs creaked a little and two doors slammed in the front. The self-starter buzzed, the engine began to tick over. The back of the car instantly filled with the stupefying fug of exhaust fumes. The car snarled round the yard on three wheels and left at a terrific pace, the tyres scrabbling at the turn out of the station yard.

Johnny, jerking up and down in the back, clung on with his eyebrows. He felt exhilarated. This was the sort of wildness that he understood.

VIII

The car roared along the road, rocking from side to side. It stabbed a path through the dark with its white headlights. Johnny gently changed his position, and tried to rub the cramp out of his forearms. Eventually, cautiously, he managed to sit upright.

He could see two heads in front, above him. Barny was apparently slumped to one side, asleep. The driver was alert. He stared ahead of him through the darkness. Johnny got a sudden, queer impression that the driver was waiting for something to happen.

There was no snow at all on the road. The headlights

sometimes showed up a white patch on the grass verge. They seemed to be doing about fifty miles an hour. Someone, probably the driver, was smoking American mixed Turkish-Virginian tobacco. Johnny could smell it above the exhaust fumes. He could also see a little dim red glow of a cigarette reflected in the windscreen. He wondered if he dared light one of his own. He thought not. He jammed his feet against the seat and leaned back. Now he was fairly comfortable. He hardly moved as the car rocked round corners, tearing towards Kesicken, through the night.

This part of the story is almost too extraordinary to tell. Johnny, afterwards commenting on it, said it was probably the *only* thing that could have happened to make him a real friend of Barny's. He still finds it hard to believe.

About twenty miles beyond Unteralp the headlights suddenly lit up a rough barrier, across the road. A man, holding a rifle, stood beside it. And he jerked the barrel of the gun sideways. The gesture clearly said 'Stop'.

The driver stopped and snatched on his handbrake. He nearly flung Johnny forward on top of him.

'What the hell . . . ' began Barny Flaherté.

'Oh, shut up,' said the driver in perfectly good English. 'Get out and shut up. It's your money he wants. Not your opinion.'

'Be damned if I will . . . ' said Barny, sulkily. 'Never heard of such a . . . '

But he climbed slowly out into the road. Johnny, crouched on all fours in the back, had seen the dark shape of an automatic pistol in the driver's hand.

Johnny dived forward and seized him from behind. He twisted the pistol out of his hand, dragged his neck back until a vertebra was about to crack, and hit him a vicious jab on the head with the automatic. The young man grunted and went limp. Johnny laid him in the back and stepped over him out into the road.

'He's out cold,' said Johnny, to himself, 'for about a quarter 'f 'n hour, I guess.'

'You've been a time, Kiki,' said a voice in the darkness, in French. It obviously belonged to the man with the gun. 'Since you telephoned I've been frozen waiting for you.'

'Straightforward hold-up,' thought Johnny. He stepped towards the voice. 'Only two of 'em evidently ... I wonder.'

The lights of the Oldsmobile made a pool of light in the road. On the edge of it was Barny Flaherté with his arms up. The man with the rifle was standing beside him.

'Hurry *up*, Kiki,' said the man with the rifle. 'Fan him over and get his wallet. He's obviously as rich as old Nick to hire a car at all. Must have the cash on him ... '

He jabbed the barrel of the rifle in Barny's ribs.

'Here,' said Barny, in a bored voice. 'Don't do that. It hurts.'

He sounded as though he were thinking of something else.

'Yeah, Mister,' said Johnny loudly.

And he hit the man with the rifle just below the ear and sprang on him from behind. A splendid rough house then took place all over the road. The rifle went clattering away across the tarmac, exploding as it went, and Barny gave a little squeal and jumped over it. Johnny sat astride his man's chest and banged his head again and again on the road.

'What happened?' said Barny, when Johnny stood up and looked down at the second unconscious thug. He brushed the palms of his hands. 'Where's the driver, Kiki, isn't it, if it isn't you? And who are you?'

Barny stepped closer and looked at Johnny.

'Goodness,' he said. 'How very unpleasant this all is. First of all I'm held up by car bandits and then I start seeing things. I thought I left a man exactly like you at Katsclöchen this morning . . . '

'You did,' said Johnny. 'I mean, this is me, here. I followed you.'

'It's all too difficult,' said Barny. 'Makes no sense. How'd you get here? Why did you follow me?'

'Tell you in a minute,' said Johnny. 'Looks like you fell in with a nicely organized lot of hold-up boys. Yes sir. Let's put 'em in the ditch an' start back over on our journey . . . '

Barny gaped for a second. Someone whose irresponsibility was equal to his own was new to him.

'You mean . . . take the *car*,' he said, slowly.

'Sure . . . ' said Johnny.

'But that, it'd be *stealing*.'

'Sure,' said Johnny.

Barny began to laugh.

IX

Johnny put Kiki and his companion in the ditch with their rifle, their automatic and their barrier on top of them. 'Never,' he said as he did so, 'was I one for takin' away a feller's means of livelihood.' Kiki was very thin and half-starved looking. The man with the rifle was older, smaller and thicker. He wore a very clean shirt and his hands were filthy with motor oil.

Barny began to question Johnny.

'Forget it,' said Johnny. 'Don't waste time. Tell you all about it on the way. Let's get crackin' before they wake up again. Seems to be plenty petrol in the tank ... '

Johnny, who did not trust electric petrol gauges, had tested it with a piece of stick and Barny had been impressed by his firm, practical attitude.

'You drive,' he said, after a second, when Johnny tested water and oil and kicked the tyres. 'I get nervous of other people driving myself, but I'm bored when *I* do it ... '

They tucked down in the front and the engine began to tick over.

'Okidoke,' said Johnny. '*There* we are.'

The car slid away from the little pile of bodies in the ditch as though they had been nothing more than a bad pothole in the road surface. They gathered speed. Soon they were humming along again.

'Let's hope ... ' said Barny, 'that the road is properly sign-posted or that Kiki kept a map in the car. Do tell me. Why are you here? I mean ... I'm positive I left you at Water Station Hotel yesterday. Today, I mean. I call it most *sinister*. Have you something dank to do with the murders?'

'Ah ... ' said Johnny. 'So you're admittin' they was murders, are you? I was waitin' for you to do *that*.'

'Dear Barbara'

The unfortunate children, Joyce and Margie Flaherté, had been tossing and turning in their respective rooms for at least forty-eight hours. Rosalie Leamington, whose talents were not connected with home nursing, was finding the way they copied each other's symptoms rather boring. Whenever she could spare a second she wrote to Miss Barbara Sewingshields and told her so.

She carried Bayer's aspirin and gargle from Joyce's room to Margie's room, four hourly, and was greeted by the hoarse and querulous screams of those whose voices are lost and whose throats are red hells covered with large white spots. She felt no pity. She only felt an exasperation about these children who spoilt her time. Madame Lapatronne crept up behind her in the passage.

'The poor ones,' she said. 'What can seem to be wrong with them?'

'Well, they've both got high temperatures and sore throats,' said Rosalie, wearily. 'I suppose it's some sort of 'flu. Gargling doesn't seem to do any good, either. And they both loathe it.'

'I have here a thermometer,' said Madame. She flourished a thermometer of the size that is usual for horses and cows. Rosalie recoiled from it with a little cry. 'We will tell how hot they are. And then we shall be bringing the temperatures *down* . . .'

'How?' said Rosalie, wearily rubbing her forehead. She supposed that Madame would not be able to compare Joyce's and Margie's heat with that of the hotel milch cow. She could not have cared less. After all, she was doing her best for the blasted children. 'The aspirins don't seem to do any good at all . . .'

'Winegar,' said Madame, firmly, and (as Rosalie thought) irrelevantly. 'Winegar cloths on the feet and winegar cloths on the throat, held on with woollen scarves. You shall see . . .'

'Really?' said Rosalie Leamington. 'Doesn't seem possible, I mean. On their *feet*? It's not their feet that are sore . . .'

'You shall see how it relieves the throat,' said Madame briskly. She shook her terrifying thermometer and plunged into Joyce's room.

II

The room was stuffy and smelt of fever and other unpleasant things.

Joyce lay in a flushed tangle of sheets and blankets. The pillow lay in a snarl on the floor. She had overturned her glass of drinking water and seemed hardly able to breathe. Large unhappy tears rolled down her face when she tried to speak. Her temperature was at least a hundred and four. Madame advanced at once with her bottle of malt vinegar, her boiling water, some cloths and woollen socks and an enormous tin basin.

The wretched child then tried to scream, but was unable. She made pathetic noises. She was more like a sick monkey than anything else.

Madame, ordering Rosalie Leamington brightly on one side, re-made the bed with a few taps and twitches.

They moved on to Margie, who lay in an unwholesome, doped, unnatural sleep. Madame thrust the thermometer under her white furred tongue. Margie began to babble deliriously round the thermometer.

'Don't talk with the thermometer in,' said Madame. 'No. You shall break it and Franz never have a new one. No.'

'If I don't speak,' said Margie, snatching at Madame Lapatronne's bony wrist, 'how sh'll anyone know who . . . '

'Now then. Do what Madame tells you,' said Rosalie sharply, tucking Margie's hand under the sheet.

' . . . Followed Kath and Pam DuVivien down . . . railway track,' went on Margie, obstinately biting on the thermometer. Madame snatched it from her mouth. Rosalie Leamington began wringing out cloths with great vigour.

'What does she speak of that worries her so?' said Madame Lapatronne.

'Some child's nonsense,' said Rosalie Leamington, shrugging her shoulders.

The door opened cautiously and Ted Sloper came in. He looked more sensible than he had in the morning.

'Wondered if there was anything I could do,' he said.

Margie sat upright and said, 'Yes' and began all over again

in her hoarse little whisper about who followed Aunt Kathleen down the railway track.

'I think Madame Lapatronne has got her well under control,' said Rosalie, putting the vinegar cloth competently in place on Margie's throat. 'She's delirious, of course.'

'Of course,' said Ted Sloper, nodding.

'I *saw*,' shrieked Margie, beating Rosalie Leamington on one side. 'I *saw*, I tell you, who followed Kathleen *and* who went into ... wen' in'o ... wen' ...'

Her voice returned with a squeak to its hoarse whisper, while Madame Lapatronne held her down with one bony hand and bathed her forehead with the other. '*Who* went into Lady Sloper's room. Before she died.'

Margie's voice died away in a low mutter. She laid her head against Madame Lapatronne's cool hand and went into a deep restless sleep.

'Funny thing, delirium,' said Ted Sloper, moving uneasily from one foot to another. 'I wonder what she means ...'

He didn't say anything else. Madame Lapatronne finished wrapping Margie's feet in vinegar cloths and pulled a pair of ski-ing socks over them. Margie whimpered and sighed like a puppy. Then Madame Lapatronne finished making the bed.

'This one,' she said, 'this one is more ill than the other. It is, of course, the worst time of night.'

'Also,' said Ted Sloper, 'seemed to me, she was talking sense. I mean, about what she thought she saw in my wife's room. Don't you?'

'Children,' said Madame Lapatronne, 'are often telling lies and wanting to be mysterious all about *nothing*. I am unable to allow a child to be ill without helping. This is me.'

'D'you think she'll wake up again and talk some more?' said Ted, looking down on the muttering child.

Madame Lapatronne straightened her back.

'We shall watch them tonight,' she said. 'She and I.' She nodded at Rosalie, who was washing her hands furiously at the wash basin. 'Then if she wakes we shall know.'

III

It was probably the knowledge of illness that oppressed Natasha. Other people felt the same thing blotting out their enjoyment. No one felt it as keenly, or reacted to it as strongly as poor Natasha, who was *so sensitive*.

'It is never *right* in a house where there are children ill,' said Kathleen, in rather a sickly way, at dinner.

'No,' said Natasha politely. 'Children, as you know, are not at all my thing. I should have thought that murders would be more likely to depress. It is most *unusual* to find me depressed because *children* are ill.'

She sat in the dining-room angrily unable to eat because of the black melancholia that engulfed her.

'Ah,' said Kathleen, 'you may have picked up influenza from them without knowing. Now *I* . . . ' and she smiled the dangerous Flaherté' smile at Natasha, 'have much better right to be uneasy over the murders than you.'

'Is that indeed so?' said Natasha gloomily. She pushed away a plate of soup. 'Why? Let us order the English Miss a drink,' she went on in an undertone. 'It must be so awfully sad to be looking after children. It must be *hell*. Have a drink, miss.'

'Thank you,' said Rosalie Leamington.

She was on her way across the room to the Flaherté table. Natasha had asked Kathleen and Toddy to dine with Pamela and her to cheer her up, as she thought. So far Kathleen had, if anything, slightly depressed her.

'There is more reason,' said Pamela annoyingly, handing a glass of sherry to Miss Leamington, who stood unhappily on one leg and drank it, 'for Kathleen to be cross, and cross over you, Natasha . . .'

'Good health to one and all,' said Miss Leamington. 'I feel one should fight it on one's feet.'

'Because Barny made sheep's eyes at Mrs DuVivien?' said Toddy. 'Before he went away? After all, Barny's not officially Kathleen's fiancé at all, yet, you know.'

'No,' said Kathleen, much cast down. 'He has probably quite forgotten asking me to marry him.'

'Expect he *has*, dear,' said Toddy cosily. 'He always does forget unpleasant things, doesn't he?'

And, oddly enough, as Natasha afterwards said, things seemed to cheer up from that moment. Kathleen became quite gay and human and called her sister a beast. Miss Leamington had another drink and went away to her own table where she began (Ted Sloper not yet being down), to write another letter to Barbara Sewingshields. And Miriam and Roger and Morris came in very late and very talkative.

IV

'He has charm, your cousin,' said Natasha earnestly to Kathleen, when Miriam and Roger had gone away to a table in the corner of the room. Ted Sloper was still sleeping in the

217

servants' dining-room (although Fanny Mayes was now in Kesicken in the Morgue) and Miriam was forced to use the ordinary dining-room. She said she hated it, and she certainly made a great noise about it.

'Who?' said Toddy. 'Barny? I should say so. Bet you two hundred francs he gets back here by the first funicular tomorrow morning.'

Kathleen nodded and smiled at her sister, agreeing with her. For a girl whose betrothed had probably forgotten all about her she looked extremely gay and had a very good appetite.

'That is *impossible*,' said Natasha, stung out of her usual indifference to Toddy's gambling. 'He has gone to Paris and so has my husband. I accept this wager of two hundred francs.'

Toddy grinned and laid her money on the table.

'Sorry, lady,' she said with her errand boy's grin. 'You don't know Barny. 'S easy money. Barny wants to enter for these damn ski-ing championships. They say he's got a jolly good chance of winning ... '

'Brigadier Shoesmith,' said Pamela earnestly. 'Up at Mönchegg. He says Barny's as fast as anything British they've got on skis, by Jove. As fast as *anything* in the French or Italian teams, too ... '

'By Jove,' said Toddy sarcastically.

'How wonderful,' said Natasha doubtfully.

'So I think I can guess he'll be back. To train if nothing else,' finished Toddy triumphantly.

'But the funeral,' said Natasha, appalled.

'Oh *that*,' said Toddy contemptuously. 'He'll put *that* off until next week, or the week after. It's different in France,' she went on carelessly.

'And he'll have to use a pseudonym for the ski-racing, any

way,' said Kathleen. 'He said he couldn't have the name of Flaherté mixed up with practically *professional* events . . . '

'Well,' said Natasha.

V

Ted Sloper approached Natasha diffidently, as soon as he came down to dinner. He stood and looked nervously across the room at the empty table and Rosalie Leamington. She was eating ice-cream with one hand and writing her letter with the other.

'I say, Mrs DuVivien,' said Ted Sloper, beside her. 'Sorry to bother you an' all that, an' Toddy an' Kathleen, too . . . '

He ducked his head at Toddy, who stared enigmatically back at him and went on cracking nuts.

'But this child of Barny's . . . ' he went on. 'Margie, is it?'

'The youngest one is Margie,' said Toddy.

'Without a plate,' said Kathleen.

'Well . . . ' said Ted. 'I don't know about plates. Well. This one, she's delirious, you know, and all that. But what she's ravin' about rather seems to make sense. If you know what I . . . ' Ted stopped, stumbling miserably.

'About what, perhaps, is this *child* making sense?' said Natasha, with contempt.

'About the murders. At least that's what it *sounds* like,' said Ted. 'Whoever went in to see my wife that evening. And then there's a piece about following you, Kathleen, down the railway track . . . '

'O-oh,' said Kathleen, sitting up. 'That time someone heaved a boulder at me. When you were ski-ing, Toddy. I'd like to know about *that* . . . '

Kathleen spoke as if that whole thing had happened five years before. Natasha reflected, and not for the first time, that half the Flaherté charm lay in the fact that none of them had the smallest idea of time.

'That's right,' said Toddy, cracking an almond between her teeth. 'So should I.'

'Well, I think someone should come and listen to this kid. She *seems* to have seen something nasty in the woodshed, so to speak,' said Ted. 'She was obviously tryin' to tell us about it. You know the way they do.'

'Who is with her now?' said Natasha, pushing her chair back.

'Madame Lapatronne is looking after them both,' said Ted. 'While Miss Thing has her supper.'

They all glanced across the room at Rosalie Leamington, whose fountain-pen still went busily across the paper. She was drinking coffee. Natasha stood up.

'Pamela,' she said. 'We will be going to listen to this child.'

'Oh ...' said Pamela nervously. 'Do you think you'll like that? I mean, children are very infectious.'

'Very, *very* infectious,' said Natasha, solemnly.

'Rather sporting of you,' said Ted Sloper, admiringly.

'I'll lend you my Red Cross apron,' said Kathleen, suddenly. 'And Toddy has a little mask she used in the M.T.C. when they all had chicken-pox.'

'That's right,' said Toddy. 'So I have.'

VI

A strange procession finally went along the passage towards Margie's bedroom. Natasha led the rout, looking like something out of an American film called *Calling Dr Kildare*. She was carrying Toddy's chicken-pox mask and wearing a stiff, rustling, well-starched apron. No one attempted to explain, now or hereafter, why the two Flaherté girls had brought these things to Switzerland with them. Natasha was followed by Pamela, regrettably giggling and trying to tie a neat bow in the apron strings, and the two Flahertés. The Flahertés were admiring their own property. They reached Joyce's door and Madame Lapatronne looked out.

'The little one she is being sick,' she said. 'Oh, the vomit.'

'How very nasty,' said Natasha, hastily putting on her mask.

'Thank God you are come,' said Madame. Natasha wasn't at all sure of this. 'The other little one is now calling also ... Go to her, I pray you, Madame. Go.'

Natasha went. She went like the Heavy Brigade at Balaclava; reluctantly, but still charging. Margie sat up in bed. Her eyes were wild and bright. There was no sense in them at all.

'Ah ... ' said Natasha.

'Margie Flaherté,' said Margie. '*Four* is a little swanky boy. See him jumping there. *All* the odd numbers are very conceited.'

'Where?' said Natasha, involuntarily glancing round her. 'Tell us what you saw. *Dear*,' she added, as an afterthought.

'The numbers,' said Margie crazily. 'I saw all the numbers. Specially One and Two and Four. Nine is eaten *up* with conceit,' she said. 'And six is a hermaphrodite.'

Natasha sat down on the bed with a thump.

'Now listen,' she said, as toughly as her husband. 'I am not coming all the bloody way to catch your damn 'flu for talk about numbers. *Crazy* talk,' she added, firmly. 'Whimsy talk. You will tell me about Christopher Robin next.'

'Christopher?' said Margie shrilly, shutting her eyes. 'Christopher? Why not? Christopher Stone is saying his prayers.'

Which, as helpful advice to someone enthusiastically investigating a murder case, was really not good enough.

VII

The night stretched out ahead of them, punctuated by the feverish behaviour of the children. Natasha abandoned all germ protection except the chicken-pox mask (which looked like a yashmak) and became extremely practical. After all, this was her nature. She had spent, she said, a more unpleasant night. However, it was full of drama.

At two in the morning, when Madame Lapatronne had been relieved by Rosalie Leamington, and Natasha had fallen asleep in a chair at the head of the stairs, Margie walked in her sleep. Natasha opened her eyes and saw Margie in pyjamas. She was standing on the top step of the stairs. The moonlight lit up her face and her tousled hair.

'Dear Barbara,' she said scornfully. '*Dear* Barbara my *foot*. Out damned Spot. I had a dog called Spot.'

Natasha sat up, excited. Dear Barbara. That obviously meant something to the child. The child stubbed her toe against the banisters and used a bad word.

Rosalie Leamington, distraught and carrying a blanket, appeared round the corner of the passage.

'Oh, Mrs DuVivien,' she said rapidly, 'I am so sorry she has disturbed you. Indeed I am. I was in with Joyce. I saw her go.'

'*Dear* Barbara,' said Margie distinctly, in tones of paralysing scorn. Natasha had stepped forward and was half-way upstairs beside Margie.

'What can she be meaning?' said Natasha. 'Who is this dear Barbara? Someone the child knows, perhaps? What a pity she is asleep ... '

Margie opened one blood-shot eye and winked at her, solemnly. Natasha was shattered. That a child could be human (or intelligent) had never occurred to her.

'Miss Leamington's friend. The Lem Bug's friend,' chanted Margie and shut her eyes again. 'A thing or two, I know. What she is always writing to. Two is a little baby boy, and eight is cosy. Such a nice woman. *Dear* Barbara.'

Miss Leamington pounced on Margie from behind with her blanket. Natasha helped to carry her back to bed. None of them enjoyed it. Margie went stiff in their arms like a starfish and they had much difficulty in getting her between the bedclothes. When they had finally pulled the clothes up to Margie's chin and opened the window and put a hot-water bottle at her feet:

'Well,' said Natasha. 'Well ... I don't know how it is you are going on with it. Being a governess I mean ... '

'I *hate* it,' said Rosalie, passionately. She stared at Natasha with burning eyes.

'Well, do not be doing it then,' said Natasha, reasonably enough. She stood at the bottom of the bed and looked at Margie, who was (apparently) peacefully asleep.

'Oh dear ... ' said Rosalie, breaking down and sniffing and sobbing in a most embarrassing way. 'I wasn't cut out for this sort of thing. Oh, dear no ... '

'Dear Barbara,' murmured Margie, turning over. Natasha wanted to laugh.

'There, *there*, Miss,' said Natasha, patting her. 'Cheer up. All will come right. It is the same way now a hundred years.'

Rosalie, still much distressed, led the way out of Margie's room across a passage to her own single bedroom. Everything in it reminded her piercingly, annihilatingly, of Barny. She found it almost impossible to sleep there. She often sat up . . . looking across the blue snow towards the mountains. Then she saw the lights of Kesicken go out one by one. She started to tell Natasha about some of this, thought better of it, and stopped.

'Poor dear miss,' said Natasha. 'Straight to bed you are going or a tiny nervous breakdown you will be having else. We will fix these kiddies for you.'

'*Oh?*' said Rosalie Leamington. But she began to undress quite obediently. Natasha was surprised.

'And now the invaluable Bayer,' said Natasha, handing aspirins when at last Rosalie was in bed. She looked extremely rum, sitting up with her glasses on. Her nose was rather pink, her hands were folded on the sheet. 'Now I will stay with you while you go to sleep,' said Natasha, looking idly round the room. 'You shall tell me the story of your life, as you say. So *comforting*.'

'Are you really kind,' said Rosalie, looking at her, 'or just curious?'

She took the aspirin and the glass of warm water Natasha held out to her. Then she laughed shortly. 'Nothing comforting,' she said, 'about *my* life story.'

'No?' said Natasha. 'But I am so sure you are wrong. *All* life stories are comforting. They are so *awful*.'

Rosalie smiled wryly.

'I see what you mean,' she said. '*You* will be comforted . . . '

'But of course,' said Natasha mildly.

'I was born at Droitwich,' said Rosalie. 'Is that the sort of thing you mean?'

She seemed to resent Natasha, who had begun to enjoy herself once more.

'Oh, *yes*,' she said. 'And where did you go to school?'

'Cheltenham Ladies' College,' said Rosalie and scowled. 'I am an only child,' she said. 'My mother is dead. She was very fond of me. My father is a chemist. He is married again ...'

'A good chemist,' said Natasha, wagging her head. 'Something in Researchs. I see. And then you went to Oxford and Cambridge. It is all so *splendid*.'

Rosalie favoured Natasha with a cold, hard stare, but her head began to droop.

'Barbara Sewingshields,' she said, her eyes slowly closing. 'Philosophy Don. Tom. The theatre. Tom Cramlington ...'

'Tom Cramlington,' said Natasha, astonished. 'Not Tom *Cramlington*?'

'The Merry Widow Theatre,' said Rosalie, opening her eyes with difficulty. 'Do you know him?'

'Know him?' said Natasha, passionately. 'He is giving me the chance when I break with Diaghilev back in the twenties ...' She paused and looked surprised. 'He is very *old*,' she said, 'even then.'

'Tom Cramlington. Barbara's Tom.'

Rosalie's head went over sideways on the pillow.

'He wasn't at all, really,' she said. 'I don't mind, now, Barbara. Don't mind anything *now*.'

She fell asleep.

Natasha looked round the room.

'Dear Barbara,' she said. 'Dear Tom. Quite enough for one night.'

Ah. This looked like something. A blue suede writing-case with a zip running round it. Natasha picked it up. She tried to move the zip and swore. It was stuck, blast it. She tucked it under her arm. Rosalie stirred in bed.

'Writing-case . . .' she said, 'M' writing case. Where is it?'

'It is downstairs in the dining-room,' said Natasha, firmly. 'I saw it on the window-sill.'

VIII

A Writing-Case

Natasha ran downstairs to Johnny's and her room, like a naughty child who has been stealing jam. She carried her loot under her arm. It is an unfortunate fact that during the rest of this long night of excitement and exhaustion she never once thought of her husband and the difficulties and dangers into which he might be running.

She locked the bedroom door and was pleased because she had Johnny's bed where she might spread the contents of the writing-case. Sometimes she looked guiltily behind her. She half expected Miss Leamington to break in and demand her property. Only once was she conscience-stricken, when she thought of calling in Miriam and Roger and Morris so that they, too, could have a good laugh. This, she decided, could come later.

There were three sorts of letters.

To begin with there were two official ones. One had Cambridge address and was written in a scholarly hand v self-conscious Greek 'e's. It began, 'Dear Miss Leamington, I am delighted to be able to congratulate you on your Good Class in Schools.' The other was typewritten and carried a printed Admiralty monogram. This said 'Dear' in typewriting, and 'Miss Leamington' in handwriting (always a sinister thing).

Dear Miss Leamington,
    I feel that you will be gratified by this small appreciation of your . . .

Natasha was bored by both these things and put them on one side.

Then there was a large, very pale blue packet with more scholarly handwriting on the envelopes. Some of these were addressed to Katsclöchen. There was another large tattered miscellaneous packet and a half finished letter to 'Dear Barbara'.

Natasha sprang on this like a leopard. She read it aloud to herself, punctuating the narrative with exclamations like 'I say!' and 'Nice thing!' and 'My word' and once, coldly, 'This goes too far'. Then she stood up and brushed her skirt. The letter was too good to waste. She went in search of Miriam Birdseye.

II

Miriam was in Roger's room, eating grapes. Her feet were in Morris's lap. They had evidently been playing three-handed rummy, for the cards were all over the room. They were delighted to see Natasha.

'Listen,' said Natasha, locking the door after her. 'I beg. Listen. It is so *extraordinary* . . . '

'What is, dear?' said Morris, taking away the writing-case. He handled it gingerly, as though it were a black mamba.

'A writing-case, *silly*,' said Roger, and slapped him. 'A girl's writing-case ... '

'Oh, I know *that*,' said Morris, sucking his thumb. 'Damn. The zip's stuck. I nearly went to Cheltenham Ladies' College myself.'

'Whose is it?' said Roger.

'English Miss,' said Natasha, and took it away from Morris.

'Goosey Goosey Governess,' said Miriam, and roared with laughter at her own wit.

'Listen, *please*, to this letter. We are all in it,' said Natasha. 'But *all* of us.'

'Read it,' said Roger, sitting up.

'*Dear Barbara*,' read Natasha. 'It seems,' she went on, turning to Miriam, 'that this Barbara teaches philosophy at Oxford and Cambridge.'

'Jolly D. Lady Philosopher Dons,' said Roger, 'always end up by bicycling round Cambridge stark naked ... '

'Goodness,' said Morris, who was an Oxford man.

'*Dear Barbara*,' read Natasha, firmly once more. '*Since the tragedy ...* '

'Which tragedy?' asked Morris. 'Mrs Flaherté or Lady Sloper?'

'Sh ... ' said Miriam. 'Fanny Mayes' death wasn't a tragedy at all. Do be quiet.'

'*Since the tragedy*,' went on Natasha firmly, '*things have been quiet and we have settled down to enjoy the peace that that common lout who calls himself a detective, DuVivien* ... I find this a little steep for my poor Johnny,' said Natasha, stopping again.

'Oh yes, indeed, dear, very poor, very poor,' said Roger. 'Go on, dear. Press on, darling.'

Natasha pressed on.

'*DuVivien and Mr Rochester have left us.* Mr Rochester will be Barny.'

'Obviously, dear,' said Miriam coldly. 'Don't interrupt yourself so much, *darling.*'

'*Left us,*' went on Natasha. 'Now here it become quite peculiar and the handwriting most vague. *Before he left, Mr Rochester's eye roamed again. This time to that common little dancing teacher I told you of before who calls herself Russian. However, even poor little me from Droitwich can detect the North Country (Manchester?) accent behind all that pseudo broken English . . .*'

'No!' said Miriam, sitting up straight.

'Call yourself a Russian, Natasha dear,' said Morris languidly. 'I'd love to hear you.'

'*It was bad enough,*' went on Natasha, '*when he was chasing that old hen, Miriam Birdseye . . .*'

Miriam gasped.

'*At least she is a genius.*'

'Ah, here's the stuff,' said Miriam, leaning forward, 'to please Mum *faster . . .*'

'*But genius excuses no one going around with two boys aged about twelve-and-a-half and thirteen. Anyway she looks as though she had been pulled through a hedge backwards . . .*'

'Not so keen, not so keen, not so keen,' said Miriam rapidly. 'Go on about your calling yourself a Russian, Natasha. I liked that bit.'

'*Anyway, Mr Rochester's taste is quite Catholic (! ! !)* I think this is a joke,' said Natasha, puzzled. '*What I cannot understand, Barbara, is why I am so taken with such an utterless, worthless set of people. They are not worthy in our sense at all . . .*'

'Worthy,' said Roger and giggled. 'Barny Flaherté *worthy*. Even by *our* standards he isn't worthy ...'

'*The Flaherté girls*,' continued Natasha, '*continue to waste their lives and their youth on gambling and drink and that dumb little DuVivien kid to waste hers with them. I must say if I were Pam DuVivien's mother (or stepmother, as she is supposed to be) I should not allow her to see so much of the elder Flaherté. Toddy, she is called. And just like that lady bull-fighter we enjoyed so much from Peru ...*'

'Damn it,' said Miriam. 'That is the limit. I don't wonder you're angry, Natasha. Give it here.'

And she snatched the letter from Natasha.

III

The party in Roger's room went on for some hours. Roger produced some baby bottles of champagne from his wardrobe, Miriam clambered on to the bed. The others spread themselves ecstatically over the remainder of the room with the letters from Rosalie Leamington's writing-case. There was very little solid news in the half-finished letter to Barbara Sewingshields.

'It's as I thought,' said Miriam thoughtfully, 'she wanted us to read these beastly descriptions of ourselves. I don't suppose she usually writes these witty little pen pictures and exquisite characterizations to "Dear Barbara" ...'

'I see what you mean,' said Roger, looking up from the pale blue package. 'Anyway, Barbara seems to answer "Dear Rosalie" pretty smartly. Listen to this. *How dreadful for you Madame Flaherté throwing herself out of the window like that. Properly handled, however, it need not affect your relationship with the husband ...*'

'Fancy the dish managing a party with Goosey Goosey

Governess as well as everyone else,' said Miriam. 'Isn't he *wonderful?*'

'What's the date on that?' said Natasha sharply.

'February 6th,' said Roger. 'As per postmark.'

'Extraordinary handwriting this girl has,' said Miriam suddenly. 'All over the place. Sometimes one thing. Sometimes another. Do look. This letter might have been written with a *fork* . . .'

She held the letter out, pointing to it angrily. The places where Miss Leamington had lost her head or changed her mind or had otherwise lost mental control, were certainly indicated clearly with blots, scratches and complete distortion of lower case letters.

'Excitable, our governess, isn't she?' said Morris.

'For an intellectual she seems to be quite illiterate,' said Miriam, 'saying 'phone, for telephone. What sort of person *is* she?'

Natasha looked up from the other miscellaneous package with a wrinkled brow.

'There is a ridiculous love letter here,' she said. 'From Tom Cramlington. You remember, Miriam? . . .'

'Remember old *Tom?* Of the Merry Widow Theatre?' Miriam rolled over on the bed. 'He must be about eighty now. Does Goosey Goosey Governess know *him?* No wonder she's so unstable. Tom Cramlington gives *everyone* the Kiss of Death.'

Natasha handed her the letter.

'Faugh!' said Miriam, after half a second. 'This certainly puts the intellectual English Miss *straight* into the *News of the World.*'

And she dropped the letter on the floor with a royal gesture and snatched the pale blue Barbara Sewingshields letters from Roger. Roger was sitting happily on the floor, reading two of them at once and sucking a large bull's eye. He was aggrieved.

'Here I *say* . . .' he said. 'That was jolly unpleas . . . Oh, it's only you . . .'

Miriam, lying on her back with one leg raised in the air, slowly beat time with it as she read Barbara's letter aloud.

'*Probably a middle-aged French-Irish Catholic with two frightful children appeals to you, Rosalie. I can't say it appeals to me. Can't you get rid of the children somehow . . . ?*'

'Sinister,' said Morris, who had (like Natasha) laid aside the congratulatory letters from Cambridge and the Admiralty.

'No one has really *tried* to get rid of the kiddies yet,' said Roger. 'But Ted Sloper is going about saying that they both know something about the murder . . .'

'No, is that so, dear?' said Morris, pleased. 'Then I think I'll add a bit more to that bet I had with Miss Toddy about Natasha being the next victim . . .'

'Are you betting *against* me, or *on* me?' said Natasha.

'I honestly can't remember, dear,' said Morris. 'I remember thinking if the worst comes to the worst we can mount a guard on you. Against, I suppose then. Yes, *against*, that's right. I'll go and have a bit more on the kiddies *definitely* being the next for the high jump. How's that?'

'No need of that,' murmured Natasha, sleepily. She was hardly thinking what she was saying. 'They will not need murdering. They are half-dead already . . .'

She suddenly stared round the room with a wild surmise.

'You can't think someone's murdering them *already*, dear,' said Miriam.

'Well, someone had better be sending for M and B,' said Natasha.

IV

Half-an-hour later they tidied up Miss Leamington's writing-case and Roger's room and put the Dead Marines of champagne bottles back into the wardrobe. Natasha made solemn notes of the dates of the letters that Barbara Sewingshields had written.

'February 6th, 10th, 12th, 14th,' dictated Roger. '*Wonderful* correspondents, these girls, aren't they? Better than *we* are . . .'

He grinned at Morris, who frowned.

'Thank you,' said Natasha, taking the list from him. 'No. Spewdo-Russian indeed! Why. I have never been in Manchester in my life!'

'You're lucky,' said Miriam shortly. 'I was once there for *weeks*. On tour.'

They crept out of the room and shut the door behind them.

Natasha parted from them and tiptoed to the top of the stairs. She went quietly down. It was about 2 a.m.

Half-way she came face to face with Rosalie Leamington. She was ghastly. Her face was white and drawn. Sweat stood on her forehead. Her mouth was half-open. Her nose seemed longer than usual.

'Why *miss*!' said Natasha, horrified.

She quite forgot about Manchester, and the Russian accent, and that she had no cause to love Rosalie.

'*You said my writing-case was in the dining-room,*' said Rosalie with maniac intensity. She grasped Natasha's wrist and shook it. 'I've been down there. It *wasn't* . . .'

'No,' said Natasha firmly. 'Of course not. I have it here. I have been seeing that you were worried, miss, so I am going to get it for you. Now come back to your bed . . .'

'*I've* heard you laughing at me with Miriam Birdseye. *No better than she ought to be.* I don't believe you. Give me back my writing-case ... '

And she shook Natasha again.

She snatched at Natasha's right arm and tore a great, furrowed scratch in her forearm. Natasha was furious.

'Oh, be taking your case, you *maniac*,' she said. She thrust the case into Miss Leamington's arms. 'Here ... '

Miss Leamington stood on the stairs in the moonlight and *gibbered*. Natasha was unafraid. She went on (most unreasonably) being angry.

'Go on back to bed and be murdering your children. I don't care,' said Natasha, and went calmly downstairs. She heard a sort of gasp behind her but she did not look back. She was too angry. 'Manchester,' she whispered under her breath.

If Miss Leamington was really going to pull her hair out by the roots or leap on her from behind, she wouldn't do it in a hotel in the middle of the night with lots of people within call. Natasha reached the bottom step of the flight and the turn round to the next landing and she looked up. Miss Leamington was still standing there, in her unbecoming dressing-gown, clasping her writing-case in her arms. She looked as insane as anyone Natasha had ever seen.

'I can scream awfully loud, miss,' said Natasha coldly, adding under her breath, '*Manchester, indeed.*'

V

Nevertheless, on the way back to her own room, Natasha stopped and knocked on Pamela's door. Pamela was awake.

'Hullo?' she said. 'Is it about father? I'm worried about him.'

'No,' said Natasha, 'it is about *me*. I am wanting you so much to come and sleep in Johnny's bed if you do not mind. Everyone seems to be homicidal. Yes, I am scared.'

'That isn't like you,' said Pamela, getting out of bed, clutching her hot-water bottle. 'I suppose you heard the news about Fanny Mayes and *that's* scared you.'

They went along the passage and their feet scratched on the coconut matting.

'Fanny Mayes,' said Natasha, halting. 'What about her?'

'They rang up from Kesicken apparently, to say she died an accidental death. Heart failure. Don't ask *me* how they worked it or if they have inquests in Schizo-Frenia. I just don't *know*. Poor Ted Sloper has nearly gone mad over it ...'

'Well, I do not wonder,' said Natasha, as she shut the door of their room safely behind them, 'that in America they have the Lynch Law. It makes one look around for Lynch Law, this Schizo-Frenia, does it not?'

'Dunno,' said Pamela morosely. 'Who're you thinking of lynching? Makes a difference.'

'I thought Miss Leamington would be nice,' said Natasha, holding her forearm under the cold water tap. It was a nasty scratch. 'She thinks you are dumb, Pam, and that I come from Manchester,' she exploded furiously.

'How do you know?' said Pamela, starting to laugh.

Natasha went secretive at once.

'I do not know,' she said. 'She tells me, I think. Yes, that is right. She tells me.'

Which, of course, did not take in Pamela for a single instant. Curiously enough, Natasha valued the good opinion of her step-daughter.

IX

Natasha Takes to Ski-ing in a Big Way

Pamela, in the bed usually given up to her father, lay awake most of the night. She worried about him (although she knew how capable he was of looking after himself) and she worried about Natasha. Natasha had obviously become involved with this rather dreary governess. A pity, Pamela thought. At this point the handle of the door moved sharply. Then the door creaked, as though someone were leaning on it with all their might.

'Hey . . . ' thought Pamela, and lay very still.

The creaking stopped. The weight against the door was removed. The visitor went quietly away down the passage. Pamela wondered if she ought to have got out of bed to see who it was. Oddly, she was not frightened.

At about seven Natasha woke and saw Pamela propped on an elbow, reading *The Schizo-Frenic Hotel Keeper's Guide to Mönchegg and District* – with an appendix on How to do a Christie.

'Have you been to sleep at all, my poor Pamela?' she said, wistfully. 'How sorry I now am that I disturb you and bring you along here. If you pass the white night?'

Pamela's mind leapt to the Tenniel illustrations to *Alice through the Looking Glass* and she laughed.

'Not much,' she said. 'But I shouldn't've slept, anyway, even in my own room. I was worried. I'm glad I came. Someone tried your door handle early this morning, Natasha.'

'Oh,' said Natasha, turning over, very bored. 'There is no *man* here it could be. Barny not back yet. Miriam, I suppose, with some of the ... ' Natasha stopped and looked guilty. 'Something to tell us,' she ended.

Pamela looked at her stepmother.

'You know quite well,' she said, 'that you were frightened of something last night. Before you went to sleep. I *might* have got out of bed and looked. Or shouted out. Or something. I wish I *had*.'

The pale light of early morning was growing stronger every minute.

'I am jolly glad you did *not*,' said Natasha, anxiously. '*Jolly* glad. Where should we be if it had perhaps been murderers with meat axes and we had let them in? Or rapers. Rapers would be more gay, of course ... '

Natasha stopped and considered the gay rapers and smiled.

'Amen,' said Pamela, and shut the *Hotel-Keeper's Guide* with a sharp snap.

'Everything,' said Natasha, as though she were speaking a magic charm, 'depends on Barny Flaherté and how *he* behaves on return. But *everything*.'

There was a brisk knock on the door and Pamela let in Nelli, who bounced in with a tray of early morning tea, said: '*Service*' and bounced out, obviously rather cross and overworked. And Pamela, pouring tea and milk, forgot to ask Natasha what she meant by her rather cryptic remark. The hour before breakfast passed serenely and reasonably. Even Natasha, confronted by the sensible rituals of Early Morning Tea, forgot the nightmares of the previous night. She lapped gratefully and comfortably, like an undisturbed cat. And at a quarter past eight, by the first funicular of the morning, Johnny returned.

II

Johnny came into their bedroom like a breath of unwanted and far too healthy fresh air. Pamela, who might have welcomed him, was already in her bath.

Natasha was trying to pick out the significant events of the previous night.

'Say, honey,' said Johnny, kissing her emphatically. 'What d'ye know? We're both back, Barny Flaherté and I. Got in on the first funicular.'

In the distance, outside the window, a faint rumble and clatter indicated the first funicular going up to Mönchegg.

'And I have lost two hundred francs,' said Natasha, indistinctly.

She said it under the bedclothes and into her pillow. She had burrowed farther down the bed when Johnny had disturbed her.

'Well ... ' said Johnny, rubbing his hands briskly together and walking round the room. 'Anything happened?'

'No,' said Natasha sulkily. 'Unless you can count Fanny Mayes passed off as *accidental* nothing. I suppose we will be having an inquest or whatever it is they are calling it out here.

But accidental is what the doctor has put on his certificate, Pam says . . . ' she ended.

'What I expected,' said Johnny. He pulled a chair up close to his wife's bed and sat on it. 'At least I gotten young Barny to admit he thinks these are murders . . . I c'n tell you, honey, he's *quite* a boy.'

'Indeed,' said Natasha drily. 'Tell me of it.'

Johnny began with the appearance of the professional mourners and undertakers at Unteralp, and told the whole peculiar tale of the hold-up. Natasha sat up, looking very astonished.

'That is *quite* fate, I think,' she said. 'So you are able to demonstrate toughness and unarmed combat and wrestling and all the things at which you are so good. I can think of nothing else would be making Barny even *interested* in you . . . '

'Sure?' said Johnny. 'Wasn't I lucky? I c'd never have gotten him drunk an' talky, you know. He takes this a-ski-ing champ-ionship thing *far* too seriously. Says he hopes the *Tatler* won't be there. Natasha, is there something not quite nice about gettin' a picture in these snob papers? I thought . . . '

'That it is being quite smart to get into them. Well, so have I always been thinking,' said Natasha, gravely. 'Lately I am not so sure.'

'Oh,' Johnny sighed as though a weight had been taken off his mind. 'Well,' he said, 'I'm glad to get back. Life Story of young Flaherté. Shook me, it did. *I* take a bit of shakin', ye know.'

'Women?' said Natasha, interested.

'He seemed to think *that* of no account,' said Johnny. 'He has the most extraordinary what's it . . . '

'Sense of proportion,' said Natasha, earnestly.

'Yeah, that's it,' said Johnny. 'Most extraordinary *lack* 'f sense 'f proportion I *ever* struck. Went to school at Winchester and went to Cambridge, was it? Or Oxford. Well, one of 'em. Came away without a degree ...'

'Whatever *that* may mean?' said Natasha. 'Why?'

'Because he fell in love with his cousin. Wouldn't tell me her name. I think Pam knows it ...'

'Yes, I remember Pam is saying that Toddy and Kathleen have told her it. Go *on*.'

'Yeah, an' that story Pam picked up about him havin' that affair with Lady What's it an' disinheritin' himself. That was OK, too. Extraordinary.'

'Who is this *cousin*?' said Natasha, jealously.

'Dunno. He wouldn't say. Seems to care for her still, yo' see. Uh huh. That's what it was. He *doesn't* think of anyone else like *that*. His face looked quite different when he spoke of her ...'

'What did he say?' said Natasha viciously. 'How did he look?'

'Eh? Oh ... Like as if he was in some world where no one else was. An' he said, an' I thought this very rum, mark you, "There is no love except for people one hasn't been to bed with ..."'

'Strange,' said Natasha. 'Very strange indeed. One wonders about this *cousin*, doesn't one?'

'Yes indeed. But he wouldn't let on about *her*,' said Johnny. 'I kinder gathered he gotten married and had all these affairs an' saw these two women murdered by *accident* kind of. As though it had nothing to do with him, because he was always thinkin' of some'hing else. Well, I mean, no one could be expected to believe *that*,' ended Johnny irritably.

'Did you *not* believe him?' said Natasha.

Johnny moved uneasily.

'D'you know, at the time, I *did*. But afterwards I got on thinkin'. It's crazy. No one can really believe that, what *he* just said. So I said, quite brisk an' lively like, because it would give him a motive for doin' these murders that he hadn't noticed himself *doin'*, see? "And now, I guess, you c'n marry this cousin o' yours, not Kathleen, an' live happy ever after?"'

'And what is he saying to *that*?'

'He says ... And, oh Natasha, an awful look come into his eyes, like *hell*, it was. "Oh no," he says, "she's not the marryin' sort. An' she loves me, yo' see," he says.'

'What can he be meaning?' said Natasha, fascinated.

'I guess he meant she had other men, you know, an' then went on saying she loved *him*, all the time. It was jealous, that boy was, honey, when he told me. A nasty, selfish, unimaginative point of view, that woman has,' said Johnny.

'We are of the earth earthy,' said Natasha. 'But I am thinking I heard you say you were *not* believing him?'

'Uh huh,' said Johnny. 'Sure 'nough. But if'n that woman *exists* an' possesses his mind like that, like what *he* said, what a first-class bitch she must be, eh, honey?'

'Bitches do not go in classes,' said Natasha. 'They are going in *waters*. First *water* bitch, one says, always, I have noticed.'

'No, but she must be hell, eh, honey?'

'I call it very clever,' said Natasha disconcertingly. 'And I should be liking to be able to do it myself.'

There was a pause.

'All the same,' added Natasha, after a second. 'I am telling Pamela just now, that *everything* depends on Barny Flaherté's getting a grasp on this situation. And if he is not even going to *try* to grasp it, but to think of something else all the time, well, *Pouf!*' Natasha blew out her cheeks to imitate an atomic bomb explosion, or some such thing. 'We have another situation like before you went away . . . "

Johnny stared at his wife, open-mouthed.

'More murders,' said Natasha. 'And now I am going to get up.'

III

It was not only the imaginative Natasha who felt the nervous tension that began to mount through the next two barren days.

The weather was glorious. There was nothing to do but ski and eat and sleep. Yet so many of the Flaherté party did not ski and were unable to eat or sleep.

Perhaps if two glamorous Austrian doctors had appeared . . . Or if there had been an extraordinary and virile ski guide in the neighbourhood with a pure gold tooth who was prepared to seduce Toddy Flaherté, some of the physical strain of sheer boredom might have been relieved. There were, however, no doctors but Kurt Vital and no guides who were not bow-legged, filthy dirty, and quite unshaven. And nothing exciting or amusing happened at all. The Flaherté party, possessed by boredom and jealousy (and other minor passions), grew daily upon each other's nerves.

IV

Oddly enough, Barny Flaherté, the cause of all the tension, was more or less immune from it.

He got up every morning at seven, sponged himself with cold

water, had breakfast and disappeared with a packed lunch into the wilds of snow above Mönchegg. He returned each afternoon at about five o'clock, completely exhausted, as brown as the sun could make him, with a raging appetite for dinner. He then fell asleep in an armchair and put himself to bed.

The only member of the party who ever caught up with him was Natasha. She had suddenly taken to ski-ing as a gentle amusement. Her dancer's muscles were perfectly co-ordinated for the sport. She was quite unafraid. A slight tendency she had for shortsight was easily corrected by a very expensive pair of tinted glasses.

She, too, was apt to leave the hotel after breakfast with hardboiled eggs, apples, rolls and butter, and garlic sausage, and did not come home until evening as exhausted as Barny.

Members of the Flaherté party, with minds like revolting little sinks (notably Toddy and the governess), imagined orgies of violent lust, enacted by Barny and Natasha, far above the snow level. They could hardly have been wider of the truth.

Barny's programme was too complicated and strenuous to allow room for such dalliance. He rushed seriously down the Ski Championship course, twice an hour, travelling like a bullet. Natasha, ski-ing slowly, or sitting apart on a mountain by herself, was aware of him only as a puff of white snow. Few things are more boring to the ski expert than a promising beginner.

Occasionally, of course, they both sat down and ate their lunch. One day, as it so happened, they did this together.

In the pinewoods below Jumping Hill Meadow there are many glorious little clearings, like heaven, where the snow has turned all the trees and fallen branches into curious and beautiful shapes and lumps. Here, when the weather is fine, the sun beats all day.

In such a clearing Barny Flaherté met Natasha. He wanted to take off his shirt and sit in the sun. She had been wondering for the last half hour if she should not leave Johnny DuVivien. She told herself that she had been finding him 'very boring' lately.

V

'I'm sorry,' said Barny. He came round the corner of a fallen log and braked himself gracefully. 'I didn't see it was you. I shall disturb you ...'

'I am not minding,' said Natasha simply. 'I *like* you.'

'Oh,' said Barny, very startled.

There was a pause while Barny looked down at Natasha, whose mouth was full of hard-boiled egg. She looked quite charming.

'I was going to take my shirt off ...' said Barny. 'You wouldn't like *that*?'

He sounded wistful.

'I am not minding,' said Natasha again. 'Now, *I* expect that you are good enough to be ski-ing without a shirt. Now if it were *me* I should fall down and hurt me terribly. I should mind *that* ...'

'I never really like to try it, either,' said Barny. He stamped his feet and undid the fastening of his skis. 'One day, maybe.'

He pulled his shirt over his head and appeared a nice pale gold all over. His face was relaxed and peaceful. He stuck his skis in the ground like a fence and leaned back on them with a sigh. This was the man who knew his wife had been murdered a few days before.

'I have some coffee,' he said, half turning his head. 'In a little flask. I expect you'd like some.'

There was peace and silence in the clearing.

'How nice it is,' said Natasha.

'The coffee?' said Barny. 'I thought it pretty frightful, as a matter of fact.'

'No,' said Natasha. 'Here. Without people. I was thinking,' she said solemnly, turning to him, 'of leaving my husband.'

'Let's see,' said Barny promptly. 'That's that rather boring nice man who helped me upstairs when I got plastered and was so tough when we got held up coming back from Unteralp? *Nice* man.'

'Yes,' said Natasha. 'This is Johnny.'

'He's *kind*,' said Barny reflectively. 'Lots of people aren't as kind as that ... '

'But boring,' said Natasha. 'And *vulgar*.'

'And common,' said Barny. And I am sorry to say they both laughed.

'Well, I dunno,' said Barny. He stretched amiably and kicked idly at the snow with one heavy ski-boot. 'One feels rather *lost* and unprotected without a wife. An' I suppose it's the same without a husband. *I* think it would be better to be the beautiful Mrs DuVivien with that Common Boring Husband than That Mrs DuVivien?'

'True,' said Natasha, who was not at all annoyed by this straight (if peculiar) way of speaking. 'It is different for a man,' she said. 'But you do not know what it is like.'

'No,' said Barny. 'I don't suppose so. Like what?'

'What it is *like*. Living with someone who cannot talk to you about *anything*. I have something unexpressed *here*.' And she beat dramatically on her breast with both hands.

Barny considered her with his head on one side.

'A good thing, I should say,' he said, finally.

Natasha was non-plussed. Barny hastened to reassure her.

'Oh, don't mind,' he said. 'Honestly. It's Schizo-Frenia. It does something extraordinary to you, doesn't it? The air is so clear. Most disconcerting.'

'What can you be meaning?' said Natasha, a little annoyed. When she came to consider it, Barny's life was in much more of a mess than her own.

'Don't be angry,' said Barny, with a sweet smile. 'Please. If you'd said that to me about your husband a week ago, I'd have sprung on you with a low growl and we would have had a *hell* of a party. I hope ... '

He grinned. Natasha was much taken aback.

'Oh, but you were protected then,' she said. 'By your wife. But I hope so, too ... '

Now, a week ago, Natasha would never have considered any such thing for a single moment.

'I feel different,' said Barny snugly. He leaned back. 'It's *all* different. I *am* different.'

'You are looking *healthier*,' said Natasha, with a little sigh. It was quite evident to her that there was to be no more discussion about Natasha, and Natasha's problems. She sat, quite prettily, ready to discuss Barny Flaherté and *his* problems.

'I *am* healthier,' said Barny. 'But it isn't only that.' He frowned and drew a little pattern in the snow with his forefinger. 'I am trying to take stock of myself. It's not easy.'

'No?' said Natasha.

The sun shone through his eyelashes. As usual he had pushed his glasses up on to his forehead.

'Not easy at all. Now I feel ... You see, I have these two rather nasty children. I don't know if you've seen them at all ... ' he turned to Natasha.

'Indeed yes,' said Natasha. 'They are both nearly dead with the 'flu and the governess.'

'That's right,' said Barny, and paused. 'Is she a good governess?' he added. 'Do the children like her?'

'I do not know if she is any *good* or not,' said Natasha. 'The children certainly hate her. That usually means that a governess is good. I see what they mean, too,' she added, looking at the long scratch on her forearm.

'Ah ...' said Barny. He was staring up into the scintillating depths of deep blue sky. 'Well, I have to find a *mother* for them, you know. I have *really*,' he said earnestly. 'It is no good putting them to schools. Flahertés *cannot* be put to schools. They behave atrociously in schools.'

Barny Flaherté seemed rather proud of this.

'So,' said Natasha. 'How long have you known that they need a mother?'

'All my life,' said Barny, startled. 'I am a Flaherté' myself. *I* need a mother's care.'

He smiled luxuriously, with his beautiful wavy mouth. Natasha was charmed, and so far as such a thing was possible for her, felt madly maternal.

'So you would not be murdering a mother?' said Natasha, 'like Regan, who would be bringing up those children?' She wrinkled her forehead. 'You would be finding this wasteful?'

'What an idea,' said Barny, dismissing it instantly. 'Now I have to find a wife, you see, who doesn't mind them. So I thought *Kathleen* ...'

Natasha grimaced. He turned to her and looked at her for the first time.

'What do you think?' he asked.

VI

'If I am now to tell you what I am thinking,' said Natasha, 'you must first tell me a thing or six.'

Barny clasped thin, gold arms round his knees and sat up straighter.

'Seems fair enough,' he said.

'First,' said Natasha, 'if it does not pain you too much. Where are you going that evening when your poor wife, Regan, fell out of the window? You remember? You were dancing with your cousin, Kathleen. She followed you.'

'Did she?'

A frown of intense concentration appeared between Barny's light eyebrows. His features seemed brittle. 'I went out ... ' He opened his eyes and stared at Natasha. They were a curious blue-green. The look he gave her was bewildered and innocent. 'I was by way of giving the governess a *whirl* at the time ... ' he said, ruefully. 'Not quite the thing, I suppose ... ' he seemed about to explain himself. 'I was *so* fed up,' he said apologetically.

'Your morals are being none of my affair,' said Natasha.

Barny flushed.

'OK,' he said. 'Skip my morals. I went out of the bar and upstairs to hurry up Regan. I thought it was about time she came down. Half-way up I thought it would be fun to see Miss What's-it ... '

'The governess,' said Natasha.

'Mm,' Barny bit his lips. 'So instead of going upstairs to Regan's room ... that was on the top floor in the front ... or *mine* ... that was on the top floor opposite *hers* ... ' He paused.

'You went to Miss Leamington's. Which is on the second floor to be near the kiddies. And she is not there,' said Natasha rapidly.

'That's right,' Barny wriggled uncomfortably. 'How d'you know all this?'

'Where are you going after that?' said Natasha.

'The writing-room ... saloon,' said Barny. 'She's always writing letters. Have you noticed?'

Natasha had noticed.

'Gives me the willies,' said Barny. Natasha said that she could not be agreeing with him more.

'Well ...' said Natasha, sensibly enough. 'She *was* in the saloon. Wasn't she?'

'No,' said Barny. 'She wasn't.'

VII

Natasha tried to be helpful.

'Well then,' she said, 'she is just *leaving*. Your wife has fallen, isn't it? She leaves to pick up your wife? Forgive me. She has *said* to me 'I see her fall past the window. I open the window and then I run down'. She must be just going to do all this, that's so ... isn't it?'

'Ye-e-es,' said Barny. His frown deepened. 'There was her precious writing-case ... The window was open all right.'

Natasha gave a little snort and instantly suppressed it.

'And her fountain-pen and everything. All laid out neatly. So I shut the window and came away. Back downstairs. Not up to my wife's room. By the time I was at the door ...'

Barny frowned again.

'I don't feel very clever,' he said. 'My mind doesn't grasp all this. It was so nasty, you know?'

Natasha knew.

'And then I got drunk almost at once. She was lying on the snow, you know. All ... broken ...' Barny put his head in his hands. He rocked to and fro. His backbone, under his golden skin, suddenly seemed sharp and white. It was a little time before Natasha realized that he was weeping. 'All my fault,' he said, brokenly. 'All my fault ... can't, can't bear it ...'

Natasha sat very still. She dared not speak. She almost shared Barny's distress.

'How was it?' she said gently. 'At the front door? Was the Governess there?'

'She came later ...' said Barny. 'Oh, I mustn't cry. I will *not*. I'll think about something else. Oh God.'

There was another terrible moment, when the only sound in the clearing was Barny sobbing. Natasha wondered if she dared touch him. She thought not. She could quite see why he had used his influence to avoid the unpleasantness of an inquest and trial.

'What you need,' she said, briskly, 'is *petting*. Like wrapping up in a cot blanket and having your nose blown. And given a sweet to suck. Poor, nervy boy. Poor boy.'

Barny laughed and sniffed and sobbed and laughed. He stopped snivelling.

'Goodness, I'm sorry,' he said. 'Goodness ...'

He turned to her with his bright resilient smile, sniffing. He held out his hand and took hers for a second. His hand was dry and warm.

'Lovely,' he said. 'Lovely person. So grateful to you, always. Please forgive me.'

His face, where the marks of tears still showed little white salty streaks, became gay. He stood up and began to put on his skis. He pointed his chin defiantly at the mountains.

'I shall *try* ski-ing without a shirt,' he said.

And with his shirt knotted round his waist, his muscles moving all over his back in perfect harmony and co-ordination, he skidded lightly sideways, stamping over the snow. He took the wood path to Kesicken.

X

In Search of Justice

Toddy Flaherté passed quite close to Natasha and Barny while they were eating their lunch in the woods. She did not look so eccentric on skis as she usually did. She might have been one of a hundred young women in trousers who were whipping down the wood path between one and two that afternoon. Probably that is why Barny and Natasha did not notice her. Toddy was still trying to work out the times that expert and very brilliant skiers would take over the Championship Course. And she observed Natasha and Barny, sitting in the clearing.

Toddy, in spite of her bluff, masculine appearance, was not the forthright, open-hearted character she appeared to be. Hers was a warped, subtle, tortuous nature. When Kathleen, in great distress, had told her that Barny seemed to have forgotten his proposal of marriage, Toddy's instinct had been to comfort and reassure poor Kathleen. Instead she bided her time. Her affection for Kathleen was a genuine (if jealous) emotion. It was obvious that Kathleen would be delighted to marry

Barny on any terms. And Toddy's jealousy (and therefore the thought that she would soon lose her sister to this marriage) overwhelmed her.

Apart from this elementary possessive instinct, Toddy's 'home' had been with Kathleen ever since Kathleen had left school. Without a mother, life can be very difficult.

Kathleen's respectable flats in London and Paris, Kathleen's Settled Accounts and Paid Bills, had always made a background for Toddy's meteoric progress through the Casinos and Race Tracks of the world.

Moreover, when Toddy was broke (and she pretty frequently was), or awaiting her quarterly allowance from 'The Lawyers', two sisters could live very nicely for the price of one. It was understood that Kathleen was always the one whose money could keep two.

That Toddy, in fact, lived *on* Kathleen, like a vampire or a Little Old Man of the Sea, was undeniable. Toddy would have been furious if anyone *else* had suggested it. However, she quite often admitted it to herself. Toddy, for all her faults, was not a liar.

Once, some years before, Kathleen had suggested that Toddy was a vampire. A terribly frightening scene had taken place. Even now, in broadest daylight, while Toddy stood on her skis in the silent woods, or skidded lightly over the icy snow by the railway track, or climbed into the funicular to go back to the Water Station Hotel for lunch, she could remember her emotion. She could still hear her own voice, harsh and uncontrolled, shouting from the past:

'You'll never be rid of me . . . never, never. You'll never escape me. I'm your sister. You know I'm always on your conscience.'

And there, on Kathleen's conscience, with all the power of her morbid imagination, Toddy intended to stay.

II

Toddy got down from the funicular and picked up her skis and climbed laboriously up to the Water Station Hotel. Kathleen and Pamela DuVivien sat outside the hotel and drank coffee in the sun. They were both a little fidgety. Rosalie Leamington and Joyce (whose first day up it was) sat near them. Pamela was so stiff from her inefficient ski-ing that she was quite unable to move when Toddy approached. They greeted each other, and Toddy sat down with a thump on the little iron chair beside them. She stretched out her gentlemanly legs.

'I saw your *beau* just now,' she said, looking hard at Kathleen. 'In the woods, with the belle Natasha . . . '

She flashed a brilliant smile at Pamela, who felt that something unpleasant had crawled down her spine. The bright sunshine was heartless.

'They looked very cosy,' said Toddy, carefully studying the effect of her words on Kathleen. 'Barny had taken his shirt off,' she ended.

Nelli came bustling out of the hotel carrying coffee and doughnuts to Rosalie Leamington and Joyce Flaherté. Joyce looked most unfortunate. Her fever had left sores all over her mouth and her hair was staring, like the coat of a sick dog. She had, too, an unpleasant, rattling cough, which always made Pamela jump. Joyce coughed now, and Pamela duly jumped.

Kathleen looked across the table at Toddy. She had gone very quiet.

'That's quite enough, Toddy,' she said. 'You can stop now . . . '

'What d'ye mean?' Toddy was angry. She promptly became forthright, bluff and open-hearted. 'If I can't protect my little sister from a two-timing cad what *can* I do?'

Kathleen shrugged her shoulders and stood up. She was wearing a short, scarlet woollen skirt and white ribbed stockings. Even against the exotic background of melting snow, indolent people and mountains that stood out against the sky like precious stones, Kathleen looked bizarre and exciting. She turned away and walked towards the railway.

'Come, Pam, *please*,' she called over her shoulder. She sounded distressed.

'Oh, good God,' said Toddy, furious. She stood up as though she had no idea what the fuss was about. She walked stiff-legged to the hotel. 'I want my lunch,' she said as she went.

Pamela, irresolute, sat at her table for half a second. Then she, too, got up and limped painfully after Kathleen.

III

'Look,' said Kathleen. 'Sit on this toboggan here where we can see everyone and no one can overhear us . . . '

She kicked a small sledge with her foot and sat suddenly on it, crushing it into the snow. They were by the railway track, looking down on 'The Bumps' and the pinewood below them.

'Have you ever been jealous?' she said.

Pamela, who had once been very jealous of a girl called Lavinia Crane who had been put into the school eleven over her head, stood kicking stupidly at the snow. Pamela's stiffness, in a queer way, was symbolic to her of her inability to help

Kathleen. She sat on the sledge. It squeaked and groaned under them.

'Sorry,' she said, as she bumped against Kathleen. 'But I *am* so stiff. What do you *feel* like?'

Kathleen considered herself, with her head on one side. She cheered up almost immediately as she tried to analyse her emotions. 'My mind goes sort of *black*,' she said. 'And I can't think. I can't be reasonable, you know. Not that I ever can, much,' she added gaily. 'But I'm less reasonable than usual.'

'Are you perfectly sure that my stepmother and Miriam Birdseye and people have no *real* designs on Barny?' said Pamela, carefully.

'I suppose so,' said Kathleen. 'They're nice people. Not like Fanny Mayes.'

'I shouldn't be too sure,' said Pamela. 'I think they probably *all* have designs on him.'

'Do you honestly think so?' said Kathleen. She was much cheered by this thought.

Pamela could not see why this should be so. She said she didn't really know, but it seemed likely and no one was really nice, she thought.

'After all,' said Pamela, 'he's *supposed* to be very attractive, isn't he?'

'Don't *you* think so?' Kathleen stared at Pamela. Her enormous black eyes seemed quite bottomless.

'Dunno,' said Pamela. 'I never thought about it. He doesn't attract me. I expect I'm very young.'

'I expect you're very *nice*,' said Kathleen, firmly.

Pamela was startled.

'No one is nice,' she said weakly.

'Any way,' said Kathleen briskly, returning to her self-analysis. 'After all this blackness and despair and all that I just get very *depressed*. Do you know what I mean? I say, "Oh well ... All these people are *much* more entertaining and fascinating and better at everything than I am. I'm very *bad*. And they are probably *much* more devoted to Barny."'

'Oh, I don't think that,' said Pamela, with a sudden blinding flash of intuition. 'Not more *devoted to Barny*. There is something depressing, though. That you think Barny is really awful hell and worthless and not worth all this misery and bother? He never tries to improve?'

'Yes,' said Kathleen miserably. 'That's quite true, I often *pray* for him. Fat lot of good it does. I pray for myself, too,' she added in a low voice.

'No,' said Pamela, who in her time had had cold experience of the uselessness of prayer. 'They do say one shouldn't pray for anything one wants. You want Barny, don't you?'

'Whenever he becomes available,' said Kathleen. 'Yes, I want him. I should go off and find someone else, like the Boss ...' she said thoughtfully. 'I'm happy with the Boss,' she added brightly. 'You've no idea ...'

'Oh, yes I *have*,' said Pamela, whose intuition was still with her. 'You get peace of mind with your Boss, or whatever you call him. Because you don't want anything from him. Don't *expect* anything.'

'That seems pretty dreary and negative,' said Kathleen. '*I* think it's because the Boss likes *me*.'

'Being dreary and negative,' said Pamela, 'is better than getting hurt all the time by something positive, isn't it?'

'Is it?' said Kathleen. 'I don't honestly know. I shall have to think that one out ...'

The enormous and glowing shape of Brauzwetter, across the valley in the afternoon sun, suddenly overshadowed Pamela's intuition. She sighed, thinking how insignificant were human beings and how comforting it was that the mountains were indifferent to their pains and horrors. Give her the mountains every time . . .

'What are you thinking of?' said Kathleen, looking up. 'You've been such a help, Pam. So kind. I shan't ever forget it . . . ' She stretched out a hand to her.

'Don't be silly,' said Pam, ignoring the hand. She stood up stiffly. 'I was thinking about mountains.'

'I shall try not to want anything from Barny,' said Kathleen. 'That's it, I think. Not want anything at all, *ever*. Oh dear . . . '

Kathleen seemed depressed again.

'Suffering,' she said, 'makes people nicer. Or so they *say* . . . '

She looked down at her gay white legs and gay red skirt.

'I think,' said Pamela firmly, 'you should take some interest in your cousin Barny.'

Kathleen looked at her in astonishment.

'And watch him practising his ski-ing this afternoon,' said Pamela.

Kathleen laughed.

'You *have* cheered me up,' she said.

IV

Little Margie Flaherté sat up in bed. Her temperature had now been normal for twenty-four hours and she was passionately bored with herself and her surroundings. She, too, had all the unpleasant manifestations of the aftermath of the germ that had attacked her sister Joyce. She had staring hair, a scabby mouth and a dry and nervous cough.

All day yesterday she had read various astonishing books that Rosalie Leamington had found for her in the saloon. There had been a splendid little number from the 1880's, for example, called *With Saddle and Sabre* and (of course) *The Hotel-Keeper's Guide to Mönchegg and District – with an appendix on How to Do a Christie*. Margie had enjoyed *With Saddle and Sabre*, which was all about racing and (disconcertingly) gentlemen blowing out their brains when they had lost a cool pony or a stone cold monkey. But as far as Margie was concerned, the sooner she got back to London and away from Mönchegg and District and How Other People did a Christie, the better she would be pleased.

She could remember very little about the details surrounding her fever. Madame Lapatronne, perhaps, and her Winegar Cloths. And Rosalie Leamington, who always got on Margie's nerves. And Natasha, whom Margie rather admired. She had detected Natasha's hatred of herself and her sister and (with the complete unfairness of youth) respected it.

Margie climbed out of bed.

Her feet, on the sun-warmed planks of her bedroom floor, squeaked slightly. She stole across to the open window, where the air was waiting. Cautiously, she pushed her head out. The sun had been shining full on to the hotel for the last six hours. The roof snow had begun to melt and so poured from the eaves in a jet of sparkling, sunlit water.

Sitting well forward, away from the spray that splashed continually on the duckboards that surrounded the hotel, were Kathleen and Pamela DuVivien. At another little table were the Lem Bug and Joyce.

If Margie *spat*, it might reach Joyce and no one any the wiser. They might think it was the water from the gutters. Margie leaned well out and took careful aim. She was short of her target by a good five feet. She tried again . . .

Presently Aunt Toddy came up to Pamela and Auntie Kathleen. Craning out, Margie could hear most of Auntie Toddy's remarks:

'I saw your *beau* just now . . . with La Belle Natasha . . . they looked very cosy . . . Barny had taken his shirt off . . . '

The words in themselves were boring to Margie, although they showed that Daddy had been having lunch with *Natasha*. Of course, it was always fun to overhear people . . . And fun the way that voices carried so sharply *upwards* . . .

Margie looked back at her sister and her governess. Miss Leamington had got up, she seemed to be coming back to the hotel . . .

Margie sprang into bed and burrowed under the bedclothes, with a quick flick of her dirty little feet.

Presently Miss Leamington came in and smiled sharply.

'Time for your rest,' she said, and went over to the window.

She drew the soothing green curtains that made the room appear translucent and interesting, like an aquarium.

Damn the old fool, thought Margie furiously. Shutting out all the light. Margie felt perfectly well. Turning resentfully over in bed, she tried to think of something that would make the Old Lem Bug *Hop*.

'*Daddy* came to see me after breakfast,' she began, without preamble.

'That's not true, *dear*,' said Miss Leamington, quietly. 'Daddy went out directly after breakfast.'

'All right,' said Margie furiously. 'It was *before* breakfast. He *thought* you'd be angry . . .'

Rosalie Leamington stood with one hand on the curtain. She (Margie felt dramatically) was excluding her little charge from the world, shutting her into a convent.

'Very well,' she said. 'Your father came to see you *before* breakfast . . .'

'He seems awfully keen on Natash . . . er, Mrs DuVivien, doesn't he?' said Margie rapidly, in her maddening, childish whine. She looked altogether repulsive. Rosalie Leamington overcame a sudden, passionate desire to *shake* her. She sat up in bed, talking on and on and on . . .

'He said to me,' went on Margie, inventing cheerfully, and noticing Miss Leamington's white, strained face with some pleasure. '"How would I like Mrs DuVivien as a stepmother?" He said he was going to meet her in the woods at lunch time and, if I *liked*, he said, he would ask her to marry him, *then* . . .'

'That's quite enough,' said Rosalie Leamington coldly.

'That's what he *said* . . .' whined Margie.

Rosalie's mind raced quicker and quicker. It was perfectly true, according to Toddy Flaherté, that Barny had been having lunch with Natasha DuVivien in the woods at lunch-time . . . And he had had his shirt off . . . Toddy Flaherté had said so. Perhaps the rest of this horrible child's revolting suggestions were true as well . . . Perhaps . . .

'Oh, go to *sleep*,' said Rosalie Leamington, the perfect governess, crossing to the bed. 'What a mess we've got our sheets into, haven't we?'

She began to tuck in the tangled cosiness that Margie had made of her bed. (The child had been imagining herself a bear and had made a nest for herself, but the less said about that the better.) When she had made an excellent imitation of the cold unfriendliness of a hospital bed, Margie spoke up again, still determined to make the Old Lem Bug *Hop*.

'I never *told* any of you what I *saw* that day when Auntie Kathleen got that boulder on her head from the luge track . . . '

'Your Auntie Kathleen *didn't* get a boulder on her head from the luge track, it missed her, and anyway, who told *you*?' snapped Rosalie, furiously.

'Auntie Kathleen,' said the child smugly. '*She* told me.'

She stared at Rosalie Leamington like an evil little monkey, with hot, sharp, accusing eyes.

V

Meanwhile Johnny DuVivien and Ted Sloper had become as angry as it is possible for two sane grown men to be.

They had spent the early morning, sitting in the various offices that surround the Department of Justice in Kesicken and had been told that (as they were not Schizo-Frenic citizens) they would be unable to plead directly against a Schizo-Frenic miscarriage of justice. No. It must all be done through the British Consul. The nearest Consul (said Authority with a happy smile), was at Unteralp. Mr Thalassio.

'Unteralp *nothing*,' said Johnny, with a sudden burst of rage. 'Thalassio, indeed. Ask me the chap'll be a *foreigner*. I'll see the Ambassador, or whoever the Top Boy is out here. Yes *sir*. Wherever *he* is . . . '

'He is at Schroeter,' said Authority, with his diplomatic grin undiminished. 'In the Fredrichstrasse. M Gaminara, C.M.G.,

C.V.O. Oh yes. You will find him in your, *Whitaker*, as you call it.'

A subordinate was sent haughtily for a copy of the British *Whitaker's Almanack*. Johnny and Ted (who suddenly remembered that he was Sir Edward Sloper, K.B.E. and had a rush of snobbism to the head) solemnly read the entry relating to Mr George Gaminara, the highest representative of Great Britain in Schizo-Frenia. Johnny was horrified, and said he was sure the feller was a foreigner with a name like that.

VI

Afterwards Johnny and Ted Sloper stood together in the street and Ted Sloper had spoken his mind. He did not see (he said) why they should go and see the local consul in Unteralp. George Gaminara, C.M.G., C.V.O., £4,700 a year (1942) was good enough for Sir Edward Sloper, K.B.E. Johnny, slightly fed up with all this talk of seniority and the Diplomatic Service being on the downgrade, said he wanted to see Justice done.

And they caught the next train to Schroeter.

At Schroeter the Envoy Extraordinary and Minister Plenipotentiary, His Excellency Mister George Gaminara, was unavailable. Johnny and Ted Sloper kicked about in various cold ante- and waiting-rooms until Johnny, growing more and more irritable and frustrated, suddenly had one of his extraordinary presentiments of danger. He seized Ted Sloper by the elbow and said in a passionate whisper that he wanted to get back to Katsclöchen as soon as possible. He had an idea, he said, *Natasha was in danger.*

'Oh, but look here,' said Ted Sloper, feebly pulling his arm away, 'I mean to say. We're almost seeing this josser by now, if you see what I—— Look here, I'm no good with me pen. Maybe you can go home and write the whole thing out? I'm damned if I can ...'

'His Excellency's Deputy will see you now,' said a shocked clerk in a short black coat, and disappeared into the cold doorway, like a rabbit into a hat.

His Excellency's Deputy was a red-haired man called Field. He was only too glad (he said with diplomatic grin) to waste a little time with them.

When he heard their business he was not so sure.

Mr Field thought it might run them into an international incident. Since the Present Government's inception, Mister Gaminara was *awfully* anxious to keep on the right side of the Schizo-Frenics. What? He would tell them what he would do.

Ted Sloper (whose innocence and naïveté in dealing with Government Departments had really to be seen to be believed) got quite hopeful at this point.

Mr Field would tell his Excellency *everything*. And if they *wrote* the whole case *out*, then he would have *something* to *submit*, now, wouldn't he?

VII

Johnny, once more outside in the Fredrichstrasse, seized Ted Sloper by the arm and hurried him furiously towards the railway station.

'Fat lot of good that was,' he hissed, passionately. '*Hurry*, can't you? Back to Katsclöchen. Otherwise the last funicular 'll have left an' then where'll we be?'

'I suppose looking for a bed in Kesicken,' said Ted Sloper, sulkily. 'An' I dunno that I sh'd mind very much . . . '

Ted Sloper halted.

'Dammit,' he said. 'That hotel gets on my nerves. An' do you *wonder*? I'd really prefer not to go back at all . . . '

'You'd prefer?' said Johnny, in tones of withering scorn. 'Say, sonny . . . ' Johnny seized him by the collar and propelled him down the cobbled hill to the railway station, shaking him a little at each step. 'You set out to see Justice done? Eh? An' *now* what's comin' over you? Eh? C'm on, I say. Let's get crackin' . . . '

'Hey . . . ' said Ted Sloper, jerking his collar free. He spoke between gasps as they crossed the station yard. 'Hey . . . After all, I suppose one oughter do things . . . proper way . . . ugh? Mus'n' one? Specially with the Diplomatic? Ugh? An' this Government in? . . . After all, we're libellin' the feller . . . doctor . . . Vital . . . aren't we?'

Johnny said nothing. He set an even brisker pace. They trotted on to the platform, panting heavily.

The great express from Schroeter to Kesicken via Unteralp came clanging and steaming into the platform as they ran up, gasping. Bells rang. Flags waved. It stopped only for two minutes today, cried an official, in German.

To their horror, it was packed from end to end.

There were noisy Swiss, angry Schizo-Frenics, smooth French and Italians, all going to Mönchegg for the Ski-ing Championships of the World.

'Oh *lor*',' said Johnny, running uselessly up and down the train.

There was only standing room for sardines in the corridor.

Eventually, utterly out of breath and on the verge of heart

attacks, Johnny and Ted Sloper were wedged in next door to an angry Italian lady and a small, smelly Swiss skier. Ted received a ski-stick in the face and recoiled, moaning. Johnny stood glaring out at Schroeter railway station, like a wild beast. He thanked heaven that Ted Sloper was now separated from him by the Italian lady, who had put an elbow in his stomach.

Johnny also thanked heaven they had 'made the train'.

'Oughter be back in Katsclöchen b' nightfall,' he said. 'Won'er what's up with Natasha?'

Nevertheless, they did not arrive in Kesicken until after the last funicular had left for Katsclöchen and Mönchegg. They were delayed by fog.

XI

Natasha Plays Poker

At Kesicken Johnny made an abortive attempt to telephone to the Water Station Hotel to let Natasha know that he was coming back as fast as he could. A peculiar force inside him said that if he were only able to get through to her it would somehow hold the danger in check. It was difficult to explain it to Ted Sloper. Ted remarked that he would try and get a bed in Kesicken and wandered off. He left Johnny, rigid with exasperation, standing in a six deep queue for the public telephone box.

Half-an-hour later, when Johnny was next in turn, Ted returned.

'Whole place in a ferment,' he said. 'Not a bed to be had. All these people' – he indicated the whispering, dimly-lit figures that moved up and down the platform – 'are sleeping here. On the floor. They *all* seem to have relations in the ski races. Most extraordinary. Some of 'em are walking up to Mönchegg *tonight* to get good places to watch from tomorrow. They're mad keen. I will say that ...'

Ted's narrative irritated Johnny far more than the queue. It went on interminably. Ted pointed out family parties of particular interest, with their own special luggage and bundles. He told Johnny what food they had with them and what time they would be having breakfast. He was *maddening*.

'That old woman there – thorough goin' ol' sport, she is. She's come all the way from Sheidegg in Switzerland to see her *grandson* race ... He's a guide there, apparently ...'

'Oh Jee-s,' said Johnny, with a groan. He was beside himself with anxiety and impatience. 'Can't you leave me alone?'

'Sorry, I'm sure,' Ted was aggrieved.

And at this moment the telephone box opened. Johnny found himself wedged in a glass sentry box with a very old-fashioned telephone like an infernal flower, a tin box with slits in the top called 25c and 50c and a great many sinister notices in German, French and English.

II

Johnny started by talking French. The operator was a woman. She was everlastingly caught up in an electric storm.

'See voo play le Hotel de Wasser Station,' said Johnny.

'Crackle,' said the operator.

'Mercy,' said Johnny.

'Spik English pliz,' said a rough and angry voice quite different from the first one. 'Thirty-five centimes.'

'Thanks very much,' said Johnny.

In his agony, working out how, when the two slits were marked 25 and 50, he might put 35 in the box, Johnny quite lost his head.

Fox crossin' river (he thought). Boy with five pint and two pint pot bringin' three pint back. Same thing. Oh hell. I'll put in 50.

'Wasser Station Halt,' said a rasping voice in his ear. It babbled angrily in German. It was the railway station.

'——!' said Johnny, dropping the receiver. It swung to and fro, crackling on the end of its flex.

Johnny left the box very very angry. Ted Sloper was still outside in the freezing February night.

'See that ol' Grandma there?' he said. 'That's the old girl's goin' to walk up to Mönchegg. Ain't she a sport?'

'We're goin' ter be sporty, *too*,' said Johnny grimly. '*We're* goin' along with Grandma.'

'Eh?' Ted's mouth fell open. He had not seen himself in the dark, climbing three steep miles to Katsclöchen up the funicular track.

'Sure . . . ' said Johnny. 'Let's get crackin', eh sonny?'

Johnny began to walk purposefully along the track with his shoulders squared.

'Well, no point in going *that* way,' shouted Ted, stumbling after him. 'That's the way to Unteralp.'

III

Eventually they started. Johnny had borrowed a small acetylene bicycle-lamp from a porter and had tied it to his belt.

It threw a fitful, dancing light before them. A leaf blew against it. It seemed to leap up and down like a living thing. Johnny shuddered. The walk up to Katsclöchen was the most unpleasant thing he had ever done.

He was cold and hungry. The wind was bitter. He had no

overcoat. It was long past dinner-time. There was little possibility that hot food would be kept for them. For welcome, (Johnny thought) there was only the cold thrill of danger. He could *smell* it, striking at Natasha, from the dark.

The night pressed close to them. It mocked their fitful, inefficient light. Once, the lamp went out altogether and Ted Sloper was frightened. He swore and struck matches and broke them until Johnny got the light going again.

It was a stiff climb. The backs of their legs, their calves and thigh muscles began to pull and ache. Behind them, above them, ahead of them, the beat of other people's feet followed and went ahead of them to Mönchegg. They echoed the rhythm of their own footsteps like delirium. Johnny began to feel that he dare not stop to recover his breath. He remembered he was not as young as he was. He would fall on the track ... He would be crushed by the unfeeling feet of those who climbed behind him ...

Damn silly ... He had to catch up with those ahead of him.

He began to fall asleep from cold and misery as he plodded.

Now it would have been a relief if Ted Sloper had told anecdotes about Gran'ma and other pleasant human beings who walked behind them up the railway track. He might have thought them ghouls or demons, he was so silent. He was as awed as Johnny by the frightening tramp ... tramp ... of feet.

When they were half-way the moon rose.

It showed them the great white heights of Brauzwetter and Glöchner and Schwab. They seemed to sway above them. It showed the dark trees and the shadowy banks of snow by the side of the track. Over their heads, suddenly, was the black and dangerous shape of the luge track.

The frost in the wind made everything keen and clear. The moon struck a bright light from the railway line, and every now and then one of the climbers ahead of them would slip for half a second and sparks would spurt coldly from his steel boot-tips. The moon, Johnny thought, made things *worse*.

His mind went ahead of him to the Water Station Hotel. *Now* he could see the lighted windows, when he was not blinded by tears from the icy wind. He wondered *why* he was frightened. *What* did he think could attack his darling, wilful Natasha?

He forced himself to be reasonable. To take the last half-mile at a steady climbing pace. If he *kept* on climbing . . . he would *get* there . . . get there . . .

Here Johnny broke into a shambling, panicky run. He jumped forward, falling, tripping over railway sleepers. The sound that he had half expected, all this horrid hour, had made him spring to life.

It was a pistol shot.

It rang up and down the valley, singing, rocking back from the high mountains.

Natasha . . . *Natasha*.

Johnny thundered across the wooden duckboard, slippery with ice. He crashed through the front door into the warm bright bar.

IV

About the time that Johnny was having trouble with the Kesicken telephone exchange, Miriam Birdseye announced that she would like to play Poker.

It was not at all surprising that Toddy Flaherté was the first person to hear her and accept, enthusiastically. Nor was it odd that Toddy seemed to have about 1,500 Schizo-Frenic francs for such a purpose. (At this time the rate of exchange in Schizo-Frenia was about seven francs to the pound note sterling and eleven to the traveller's cheque. It was driving tourists insane with exasperation.)

Miriam opened her pale blue eyes wider when she saw Toddy's gambler's wallet. She drew it from her armpit. It bulged with notes from every country in Europe.

'I thought you said you were hard *up*,' said Miriam, accusingly.

'So I am,' said Toddy, cheerfully. 'Very, *very* hard up.'

'Well then, what's all *that*?' said Miriam. She leaned forward and ruffled the startling green and mauve notes with her forefinger and thumb.

'*That*'s my gambling purse,' said Toddy. 'Not to *live* on. The lawyers send me money to *live* on.'

'Goodness,' said Miriam.

M Lapatronne came in. He carried two new packs of playing cards (sealed), and an old-fashioned revolver.

'Goodness, dear,' said Miriam. 'What are you doing with *that*?'

It was a very heavy six-chamber army revolver that had been oiled quite recently.

'OK,' said M Lapatronne. 'She unloaded it. Quite safe. I am starter tomorrow. In ski racing. Therefore very proud tonight.'

He smiled at Miriam reassuringly.

'Drinks all round, isn't it?' he said.

'Is it?' said Miriam. 'It all depends. Mostly on who's paying for them. I don't fancy buying drinks for everyone in the hotel *myself.*'

M Lapatronne went on playing with the revolver. When it was understood that drinks were to be on the house, Toddy slouched across to the bar to get them. She looked more like a square-jawed young man than usual.

'Twenty-one years I have had this one,' said M Lapatronne to Miriam. 'From the last war. When everyone was neutral.'

Schizo-Frenia had been an ally of Great Britain in the first World War and M Lapatronne often spoke of it.

'Got any ammunition?' said Toddy. She stood with her shoulders against the bar and one leg crossed over the other. She had put her notecase back in the pocket of her shiny black leather Tyrolean jacket. 'We might shoot rooks,' she said.

'There are no rooks here, miss,' said M Lapatronne, glancing at her uneasily. 'Yes. I have ammunition. But tomorrow with blanks she will be loaded. I have four hundred skiers to start. One after each other. That is why I am oiling her. Nothing must go wrong ... '

The electric light shone down on his bald head and on the barrel of the revolver. The revolver was blue and iridescent with oil.

Kathleen Flaherté and Rosalie Leamington came into the room almost together and bumped into him almost together.

'Putting the children to bed,' said Rosalie, and jumped as she saw the gun. 'Ooh!' she said. 'How horrible.'

Toddy handed her a drink.

'Look at that,' said Kathleen. 'Don't show Toddy. She adores guns. Oh, there you are, Toddy.'

'Don't be silly,' said Toddy amiably. 'You're better with a revolver than I am.'

Kathleen smiled her pointed smile.

'You'd never think it to look at her,' said Toddy. 'But she *is*. Glass balls in the air, and all. Little Sure Shot.'

Natasha came in and said she did not want to play poker. Then she saw the revolver. Toddy now had it. She was still leaning against the bar. She squinted along the barrel, clicked the chamber open and tossed the gun up into the air.

'You look,' said Miriam coldly, 'exactly like one of those nauseating young men in *Dead Wood Gulch* or the *Luck of the Six by Two*.'

Miriam then took the gun away from Toddy and handed it back to M Lapatronne. Toddy seemed pleased by Miriam's remark.

'What a pretty little gun,' said Natasha, in her soft, slow voice.

Toddy went across to the table and slid her thumb under the seal of one of the packets of cards, broke it and scattered the cards on the table. She threw the Joker on one side and began to shuffle.

'Play with the Joker?' she said to Miriam, jerking her head. She sat down with her legs rather far apart.

'Certainly not,' said Miriam. She had begun, rather crossly, to think that Toddy was, perhaps, a class above her as a player.

'All right, all right,' said Toddy, as though she read her thoughts.

Roger and Morris came in, twittering with excitement and carrying a little packet of francs. Natasha said again that she begged to be excused. Pamela came in and stopped short when she saw her stepmother.

'Oh,' said Pamela. 'Do you think I *ought* to play, Natasha?'

'I am not knowing,' said Natasha, solidly. 'Do you know the rules and all of these combinations? The House Full? The Flush? The Straight, and all of these?'

'Yes,' said Pamela.

'And how much money are you having?' said Natasha. 'And how much are you prepared to lose?'

'Five pounds,' said Pamela. 'Same answer to both questions.'

'Don't worry, Mrs DuVivien,' said Toddy, suddenly, cutting in. 'I'll see she comes to no harm ...'

Natasha looked candidly at Toddy. Natasha's eyes were limpid and cold as a trout stream in winter-time. Toddy's eyes were black and bright with excitement.

'You will do that, will you?' said Natasha. 'I think perhaps I am taking a hand for one round for the hell of it.'

She sat down. Kathleen and the governess wandered out. M Lapatronne said he would put away the revolver. At the door Rosalie Leamington said brightly that she had letters to write and Roger and Morris began to giggle.

Miriam quelled them with a look. They cut for deal.

V

Roger was dealer. Natasha sat gently down beside him, on his left. Miriam, Toddy, Pamela and Morris disposed themselves around the table.

'Five,' said Morris, suddenly. 'Perfect number for Poker. Goody, goody. We're going to have quite an evening.'

Roger began to deal in pairs.

'No,' said Natasha, returning the cards to him. 'One at a time, 'if you please.'

Toddy looked at Natasha with respect and grinned. Roger flushed, shuffled and re-dealt.

'Are you agreeable to me,' said Natasha slowly, 'if I am only playing with one hand? And please what is the limit to be? And what the ante?'

'Oh, on *one* hand the sky's the limit,' said Roger. 'No fun unless it's the sky.'

'I don't know,' said Toddy, doubtfully, glancing at Pamela.

'Oh *hell*,' said Roger.

'Be quiet,' said Miriam, and tapped him with her long, thin hand.

'The sky,' said Natasha, suddenly, firmly, 'is the limit. And the ante is one franc.'

'My eye,' said Miriam. 'One Schizo-Frenic franc?'

'Why not?' said Natasha. 'And as I am only playing one hand will someone please promise to declare Pamela stopped when she has been losing £5?'

'All right,' said Toddy. 'I promise.'

And, oddly enough, Natasha trusted her.

VI

Everyone looked at their cards. Natasha had two pairs. Two aces and two sixes. She came in. Everyone came in. Natasha asked for one card. She looked at it furtively. It was an ace.

Well. She looked at it again. Then she laid the whole lot in a little pack in front of her and waited to see what she had against her.

Miriam took two cards and stayed. Morris took three and threw his hand in. Pamela took one and stayed. Toddy took one and stayed. Roger took two.

The betting started. It was slow to begin with. By the time Natasha spoke Pamela and Roger had gone. It was obvious that she and Miriam and Toddy had the hands.

'I'll see you and I'll raise you ten,' said Miriam to Toddy.

'All right,' said Toddy, laconically. 'And *you* ten.'

'And I,' said Natasha, slowly. 'Will see you both and be raising you both fifteen ...'

'You must have a good hand,' said Toddy, turning to Natasha.

'Oh, yes,' said Natasha. 'I have. A very good hand. I think ...'

She suddenly picked it up to make sure and clutched it to her bosom. Everyone laughed. Natasha was angry.

'Then I'll see you and I'll raise you thirty,' said Miriam as the laughter subsided.

'Oh, the hell with these francs,' said Toddy. 'Call 'em ten to the pound. All right? Three pounds. Yes. This hand is worth *six*. Six pounds.'

She turned to Miriam.

'Twelve,' said Natasha.

'Twelve pounds is a lot of money for mum on one hand,' said Miriam, suddenly. 'Let those lunatics fight it out ...'

And she paid into the kitty a cheque for thirty shillings payable to the Ivy Restaurant, a book of stamps and fifteen shillings. Toddy expostulated and then began to laugh. Miriam sat tense and frowning, waiting for Toddy and Natasha to finish.

In the end they saw each other for thirty pounds.

Toddy put down the ace and a king and three queens. Natasha, very slowly, one by one, put down two sixes and then, in three quick jerks, her three aces.

'Full house, aces high,' said Miriam. 'Well. What an extraordinary hand for a first ...'

'First and last,' said Natasha. 'Oh, yes ...'

She gathered up the kitty. She had won about fifty pounds.

'Here, I say,' began Roger, eagerly flipping the cards down. 'You can't do that. We've got to have our revenge . . . '

'Oh?' said Natasha. 'Why? My agreement was that I stay for one hand only . . . '

Pamela was confused and silent. She felt that games brought the worst out in Roger and Morris. She was perfectly right.

'Oh, well . . . ' said Roger, sulkily. 'If you like to . . . '

'I am certainly liking to,' said Natasha, coldly. She left the table.

'Now the numbers are all wrong,' whined Morris fretfully.

'Be quiet, child,' said Miriam and slapped him.

M Lapatronne suddenly reappeared on the edge of the circle.

'But I will play,' he said. 'I will certainly make up the numbers. Oh, but certainly . . . '

'I say,' said Roger. 'How awful if one of us wins the hotel?'

Natasha stole quietly out of the room.

VII

The ground floor passage of the hotel was cold after the warm bar. Natasha thought about central heating. She went upstairs to put away her winnings.

Johnny had a very stout leather suitcase that locked. Natasha planned to put the money in that.

Toddy Flaherté had certainly a nerve to bet a third of her purse on three queens. Natasha wondered if she would have done the same. She was so *sure* she would on a first hand.

In their room, Natasha reached under Johnny's bed for the suitcase and pulled it out. There were some shoe bags inside, heavily embroidered J. Du.V. There were also some loose, much crumpled sheets of newspaper. Natasha stuffed the notes carefully into one of the shoe bags, closed the case, turned the key in the lock and dropped the key in her bag.

She went across to her wardrobe and took down her dark mink coat. A walk in the moonlight was attractive, but cold. She would need the fur coat to keep warm and the frost would do the fur good.

Outside the snow was freezing hard, Natasha could almost *hear* it freeze. It seemed to hiss in all directions. The moon like a blank, new half crown, stared dangerously down at her. The moon sailed through the clouds above Brauzwetter . . .

Natasha tried to think. With her hands deep in the pockets of her mink she stalked along the duckboards outside the hotel. She could look in on the card players. M Lapatronne, very intent and very small. Miriam, roaring with laughter, her head back and her teeth showing. Toddy, chewing on her little finger. Natasha had a hunch that with herself out of the game, Toddy would take all the luck. For some reason Natasha hoped so.

Then Trudi pulled the curtain and Natasha was back again, trying to think. She tried to retrace her thoughts.

Now (said Natasha fiercely to herself) it was *not* necessarily the same person who had been pushing Regan out of the window *and* who had been poisoning Fanny Mayes. Now a murderer (thought Natasha) usually sticks to one method. The French murderers in the Terror always murder the poor aristocrats at the guillotine. The pusher over heights on impulse always push over heights on impulse, like poor, mad Sadie Dobson.* The poisoner always poisons. The postman always rings twice . . .

_____

* *Murder, Bless It*

281

Natasha, in fact, had a hunch that there were two murderers on the loose. The whole thing was very nasty.

Natasha went over the suspects (*including* those vile kiddies, she said, tartly, to herself) and wondered if Ted Sloper would poison his wife. Natasha thought Barny had not murdered *his*.

Barny. She wondered where he was now. He had almost fallen asleep in the middle of dinner. He had not even appeared in the bar when they cut out for the poker game. He had simply disappeared. To bed? wondered Natasha.

So for that matter had Kathleen Flaherté and the Governess. With a sudden, cruel little stab of jealousy Natasha wondered if either of them were with Barny. So what? said Natasha to herself, finally. At this point she began to think again that she should leave Johnny ...

Her abstracted pacing had taken her to the end of the terrace and back again several times. Now she stood still ... a dark, slender figure sharply outlined against the snow in the moonlight.

In fact, she was a sitting target.

VIII

Toddy Flaherté's two square boyish hands lay flat on the table in front of her. Her agate signet ring winked from her little finger.

Miriam had a pair of queens. She was trying to make up her mind if Toddy was bluffing. Toddy was impassive, untroubled. Her cards lay between her hands in a neat pile. She looked as though she were thinking of something else.

'Oh, damn and blast, I give *up*,' said Miriam, abruptly,

throwing her hand in. There was £20 in the kitty. Miriam added her stake. It consisted of a cheque (very dog-eared) for £5 (signed Noël Coward), a Post Office money order for the unlikely sum of £17 3 0, and some pound notes.

'Let's see what Toddy *had*,' said Morris. He reached across the table.

'Oh, *no*,' said Toddy, good temperedly. She took his wrist and twisted it sharply.

'Hey!' said Morris. 'That *hurts*.'

Toddy mixed her hand among the other cards with her free hand. Then she let go and drew the kitty towards her.

'What's the matter?' said Morris, angrily, looking round him. 'Why are you looking at me like that, Miriam?'

'I thought you knew the rules of poker, dear,' said Miriam. 'Wouldn't have let you play if I hadn't . . . oh, my lor', what was *that*?'

Morris was hurt and angry. Everyone's nerves were inflamed with excitement, exposed and shocked. And it was at this moment that someone fired the revolver, that slammed the echoes across the valley, to go reverberating up the mountains.

IX

Everyone stood up as Johnny burst into the room.

M Lapatronne said, 'My God, my gun,' and rushed to his office. Johnny passed him, thundering with his boots on the polished floor. He sprang upstairs, two at a time. He collided with Barny Flaherté. Barny was in pyjamas. His hair was ruffled.

'Where was it? Where was it? Quick man, quick,' shouted Johnny.

'I was on the top floor. I *thought* it was this floor, why I came down ...' said Barny rapidly and sensibly. 'I *thought* the saloon ...'

Johnny flung himself at the saloon door and burst in. The room was dark. A chill wind came from the open window, carrying the reek of gunpowder. There was a figure by the window, half lit by the moon. It was a woman. The gun was smoking in her hand.

Johnny snapped the light on.

He did not know who he expected to see.

It was Kathleen Flaherté.

XII

Part of the Puzzle

The saloon was silent, like the grave. The faint film of dust that lay along the mantelpiece and on the broken clock had stirred a little, to settle again.

Johnny stood by the window and stared down on to the moonlit terrace. He could hear the feet still tramping up the railway line.

He heard Barny behind him.

'Have you gone *mad*? For heaven's *sake*, Kathie. Whose is that gun? Where did you get it from?'

He heard Kathleen answer him. The terrace below him was empty. The woodpile threw a dark shadow.

'It's Monsieur Lapatronne's. He left it in the office. I took it. An' two cartridges . . . '

'*How dare you?* Give it here.'

'Yes, Barny.'

Johnny turned round. His powerful shoulders blotted out the moon. He pulled the curtains across. It rasped. The dangerous night and the tramping feet of the ski enthusiasts were shut out.

'*Please* . . . ' said Johnny. 'There's nothin' down there. What . . . *who* did you shoot at, please?'

'It . . . it's all right,' said Kathleen, hysterically. 'It . . . I missed . . . '

'Kathleen!' said Barny, sharply.

She dropped into one of the ridiculous, over-upholstered chairs. She put her head on her hands. Her hair, like black water, poured over them. Her forehead was broad and white and smooth as it had always been. She did not *seem* mad.

'*Are* you mad, Kathie?' said Barny, roughly. He knelt down beside her. He put an arm along her shoulders and shook her. 'Who did you miss? And why?'

Kathleen shuddered and laid her head back against his shoulder.

'She is firing at *me*,' said Natasha's quiet, unhurried voice from the door. 'Because she is jealous just exactly like hell of you, Barny. You and me.'

'Wha'?' Johnny felt the saloon tip up and go endwise. He grabbed the edge of the curtain to steady himself. 'Wha'?' he repeated, stupidly.

Natasha locked the door.

'Shut that damn window, DuVivien,' said Barny, suddenly, 'I'll catch cold . . . '

He had pushed Kathleen from him when Natasha came in. She was, consequently, crying again. Barny looked thin and young and angular in his striped pyjamas. His bare feet were already cold and he was shivering. He looked pitiful.

'I don't understand,' said Johnny, suddenly. He seemed to himself to be the only human being in the room. 'I do *not* understand.' He shut the window.

In the passage outside the excited crowd was gathering. Natasha had shut the door only just in time. They could hear the noises. Voices shouted: 'What's going on there?' and 'I wish my pistol, pliz,' and 'Let's finish the game, for God's sake . . . '

'Oh,' said Barny, wearily. 'Give him his gun and let's get this settled. Don't let anyone else in. This only concerns ourselves.'

'That is true,' said Natasha.

Johnny was not at all sure.

Natasha picked up the revolver from the floor where Barny had laid it. She unlocked the door and handed it to someone outside. She shut the door sharply, leant against it, locked it.

'Hairy hands Herr Lapatronne has,' she said conversationally.

'Hell's teeth . . . ' said Johnny.

'Well now, Kathie,' said Barny. 'What *is* all this?'

He sat in a heap as he had sat in the woods, his hands locked round his knees, his face thin and peaked with worry.

Natasha took off her mink coat and wrapped it round Barny's shoulders. He tucked his feet under him in the chair and looked grateful. He said nothing.

'*You* do not be needing any explanation at all,' said Natasha. She looked down at him gravely. 'You know that Kathleen is murdering your wife because of you . . . '

Kathleen began to cry quietly.

II

'My lor',' said Johnny DuVivien. He also said something extremely coarse and quite unquotable. It comforted him a lot.

'Perfectly true,' said Barny, with his appealing, sweet crazy smile. 'Do stop *crying*, Kathie, there's a dear. No one can *do* anything to you. This isn't England.'

He turned his head from Johnny to Natasha. When he looked at Natasha he lowered his eyes. 'I was horrified,' he said quietly. 'I met Kathy coming out of Regan's room. There was no doubt about it at all. I *had* to hush it up for the family. Do you see that?'

Johnny did not see that. He said nothing.

'I was horrified,' said Barny again, lamely. 'I got drunk,' he ended.

'It was so awful,' said Kathleen. 'And then I thought Barny might get hanged. Oh dear, I am sorry. Really I am ... '

'God,' said Natasha slowly, 'will no doubt have mercy on your soul. It is not for us to forgive you.'

'Oh, no,' said Kathleen. She lifted up a blank, cold face. Tears poured down it and she paid no attention to them. 'But what,' she suddenly, piteously cried, 'will become of *me?*'

Johnny was rooted to the spot, fascinated and horrified. He felt very tired.

'You'll go into that nice convent near Passy,' said Barny brightly. 'You'll be OK. You'll see. It's the *world* she can't cope with,' said Barny, turning anxiously to Johnny, to see if he saw the point. 'She's quite all right, really. I mean, not *homicidal* or anything.'

Johnny exploded.

'You mean to sit there, ca'm as ca'm, an' tell me that gal ain't homicidal? Why, she jest tried to shoot the hat off'n my little Natasha!' he shouted. 'What's wrong with you all? Nasty corrupt lot. Can't buy *our* silence like you could buy the police. We ain't Schizo-Frenics!'

'No?' said Natasha. 'Be silent, Johnny, please.'

'An' what about *Fanny Mayes?*' shouted Johnny. 'I don't

suppose Ted Sloper's so tarnation fond of you as that cousin o' yours . . . ' He glared at Barny and Kathleen alternately.

Kathleen looked up, startled.

'I *swear* I didn't,' she said. 'Honestly I didn't . . . '

'What?' said Johnny, irascibly.

'Have anything to do with Lady Sloper – Fanny Mayes, I mean. I'm very sorry about Regan and it was very wrong of me and I'll forsake the world and be a nun (because I don't want to a bit) . . . ' She began to cry again here. 'And I *did* shoot at Mrs DuVivien out of the window and miss her, and I'm very sorry, *glad* I mean, that I missed her. But I had *nothing* to do with Fanny Mayes. Oh, do *please* believe me . . . '

Johnny turned his back.

'Oh, all *right*,' he growled. 'Go on. Put a sock in it. I believe you.'

There was a pause.

'Thousands wouldn't,' said Barny, brightly.

There was another pause.

'There's one thing . . . ' said Johnny, turning back to Natasha. 'One thing I don't understand at *all* . . . '

'There's a whole murder I don't get,' said Barny cheerfully.

'Who in tarnation threw that boulder at Kathleen?' asked Johnny.

There was a pause as Barny drew in his breath.

'I did,' said Natasha simply.

III

Natasha offered no one an explanation of her behaviour. And no one but Johnny would have asked for one. Kathleen seemed to think that Natasha and she were now tit for tat and that no one need worry about (*a*) revolvers and (*b*) boulders. Barny, accepting things as they appeared to be, shrugged his shoulders, handed back Natasha's mink, and went back to bed. He had, after all, the ski-ing championships to think about in the morning.

'So you'll write to the Mother Superior, Kathie . . . ' he suggested earnestly at the door. 'And tell her *everything*. After all, she will believe it was an accident.'

The door shut behind the Flahertés and their inconsequence and their lunatic arrangement of the principles of civilized behaviour. The passage seemed to be empty. The DuViviens were left in the saloon.

'Well, I'll be made up into dress lengths!' said Johnny, and began to laugh. He sobered suddenly. '*Was* there any reason, puss, f'r that there Kathleen gettin' so jealous?'

Natasha did not reply to his question. She pushed back the curtain and traced a little man on the windowpane with one of her fingers.

'Johnny,' she said, 'I have been thinking for a long time now.'

Johnny looked up, startled.

Something shocked him.

'Ever since Sadie Dobson,' said Natasha.

Johnny groaned as he recollected his Irish indiscretions.[*]

'That perhaps we might live *alone* a little while instead of together. You are getting always on my nerves now, you know. And most of the time you are not understanding one word I say . . . '

'That's always bin true,' said Johnny, crestfallen. 'I never

_____

* *Murder, Bless It*

have. Gettin' on your nerves is new. Uh huh. That's new . . . '
he added reflectively.

'Well, anyway,' said Natasha, 'I am thinking it only right to
tell you that is what I *want* to do. For a little while.'

'Do I pay you alimony, or what have you? And what happens
to Pam?' said Johnny. He sat abruptly on the chair that Barny
had just left.

'There is no reason for going into all of that now,' said
Natasha coolly. 'It was not right, though, that you should not
know what was in *my mind*, Johnny.'

Johnny said he supposed not. He stared miserably at the
floor.

'Oh, do *not* be looking like this,' said Natasha. 'Nothing has
been happening yet. And you have still to find out who killed
this awful Lady Sloper . . . Fanny Mayes. *If* they did at all.'

'Yeah,' he said. 'That's so. Wal, I guess I c'n seek out li'l ole
Hans Grübner and get the real truth, the whole truth, an'
nothin' but, so help him.'

'Oh yes, dear Johnny,' said Natasha. 'That will cheer you up.
You will be so *glad* and *good* at all of that.'

Johnny looked at the time and yawned hugely.

'Half pas' eleven an' nothin' to eat all day,' he said. 'No
wonder I feel so depressed . . . '

Which, as Natasha told her afterwards, was exactly the way
that she had *expected* Johnny to react. Johnny was, however,
upset enough to skip the question about why Natasha had
thrown a boulder at Kathleen Flaherté. Which, from Natasha's
point of view, was just as well.

BOOK FOUR

THE OTHER PART
OF THE PUZZLE

I

The Ski Championship

Since dawn the Lavahorn and all the white surrounding countryside had crawled with people. Spectators who had walked up to Mönchegg the previous night were already strung out, frozen stiff, along the course. They waited patiently for the first competitor.

Each funicular that arrived from Kesicken and beyond brought more and more people, in brighter and brighter clothes. They swarmed over the railway track and ran about riotously at Mönchegg. Those who were drunk were quietly drunk and caused no trouble.

Mönchegg was unbelievable. It was impossible to see a square inch of snow in front of the hotel. A photographer in an aeroplane might have diagnosed a wedding cake, smothered in hundreds and thousands. This was the general effect from the air.

The ski lift, creaking and groaning most distressingly, had been hard at it since 8 a.m. carrying competitors and officials to the top of the Lavahorn. M Lapatronne was quite lost from view. He stood amongst a crowd of unfamiliar judges with yellow arm bands. He wore a sporting costume of green tweed and a flat green cap. He carried his revolver.

Hans Walter and his fellow guides, looking just as usual except for arm bands with red crosses that said they belonged to an official party for mending broken necks, stood about in attitudes full of negligent ski-craft.

Barny, with his frightening new bristle-headed friend from Mönchegg, Brigadier Shoesmith, had left the hotel at seven-thirty and had breakfasted at Mönchegg with the British ski-ing team. They were a sidey lot of young men, with vast R.A.F. and desert moustaches. One or two of them wore modi-fied battle-dress and a great many campaign ribbons on their bosoms. Barny hated them all at sight.

'Let's see now,' said one young man with a corn-coloured moustache and double row of medal ribbons. 'Navy type, aren't you, eh? Didn't I meet you at Shepheards in '42?'

'What racket *were* you in in '42?' said someone else.

'The Black Market,' said Barny. He had entered himself on the official competition sheets as 'Grahamstein'. And this put a stop to all further conversation.

II

The course started on a little plateau on the top of the Lavahorn, shot over an almost perpendicular precipice and turned abruptly to the left over a shelf of frozen rock.

A mistake here (it was said) meant almost certainly a broken leg. Spectators were not allowed to clutter up the course. The dense crowds began about twenty feet below, where the course began to go across the first of several flatfish snowfields. The course was outlined with spectators all the way from here to the drop over the lip of the gulley that passed under the railway at the Water Station.

Barny was scared stiff. He had skied over the course often enough, but these spectators (who seemed eternally pressing forward), these judges (who were as blasé and maddening as English judges at a point-to-point), his horrible team mates and the ghoulish stretcher parties, all these things combined to make him think he would shortly break his neck. He seemed to be in hell already. There was therefore no point in having a drink. Damn them all. Barny had a good mind to do the whole course like a slow bicycle race, as slowly as possible.

III

Johnny DuVivien clattered out on to the peaceful terrace of the hotel. He began to think that the previous night had been a series of unpleasant stories thought out by an unkind person to upset him.

Kathleen Flaherté, a murderess. It weren't credible. Natasha throwin' boulders. Natasha leavin' him. Goodness knows, *that* was only too possible. Johnny stood, unhappy and uncomforted, kicking at one of the iron tables.

Two young men on skis, wearing red cross armlets, dropped rapidly down the hill behind the hotel. They were on duty at the twist below the Bumps that led into the wood path. They were hurrying.

'Hey!' shouted Johnny. '*Hans Grübner?*'

'Ja, ja.' They nodded their heads as they flew down, turning in sharp, neat half-circles.

'Is he on duty? Wo?' shouted Johnny. 'Please?'

'Ja, ja.'

One of the young men stemmed abruptly and shouted through his cupped hands that he was at the turn above the ravine, by the luge track. Johnny repeated this and the young man nodded. Then he stamped twice on the snow and flew away again, down the white hill, behind his chum.

'The turn above the ravine,' said Johnny slowly. 'That's just before the course goes under the railway. Oh *hell*. With all them people about, too. The snow up there's about fifteen feet. I'll never *make* it on me two flat feet. I'll have to get skis . . . '

And he stumped angrily into the ski shop.

IV

When Kathleen told Toddy that she had decided to take the veil, Toddy did not seem at all surprised. She said that she had always expected that Kathleen would do this sooner or later. She asked for no reason. Her voice went a little gruff with emotion, and that was all.

They were packing lunch into Toddy's rucksack. They were going to watch Barny's descent. They had agreed to find the *easiest* stretch so that he could not say afterwards they had put him off if they lost their heads and cheered him. So they had decided on the flat half-mile above the hotel, where competitors had to use their sticks to urge them along, to achieve any speed at all.

Toddy was now filling a brandy flask at the bar.

'Will the rent from 68 Rue Maubart make part of your *dot*?' said Toddy, confusedly. 'And' – she showed signs of emotion – 'you will go into an Order we can come and see you in sometimes, won't you?'

Kathleen thought the rent would certainly be a part of her *dot*. 'It belongs to me, after all,' she said.

'Perhaps *I* could take it,' said Toddy. 'It would save trouble about writing-paper. What does Barny say about it? I bet *he* . . . '

'It was his idea,' said Kathleen, with great control.

'*Barny's* idea!' Toddy was aghast. 'He was always so *against* it when you suggested it before . . . '

'Yes,' said Kathleen, vaguely. 'He was, wasn't he?'

And with this explanation her sister had to be content.

'Look,' said Kathleen, two minutes later, outside the hotel. She was quite gay again. 'There goes that Miss Thing, the Governess, on skis. Doesn't she look funny?'

Toddy gave an abrupt roar of laughter like a sea-lion.

'*That* one's in Attitude Shopping Basket, all right,' she said. 'Look at that great big DuVivien clambering about by the luge track. Goodness, isn't he clumsy? I wonder why he's going to watch up there?' Toddy rambled on. 'Barny does look nice on skis . . . '

A bang from the top of the Lavahorn made Kathleen flinch and show the whites of her eyes. The starter's gun.

'By the by . . . ' said Toddy, brutally. '*Did* we ever find out what happened to that revolver shot last night? Or who fired it? Or what those DuViviens were up to in the saloon?'

'Yes,' said Kathleen.

And Toddy, to her own surprise, was silenced.

V

Hans Grübner, looking very unlike a policeman, sat on the snow by the turn into the ravine. He sat in the attitude of the Lincoln imp.

'So . . .' he said as Johnny plodded up to him. 'The eminent criminologist.'

He went on sitting there.

'Yeah,' said Johnny. 'Yeah. C'n I sit beside you?'

Hans Grübner was surprised.

'If it is not too wet,' he said. 'I am a stretcher party,' he said, proudly. 'Last year there have been two deaths here. And that was only the Schizo-Frenic championships. This time, Championship of the World, who knows? I hope your trousers are waterproof . . .'

''N so do I,' said Johnny, fervently. He sprawled beside Hans Grübner. 'You talk excellent English, don' you?' he said.

'I do,' said Grübner, gratified. 'Several English ladies have been teaching me when I am younger,' he added with a lecherous smile.

'Sure,' said Johnny. There was a silence while Johnny, a good Australian, thought of 'his sisters, Englishwomen generally'. 'We have a proverb,' he said, finally, 'in the British Empire. "Money talks" we always say. Did the ladies teach you *that?*'

And Johnny, too, smiled lecherously.

Grübner laid a finger on his nose.

'In Schizo-Frenia we too have a saying. "Show me colour of your sow's ear and I will tell you if we can make a silk purse".'

'A thousand,' said Johnny, without hesitation. He took a note from his note-case and dropped it into Grübner's lap. 'I want to know about Lady Sloper,' he said.

Grübner slid the note into his hip pocket.

'You know about the first one?' he said. 'That was sad, was it not, sir? The young lady pushes her sister-in-law out of the window quite by mistake.' Hans Grübner's face showed clearly that he thought Girls, after all, would be Girls. He sighed. Johnny wanted to shake him.

'Lady Sloper,' said Hans Grübner. 'Now this is quite different. I only decide to drop *this* case because the ski-ings are so near ... And I need *all* my time for the ski-ings ...'

Johnny remained silent wondering if everyone in Schizo-Frenia had this extraordinary callous attitude towards life and death.

'This lady, is, we all think, murdered. By these mad pills of barbituric with a label *Mrs Flaherté* which we find by the body.'

Grübner was silent for a minute and then he looked at Johnny closely. His eyes were brown and slightly blood-shot.

'What do you wish this information for?' he said.

'The truth interests me,' said Johnny.

'Will this go farther?'

'To my wife.'

The starter's gun crashed a thousand feet above them.

'Here they come,' said Grübner, with a happy grin. 'The Italians come first, I think. Italians often break legs, backs, necks, eh, anything ...'

Johnny waited.

'This lady,' said Grübner, gabbling rather fast, 'we find from autopsy had been most horrible intoxic before death. What a *lot* you English drink. But she die of barbituric poisoning. Taken through the mouth. Vital performs autopsy. He is right, I expect ...'

A figure shot down to the lip of the ravine, performed a breathless christie and shot down the ravine, rocking towards the railway track. For the next hour their vision was full of nothing but flying figures. And Grübner did not say anything more about Fanny Mayes.

VI

Margie and Joyce, whose looks since the influenza had resumed their usual low level, walked along the railway track. They had been told by Miss Leamington to meet her on the bridge over the ravine. They would (she had told them) presently see their father rush under the bridge, representing Great Britain. They ought to be very proud.

Margie nudged Joyce.

'Are you proud?' she said.

'Why should I be?' said Joyce. 'I'm half French an' half Irish.'

'Mummy,' said Margie, 'was Canadian.'

'I didn't like Mummy at all,' said Joyce pensively. She had her head on one side and was wondering how the words sounded.

'Joyce didn't like Mummy at all,' said Margie, repeating the words in a sort of chant. 'What's Daddy wearing? Red hat, yellow jersey and black trousers, like he always does? Or will he be dressed entirely in Union Jacks?' A most adult sneer came into her voice. 'That's what Miriam Birdseye said,' she added in a different tone.

'You sound like the racecards in *Saddle and Sabre*,' said Joyce. She, in her turn, had borrowed this exquisite work from the saloon. 'Only it ought to be black *sleeves*, not trousers.'

'Don't be silly,' said Margie. 'He can't ski without *trousers*.'

302

These formidable children began to squeal with laughter at their joke. Finally Margie went too far and crossly pushed Joyce into a snowdrift. Joyce said she supposed Margie thought she was *jolly* funny.

'Auntie Kathleen came and said goodnight to me last night,' said Margie. She no longer sneered.

'Well ... ' said Joyce, jealously. 'So did she me. She told me she was going into the Sacred Heart at Passy ...'

'*I* shall be a nun when I grow up,' said Margie, uninterested in Auntie Kathleen. 'I shall be a Mother Superior and very, *very* well bred, and one day I shall lay hands on a consumptive and it will be a miracle and I shall be Saint Margie. Ann Todd will play me. Or Katharine Hepburn,' she added.

There was a shocked silence between them.

'Do you know?' said Joyce, interested. 'Sometimes I *actually* hate you.'

'Well-do-you-so-do-I,' said Margie all in one breath. She began to cough rather pathetically.

'Good morning,' said Ted Sloper, catching them up. 'Little gel,' he added.

'Which of us,' said Joyce coldly, 'are you describing as "little gel"? I am the oldest.'

'Would half-a-crown cure that cough?' said Ted to Margie, who was deep in a nauseating imitation of Saint Margie's death-bed scene. She had imagined herself straight into a dimly-lit convent. There were hundreds of Flahertés gathered round to see the last of her. 'She saved thousands, herself she cannot save' they were saying. One of them looked just like Tyrone Power.

'A Schizo-Frenic franc might cure it,' said Saint Margie.

She looked out of her death-bed to play her last exquisite and touching comedy scene.

'What faces kiddies make,' thought Ted. Out loud he said boisterously, 'And whither are we away?' and fell into step beside her.

'Bloody old fool,' said Margie.

'To see the ski-ing,' said Joyce politely.

'Ah, yes,' said Ted judiciously. 'I don't think I've seen either of you since you were ill? Eh? Isn't that so?'

'I was very, *very* ill,' said Margie solemnly.

'Indeed you were,' said Ted. 'You nearly died.'

This simple speech sent him far up in the children's estimation. They looked at him with a new respect. When they had walked another hundred yards Ted found a nasty little paw, in an unclean mitten, thrust into his hand.

'I nearly *died*,' repeated Margie.

'Certainly were delirious,' said Ted brightly. 'Talkin' all sorts of rot about who threw the boulder at Auntie Kathleen ... '

'Everyone knows *that* was Aunt Natasha,' said Joyce coldly.

'Oh ... ' Ted was startled. 'So you call her Aunt now, do you?'

'Sure do,' said Joyce brightly.

'You went on about who went into m'wife's room. You remember her. Aunt Fanny?'

'Joined God's Holy Angels,' said Margie briskly. 'And any way she wasn't Aunt Fanny. She was Lady Sloper.'

Snubbed, Ted bowed his head. He doubted whether his wife had joined God's Holy Angels. They were still walking along below the flat snowfields. From time to time a skier shot past, scornfully. The skiers were still Italians, dressed in black from throat to heel and looking Fascist, but *chic*.

'If you like,' said Margie. 'I'll say who it was I saw go into your room.' She stopped and looked at him. 'They came off the funicular . . .'

'Who did?' said Ted sharply. He almost expected the reply God's Holy Angels.

'Bend down,' said Margie. 'And I'll tell you . . .'

Ted Sloper squatted down on the railway track. Margie supported herself on his shoulder with one sticky mitten and whispered hoarsely in his ear. He drew back nervously from the fumes of peppermint and milk chocolate.

'Come here,' said Margie, imperiously, pulling him down. 'You can't hear me away up there . . .'

A look of blank incredulity spread slowly over Ted's flat, pleasant face as he listened.

VII

It was an interesting fact that few people knew Roger's and Morris's surname. Their names were a matter of some uneasiness to both of them. They were relentlessly hyphenated. Whether Morris was called Birchwood-Watson or Watson-Birchwood only Morris and Roger knew. And they seldom told anyone.

Roger's was more simple to deal with. His name was Partick-Thistle. And (or so Roger would tell you) no Scotsman could ever put 'Thistle' in front of 'Partick'.

Ted Sloper, slightly out of breath, because he had been hurrying up the railway track from the young Miss Flahertés, accosted Miriam Birdseye and asked her for Roger's surname. They were outside the hotel. Miriam looked vague.

'Don't understand, don't understand, don't understand,' she

said, rapidly. She was wearing an elegant *ensemble*, based on an American Petty Officer's pea jacket, which she wore with some *panache*.

'*Spectator* sports,' she said, proudly, smoothing it over her stomach. She watched Ted, warily.

'Why do you want to know Roger's surname?' she said, suspiciously. 'And Morris's. It has nothing to do with you.'

'Oh, but look here, Miss Birdseye,' said Ted, angrily. 'I'm tryin' to collect data about poor Fanny's death. That demon Flaherté child tells me that . . . '

'Don't want to hear, don't want to hear, don't want to hear,' said Miriam – she looked at him with enormous pale blue eyes – 'anything that little bastard says. *One* of them,' said Miriam, evidently returning to Roger and Morris, 'is called "Thistle". He's my milkman's son, so I know. But they are both *very* dear friends of mine, and I will not have them worried . . . '

'*Which* one is called Thistle?' said Ted Sloper.

'Don't like your tone,' said Miriam, turning away.

'*Which one is called Thistle?*' shouted Ted, his face turning slowly mauve.

'I forget now,' said Miriam. This, as it happened, was perfectly true.

She went to the front door, where she met Morris. He carried a large basket, evidently full of food, and they walked away together down the railway track.

Miriam pulled a little toboggan that she had unearthed from the ski hut. Sometimes it banged into the calves of her legs and Miriam swore. Sometimes it ran on ahead, leaping and bounding.

Ted Sloper stamped into the hotel. If anyone presented him

with any more of this pretentious inconsequence he felt that he would go *mad*.

He borrowed M Lapatronne's typewriter. He sat for the next twenty minutes opposite it. He was trying to write an understandable account of his wife's death for the British Ambassador. The facts, as he tried to recall them, were accurate. The typing and the diplomatic style left a great deal to be desired.

'On the morning of the . . .' typed Ted, carefully, and stopped. 'Oh God,' he said out loud. 'What day *did* it happen?'

The typewriter was possessed by a demon that wrote p and q and 6 all the time. He got up and walked fretfully up and down the dining-room. He tried to work out the date. He couldn't do it. He hadn't got his pocket diary. He went back to the typewriter and left a space.

```
On the morning of the . . . . . . . . I had
an argument with my wife. pqvs. She was
expecting a child and qconsequently was
not her sweet brightself. She hit me with
the qbedside light. 666. After this she got
even angrier. She ptold me the child was
not mine, but Barny Flaherté's. There was
more, but I think it irrelevant. I did not
know . . . I still do not know whether she
was ptrying to upset me or whether she was
speaking the truth.
```

Ted, remembering the horror of that morning and the more distressing ghastliness of the evening, blenched and laid his head on the typewriter again. The typewriter, possessed by its poltergeist, slapped out a row of 6's.

'Oh,' groaned Ted. 'I can't do this. I *can't* do it. I'm not a novelist. I haven't got any detachment. Can't even type. It's too *much* . . . '

And a large tear rose in his eye and threatened to overflow it. Roger Partick-Thistle, that student of human nature, now came into the dining-room. He had a rough transcription of his new musical version of *Dracula* under his arm.

'I hear you've got the typewriter, dear,' he began, jauntily. 'Mind letting me know when you've finished? I've got my . . . Oh *dear*,' he added, with a complete change of tone. 'Whatever is it? Something beastly's happened to you. Or you don't feel well . . . '

Ted lifted his head from the typewriter and shook it. He blew his nose rather noisily. Roger winced.

'Trouble is,' said Ted, 'I'm not a novelist or a typist. If I *were* I shouldn't be so upset . . . '

'What is it?' said Roger, with interest. He sat on the table swinging one leg. One hand went up to play with his little bright bow tie.

'Account of my wife's death for the Ambassador,' said Ted, looking down and mumbling. 'They won't *do* anything, they say, until I submit them a case. And I can't do it. I get muddled. And this typewriter won't type.'

'Well, look here,' said Roger, running a hand over his hair. 'I don't want to push *in* or anything, dear, but I even know that typewriter. If you'll let me help . . . well, I *will*, that's all . . . '

'I don't even know your name,' groaned Ted. 'And I insist on knowing it because . . . '

'That stinking little kiddie,' said Roger amiably. 'Well, I expect I'll even be able to add to your facts, dear. I saw your wife alive at six-forty-five, just after I got off the funicular. She was on her bed. Drunk and shouting, as I expect you know. That kiddie saw me coming out of your room ... '

'Why didn't you come forward before?' shouted Ted. 'Why are you telling me this? *What were you doing in there?*'

'It was a bit eccentric,' said Roger. 'I went into your room by mistake. Never so shocked in my life. I certainly couldn't have told you at the time. When I knew she was dead, I mean. You'd have suspected me of God knows what ... '

'I do now,' growled Ted.

'Well now, look, dear,' went on Roger, ignoring this. 'You get up from that typewriter, dear. I'll type. You dictate. We'll soon have it done ... '

He shook his head at Ted's transcription, with its liberal sprinkling of 6's and p's and q's. Ted got up. Roger pulled out his typescript with a quick rattle of rollers and screwed it up into a ball. Ted was insulted.

'Look here,' he said. 'This is all fine, but ... Oh, damn. Well, I'll take it in the spirit in which it's meant. But *tell me your name ...*'

'In a spirit of cold curiosity, dear,' said Roger, and told Ted his name. Ted roared with happy laughter. It was Roger's turn to be insulted.

VIII

I have the honour, sir, to submit the
following facts for your consideration,
typed Roger briskly. They relate to the death of
my wife, Lady Sloper (better known as Fanny
Mayes) who I believe to have been murdered
on . . .

'On when, dear, was she murdered?' said Roger. 'Oh, well,
never mind, we'll put that in later . . .'

. . . at about seven in the evening. A
hotel guest, Mr Roger Partick-Thistle, saw
her alive at 6.45. We may conclude from his
evidence that the poison (barbituric) on
the testimony of another hotel guest, Mr
J. DuVivien (who has this information from
Schizo-Frenic authorities), was not in the
room at all. My wife was alive and noisy
and not sleepy as she might have been under
the influence of barbituric. The poison must
have been introduced later by some other
person.

The events leading up to this tragedy
were complex. I had had a serious quarrel
with my wife that morning. She hit me . . .

'You poor *dear*,' said Roger at this point, rattling the keys of the typewriter in a *dance macabre*. 'How awful for you. What a vixen Fanny *was* ...'

'She was my wife, sir,' said Ted, frowning.

'Oh, all right, dear,' said Roger, and went on typing.

```
My wife afterwards wrote me a letter which
indicated her intention of returning the
next day to England. This disposes (I feel)
of any possibility of suicide.
    I submit, sir, that I have produced enough
evidence to show that this case should
be reconsidered in the light of British
Justice, if necessary on British soil. And I
have the honour, sir, to remain ...
```

'Now then, dear,' said Roger, 'sign it and put all your titles and all your orders of companionship to impress the Old Buzzard. And then we'll post it.'

Ted, with his head on one side, looking miserable but resigned, read the letter through.

'I shall put my English address at the bottom,' he said solidly. 'And then, if there's a delay, they will be able to contact me in England ...'

'*If* there's a delay?' said Roger scornfully. 'Where *can* you have spent the War, dear? Or the Peace?'

Ted was already thinking of something else.

'You're *sure*,' he said earnestly, 'we oughtn't to have drawn attention to the bad behaviour of this policeman feller, Grübner?'

'Certainly not, dear,' said Roger. 'Give the man the facts that you can see and what you have deduced from them. Then no one can complain or bring a libel action or *anything*. Now sign it.'

Ted signed. His signature was over-elaborate and pretentious. Roger sighed when he saw it.

'And now an envelope,' said Roger, 'which you can address better than me, knowing the Ambassador's style and all. And then you can post the whole *thing*, dear. And then I can get on with *my* typing.'

Ted suddenly realized that he had taken advantage of this eccentric young man.

'I say,' he began. 'Thanks very much, I ...'

'Don't mind me,' said Roger airily. 'I *liked* doing it. You run along and find who had barbituric and who made your wife take it and who went into your room after me. I don't think she took it all by herself y'know ... She had a skinful of alcohol actually ...'

'No ...' said Ted reflectively.

'And then *do* come back and tell me,' said Roger. He patted Ted lightly on the shoulder.

He rolled the sheet of quarto rapidly into the machine and typed fiercely 'Enter the Countess Dracula in a red spot. Song: *Blood Relations*.' He underlined it furiously. The typewriter promptly wrote a neat line of sixes.

II

Natasha Gets Involved

Ted Sloper, when he had posted his letter, was at a loose end.

As a matter of fact his whole idea in writing to the Ambassador at all had been to relieve himself of the responsibility of finding out about his wife's death. And now, to his annoyance, he discovered that the only way he might ease his conscience was by finding out more and still more.

He stood outside the hotel in the sunlight, with his hands in his pockets. Roars of applause and shouting up and down the Laverhorn now showed that the Schizo-Frenic team had started their descent. The entire neighbourhood gave tongue. Natasha came out of the hotel in ski-ing clothes. She looked beautiful. She came up to him.

'Why are you not watching Barny Flaherté do the ski?' she said, without preamble.

'I've been writing to the Ambassador,' said Ted, pompously. 'And now I've decided to find out who possessed barbituric sleeping-pills in the hotel. I'm quite sure someone helped poor

Fanny to take it. She was awfully drunk, you know,' he said, confidentially. 'She wouldn't have been able to take it all by herself.'

Natasha looked at him.

'You cannot have been thinking *that* one out all by yourself, Sir Sloper,' she said, gently. 'It does not sound like you.'

'Of course I thought it out for myself,' said Ted, crossly. 'What on earth do you mean?'

'I mean nothing.' Natasha shrugged her shoulders. 'I tell to you,' she said, 'except for Mrs Flaherté's sleeping-pills *I* have never heard of any barbituric in the hotel. No.'

'But there *may* have been some more,' said Ted. 'Miriam Birdseye might take it. Or her friends. They may be drug addicts. Or you might. Or your husband.'

'Thank you,' said Natasha, 'but you may be counting out my husband and myself. We none of us ever have to take something for sleep but aspirin. And Pamela. She never take even aspirin. But what about Toddy and Kathleen?' she added, 'Toddy looks more like morphia, if she is anything, but with those black eyes you never can even see any pupil. But I should talk to *them*. *They* are on that nice, flat bit of snow up there. Waiting for Barny.'

Natasha pointed with one catskin mitten. Ted followed the line she gave him.

'After all,' said Natasha, 'it has been *Toddy* who has taken your wife upstairs when she is getting so dead drunk and she is *so sure* to tell you something new.'

Ted sniffed the air like a large and unintelligent dog.

'Not a bad idea, Mrs DuVivien,' he said. 'And what will *you* be doing meanwhile?'

'I,' said Natasha, 'will go up to the top of the Laverhorn and see Barny start.'

'You might ask him about his wife's sleeping-pills when you're up there, then,' said Ted, heartlessly.

'Oh, I *will*,' said Natasha, solemnly.

But when Ted had gone lumbering off towards Kathleen and Toddy, Natasha went into the hotel to interview Trudi, the chambermaid.

II

Trudi Gertuchen was in the kitchen. She got up when Natasha put her head round the door and came towards her, trailing knitting. She was a plump, bun-like young person with a round face and eyes like burnt currants. She walked as though she were an excellent dancer.

'A vot' service,' said Trudi.

'See, Trudi,' said Natasha, '*do* be coming into the dining-room that Miss Birdseye now has . . . '

Trudi followed Natasha into the servants' dining-room. Ted's bed had been moved. Natasha began to speak enthusiastically in French of Trudi's intelligence and attention to detail. Trudi bridled. Natasha pressed a 250 franc note into her hand and asked her if anyone had ever lost any sleeping-pills in the hotel. Trudi seemed surprised. Then she thought, with one plump finger in her mouth, that she remembered Mrs Flaherté tell her, Trudi, on the night before she fell so tragic that her pills were missing. But no one else.

Natasha was pleased. Trudi went on to say how sad Regan had been and how she said no one could help her now, not even

Kathleen. Natasha smiled a little bitterly at this and pressed another 250 franc note into Trudi's hand.

Could Trudi perhaps recall, without too much trouble, if everyone in the Flaherté party woke up easily every morning when the early tea was brought them? She was speaking, Natasha explained, of the days before poor Lady Sloper had died of heart failure.

So tragic, Trudi thought. So did Natasha. Trudi could not remember anyone *she* had served with early tea. But she would send Nelli Gertuchen, her sister. Nelli did more early teas than she did.

And out she went.

Nelli's resemblance to her sister was so exact as to be quite embarrassing. But she was not very helpful. On the two or three mornings following poor Madame Flaherté's death Monsieur Flaherté had been *very* hard to wake. He had been most soundly asleep. She could remember no one else. Miss *Toddy* Flaherté was always difficult to wake. Some of the other members of that party did not have early tea. The Governess, for example, and the two children.

Natasha thanked Nelli very much. And the Gertuchen sisters were richer by 500 francs.

III

Natasha went up to Mönchegg on the afternoon funicular. She was fussed. She found it hard to arrange the facts that she had learned about the elusive bottle of barbituric pills.

If indeed they had been used to poison Lady Sloper (which now seemed likely) then the murderer had probably stolen them in the first instance. They had obviously been stolen for a *use*. Perhaps the murderer-thief was a bad sleeper ...

They were obviously careless and daring and impulsive and foolhardy. Otherwise, why leave the bottle loosely on the bedside table? Unless ... it was someone who hoped that more suspicion might fall on Kathleen. Who *knew* that she had killed Regan?

Either way, Natasha was determined to see Barny as soon as possible.

She sat on the shiny varnished seat and looked out with some horror at the pushing, boisterous crowds at Mönchegg. She walked along to the ski-track and took down her skis and walked over to the ski-lift. It was still carrying spectators to the top of the Laverhorn.

I have always found it difficult to explain Natasha's behaviour at this point. She had never been on a ski-lift before. Possibly the early stages of her infatuation for Barny Flaherté made her take a physical risk that she would not normally have considered. Or it may have been her love of drama. Certainly, if she had remained in the Water Station Hotel she would have been bored to death.

Natasha now stood by the shaking, vibrating apparatus that came snaking out of the hut.

There was a wire that went up to the top of the mountain.

Running up it were hooks like anchors. Against these leaned the experts, negligently. To these clung the inexpert, most desperately.

By holding the skis parallel and rigid, and paying great attention, even the inexpert eventually gained the top. After a time it was exhilarating to see the pine trees of Lavadün dropping into place on the right, to pass ecstatically over small bridges

317

and other pine trees, to see swarms of people like coloured ants cluster about beneath one's feet. To mount, in fact, to the peak of the Laverhorn. Natasha went up on her ski-lift alone.

She adored every minute of it.

IV

There was a small plateau on the top where wooden huts had been built for the judges and teams. It was crowded with people in different-coloured arm bands, or with disfiguring and embarrassing numbers on their chests. They were all shoving about, drinking brandy out of flasks and talking to each other. Every now and then the revolver would crack. There would be shrieks of excitement and a roar of applause. And yet another skier would shoot away, over the precipice into mid-air and certain death, flying down to Kesicken. Or so it seemed to Natasha.

On a lower shoulder slightly to her left was an angry mob of Very Gamesy Women, milling about like the men. Natasha was bored by them and looked back at the higher crowd. She saw now that this was entirely masculine, and therefore slightly less Gamesy.

Among it (and rather noticeably) moved five haughty young men covered with medal ribbons and obscured by moustache, calling each other 'Rinso' and 'Bunjy' and 'Squeaker'. Natasha assumed, and rightly, that this was the British team. On the ground behind them, looking cold and frail and mauve and intensely miserable, was Barny. When he saw Natasha he was delighted.

'Darling Natasha,' he cried. 'I can't move. I've got pins and needles with terror. How brave of you to come up here among these unpleasant people. They are like Dunkirk. I *love* you for coming.'

Natasha, of course, was delighted.

V

They held hands.

'I am coming to wish you luck,' said Natasha.

'I need it,' said Barny. 'I have pins and needles *all* over. But all over. I've been here for hours and hours. If it goes on any longer I shall *die*.'

'My poor Barny,' said Natasha, helpfully. 'And it is looking so offully steep, just now, too, isn't it?'

Barny groaned.

'*Oh*,' he said. 'Let's talk of something else.'

'Well, what about?' said Natasha. 'Now will you be making a suggestion? I know ...' she added, happily, putting an arm round his neck. 'Tell me of Mrs Flaherté's sleeping-pills.'

'*That's* cosy,' said Barny, moving his head gently against her arm. 'Sleeping-pills. Regan's pills. *I* took 'em ...'

'No ...' Natasha was horrified.

'Yes, and lost them again,' said Barny, cheerfully. 'Whatever is the matter, Natasha, darling? You've gone quite *white* ...'

'It's the cold,' said Natasha. 'Soon I get pin and needle, too. Tell me how you lost them.'

'Well dear ...' Barny wrinkled up his face and pushed his horn-rimmed glasses up on to his forehead as he always did when he thought. 'That night, you know, I got drunk ...'

'Yes ...' said Natasha, encouragingly.

They were in a strange little warm vacuum, surrounded by

the cold and other people's legs. The world did not exist for them at that moment.

'And later in the middle of the night I woke up. Oh, I had a head. An' I remembered Regan's pills and went across the passage to her room to get them ... She wasn't there, of course ... '

'Of course,' said Natasha, and remembered, with pity, that broken figure in the snow.

'And I took two, and oh, how I slept. I had remembered, you see, about Kathleen ... and everything. It was like heaven to be asleep. When I tried to find 'em to take two more the *next* night they'd gone. Now wasn't that odd?'

'*British Team! Grahamstein!*' screamed an angry Schizo-Frenic voice from the wooden hut.

'That will be the Great British Team,' said Natasha with interest. 'Grahamstein. What a funny name.'

'Oh goodness,' he said miserably. 'That's me. Oh hell.'

He rose painfully to his feet and shuffled forward to the lip of the precipice. To Natasha, suddenly, he seemed like Lucifer, son of the morning, before his fall. Someone barked orders at him and he shook his head. 'Good luck!' screamed Natasha. Barny turned and waved. The gun cracked. Natasha shut her eyes. When she opened them he had gone.

VI

'Excuse me, madame,' said a bullying voice in Natasha's ear. 'You should not be here. You should be down there with the other ladies.'

'Oh ... ' said Natasha. She said she was sorry. Her eyes were blinded with tears and love. Her heart had gone with Barny, down the mountain. "Four summer days from morn till dewy eve he fell",' she said confidentially to the official. He was not an admirer of Milton.

'I beg your pardon, madame,' he said. 'Down *there*, please. Among those other ladies and wear *this*, too, please . . . '

Natasha had hardly noticed that she had been branded between her shoulders and on her bosom with a large white figure six. Reluctantly she stood up. She thought of Barny, flitting down the mountainside on angel's pinions. She shuffled forward.

Presently she was with the Gamesy Ladies on the Lower Shoulder.

'Numero 6?' someone shouted. 'Number 6? Ah. There she is . . . '

And Natasha was impelled forward by rough, friendly hands.

'You're next but one,' said a stout bronzed Englishwoman in her ear. 'You nearly missed it. I'm so glad you didn't . . . '

Natasha wondered what it was that she had so nearly missed, and said politely that she was glad also. The revolver had cracked twice more, and the ranks had opened all round her like a dream, before Natasha realized that she was, in fact, poised at the top of a precipice only slightly less steep than Barny's, with Number Six on her bosom. Ahead of her a double line of silly little flags writhed about the snow like two mocking snakes . . .

Natasha nearly died.

And then the pistol barked and she went over the precipice with no sense of initiative and precious little sense of balance.

Roger typed industriously.

> I'm one of the blood relations of the
>   Countess Dracula
> We've been vampires for generations and
>   Great Great Grandmamma
> The first of the vampires in Debrett and
>   also in Who's Who
> Was a bright young thing in the Were Wolf
>   set in 1822
> Frightf'lly partic'lar
> An absolute stickler
> For blood of the deepest blue . . .

It was the finale song and the climax to Act I of *Dracula – A Musical Extravaganza* by Roger Partick-Thistle, based on the novel *Count Dracula* by Bram Stoker. It was to be sung by the juvenile lead, Vamparine Camilla, with orchestra and full company. For Roger it meant that the end of his typing was in sight. He was thanking God. He began on the chorus.

> The last time I saw the Countess
> The Day the Bastille was freed
> She was walking the Champs Élysées
> With her pedigree wolf on a lead.
> Ah! for the Revolution
> Dear Madame Guillotine

> I founded my Constitution
> On Blood that was Ultramarine.
>
> *(Pom Pom)*

'Of course,' said Roger, brightly, to himself. 'The Champs Élysées wasn't built when the Bastille was freed. I shall have to tell Freddy. Damn. He'll be furious. So will Miriam ... '

And he began on his second chorus. Twenty minutes later he tucked the mass of quarto paper under his arm, slid it into a cardboard folder and staggered back to the office with the typewriter. He was anxious to tell someone about the Champs Élysées. He went upstairs to put on his fur coat and his boots. As he went he sang, in an unpleasing tenor:

> *Oh! The tombs where the moon shone brightly*
> *Oh! The Castles on the Rhine,*
> *We used to play twice nightly*
> *In 1879.*
> *Oh! The Banquets in Bohemia*
> *When the neighbours came to dine*
> *And left with pernicious anæmia*
> *I'm afraid that the fault was mine.*
>
> *(Pom Pom)*

Miriam and Morris, sitting on their toboggan beside the Championship Course, heard him coming and greeted him fairly friendlily.

'I *say*, dear, that song ... ' began Roger.

'That awful boring Sloper man was looking for you,' began Miriam. 'He wanted to know your surname. I didn't

323

tell him . . . ' she paused doubtfully. 'At least . . . I don't think so . . .'

'He found me,' said Roger. 'And we wrote to the Ambassador. It was *fascinating*. The Hunt, dears, is *up*.'

'It had better be,' said Morris, sourly. 'We have to go home at the end of the week.'

'Oh,' said Miriam casually, 'we'll catch the murderer before *then*.'

'Was it any of us?' said Roger, doubtfully.

'It was *not*,' said Miriam, crossly. '*That* is the sort of remark, Thistle, that has got you where you are today. Though it might well have been me. I *loathed* Fanny Mayes. And you were no friends of mine,' said Miriam, unfairly, looking back and forth at Roger and Morris, 'if it might not well have been you, too.'

'Oh yes, dear,' said Roger. 'She was quite utterly the beastliest thing I've ever *seen*.'

'*I detested* her,' said Morris quickly. 'So did everyone.'

'It was probably Linnit and Dunfee in disguise . . . who did it,' said Miriam.

'Or George Black Limited.'

'Or any theatre management, dear. She was a bad, bad actress,' said Miriam.

'So we must find the murderer and press him warmly by the hand,' said Morris, 'well, any way,' he ended, lamely, 'find him.'

'And before Saturday night,' said Roger. 'Oh! *Well skied, sir!*'

'*Well skied, Barny!*' screamed Miriam. '*Well skied, Dish!*'

VIII

Barny, dropping to his first christie at about sixty miles an hour, was conscious only of exhilaration and intense excitement.

The *second* christie would be the tricky one and he knew it. If he could brake slightly and turn it into a *stem* christie it would be easier. He made it. Breathless poised, he swooped down towards the upturned faces of the crowd. They were a pink blur.

He took the third christie almost level with Miriam and Roger and Morris. He heard their screams, vaguely.

From here to the ravine was a long slog along the flat. Barny urged himself with his sticks. The turn to the ravine was an absolute *stinker*. Barny took it as fast as he could. He shot down the ravine unaware of Johnny DuVivien's sour admiration, or Rosalie Leamington's breathless adoration, or his children's surprise that he looked as good as the others. He was also unaware of two fat strangers in musquash coats who said:

'They don't seem to be goin' very fast, do they, Mabel?'

Barny at that moment had achieved seventy miles an hour.

IX

'They're mixin' some women in with the men now,' said Mabel.

'Women are even *slower*,' said her friend.

'Don't seem to be travellin' at all. I don't suppose anyone will break a leg at *all*,' said Mabel, disappointed.

'Not till the jumpin', darlin'. Let's go down an' get good places for *that* . . .'

So Mabel and her friend left the most astonishing episode of the afternoon (Number 6, an unknown Russian lady from Wasser Station Hotel), who careered down the course entirely out of control.

'I simply pray to God not to fall and to good Saint Stanislaw of Lwow,' said Natasha, afterwards. 'I know if I fall I die.'

It was, of course, Miriam who first noticed her slight, flying figure and drew everyone's attention to the phenomenon with a scream that would have done good duty at a soccer football match. Roger and Morris joined in with the long, uncanny howls of two whips viewing fox leaving cover. Natasha, now spanking along the straight to the ravine, had achieved the impossible by ignoring all the turns and ski-ing straight down the middle of the course, leaping over all the little bumps she should have twirled around. She was therefore travelling four times faster than anyone else.

'She'll break her neck at the ravine turn all right,' said Morris, gloomily. 'Let's go an' look.'

To his annoyance Miriam slapped him violently in the face. She flung herself on her toboggan and covered the twenty yards to the railway bridge down the railway line in exactly the same time that Natasha did her thousand. Consequently she was in time to see Natasha take the twist into the ravine with her knees bent double and knocking furiously. She shot under the bridge and down the Bumps like a hundred-pound shell.

It was afterwards agreed to be the most astonishing performance ever witnessed at Kesicken. Only a dancer could have done it. Natasha explained to anyone interested that she had not existed at all during her descent, but had hovered uncertainly above her own head in a state of levitation, engaged in a long dialogue with Saint Stanislaw of Lwow. No one believed this but Barny. You may perhaps understand why Natasha loved Barny.

'And when I come to the woodpath,' said Natasha afterwards, 'good Saint Stanislaw of Lwow he say, "It is all ice here, little Nevkorina, and if, beloved, you do not turn your skis sideways you will join the Holy Saints, which, charming as you are, would not be quite the thing". So I turn the skis sideways as he tells me.'

'Go on, go *on*, darling,' screamed Barny, off his head with excitement. 'What happened next? So you skidded like mad . . . '

'And *then* I come to the smooth snow and the winning post and Saint Stanislaw leaves me and I am quite at a loss. And I go like hell. And I fall down and tie my feet behind my neck. It is very difficult, this. And you come and take my skis off, darling, *darling* Barny,' and she kissed him passionately, with her lovely hair falling into her eyes, 'and I should never,' she said as they limped off the field together, 'have gone *on* at all if you had not been waiting for me at the bottom, *Barny* . . . '

And one of the judges said, in tones of the deepest disgust, 'That little Number Six is ten seconds ahead of them all. Even the Schizo-Frenics. We shall *have* to give her the trophy.'

But Natasha said it should be given to Good Saint Stanislaw.

III

'A Little, Little Moment'

Dazed, gay, and out of breath, Barny and Natasha went on down into Kesicken to catch the funicular back to Katsclöchen. Nothing, Natasha said, would make her stay on skis half-a-second longer than she need. Accordingly, they took them off and walked the last half-mile through the mud and manure and slush to Kesicken. Their behaviour was considered extremely eccentric by the Schizo-Frenics.

In Kesicken, Natasha looked so pretty, her face so pink and white with fresh air and unnatural exertion, and her lovely ash-brown hair disarranged and floating in the wind, that Barny said he must buy her a present to commemorate their boldness. They went down the main street of Kesicken in a happy swoon.

Barny thought a scarf would be nice. Natasha wanted a pair of very tight Schizo-Frenic trousers made of black felt. She said that she had many, many scarves and all special, but *no* special trousers. Barny was delighted with her.

They sat in a shop called *Chocolat, Praliné, Doughnuts* and ate Marron Glacé (Natasha) and doughnuts (Barny) and drank chocolate. Neither of them saw the envious face of Rosalie Leamington, pressed for a second against the steaming window pane. It vanished into the crowds like a ghost. A drowned ghost. It was hot and noisy and crowded inside the tea-shop. The pale, unhappy spectres outside did not concern Natasha and Barny. They would have denied their existence.

Yet, later, they saw Miriam and Roger and Morris in the main street, looking brightly coloured and cheerful and Barny rushed out of the shop to drag them in to share. Miriam was always enchanted by the success of others, and her excited con-gratulation of Natasha in what she called her 'Death-Defying Leap' was genuine and infectious. Soon everyone was drinking coffee or chocolate and ruining their teeth with sweet things. Soon, too, Roger was entirely happy. He crooned the third chorus of his vampire song:

I'm the Vampire Queen,
My mental age is seventeen;
Here I am – and don't you think I'm smart?
Which of you fine boys'll put a stake through my heart?

It went with a great swing. Barny was happier than he had ever been. Natasha described her dialogue with Saint Stanislaw and Miriam also believed in it. Morris wondered if Saint Stanislaw would help them find out who poisoned Fanny Mayes by Saturday.

'*Roger* says that Linnit and Dunfee did it, heavily disguised as nuns because she was such a rotten actress,' said Miriam. Everyone roared with laughter and the temperature in the café mounted.

'It couldn't really be in worse T, now could it?' said Miriam.

'T?' said Barny, doubtfully. 'I know Linnit and Dunfee are theatrical agents ... but ...'

'Taste, dear, *taste*,' said Roger briskly.

'Oh,' said Barny. 'I see.'

'And Barny is *saying* on the mountain,' said Natasha, putting her hand in his, 'that he stole his wife's sleeping-pills which my old Johnny say are used for killing this Fanny, and he lose them. Someone, he think, took them back from *him*.'

'Ah!' said Roger. 'Now who's been in Barny's room?'

'Well *I* have,' said Miriam, and smiled at Barny through her six-inch-long false eyelashes. 'But not since the first day I knew him.'

'Miriam,' said Roger sharply. 'Think back. You've got a wonderful memory for that sort of thing. Photographic. She has honestly ...' he turned to the others.

'Memorize the roo-oom,' said Morris in a languorous imitation of Greta Garbo as Queen Christina.

'What for?' said Miriam.

'To see if you can remember a bottle of sleeping-pills anywhere about,' said Roger. 'What colour were they, dear?' he asked Barny.

'Red,' said Barny. 'Capsules. They were in a little squat bottle with a label. It was a Heppell label, I think.'

Miriam screwed up her face and achieved a startling likeness of Hermione Gingold. She shut her eyes. Then, in a rapid undertone she began to describe Barny's room as she had seen it.

'Bed made. Not turned down yet. Chambermaid coming soon ... Window half open. Ski-ing boots under window. Ski-ing socks on radiator.'

'What colour socks?' said Morris helpfully.

'Yellow socks. On chair grey flannel trousers. Red sweater. Dressing-table ... '

'Ah ... ' said Roger, sitting up.

'Brushes. Men's hairbrushes. Clothes brush. Stud box. Comb. Clean handkerchief. Bottles ... '

Everyone sat up.

'Dettol. Peroxide. Tooth paste. Gargle. Aspirin.'

Miriam opened her eyes.

'No little bottle with red pills,' she said. 'Mum's *tired*.'

Natasha pressed another marron glacé into her hand.

'Beside the *bed*, Miriam, beside the *bed*,' clamoured Roger and Morris.

'More chocolate,' said Miriam. 'More chocolate for mum ... '

'Hey! Waiter, please,' said Barny, gesturing.

Fortified, Miriam began her Kim's Game all over again.

'*Bed*,' she said firmly. Roger choked and had to be patted on the back. Miriam frowned.

'Bed,' she repeated. 'Red pyjama-case. Scarlet dressing-gown on door. Exercise book, fountain-pen on top of cupboard. Bottle-of-little-red-pills ... '

Miriam opened her eyes in triumph and drank a whole cup of chocolate without a pause.

'And *that* ... ' said Roger, 'was in the evening, because otherwise you wouldn't have mentioned the *chambermaid*. The evening that Fanny died. Now wasn't it?'

'It was,' said Miriam. 'I came off the funicular and went upstairs and Barny and I talked about our *Souls* ... ' Miriam fluttered her eyelashes like a charming pantomime horse. 'And then I went and got changed,' she said.

'I am remembering that Johnny and I are leaving you both down *here*,' said Natasha, 'at a *thé dansant* or something and you are come back on the same funicular as Pamela.'

Barny frowned, trying to remember something. Morris and Roger heaped presents on Miriam's plate and made much of her. Roger said 'the educated pig will now eat' and it was considered that he had gone too far. Natasha was sitting in a happy and exhausted daze, wondering why Roger and Morris and Barny and Miriam did not bore her or get on her nerves.

'*Fanny*,' said Barny with an effort, 'was found dead at seven o'clock. So my ... er ... Regan's pills were taken between five forty-five and about a quarter to seven. Anyway, to take enough to *kill* a person they'd have to be dissolved in water. Prob'ly *hot* water. *No one*, however drunk, would take about thirty little red pills off someone's hand like a *horse* ...'

'Strange horses you know, dear,' said Roger.

'Who else, but dearest Miriam, darling Barny,' said Natasha, laying a hand on his knee, 'was in your room between six forty-five and seven?'

Barny shut his eyes.

'Hundreds of people,' he said.

'In what order?' said Miriam, producing from a large leather hand-bag a little battered diary and a much-chewed lump of pencil. Faintly written in the diary Natasha could see *Lunch* – Noël and Ivor. *Tea* – The boys at home. *Dinner* – Major P. *Savoy*. 9.00. She averted her eyes.

Clenching her pink tongue between her teeth Miriam scrawled to Barny's dictation: 'The chambermaid. My elder child Joyce. My younger child Margie. The governess, Miss Leamington.'

'I changed after they had gone,' he said. 'And came down to dinner.'

'Where were you being when you heard about Fanny?' said Natasha.

'I was . . .' said Barny, 'in Kathleen's room. Asking her to marry me.'

There was a frightened silence. Barny looked unhappy. Roger stared wildly round him and tried to re-create the party. Morris ordered more and more doughnuts in a daze and Natasha put her hand firmly in Barny's.

'Dearest boy,' she said. 'You do not *need* to marry anyone now that Fanny is dead. You will not be *needing* protection.'

'Much,' said Miriam.

'It's my awful children,' said Barny. 'Miriam has some. Miriam, what did you do with *yours*?'

'Set them to fiddles,' said Miriam, instantly. 'I set one to a fiddle when he was five. *Now* he's the best billiard sharp in New York.'

'Don't tell Barny,' said Roger, 'about your *other* son with poetry in his soul who wrote "When Cares pursue yah, Sing Hallelujah".'

'That was not my son,' said Miriam indignantly, and the party was saved.

II

In the funicular going back they quarrelled among themselves about who should interview what. Roger, particularly, having (as he considered) managed *well* with Ted Sloper (and all by himself) could not see why he should not be allowed to interview Trudi about the sleeping-pills.

'I should *like* to ask Trudi,' he said sulkily, kicking at the shiny yellow carriage door. He left a long scratch on the varnish.

'The Growing Boy,' said Miriam Birdseye, fondly. Then she added, in tones of the purest menace: 'Explain to him, Morris, that *Natasha* is already dealing with Trudi and Trudi trusts Natasha. And it would be a pity to alter that, I should say ...'

'Couldn't A with you M,' said Morris.

'The Governess, then,' said Roger, pouting.

'I am thinking the Governess and Toddy and the children are all being Barny's problem,' said Natasha. 'They are *his* children and *his* governess.'

Roger dropped his mitten on the floor and growled among their legs savagely that he didn't trust Barny one *inch* and still considered that he had murdered both his wife and Fanny Mayes. Barny did not hear him.

'Why should he do that, dear?' said Morris. Morris was the only member of the party who had dived down to help Roger pick up his glove. 'In heaven's name, why?'

'Well, because he likes it. And to get rid of them,' said Roger savagely.

'Don't be silly, dear,' said Morris. And that was that.

Roger, who had been imagining himself the life and soul of the party, was furious.

III

The Water Station Hotel looked as sweet and pretty in the twilight as a nest of thrushes. A large number of newspapermen of all nationalities and all the local representatives of the Schizo-Frenic organs (of which there were a great many) had moved in. They had been piled up against the bar since tea-time waiting to interview Natasha. The representative of *Pravda* was particularly restless.

Natasha went through the bar like a comet and upstairs. The newspapermen rippled, clinging to one another's shoulders like lice.

'That M'me DuVivien just went by?' said the *New York Times*.

'Yes,' said Roger, haughtily.

'Are you a friend of hers, dear boy?' said an unknown gentleman.

'I've got a cable to send,' said *The New York Times*.

'Come now. Help us. What nationality is she?' said *Pravda*.

'Drink up, dear boy,' said the unknown gentleman.

'USSR,' said Roger vindictively.

And, as a result of all this, some days later, Stalin crossly examined a cable from the Schizo-Frenic hierarchy of ski-ing that congratulated the USSR on now holding the world ski record for ladies over four picked miles. It appears that Stalin was unimpressed.

And the next half-hour was spent by Roger and the newspapermen in a state of mutual self-esteem and drunkenness; by Natasha and Barny in separate (but equally hot) baths and an identical dream of excited sentiment; and by Johnny in the deepest gloom with Hans Grübner in Kesicken.

IV

It was a good thing that Natasha was unaware that the USSR had been ear marked as her homeland. Darling Natasha was, perhaps, a little old-fashioned and *silly* about the New Régime.

335

When she was out of her bath, dusted all over with talcum powder and seated cosily in front of her dressing-table, Trudi knocked. Natasha wrapped herself in an exiguous garment of pale blue satin and said 'Herein'.

Trudi bounced in and began to turn down the beds.

'A vot' service,' she said as usual.

'I say, Trudi . . . ' said Natasha, 'are you remembering what I was asking you about all those sleeping-pills this morning?'

'Oh yes, and may I congratulate . . . ' began Trudi.

Natasha stared. It had not struck her that her behaviour on skis had been anything but foolhardy.

'It was nothing,' she said, with a graceful wave of the hand. 'But nothing at *oll*. Mister Flaherté was telling me about these pills and saying that he took them and they are disappearing again. Now what I am wondering *is*, if you can be remembering if they are lying beside the bed that night? On the little cupboard? When you turn down the bed?'

Natasha reached for her bag and began to rustle about in her Schizo-Frenic notes in a very rich way.

Trudi considered.

'This will be the night Lady Sloper die?' she said. 'The night my sister Nelli do Lady Sloper's floor, middle floor. I do top floor. Then I go back to the bar.'

'Yes. The night Lady Sloper died,' observed Natasha, holding 200 francs between her finger and thumb.

'Yes,' said Trudi, with her eyes fixed brightly on Natasha's hand and (let us face it) her note case. 'They *was* there when I turn down Monsieur Flaherté's bed. For I knock them on the floor by mistake. And this was about the same time in the evening as now . . . '

'Six o'clock,' said Natasha, nodding sagely.

Trudi agreed and said Natasha was far too generous and kind. 'Service, madame,' said Trudi, and bobbed out of the room.

V

Barny, pink from his bath, with his light hair plastered down on each side of his face, went in search of Toddy. He was wearing his scarlet dressing-gown. He knocked on her door.

She sounded angry when she said come in. She was lying on her bed reading a book by Collette called 'Ces Plaisirs'. She had already changed. She looked up as he shut the door behind him.

'Well,' she said. 'Your girl friend upset every book in Mönchegg but mine. Congratulate me. Damn grateful I can tell you. Made a packet.'

She swung her legs over the bed and sat up. Barny offered her a cigarette and she screwed it into her frightening holder. She bit on it savagely.

'Tiring, isn't it?' she said.

'My girl friend, or your cigarette holder?' said Barny. He looked at his cousin with hatred.

'Well, I meant your girl friend,' said Toddy. 'But don't take it so hard, chuck. What's the matter with you?' she added, brutally. 'Taken the veil, too?'

Barny made an exclamation of annoyance.

'I came to ask you to give back the thing you stole out of my room the night that Fanny died,' he said, coldly. He put his hands in his dressing-gown pockets and pulled it tightly round his hips. He looked decorative and he knew it.

337

'Oh . . . ' said Toddy, non-plussed. 'So you've found *out*, have you? What a family.'

And she handed him a 500 franc note.

VI

Miriam Birdseye met little Joyce Flaherté on the stairs. She greeted her with a wolfish grin.

'Well, *dear*,' said Miriam, falsely.

Joyce shuddered.

'We were talking about you this afternoon,' pursued Miriam. 'In Kesicken. Your daddy and me.'

'What did you say?' said Joyce, in spite of herself. She came up quite close to Miriam and breathed heavily. She also trod on one of Miriam's toes.

'Little bastard,' said Miriam.

'What?' said Joyce.

'He was plastered,' said Miriam hastily. 'We said that you . . . you should learn the violin,' she said. 'To support your father. In his old age, of course . . . '

Joyce was taken aback.

'What did you do with the bottle of red pills you took out of your father's bedroom?' said Miriam quickly, before Joyce could recover. Joyce looked sulky.

'Miss Leamington took them away from me,' she said. Then she stared at the floor.

'Why did you take them?' cried Miriam.

'They reminded me of my mouse,' said Joyce.

VII

Miriam collided with Barny on the stairs.

'Joyce took it ...' she began.

'Toddy didn't ...' began Barny. They both roared with laughter.

'We must tell Natasha,' said Barny unnecessarily. They wheeled and ran foolishly along the corridor to Natasha's room.

(In Kesicken Johnny bought Hans Grübner his fifth drink and said he wouldn't go home till morning.)

Natasha greeted them with exquisite politeness and a hair brush in one hand.

'Joyce took the bottle of sleeping pills because it reminded her of her *mouse*,' cried Miriam.

'But the Leamington took it away,' said Barny.

'After Trudi is turning down your bed,' said Natasha. They looked at each other and Miriam sat suddenly on the floor.

'Mum's tired,' said Miriam. 'Mum will have supper in bed.'

'*Not* in Johnny's bed, dearest Miriam,' said Natasha. 'There is already too much running about in dressing-gowns and nervous chaperonage. I will be calling Roger and Morris and they can be putting you to bed if you are liking.'

'Mum's tired,' said Miriam, again fretfully.

'Someone,' said Barny, 'must interview Miss Leamington.'

'Mum's too tired,' said Miriam. 'And who,' she added, in a brisk voice: 'would be more suitable to do that than her employer, you dope?'

And she kicked him on the ankle.

VIII

Morris eventually put Miriam to bed. Roger was still with his new friends, the newspapermen. After drinking for some time they had sent off a number of cables. They were now drinking.

Miriam ate roast chicken, sitting up in bed. She looked baroque. When she finished she told Morris (cosily eating dinner from a tray on a chair, to keep her company) that she must see Natasha and Barny at once. They must, she said, be brought to her. What were they doing?

'Dancing,' said Morris. He leered. The swift, bouncing rhythm of the little Schizo-Frenic dance band was beating through the hotel once again. 'It seems a pity to disturb them,' said Morris, doubtfully.

'Don't be ab-*surd*,' said Miriam. '*I* want to see them. Time, Tide and Miriam Birdseye wait for no man.'

'That used to read *The New Statesman*,' said Morris.

'*That*,' said Miriam, 'is the sort of remark that has got you where you are today.' She threw a shoe at him. 'You're nothing but a nark,' she said.

'I am *angry* with Barny and Natasha,' said Miriam. 'Think of that nice little step-child, Pamela ... ' Miriam practised a grimace that looked like something out of a ghost story by M. R. James. Morris, terrified, hurried out. 'I must,' she said to herself, as the door slammed behind Morris, 'upbraid them about that.'

But when they stood at the bottom of her bed she asked nothing but:

'What did the Governess do with the bottle of sleeping-pills?'

Possibly this question was nearer to her heart.

IX

Barny and Natasha were beautiful. Natasha's white dress frothed round her feet like a frozen waterfall. Her hair was as artlessly well-brushed as a child's. Her eyes were enormous and innocent and untroubled. She looked like a girl of twenty-two and not a very knowledgeable one at that. She was, in fact, happy.

Barny, in a double-breasted dinner-jacket, was less unself-conscious. But he, too, was happy. He blew his nose on a white silk handkerchief.

'No,' he said, guiltily. 'I never asked her yet.' He looked at Natasha. 'The night is yet young,' he said.

'You must never, never, *never* say that again,' said Miriam, furiously. 'I will not have it.'

'Neither will I,' said Natasha. 'It is a disgusting thing to say.'

'Ask the Governess,' said Miriam. 'And look after that child, Pamela.'

She dismissed them both with a regal wave of the hand. Natasha's hand flew to her mouth.

'I had forgot her,' she said. Her happiness was snuffed out. Her hair seemed to lose its curl. It was possible to see there was a small coffee stain on the radiance of her dress. She was, in fact, no longer happy.

X

Natasha had never considered Pamela as a duty before. As she left Miriam's room her mind was no longer untroubled in the enjoyment of dance music and the smell of expensive scent.

Instead, it was grasped by the strain of a conflict far bigger than any she had lately endured over the relative importance to her of Johnny and Barny.

Pamela. Natasha forced herself to consider Pamela. Natasha was genuinely fond of Pamela. She had intelligence and the same downright common sense that Natasha had originally enjoyed in Johnny. And to her horror, Natasha now found herself looking on her darling Pamela as a nuisance. Poor Pamela. A *nuisance* because Natasha could not indulge herself in Barny without hurting Pamela. (Natasha took it for granted that *men*, like Johnny, got hurt and considered them perfectly fair game.) Pamela, however, was defenceless and her home was with Natasha and Johnny. She surely would be too young to understand the sick feeling of exasperation that Natasha now felt for Johnny. Johnny, of course, understood it only too well. That was why he was now buying Hans Grübner his tenth drink.

Natasha stood at the top of the stairs, the light gone from her eyes, her hands to her face, concentrated essence of tragedy expressed in the droop of her white shoulders. The tragedy was for herself, Natasha Nevkorina, the Pagan, the pleasure-loving, held down by Puritan Duty. She was horrified.

'Darling Natasha,' said Barny, and ran a warm finger up her forearm. She didn't even notice him. 'What *can* it be? I love you, you know. Surely that makes everything all right?'

'You are a thing of a moment, Barny,' said Natasha. 'A dear thing. But it is only a little, little moment. And a moment is not worth one's whole life's peace. Of the *mind*, I mean, of course,' she added, in a lighter tone.

Barny tried to sweep her exquisite sorrow into his arms. She eluded him with a delicate gesture, absently, uncoquettishly.

'Ah ... ' she said. 'It is so *sad*. And therefore, of course, so *beautiful*.'

And to Barny's consternation she began to laugh merrily at herself.

Barny Flaherté had met his match in inconsequence.

XI

Natasha had, of course, under-estimated Pamela, who was as intelligent and sensitive as it is possible for a reserved child of twenty to be. Pamela had long ago decided on her future. It would certainly be lived without Natasha and without Johnny. And preferably, without *anyone*. Pamela's intention was to live alone, in London, and earn her own living as a journalist. She confided all this to Ted Sloper as they danced round the room in time to a rather bouncing waltz.

'*One*, two, three, *One*, two, three,' said Ted under his breath, adding in a rather louder tone, 'well, that's very interestin'. I might be able to do something for you *there*. I know an editor or two, y'know. Oh, sorry, was that your toe?'

'No,' said Pamela politely. 'But do tell me about these editors. Which ones do you know?'

'Mind you,' said Ted, and glanced at the bar where Roger and the journalists now sang a modified version of his 'Vampire Song' and beat time on each other's shoulders. 'Newspaperin' is a rough business ... '

Pamela laughed.

'It sounds as though you were talking about wall-papering and distempering,' she said.

'Well, it's about the same,' said Ted. 'Has anyone ever told you that you're a very beautiful young person? Eh?'

With dexterity he waltzed her through the door on to the moonlit terrace, where, in the cold, they spun abruptly to a stop.

'No . . . ' said Pamela doubtfully.

'About time then,' said Ted. 'Suppose you've no time for an old codger like me? Eh?'

And he kissed her most emphatically.

Oh hell. I've got to be kissed sometime. I must go through with this, thought Pamela. She did not enjoy it at all.

XII

Natasha left Barny at the top of the stairs because she wanted to find Pamela. Barny, alone, felt something twist in his heart. He was unused to the sensation. Irritably, he went in search of Miss Leamington.

As he came into the bar Pamela and Ted Sloper re-entered the room through the front door. Ted's eyes were bright. His lips were compressed in a thick line. Pamela shuddered as they began to dance again. The Schizo-Frenic band were playing a selection from *Oklahoma* far too fast.

'One, two three four five six seven eight,' counted Ted under his breath. They went hurriedly past Barny, who grinned. He had seen old Ted on the dance floor before.

Miss Leamington was sitting by herself in the far corner of the room.

'Come along, Miss Leamington,' said Barny pleasantly as he approached her. 'Do come and dance. The band's playing far too fast. We shall probably break our necks.'

Miss Leamington looked up suspiciously. She glanced round the room and saw no one there to rival her. She drew a deep breath. Her dull, rather long face was at once less heavy. She stood up.

'Why, of course,' she said carefully. 'What is this pretty tune called?'

'*People will say we're in love*,' sang Barny in his gentle baritone. He thought, with a pang of tenderness, of Natasha. He grasped Miss Leamington carefully. They moved off, doing a slick series of quarter turns left and right.

'*Don't laugh at my jokes too much* . . . ' thought Barny grimly. '*People will say we're in love* . . . '

Their feet moved in an intricate pattern as they went round the outside edge of the room. Miss Leamington danced quite well. She was a little fond of 'taking the lead', and Barny found her a little heavy in his hand. Bit by bit he followed her more and more, and he managed better. The world (he hoped) still had the impression that he was in charge. Miss Leamington concentrated fiercely as she set the pace. Barny kept up with her.

'You dance well,' he said wickedly. 'Where did you learn?'

'Cambridge,' said Miss Leamington shortly, and thrust herself purposefully against his thighs.

'Oh . . . ' said Barny. 'Fancy. Bachelor of *all* the Arts.' He laughed pleasantly. 'I must have you teach Joyce and Margie,' he said.

Miss Leamington did not reply. Her feelings about Joyce and Margie were, at that moment, of the purest hatred.

'Funny children aren't they?' said Barny. 'Extraordinary thing, wasn't it, Joyce taking those sleeping-pills out of my room? Don't you think? She thought they were like her *mouse* . . . '

345

Miss Leamington's heavy features expressed refined disgust.

'She gave 'em to you, didn't she?' said Barny. 'What'd you do with 'em?'

There was a pause while Miss Leamington grasped Barny more firmly to her.

'What did you do with 'em?' said Barny again. The music stopped and Ted and Pamela clapped perfunctorily.

'I put them back in your room,' said Miss Leamington slowly.

And at this moment Natasha, looking as though she were made of starlight, moonlight and candlelight, came into the brilliance of the room, with the dark night behind her. Barny stared at her like a drugged moth. And Miss Leamington's arms fell slowly to her sides as she followed the direction of his eyes.

IV

'You'll Never Prove it . . .'

Even someone less sensitive than Natasha must have observed the aura of hatred that suddenly burned round Rosalie Leamington. Natasha was looking at Pamela, uncomfortably fox-trotting in Ted Sloper's arms, when she became aware of a feeling of constraint. She was also aware of Barny. And then she noticed Rosalie Leamington.

Morris appeared at her elbow, mildly anxious to dance, twittering with dry and facile compliments. In his tall, sallow way Morris was not unpleasing. He was more kindly than the waspish, kiddie-like Roger, who now thumped the representative of *Pravda* on the back and sang:

> 'YOU be my succubus
> I'll be your incubus
> You are a lucky cuss
> You are the Lily of Drac-ULA
> You are my littul bleeding rose.'

Toddy, also, had joined the newspapermen and 'the unknown gentleman' was teaching her the words. Natasha said she would dance with Morris. In his impersonal embrace she swayed round the floor.

'I cannot,' said Morris, gravely, 'bring myself to *roister* in the ballroom. And I hope that if this somewhat *boisterous* rhythm continues you should not mind if we dance *against* it? Perhaps in six-eight time?'

'That will be being most *interesting*,' said Natasha, who seemed, in Johnny's absence, to have forgotten all her scruples about ballroom dancing.

'Your friend – *our* friend – Mister Flaherté, seems anxious to attract your attention,' said Morris, delicately, near to her ear.

'What is he looking like?' said Natasha. She lowered her eyes to regard Morris's bow tie demurely. It was an inch from her face. Morris looked over the top of her head and sniffed reverently. He said he thought Barny looked unhappy.

'*That* Miss Leamington is absolutely crushing him to *death*, poor darling,' said Morris. 'I wonder if he has managed to extract the information about the pills?'

'I am expecting that that is why he is signalling,' said Natasha. 'Morris. Would you be so offully kind?'

Morris, after a slight pause for reflection, said that he might.

'When this dance is being over will you rescue my poor Pamela from Sir Sloper? She *cannot* be happy with Sir Sloper. He is so *flat* and kind and nice and *nobody* could be happy with him.'

'How curious,' said Morris. 'Now, if *Fanny* had said a thing like that about him we should *all* have thought her bitchy.'

Natasha smiled divinely.

'So am I bitchy,' she said. 'But I am never allowing myself to be saying *anything* nasty to anyone. It spoil my face.'

Morris, laughing helplessly, wound his waltz to a close. He poured Natasha a glass of champagne and then took Pamela elegantly away from Ted Sloper.

Ted put his hands in his pockets and loafed over to the wall where Barny had deposited Miss Leamington. Ted, perhaps, was a little full of brandy. He was, as a widower, enjoying a sense of exhilarated emancipation that was not in the best of taste. Fanny had been buried in the Kesicken cemetery that afternoon. Ted began to wonder if sleeping dogs and sleeping murderers might not be allowed to lie. He stretched out a broad, pink hand and pulled Miss Leamington from her chair.

'Come along, little girl,' he said, foolishly. The band broke again into its selection from *Oklahoma*. (It was very proud of this selection.) 'Let murderers lie,' said Ted.

Miss Leamington went stiff in his arms and said: 'I beg your pardon?'

'Well . . . ' said Ted. 'You know how it is, what? Justice an' all that. P'raps I'll let these Schizo-Frenics get on with it. Probl'y not got much chance 'f catchin' the murderer now, *I* should say?'

'Get on with it?' said Miss Leamington, frozen, stepping grimly backwards roughly in time to 'I caint say No'. 'Get on with what?'

'Why, with catchin' the lunatic who murdered my wife.'

There was a silence. Ted Sloper thought what an uncommonly bad dancer Miss Leamington was and tripped over her toe. She said: 'Pardon' and then, tentatively:

'You're sure . . . it was . . . a lunatic . . . who did it?'

'My *dear* lady, *positive*,' said Ted and beamed. '*One*, two, three, four. Sorry. *All* murderers are mad, what? I mean, one just doesn't kill people, does one? Or perhaps you *do*?'

He laughed heartily at his joke, tripped again and went on laughing and Miss Leamington coldly bared her teeth.

'I should have thought,' she said, icily. 'That even you could see there were occasions when to kill someone might be the only course open to a man or woman of integrity. It is, after all, only the breaking of a tabu of so-called civilization.'

'Eh?' said Ted.

'Not murdering people is as much of a convention as time,' said Rosalie Leamington.

All this shook poor Ted Sloper a lot. He had no love of 'brainy women'. The word 'integrity' alone was enough to make his eyes float away like small balloons. Having therefore acquired a brainy woman by mistake he wished she would be quiet.

'What rot!' he cried, explosively. (It was, of course, the brandy speaking, and not Sir Edward Sloper K.B.E.) 'Murder's a matter of right or wrong. Er – ethically . . . '

And Rosalie Leamington smiled pityingly at him.

II

Pamela and Morris had both seen *Oklahoma* and so were able to talk happily to each other. Morris had been at the first night and had also been at the first night of *Annie Get Your Gun*. Pamela therefore regarded him much as the mortals regarded the various gods from Olympus who took such interesting fancies for the mortals. (Goodness! A *god*! Dancing with me!)

'Are you,' Pamela hardly breathed word, 'a *dramatic critic*?'

Morris smiled and nodded. ('Really,' said the gesture of his head, 'this little mortal is quite charming.')

'And you go to first nights? All the time?'

'Why, yes.' Morris looked down at her. 'Of course it's very boring really. All the plays are so *frightful*, as a rule. *Annie* and *Okla* were different, I grant you. Exactly my tea,' said Morris.

There was a pause.

'I work for a perfectly frightful Sunday newspaper,' said Morris. 'I hate it as a matter of fact.'

'Why aren't you over there drinking with *Pravda*, then, and all that lot?' said Pamela.

'My dear girl,' said Morris. He pronounced it to rhyme with real. '*Those* are reporters. *I* am a "Feature Writer".'

'Oh I see . . . ' said Pamela.

In fact, she did not.

III

Barny, left with no Miss Leamington and with two glasses of champagne, drank them both. Then he saw Natasha, drooping like a camelia. He approached her, warily, with two more glasses of champagne.

'Both,' he said, owlishly, 'for you.'

Natasha drank them, absently. She looked over the rim of the glass with approval for Pamela and Morris. As they danced past, Morris said: 'Well, if you come down the Street when you get back I'll introduce you to my Editor. Yes I will. He's a funny little man and it's a rotten paper . . . but . . . '

'Ah,' said Natasha. 'This is better.'

Barny thought she meant the champagne and said he would

351

get her some more. She turned her enormous, shadowy eyes on him and said, 'No. Not champagne. It is just more *convenable*, that is all.'

Barny was non-plussed, but then they danced together. And here my story ought to end. For the grace of their movement and their variations and the delicacy of their footwork were all so beautiful that I should like to say: 'And so they danced happily ever after,' and never write another word. But Barny spoke.

'I asked Miss Leamington,' he said against Natasha's ear, 'about the sleeping-pills. And she took them from Joyce and she handed them back. I mean, she put them in my room.'

Natasha said nothing.

'That means,' said Barny, nearer and nearer to her ear, 'either the *murderer* took them *after* that——'

'Yes,' said Natasha.

'Or the murderer had some of its own.'

'Yes,' said Natasha.

'Or Miss Leamington is lying,' said Barny.

There was a pause filled with the harmony and excitement of music and movement.

'Say something more than "yes", beloved heart,' said Barny.

'That,' said Natasha, 'is *it*. Miss Leamington is lying.'

IV

They woke up Miriam Birdseye to tell her. Miriam yawned hugely and said she might as well get up again if people didn't let her sleep. It took a lot of determination on both their parts to keep her in bed.

'Of *course* she's lying,' said Miriam, finally. 'And of course she murdered Fanny Mayes. Because she thought Fanny was preg by you, Barny. She did it *for* you, dear. What a lot of trouble you cause. But I'm damned if you'll ever prove she did it. She's too clever ... '

Miriam yawned again, even more widely, and her teeth reminded Barny of the stalagmites and stalactites in the Caves in Cheddar Gorge. He held tightly to Natasha's hand in an agony of fear.

'I am believing,' said Natasha, slowly. 'That Miriam is right. Everything is pointing that way.'

'It fits,' said Barny, doubtfully.

'Of course I'm right,' said Miriam, briskly. 'But I'm damned if *I* could prove it. I thought she'd pushed your wife, too, out of the window, Barny ... ?'

'No,' said Barny, blankly. 'Kathleen did that.'

'Oh well,' said Miriam, in the same tone as one who has written in the wrong clue in *The Times* crossword puzzle, 'Do go away. Mum's sleepy.'

Natasha and Barny poured out into the corridor.

'Natasha, Natasha,' said Barny, helplessly. 'Don't leave me, don't leave me. I'm frightened.'

Natasha did not leave him.

V

The Last Day

The next day was the day before everyone went home. It was a sad day, made even sadder by the beautiful weather, by the dark blue sky and the dazzling, newly fallen snow.

Johnny arrived back in the middle of the morning, with a three-quarter-inch stubble on his chin (his was a fast-growing beard) and began, soberly, to pack. There were skis to be returned to the ski shop with labels on them. There were bills to be paid. Perhaps Natasha would not want to travel with him.

He wandered through the half-deserted hotel to their room and pulled out their suitcases. He smiled wryly when he saw his shoebag full of Natasha's poker winnings. Darling Natasha. He would miss her so much.

He sat for a long time with his hands full of francs and did not notice the bright sunlight outside, nor the heartless cries of the skiers who passed the hotel, praising God. Johnny was too sane and too unselfish to attempt to fight to regain Natasha. He was also, of course, too fond of her.

The day spread out, punctuated by the arrival of the various members of our party at the hotel for meals. Morris and Pamela went off together early in the afternoon, discussing the magazine market for the short story. Miriam Birdseye paid her bill. This was a major operation involving almost every member of the hotel staff. There were last minute telephone calls to Schröeter and Thomas Cook and Son to confirm the bookings of the *wagons-lits*. Barny and Natasha, with lunch in rucksacks, went for their first and last ski run together round Verboden, Glöchner-gleicher and Mönchegg. Only Rosalie Leamington was not happy.

II

Rosalie Leamington, biting her lips, sat in the funicular that took her up to Brauzwetterjoch. She was determined, she said, to see this famous view before she returned to England. Consequently she left the children behind at the hotel. She was anxious to think.

Her passion for Barny was all-absorbing. She could not believe that the tenderness and pleasure which she had experienced at his hands meant less than nothing to him. She was so certain that her burning intensity must have fired him also. It had not even singed him.

Brooding in the funicular, carried into the still, cold air far above the small peaks of the Lavahorn and the Bleaderhorn, Rosalie Leamington, with all the misplaced and disciplined processes of the lady philosopher, worked out the behaviour of Barny Flaherté.

Her first false premise was that he truly loved her. She

supposed, poor Rosalie Leamington, that that was why he had made love to her. *Therefore* all his strange behaviour with Mrs DuVivien (nasty common cheap scented thing) had been to 'put in time', until the children were safely under someone *else's* care.

It was certainly not right for a governess to allow her employer to make love to her. So she must give in her notice, writing a formal letter with her London address on it. And then, when Barny was *free*! Oh then, surely he would come and find her there? Waiting for him.

Rosalie Leamington had too good opinion of herself (and this was her second false premise) to suppose that she could ever have fallen in love with anything but the Best and Most Good. That Barny Flaherté was not the Best and Most Good, but was (into the bargain) pretty cheap and second-rate, would not have occurred to this besotted woman. Her affection was the fruit of a nature warped by intensity and concentration to the point of insanity. It was, in its own awful way, sincere.

She did not appreciate the view from Brauzwetterjoch.

III

Kathleen Flaherté told her beads and promised to try to atone for her great sin. She found some sort of peace and comfort. With Toddy's help she packed and strapped up her suitcases.

'It will be quiet in Paris,' she said to Toddy. 'But the nuns will be nice. How awfully unhappy I have been here. How sad it is. I am glad we are going home.'

Toddy wondered if a nice long rest in an institution might not be even better for her little sister. She took a pipe from her

jacket pocket and put tobacco into it with quick, firm movements. She struck a match. Soon Kathleen's bedroom filled
with the unpleasant smell of her tobacco.

'You should come back to Schizo-Frenia in the Spring,' she
said, 'when you are in the Order. You'll like the little flowers.
They are more peaceful than ski-ing. Edelweiss and that.'

Kathleen's eyes slowly filled with tears.

IV

Joyce and Margie Flaherté were both glad to be going home, as
we know. Johnny and Pamela had not, truthfully, enjoyed their
holiday. Miriam Birdseye, full of new-found vigour, was going
straight into rehearsals of a new revue called *Absolutely the End*,
and so was impatient to see London again. Wherever and whenever Miriam went Roger and Morris were content to go. Only
Natasha and Barny were leaving Kesicken and Katsclöchen with
that odd, poetic feeling of poignancy and impending disaster
which spells the end of a really good holiday.

They stood now in the gathering dusk at Mönchegg, on their
skis, preparing to run the three miles back to Katsclöchen and
the Water Station Hotel. The sun, broad and red (but never
as broad and red as the English winter sun), dipped behind
Brauzwetter. The enchantment was gone.

'Dearest Natasha,' said Barny, and stared at her slight figure,
at her face, milky in the twilight, and her enormous eyes. 'Dear,
dear, Natasha. And I haven't even kissed you ... '

Natasha smiled. And she fled down the icy snow trail
towards Water Station like a beautiful ghost. Her skis hissed
as she went.

VI

The End

Barny Flaherté travelled to Paris and attended the funeral of his wife, Regan Flaherté, in the Madeleine. Flahertés and Rastignatts and some Menzies came from all over Europe and Canada, in deepest mourning, and said how awfully sad it was about darling Regan and her ski-ing accident. Joyce and Margie, smiling brightly and shaking hands with everyone, behaved more as if they were at a wedding than at a funeral. It was arranged (by one of their quite other aunts, a Rastignatt, from Marseilles) that they would now be sent to an expensive English boarding school. Here, they had not time to think at all. Barny had had enough of governesses.

He travelled on to London, where he lived in his club for a while. He hardly bothered to open the letters that he received. Amongst others he tore up Miss Leamington's letter, giving notice, quite unread.

Barny was still enchanted by Natasha, although she had told him that she intended to elude him. By every post he expected a letter from her. Every time he was summoned to the telephone he thought it might be her. He had almost reached the point where he would ring up the husband. Barny was not, as a rule, good at husbands.

However, one day in March he received a letter, forwarded from Paris. It was postmarked 'London. Notting Hill' and he pounced on it, his heart leaping. From Natasha?

No. It was from Rosalie Leamington.

II

Sir Edward Sloper settled back into the routine of bachelor life and began to forget that he had ever had a wife. Occasionally when he was summoned to the Film Studios at Caversham Lodge, he recalled his foxy Fanny and the horror that he had suffered at her hands. But soon he fell in love with a red-haired singer and forgot Fanny entirely. He did not marry the singer and he began to think that Fanny had truly died of heart failure.

One day, he, too, received a letter that disturbed him for a second. It was from the Representatives of H. M. Government in Schizo-Frenia.

They considered that there was inadequate evidence to justify re-opening a case which had already been dealt with by Schizo-Frenic law. They had the honour to remain his and were George Gaminara, Minister Plenipotentiary, etc., etc.

Ted tore up this letter and used it for spills, and the red-haired singer complained because he dropped thick black ash on her dress. So far as Ted Sloper was concerned, this closed the case.

III

Rosalie Leamington, however, re-opened it with a blowlamp.

Dear Mister Flaherté *(she wrote)*

You cannot leave me without a word. I know, too,
that you are in London. Your cheque was not enough
acknowledgment to my letter of notice. I require a
reference but – I *must*, I must see you as soon as possible
and at the above address. Please, please come to me.
Do not fail me. It concerns you and me and Sir Edward
Sloper. Oh, pray come. I love you.

R. Leamington.

The flat is the basement one. Ring twice. ——R.

Even so, had Barny had something else to do that afternoon he might have paid no attention to that wild, silly
letter. The weird, unconcentrated scholar's hand touched
nothing but his curiosity. Yes, he remembered the governess.
But only vaguely and certainly not in a sentimental way.
Perhaps she had something new to say about Fanny Mayes's
death. If she *had* been lying about those pills he would need
to be clever to get her to confess. But it would all interest
Natasha.

This would be an excuse to approach Natasha. Her love of
drama could never resist a splendid complication like *this*.

For a long time Barny stood in the hall of his club and
turned the letter over and over in his long, thin hands. And
if a terrifying old man called Bexhill had not lurched up and

asked Barny to buy him a drink, Barny might *still* not have done anything about Miss Leamington's letter.

'Sorry, Bexhill,' he called back over his shoulder, as he ran down the steps. 'Got to go out.'

He hailed a taxi and looked down at the letter in his hand.

'Varley Gardens,' he said to the driver. 'Number Six.'

'Uh huh,' said the driver. 'I knows it. By the Water Tower on Campden 'ill ... '

The driver swung the flag round with a savage 'ping'. As he twirled round and went towards Notting Hill Gate it began to rain. The wind blew against the windscreen and the rain ran down the glass like tears. Barny sat upright in the back, the letter clenched in his hand. Soon he would find out all about it ...

IV

At Notting Hill Gate it was still raining. Most people were indoors, or hurrying to get there. The sun occasionally came out, unsuccessfully. It was a cold afternoon. Barny felt in his pocket to pay the driver.

He got out. The water tower was tall and gaunt above the whole district, like a frozen finger. The taxi gave another sharp 'ping' and went away. Barny was marooned.

Varley Gardens consisted of about fifteen very tall grey houses. Number Six was in very bad repair. Paint peeled from the front of the house. The wood showed plainly through the broken blisters on the front door. The railings were grey with dirt, and flimsy with rust. A thin cat ran like a shadow across the road to slide behind a dustbin.

Six miles away, in Hampstead, Natasha was suddenly aware of a burning sensation of disquiet.

V

Barny rang the basement bell twice, as he had been told. He stood at the bottom of the area steps, horrified by the damp that seeped up at him. He put his hands in his pockets and jigged his feet. The cat hissed and spat at him from the dustbins.

He could hear thudding feet inside and the bolts and keys turning and being drawn back. For no reason his heart began to beat very hard. He smiled uneasily.

The basement door swung in. There in the dark stood Rosalie Leamington. She gasped, and her face worked. There was a stone-paved passage behind her, going back in the bowels of the house. He took off his bowler hat.

'You wanted to see me?' he said, vaguely.

'Nice of you to come,' said Rosalie, gruffly.

She stood on one side to allow him to pass her. There was a lavatory on his left and a dank, cold cave that could only have been a bathroom. Their feet rang on the stone flags.

Rosalie Leamington now went ahead of him, limping a little. And she apologized for this, poor devil, and pushed her heavy hair out of her eyes with one hand. In her left hand was an axe.

'I have been chopping wood,' she said. 'Come in.'

Barny stepped over yellowish splinters and chips that lay about the floor.

'Oh yes,' he said. 'Wood fire. Capital things, wood fires.'

He shivered and turned his hat in his hands. They were now

in a living-room that also ran back into the house, like the passage. It was a shadowy cavern.

'Take the comfortable chair,' said Miss Leamington. She turned a switch. A jointed reading-lamp poured white light down upon the chair. It made things worse. There was silence. Barny sat down. It was not comfortable. He held the letter out to Miss Leamington.

'Oh ...' she said, 'I wrote that four days ago. When I was mad. I'm not mad now.'

Barny looked at the heavy face, sagging with emotion, at the eyes, red-rimmed and swollen behind their thick-lensed glasses. And he saw her cold dry hands that twisted together, rasping as they did so.

'You don't *look* very sane,' said Barny.

The awful silence rose more tightly between them.

'I suppose you want that reference,' said Barny. He made a movement to take his fountain-pen from his pocket. He looked round him for paper. And he could not avoid seeing the walls, where damp spread in dark patches. Here, idly, a spider sat. One wall was a bookcase. There was a drawing of witches by Mervyn Peake. There was a reproduction of Dürer's 'Melancholia', and there was a reproduction of an El Greco. Otherwise, draughts furnished the room.

Barny was aware, but only dimly, of a bed in a corner. He hastily turned his eyes back to Miss Leamington. She now sat on a rough milking-stool. She banged her knee with her clenched hand.

'How can you, how can you, how *can* you – be – so insulting?' she was saying, over and over again.

Barny was amazed. His glance was candid and surprised and tolerant. Rosalie Leamington saw it.

'*Once* you didn't despise me,' cried Rosalie Leamington, '*Once* you didn't look at me as though I were a poor thing. Now I am worn out with misery, with fighting intolerable despair——'

'Here,' said Barny. 'What's wrong?'

He wished he had not come. He looked around him for the door.

'Oh no. *No.* You'll hear me out.'

Barny looked back at those angry, glittering eyes. Rosalie sprang from her stool and paced the room, tears pouring down her face.

'Hey,' said Barny, and again: 'What's wrong?'

He remembered his taxi, cosily going back to St James's. He even thought with pleasure of old Bexhill.

'Wrong ... wrong ... you ask me *that*? Do you know the difference between right and wrong? You ... you ... moral anarchist!'

Barny stirred in his chair.

'I do know the difference between right and wrong,' he said. 'What's the matter?'

Miss Leamington knelt suddenly at his feet and flung her strong lean arms round his knees.

'Then you love me?'

Barny drew back, nervously.

'No,' he said. 'No. Not exactly.'

'Good heavens,' cried Rosalie, explosively. 'Then why did you tell me you did? Not once, but many, many times. I could forgive anything but those lies. Anything but that. That shameful, terrible evening ...'

She sobbed, however, without reticence or shame and beat

out the rhythm of her speech on her knees. Barny looked at this odd face, all twisted with grief into a caricature. Had he been able to show pity he might still have saved them both. But Barny was also, in his own awful way, sincere. He felt only distaste.

'It is ... conventional,' he said, hesitantly. 'And I felt ... you know ... that you are, *as* you are, an intelligent woman, you might have *preferred* me to say something like that. I'm sorry.'

'Prefer it?'

Miss Leamington sprang to her feet.

'*Prefer* it? Sorry? You! You aren't fit to think what I prefer. Men like you, who use your vile charm and call it love, and say tender things and make gestures, meaningless and *empty* gestures. Used a hundred years. Destroyed a hundred years. Ah, what a destroyer you are, my love, my dear, my *very* dear ...'

A strange bright smile played now on her face. She stepped back against her cold fireplace. She was a tall girl. She towered over Barny in his chair.

'Destroyer?' said Barny, interested detachment in his voice, 'What do you mean? You know ...' he said, 'the trouble with you is you have no sense of humour.'

He nodded as though he had found a fundamental truth.

'Love is funny, you know,' he said. 'And nice and warm. Not tempests and whirlwinds sort of,' he ended, inarticulately.

'*Everything* is not funny,' shouted Miss Leamington, with a terrible cry. If only she could convince this young man, all might still be well between them both. 'How can you say so? And of love? Ah, love is not funny. My love is not funny. It is a king. A fierce, trampling king. *You* ... and those like you, will go on ... from woman to woman ...'

Barny looked at her in astonishment.

'Taking your pleasure from them, trampling them down, you sensual beast ... seeing them *die* for you ... '

Barny was not very uneasy.

'Ah no, you shall hear me out——'

She thrust him back into his seat. She tossed her head. Her glasses had fallen off. She looked rather fine.

'I sent for you to tell you of the hells that you have caused. The death of your poor wife. Poor Regan. Did that mean nothing to you? Your cousin, poor Kathleen – living in hell, a death in life because of you——'

'Convents are quite comfortable, not hells in life in death,' said Barny. 'Don't go too far. And what about Fanny Mayes?'

'And you dare to use that mocking tone to *me*? You are not *human*. Is it any wonder you kill souls? I tell you. You feel *nothing!*'

'I feel a very great deal,' said Barny, indignantly. 'I'm *very* sensitive.'

Miss Leamington swung round at him, roaring.

'Sensitive? Ah, what do you know of sensitivity? *All you* know is *sensuality*. I killed Fanny Mayes. And what about me? For you. Because *your* safety was menaced by her. Because she told the world and half the city that she was to bear *your* child. Yes. I killed her. I was proud to kill her.'

'You're too proud altogether,' said Barny, contemptuously.

Rosalie Leamington still held the wood-axe in her hand.

And she hit him again and again on the back of the neck. And so, with a look of astonishment, of ghastly humour and his usual detached interest, Barny Flaherté slid from his chair and died at her feet. His bright blood was only one more stain in that dreadful room.

VI

When she came out of the flat she leant her head against the unpleasant wall. An hour before, the rain had been falling. Now, little pools stood in the pavement. Someone's wireless blared the news and made everything seem very still and quiet.

Rosalie stumbled up the steps that led to the street. She started down the hill towards the tube station, moving slowly.

Some children played viciously at the corner of the street with an old tennis ball. It came bouncing towards her. One of the children ran after it and butted Rosalie's legs and said 'Sorry, miss' and gaped because she had not paid attention.

Life went on all right and Rosalie went on, somehow, down the hill to the tube station, moving like an automaton.

At the Underground the entrance was stale with dust and old pieces of ragged paper and straws and filth. A hot wind roared up the staircase whenever a train came in. There was no one in sight. Three public telephone boxes stood empty, with lights burning in them. The A–K – and L–Z swung listlessly on their strings.

She went into the middle box and picked up the receiver.

Then she dialled 999 . . .